Beth s DECISION

"In memory of my mum – Janet Hughes"

Beth's DECISION

By
Tricia Hughes

Bookaholics Publishing, 2019.

Published by Bookaholics Publishing

imprint of

Estuary Media Group Ltd
19, Carters Garth Close, Grainthorpe, Louth,
Lincolnshire, LN11 7HT

ISBN: 978-1-9160289-3-7

Page design by Pageset Ltd, High Wycombe, Buckinghamshire HP11 1JR.
Printed by Ridgeway Press, Easton Royal Pewsey, Wiltshire SN9 5LU.

Contents

--ooOoo--

Chapter One

--ooOoo--

*A*s Beth looked out through the front room window she noticed her husband was talking to their next door neighbour. He had parked his car in the driveway and stopped to speak to Mrs Hall as she was trimming the hedge between their gardens. Phil was obviously joking with her as they both began laughing at something he said.

It was always the same with Phil, he could make anyone laugh. Only, sometimes when you lived with someone like that all the time, the jokes wore a bit thin.

Beth chided herself from criticising her husband in this way and moved away from the window. She walked across the front room and out into the hallway.

She could hear the saucepans bubbling in the kitchen and quickly went to turn the gas down slightly before they boiled over. She was cooking a familiar meal of spaghetti bolognaise tonight, something she could manage on auto-pilot.

The children were upstairs in their bedrooms tussling with their homework which she liked them to finish before they ate dinner together. It meant that everyone could relax at the end of the working day. But, she reflected, how could she relax tonight?

She slipped her hand into the pocket of her jeans and felt the piece of paper she had pushed in there earlier.

"Hi everyone I'm home," called Phil as he slammed the front door shut behind him. "What's for tea tonight?"

"It's spaghetti bolognaise," she called back quickly.

"I'll just go and change, be down in a sec," he said running up the stairs.

Beth was glad she did not have to face him immediately. How was she going to react? It was not everyday you came across a piece of paper in your husband's jacket pocket that could change the rest of your life.

As Beth stirred the pasta she thought back to earlier that afternoon when she had been collecting some clothes together to take to the dry cleaning shop.

Her best dress needed freshening up in time for the annual office party and Phil's suit needed cleaning as well. She had slipped her hand into his jacket pockets as a matter of routine only expecting to find a business card or pen to be removed. But instead, she had pulled out a small slip of paper with a telephone number, the name Lisa and a heart shape drawn with 'I LOVE YOU' written inside.

Beth's heart had skipped a beat as she read the words.

Surely this could not be true? Why would Phil have kept this incriminating piece of evidence in his pocket – could it be that he actually wanted her to find it?

She had no reason to suspect that he was having an affair – or was even contemplating one. Their marriage was going through a bit of a stale time but she thought this happened to everyone.

Beth and her friend Amanda often talked about their husbands over cups of coffee in their kitchens when neither was at work. They would sit and discuss their men, children and other domestic trivia at length. As far as Beth knew, neither Amanda nor her husband had ever strayed from the marital path.

Phil had seemed happy enough recently although a bit distracted perhaps and working plenty of overtime. Now she thought about it, he probably was working late more often than ever before but had said this was due to falling sales and the pressure exerted by his boss to ensure he reached his targets.

Anyway, Beth felt her mind wandering from where she wanted it to be.

Dragging her thoughts back to the piece of paper in her hand she had sat down slowly on the bed. Should she ring this number and find out who 'Lisa' was?

Could it be that this was not meant for him or maybe someone had slipped it in his pocket as a joke. But who would do that? And surely Phil himself would have found it and either shown her to share a laugh about it or binned the scrap of paper.

Beth looked up and stared at herself in the dressing table mirror in front of her. Her grey eyes looked large and startled at the shock of her find. She felt cold and shivery as she suddenly felt that her life seemed to belong to someone else.

What should she do?

Should she show it to Phil and confront him?

"I just don't know what to do," she said aloud to herself in the mirror.

After a few minutes, she got to her feet and pushed the paper into the front pocket of her jeans. She took a deep breath and picked up her brush to pull through her shoulder-length fair hair a few times. As she laid it back down she decided not to say anything yet.

Beth had a tendency to blurt out the first thing that came into her head when faced with a problem and this was not a good policy. It often meant that what she said was either an accusation or a condemnation.

Beth realised she could afford neither of these in the present circumstances. She would have to be sure of the facts before she could confront Phil with the situation.

Although he had a good sense of humour she doubted that a full-on accusation from her that he was having an affair would go down very well with him, especially after a busy day at work.

So, probably best to say nothing for a while and try to carry on as normal. Go downstairs and start the preparations for the homecoming of her three children.

When they arrived home, and before they started their homework, it was customary for Beth to prepare a little snack for her children. It was a ritual that they sat together for a few minutes and talked about the day at school.

Beth had noticed that Annie had become a little reticent of late, leaving most of the talking to the younger two. This might just be the usual way of teenagers as they grew up and became more secretive about what they got up to.

Beth decided she would try and spend some time with Annie to make sure she had no problems that needed her help or advice.

Running down the stairs to the kitchen, Beth quickly got some flapjacks out of the biscuit tin and began mixing three banana milk shakes ready for the invasion. She took some straws out of the cupboard for their drinks and put the kettle on ready for her own cup of tea.

Just as she had finished she heard the gate bang and James and Christina ran in through the back door.

"Whoopee it's Friday," sang Christina, at twelve years old, the youngest of Beth's children She was a small pretty girl with long straight hair the same colour as Beth's and big blue eyes that could melt the strongest heart.

"And it's half term!," yelled her 14-year-old brother punching the air with his fist as he threw his school bag on the floor and jumped over it. James was a slim dark-haired boy of average height who had inherited Phil's good looks.

"All right, calm down you two," laughed Beth. "Where's Annie?"

"Oh she's coming in a minute," said Christina. "She stopped to talk to that boy who lives in the house behind us. You know, the one with the hot tub in the garden."

'Aha,' thought Beth, 'that's why she has been quiet recently and keeping her thoughts to herself'.

As James and Christina sat down at the table and grabbed a handful of flapjacks, Annie walked in through the back door.

Beth looked at her and smiled. Annie was growing up very quickly with long, silky dark hair falling to her shoulders and developing a nice figure – despite the school uniform.

"Hi Annie, how was your day?" asked Beth.

"Fine," was the muted response.

"Anything exciting or different happen today?" probed Beth. Annie shot her a quick look and almost blushed.

"No, not really," she replied. "But I have been asked to a party tomorrow night. It's at the house behind us with the hot tub in the garden. Ben and Joanne are having a party while their parents are out."

"Oh," said Beth. "And do their parents know about the party?"

"Yes," said Annie. "They don't mind as long as there are no gate-crashers and it finishes at midnight. They are only going across the road to some friends for dinner so they'll be able to hear if anything gets out of hand."

"Sounds great," Beth responded. She was relieved to hear it was not going to be the sort of party where anyone could turn up – including the police – during the early hours!

"What will you wear?" Beth asked the perennial female question. "How about that new dress we bought a couple of weeks ago?"

"Don't think so," Annie replied as she sat at the kitchen table and picked up her glass. "It isn't the sort of party where you dress up. I'll just wear jeans and a top."

"Are any of your friends going?" asked Beth as she fiddled with her cup. "Will you know anyone else there?"

"I think some of the people in my class will be there, but Linda, Sheila and Marilyn aren't going," replied Annie.

James and Christina stood up, bored now that they had finished their snack, They picked up their school bags to go upstairs to their rooms.

"Are you going to do your homework now or leave it till later during half term?" asked their mother.

"Now," they both said at the same time. "Then we are free to do whatever we want," said Christina twirling around with her hands in the air.

"Mind your bag against the units," said her mother. "OK. We'll have spaghetti bolognaise for tea tonight and I'll call you when it's ready."

She looked at the clock and added, "Dad will probably be early tonight too."

And now, here she was stirring the pasta and wishing that she had not found the piece of paper now resting in the pocket of her jeans.

Beth moved about the kitchen collecting plates and cutlery. She heard Phil talking to the children upstairs and then they all came clattering down towards the kitchen.

"OK everyone, it's ready," she said as she began dishing out the pasta, meat and vegetables. She realised she was lucky as no-one began saying they did not want any or part of the meal. Her sister's children were very fussy about their food and only ate what they were used to.

"Right," said Phil as he picked up his knife and fork. "What's new today then?"

Beth looked at him across the table but he was not looking at her. The two younger children competed for his attention with their tales of school and what they wanted to do during half term.

Annie and Beth sat quietly eating their spaghetti and let the others talk.

"I need to go into work at the beginning of next week' said Phil to Beth when James and Christina became occupied with their dinner. "What about you Beth, are you having any days off next week?"

"Yes," she said. "I've booked the whole week off and I am sure I told you that a couple of days ago."

She looked at him as he struggled to remember the conversation. She couldn't stop herself thinking, 'This is another clue towards the puzzle of the telephone number. He forgets our conversations!'

"Yeah, I think I do remember now, you saying something about taking the last of your holiday entitlement. So what will you do at the end of the year at Christmas?" he asked.

"I told you that too," said Beth sharply. "The offices are closing down for a few days as there is not usually much to do and it will save on heating costs."

"Oh right," said Phil as he finished his dinner. "Yep, I do remember that now too."

Beth looked down at her plate as she scraped up the remains of her meal. She asked herself if she would have noticed this seeming lack of interest in her life if she had not found that dreaded piece of paper?

Everyone had finished now and looked round to see what was going to be served next.

"Have you made a pudding?" asked James.

"Not today," said Beth. "But there are choc ices in the freezer and the rest of the bowl of fruit salad in the fridge if you want to help yourselves."

The three children needed no further reminder as they got up from the table and took their choc ices out of the top basket of the freezer and went towards the back door.

"Whose turn is it to fill the dishwasher?" asked Beth.

"Mine," replied Christina turning back, "I'll come back in when I've finished and do it – OK?"

"Yes, that's fine," responded Beth. "Do you want an ice cream or a coffee?" she turned back to Phil and asked him.

"Just coffee I think. I'll go and put the telly on and watch the news while you make it," he said.

Beth got up and switched on the kettle. She purposely left the dishes on the table for Christina as she believed in everyone taking their turn to help out in the house.

As she spooned coffee into the cups she felt edgy and disorientated. The spoon fell out of her hand and onto the floor. She bent to pick it up and banged her head on the cupboard door handle.

'I need to talk to someone,' she thought. 'I'll have to ring Verity or Amanda.'

She took the coffee cups into the front room and sat on the chair furthest away from Phil. He didn't notice as he was listening to the sports editor talking about tomorrow's local football match.

Beth sat quietly and sipped her coffee. How was she going to speak to Verity or Amanda without anyone hearing their conversation? Maybe she should pretend she needed something from the shop and ring from her mobile? It was obvious that there would be no peace in the house for the next nine days now that it was half term holiday. Or perhaps she should try and deal with this herself first before speaking to anyone else.

Beth leaned back in the chair and closed her eyes. She felt very weary and might have dropped off to sleep had the phone beside her not chosen that very moment to ring.

"Hello?," she said into the receiver. "Oh it's you Verity – what's up, you sound strange?"

Beth listened to her sister and suddenly sat up straight in the chair nearly dropping her cup.

"What's happened? You've done what?" she asked.

"We've won some money on the lottery that John does at work," her sister said down the phone. "Can you believe it? We can't. We've talked about it for the last hour since he got home and we still can't believe it!!"

"How much have you won?" asked the ever-practical Beth.

"You won't believe it," said Verity. "We've won over two hundred and fifty thousand pounds. And that's each, everyone in the syndicate has won that much."

"I don't believe it," said Beth, emulating Victor Meldrew. "I just don't believe it. When did you find out?"

"About an hour ago when John got home from work," repeated Verity. "He didn't tell me until he got home. He knew at about four o'clock when the chap at work checked the ticket at the newsagent shop."

"Wowwee!" Whooped Beth. "I'm so pleased for you!"

She swung round in the chair to look at Phil and said to him, "Guess what? Verity and John have won the lottery!"

He looked stunned and pleased and yelled out, "Well done!," for Verity to hear down the phone line.

"Thanks," shouted back Verity. "We don't know what to do yet. We don't know what to spend it on but I know we are going to have a really good holiday. John wants a new car, Sam and Lucy are making a list and I just want to go shopping!!"

"I should think you do," agreed Beth. "Can I come with you?" she joked.

"Yes, definitely," said her loyal sister. "You can have some new clothes too."

"Oh I didn't mean that," Beth said immediately. "I just wanted to come and watch you buy some."

"Well we will sort that out very soon," promised Verity. "We have not actually got the money yet. We will probably have it in the bank sometime next week. Anyway, I am going to ring mum and dad now and tell them. They'll be knocked over,"she chortled.

"OK," said Beth. "Ring me again if you want to. We are so pleased for you all." She smiled at Phil as she spoke. "Bye then." Beth put the phone down.

"What fantastic news." said Phil, his attention taken away from the football. "What are they going to do with all that money? Pay off the mortgage?"

"The mortgage wasn't mentioned," replied Beth. "Only new cars and clothes shopping."

"It's so great to hear of someone you know actually winning a sizeable amount," said Phil, leaning back in his chair and yawning. "Reading about people in the newspapers isn't the same."

"I'm going to tell the kids," said Beth getting up from the chair and carrying the cups outside to the kitchen. "I'm sure their cousins will become their new best friends now," she laughed.

"Hey kids! Some great news!" She called from the back door.

They came running in and listened with amazement as Beth told them about the lottery win.

"Oh brilliant!,"yelled James. "Can we go round and see them now?" he asked.

"Oh yes," agreed Christina. "Let's go now."

"We can't do that," Annie told them. "You can't just go round to people who have won money and beg from them."

"We won't beg," said James indignantly. "I'm sure they will just give us some, won't they?" He looked at his mother for support.

"We aren't going round to their house now," said Beth firmly. "They want some time alone to discuss what they are going to do with the money. And we won't be begging either."

She looked at James. "You are not to text or ring unless you just want to say well done to them. Congratulate them on their good luck. You are not to ask for anything – do you hear?"

"Oh, OK," he sighed in agreement, looking rather disappointed.

"But we can still go and see them soon can't we?" Christina asked, brightening up a bit.

"Of course. We will see them sometime during half term. We always have a day out with them don't we?" their mother promised. "Now Christina – fill the dishwasher please and then has anyone still got homework to do or have you finished?"

As the family dispersed to go their separate ways, she realised that Verity could not be confided in now and wondered about ringing Amanda. She could use the excuse of spreading the good news.

Beth picked up her mobile phone and wandered out into the back garden towards the swinging chair. She sat down and looked back at the house. She could see Christina's head bobbing up and down as she bent to fill the dishwasher. Annie was upstairs in her bedroom which was confirmed as her music had started again. James had probably gone through to the front room to talk to Phil about whether his cousins would give him a share of their windfall.

Beth prodded Amanda's number on her phone and put it to her ear. The phone rang twice and then went straight to answerphone. Beth cancelled and pressed call and rang again but got the same response. She left a brief message for Amanda saying she would ring again later or the next day.

She swung her legs despondently on the swing and contemplated her feet as they moved backwards and forwards. Her toes could do with a new coat of nail polish, she decided, and her sandals were beginning to crack at the sides due to constant use during the hot summer weather they had enjoyed that year.

As Beth swung idly she decided to leave worrying about her

problem until tomorrow. It was getting quite dark now and if she went inside and opened a bottle of wine, Phil would join her in drinking it and they could live through another evening without Beth's fears coming between them – at least until tomorrow.

Tomorrow was another day – and as an ending of a famous novel it could also be applied to Beth's present dilemma.

Yes, she would deal with the problem tomorrow.

Chapter Two

*W*hen tomorrow came at just after 7am, Beth groaned slightly as the consequences of drinking nearly a full bottle of red wine became apparent. A slight headache, a dry mouth and sore throat was not a good start to a day when major problems had to be confronted. Beth did not indulge in alcohol very often but last night had felt the need to become a little tipsy.

She turned over in bed and tried to get comfortable enough to return to sleep for a bit. But once her mind had begun to work through the events of yesterday, there was no getting back to sleep. She carefully sat up so as not to disturb Phil and slipped out of bed.

Quietly walking across the door she picked up her lightweight dressing gown and pushed her feet into her slippers. She opened the door as quietly as possible and pulled it softly behind her.

Beth hesitated on the landing making sure that Phil's slight snoring could still be heard before she tiptoed to the stairs. When she reached the kitchen she shut the door behind her and went to put the kettle on. She took out her favourite mug covered with red poppies and put in a tea bag. The boiling water steamed out of the kettle as Beth filled the cup. After milk had been added, Beth took the cup out into the conservatory to sit and reflect.

Again, the question – what should she do? Phil had acted perfectly normally during the evening and they had enjoyed drinking the wine and idly chatting about her sister's good fortune. They had even planned what would be their 'dream' future together if they had won the money.

But did they have a future together? Beth and Phil had always been adamant that their marriage would not be invaded by any other person. Beth had never been tempted to stray into an affair, in fact the opportunity had never really ever presented itself to her, she realised, almost with a tinge of regret.

But what if it had? How far would she go? Would she consider her options? Of course not, she thought with a touch of anger. When they had exchanged their wedding vows they had meant them – forever. Probably most people do – at least at the time, she pondered.

There was nothing wrong with their marriage apart from a bit of apathy. They spent time together, although mostly with the children as well. They did not go out on their own very often apart from their annual wedding anniversary meal and the occasional 'work' do organised by Phil's boss.

Beth thought back to their anniversary meal this year which had been a bit of a disaster. They had booked a table at their usual restaurant but when they arrived it had obviously changed hands. The menu was not to their taste with most dishes served being covered in rich sauces. Too many extra tables had been added and the waiters spent all night bumping from one chair to another as they hurriedly tried to hand out the meals.

The background music had been slightly too loud adding nothing to the ambience but making conversation a strain and they had waited a long time between their starter and main course due to a mix up with the orders.

Beth had chosen a pasta dish for her main course, which had turned out to be just that – a plate of pasta. There was no recognisable sauce with this meal just a sprinkling of peas and asparagus. She had forced down as much of the dry food as possible not wanting to make a fuss on their special night out.

Phil had chosen a steak as usual, but he had not enjoyed the accompanying sauce or the lack of sufficient food to fill him. Nouvelle cuisine looks very nice on the plate, almost a shame to eat it, but it is not very sustaining to someone with an appetite, man or woman, she thought.

The dessert menu was no better with very rich and delicate offerings that did not satisfy. They had not lingered over coffee as they usually did but paid the bill and left, vowing to try somewhere else next year.

Anyway, back to the problem of the telephone number. Beth decided that she did not want to speak to Phil about it before she had talked it over with someone else. This would get things sorted out in her mind better and help her to approach him with a slightly calmer attitude. She could take out her indignation and upset on somebody else first.

Beth finished her cup of tea and leaned back with a sigh of relief. It was always a good thing to make a decision, somehow it felt that the task was almost completed. She would ring Amanda later today and arrange to meet her somewhere so they could have a private conversation.

Four hours later Beth was sat in the café at Morrisons with her excuse for being there – a trolley-load of shopping already piled into her car. She sipped her cup of coffee as she looked out of the window waiting for Amanda to arrive.

Amanda's bright yellow car swept into the car park and she parked with a flourish as close to the entrance as possible. Beth watched as Amanda got out of the car and locked it before walking towards the swing door. As usual she was totally oblivious to the men looking at her as she swung her long blonde hair from side to side.

With her height of five foot eleven, Amanda was striking enough but her looks certainly drew even more attention wherever she went.

Beth smiled fondly at Amanda as she made her way across the cafeteria to the cappuccino placed ready for her.

"Hiya babes," she said kissing Beth on the cheek. "Well, what's all this cloak and dagger stuff about, meeting in Morrisons?! I don't think I've ever been in this café before," she added looking around at the sparsely populated tables.

"Have you been shopping already?" she asked Beth.

"Yes," replied Beth. "How are you? I haven't spoken to you for a few days. What's been happening?"

"Oh just the usual. A bit of work, sorting out kids stuff, you know how it is. Anyway, what's more important, is what's happened to you?" she repeated.

"Well a couple of things really," began Beth, methodically stirring her coffee. "One good and one…well, weird I suppose."

"Right then, come on let's have the weird one first and save the best till last," said Amanda

She settled back in her chair and looked closely at Beth's face for the first time since she had arrived. "I can see something has upset you so let's hear it."

'Well, it was yesterday afternoon as I was sorting out some clothes for dry cleaning. I took Phil's best suit out of the wardrobe and felt in the pockets for pens, loose change, that sort of thing' explained Beth. "And I found a piece of paper."

"OK," nodded Amanda slowly. "And what was on this piece of paper."

"A phone number," stated Beth.

"OK," Amanda said again. "Anything else?"

"Yes," Beth looked down at her cup almost ashamed to carry on with her explanation. It wasn't her fault though – she didn't ask to find this 'incriminating evidence'!

'Look I'll show you' Beth reached into her handbag and opened her purse.

She had scrunched up the piece of paper and fitted it into one of the pockets of her purse. Beth handed the small item over to Amanda who opened it up immediately.

She glanced at the writing and looked up at Beth.

"Who's Lisa?" she asked.

Beth shrugged her shoulders and said, "I don't know. I don't know anyone called Lisa but obviously Phil does."

Amanda studied the writing again before handing the paper back to Beth.

"Have you asked Phil about this yet?" she asked.

"No, course not," replied Beth. "I haven't had a chance and I want to get it right. I don't want to do my usual way of just blurting out something and regretting it later."

Amanda nodded in agreement as Beth folded the paper back to its small shape and replaced it in her purse.

"If you ask him there will probably be some simple explanation," said Amanda as she tossed her blonde hair back over her shoulders and picked up her cup to take a sip.

"And what if there isn't?" asked Beth. "What do I do then?"

"Ah that's the thing isn't it? You haven't said anything in case he tells you something you don't want to hear. I am right, aren't I," pressed Amanda.

"Of course you are," snapped Beth. "It doesn't take an amateur psychologist to work that out. But it still doesn't solve what I am going to do."

They looked at each other over the table top and sighed. Amanda may be a 'blonde bombshell' but she was not flighty. She was mostly unaware of the effect her looks had on men. Her marriage was a good one and Brian, who was eight years older than Amanda, knew how to keep his wife happy. They had two teenagers both of whom were looking forward to going to university and Amanda had a part time job at the local garden centre. She loved growing plants and her garden was always a picture, whatever time of the year. Amanda was happiest in her scruffy jeans, hair tied back with a band and a trowel and trug in her hands. She was very knowledgeable too and spent many hours reading books or surfing the internet to gain further information about her precious plants.

Beth often envied Amanda for having such a passionate lifelong interest.

They had known each other since meeting in the maternity unit at the local hospital. Amanda had been having her second baby, Claire, whilst Beth was giving birth to Annie. Their babies had been born within 24 hours of each other and Amanda had helped and advised Beth during the first few weeks of new motherhood which led to them forming a lasting friendship. Their daughters too were quite close although they did not count each other as 'best friends'.

The two families did not meet often as the men weren't on the same wavelength. Amanda's husband, being a bit older, seemed almost like he belonged to a different generation and he was not interested in sport. Phil, on the other hand, loved football and cricket and had played both for many years.

He had given up playing football on Sunday mornings a couple of years ago but had become involved with the local team of under 14's as James played in goal. Phil had tried to encourage him to play a more energetic role, but James was happy waiting for the action to reach him before leaping out and saving as many balls as he could reach.

It was therefore Amanda and Beth who continued their friendship, mostly meeting when they were able to fit it in with other family commitments.

Amanda sat up straight in her chair and looked at Beth. "You know the only way to sort this out is to actually talk to Phil and ask him. There's no other solution."

"I could ring the number," suggested Beth. "Pretend I was someone else and find out who answers."

"Yes but that could still give you the wrong idea, or even no idea at all. The person might not be Lisa, and anyway how do you ask if she knows Phil at all?" asked Amanda.

'I haven't thought all that out yet. I've been so shocked and I wanted to talk about it before I did anything. You know what I'm like: act first, think later and this is too important to make a mistake," said Beth. "I know I could ring the number and just ask for Lisa. See what happens. But I need to know what to do, or say, after that."

"I don't know," responded Amanda. "I've never been in this situation and don't know anyone who has. What about all those chic-lit books you read? What happens in them to someone in this situation?"

"Oh that's easy, they always do the right thing. And if they don't, it still comes out right in the end. How can I know this will? If Phil is having an affair, there I've actually said it now. what am I going to do? I never ever thought that this might happen to us so I don't know the right way to deal with it!"

Beth slumped forward with her chin on both hands and her elbows on the table.

"Come on, cheer up – you don't know that Phil is having an affair."

Amanda leaned forward to pat the top of Beth's head. "Why don't you just throw the piece of paper away and forget about it? Pretend you never found it?"

Beth closed her eyes and groaned. She took a deep breath and sat up.

"You know I'm not the type of person to brush things under the carpet. I like to find out what's going on and why. Anyway, I would always have a doubt in my mind and will probably blurt it out one day when we are having a row or something."

"No, I need to know who Lisa is and what this piece of paper is doing in Phil's pocket. I'm going to ring the number and pretend to be someone selling something. I'll ask to speak to Lisa and say I've got her number from someone she works with. That might give me a clue to find out if she works with Phil,"

Beth's voice became more decisive as she worked out what she was going to do.

"OK," said Amanda. "Then what?"

"Then I will…Oh I don't know" I'll have to work it out and write it out so I don't get stuck on the phone not knowing what to say," said Beth.

"That's a good idea. Get something down on paper and then you won't have to think fast and get it wrong. But can you cover all possibilities?" asked Amanda.

"Well obviously not everything, but if I spend a bit of time working out a couple of different replies then I might cover most things. Also, I'll have to remember to withhold my telephone number."

"When do you think you will do this? Remember, it's half term now so not much peace and quiet for a few days," Amanda reminded Beth.

"I know." replied Beth. "I'll have to wait for everyone to go out or leave it until the next week. How am I going to get through the next few days with this on my mind?' she asked.

"You could always come over to me for an hour one day and make the call from my phone. I could keep Paul and Claire busy and you could have the front room to yourself for a bit. You could work out what you want to say and write it down and then ring the number. You'd have privacy from anyone in your family bursting in on you," offered Amanda.

"Oh that's great, thanks a lot," said Beth smiling at her friend. "I think I might take you up on that offer. What I'll do is find out what we're doing next week and see if I can come over to your house for an hour or so."

"Right, that's settled then. I'll have to go now. I promised to take the kids into town for some new trainers. I expect I will end up buying more than that but it will be their half term treat. What are you doing now?" asked Amanda getting to her feet and gathering her coat and bag.

"'I'm going to take the shopping back home and then they should be back from Phil's mum's soon. They went to clear her garden up a bit and I think she wanted to give the kids some half term spending money. That's why I managed to get away alone to do the shopping," explained Beth.

"Hey I've just remembered – what was the good news you were going to tell me?" asked Amanda.

"Oh yeah – you'll never guess – not in a million years," teased Beth.

"No, okay I won't guess, then tell me."

"Verity and John have won some money on the lottery. And I mean big money – life changing money," said Beth. "They are hoping to buy new cars, go on holidays, pay off the mortgage probably."

"Oh great – it's good to actually know someone who wins a big amount, not just a tenner," said Amanda.

"That's what everyone says," Beth agreed. "I'll find out more about it when I see Verity this week. I'm sure they will do something for mum and dad too. James is hoping for a share I think, I've had to tell him not to 'beg' for a handout." Beth laughed at the memory of her son's disappointed face when she had told him to wait to be offered a present.

They walked together out of the café and into the car park, stopping next to Amanda's custard-coloured vehicle.

'I wouldn't change my car but a nice holiday in a hot and exotic place for a couple or three weeks would be nice," Amanda mused.

"Yes," agreed Beth. "Do you do the lottery?"

"No," said Amanda, laughing. "Looks like two weeks in Tenerife again next year – it's not so bad though," she said.

"Well we'll probably be in the caravan again next summer – and that's not so bad either' said Beth kissing her friend on the cheek. "I'll ring you on Monday and arrange a time to come over. And thanks, thanks a lot for listening to me and trying to help."

"Chin up, it's probably not as bad as your imagination is making it," said Amanda, unlocking her car. "I'll see you some time next week. Take care."

Beth set off across the car park towards her car and waved when Amanda swept passed her.

She felt better for having talked about her dilemma with her friend. Again, she could put off having to do anything for a couple more days and try to get on with her life.

Beth drove home with the radio blaring out Saturday afternoon pop songs and tried to sing along with the ones she knew. She would put the shopping away and wait for her family to arrive back home. They had planned to go to Pizza Hut for a meal that evening and she would soak in a hot bubble bath before putting on the new jeans she had bought in the sale last week when she was having a shopping browse during her lunch break.

Of course, Annie was going to the party that night, Beth suddenly remembered. Perhaps it would be better to have a take-away pizza to make sure that Annie ate with them in case there was the possibility of alcohol consumption that evening.

Beth could remember going to teenage parties held at her friends' houses when their parents were out. Bottles of cider and beer were the usual drinks in those days but now they had these alcopops and Barcardi Breezers.

Beth did not know the parents of this lad but as they were only going to be across the road at a dinner party, she did not think that things should get out of hand in their absence. But you never knew for sure. Maybe they did not mind a bunch of befuddled teenagers let loose in their house? She was sure that Annie had said it would not be a late night, though, so that did bode well. Anyway, they would definitely eat at home tonight so that Annie could not excuse herself from joining them. They could go out to Pizza Hut another night.

Beth swung the car expertly into the drive and noticed that Phil's Audi was not there. She unloaded the shopping and filled the fridge and freezer.

As she put the kettle on to make a cup of tea she heard Phil's car pull up outside. A few minutes later they all bundled in the front door and the children excitedly began to tell Beth what they had been doing all afternoon.

From the three of them she gathered that Phil's mum had given them £10 each to spend at half term, they had helped with the gardening work and been to see the litter of puppies next door.

"Can we have one?" asked Christina hopefully to her mum. "Oh please, let's have one. I liked the smallest puppy best, it was so cuddly and sweet."

"I don't really think it would be fair to have a puppy, or a dog, when we are all out all day," Beth told her. "They need a lot of looking after and we really haven't got the time."

"I knew you'd say that," said Christina, dismally stubbing her toe on the floor.

"Do you think we'll ever have the time for a puppy?" she asked her mum.

19

"Not at the moment," Beth gently replied as she continued to make the tea and pour out

some squash for the children.

Phil came into the kitchen and washed his hands at the sink. "Are we still going to Pizza Hut tonight?" he asked his wife.

"Well I think we'll give it a miss tonight. Annie is going to a party so we don't want to be late out and her to miss any of it," she said looking over at her eldest daughter.

"I think we'll make do with a take away pizza tonight and go out another time this week," she compromised.

"OK." said Phil, "That's fine with me."

"What time are you going to the party Annie?" asked Beth.

"Oh about eight o'clock I think. Ben said he would look out for me at that time. So I'll leave here just before eight," Annie answered.

"Are you walking round there on your own?" asked Phil.

"I'll be OK, it's only round the corner," replied Annie.

"Yes but it will be dark at eight so I think I'll walk round there with you." said Phil.

"'No dad, it's OK,' Annie assured him, looking a little flustered.

"Don't worry, I won't come to the door or even to the gate," laughed Phil. "I can remember what it's like to be a teenager, you know. I'll walk as far so I can see you go into the front gate. But what about getting home?" he asked Annie.

"Ben said he will bring me home, probably about midnight," Annie looked anxiously from her dad to her mum and back again. "That's ok isn't it?"

"Yes that's fine." reassured her mother. "As long as you take your mobile and ring us if you need collecting. Your dad can pop round and meet you as you come out if necessary. But only if Ben can't bring you back or you want to come home earlier…or something."

"And I do want you home by midnight," her dad said as he sat down at the kitchen table. "I know it's your first big date but you are still only sixteen," he added.

"Oh dad, I know," Annie rolled her eyes at the ceiling. "I'll be back by midnight and it's not a date – just a party."

Beth smiled to herself. She could remember similar conversations with her parents when she and Verity had begun to spread their wings a bit. They had been lucky though, as Vera and Jack were lenient parents – obviously concerned about their daughters but not taking it to extremes.

"Are you having a bath or shower before you go?" asked Beth.

"Of course," said Annie. "I'll go and get started now. What time will the take-away be here?"

"We'll order for about seven so that will give you time to eat before you rush off," said Beth. "Do you want to go to the video shop and get a DVD for tonight?" she asked the younger children who were feeling a bit left out.

"Oh yes, wicked!" James said. "Can we have one each?" asked Christina.

"OK, just this once but you will have to start watching early enough 'cos you two aren't staying up until midnight," said Phil looking at his watch.

"It's just gone five o'clock now so we'll go and get the DVDs and order the food for seven." Phil got to his feet and picked up his car keys again.

"Come on then," he nodded at Beth and said, "Why don't you go and have a relaxing bath too as you've got the night off from cooking?"

"Yes I might just do that." she agreed as she started to put the cups and glasses into the dishwasher. "What a good idea."

She looked at Phil to see if he was really concerned about her but he had already left the room.

Annie said,"I'll have a shower in your en suite if you want to use the bathroom for your bath."

"That's a good idea," agreed Beth. "We can both make ourselves beautiful at the same time."

They went upstairs together and Beth spent the next hour soaking in a hot bubble bath before getting dressed and wandering into Annie's room to see how she was getting on.

Annie had showered and washed her hair and was sat at her dressing table putting on her make up. Her jeans and top were placed on the bed and Annie turned round as her mum walked in.

"Mum, do you think I could borrow those sparkly sandals you bought a while ago?" She asked. "The one's you wore to Verity's birthday party?"

"Yes you can borrow them for tonight – but I want them back to wear again myself. I'll go and get them." Beth turned round and went back to her bedroom.

As she opened the wardrobe door to find the shoes, her thoughts went back to yesterday – was it only yesterday? – when she had taken Phil's suit out of the wardrobe and found the piece of paper.

She rummaged about at the bottom of the wardrobe to find the shoe box containing the sandals.

"Try to forget it for a while," she told herself. "Give yourself a break."

She then considered Phil in the kitchen earlier. 'He doesn't seem like a man with a secret lover,' she thought.

Beth took the sandals in to Annie and sat on the bed watching her stroking mascara through her eyelashes.

"Are you excited?" She asked.

"Oh Mum, it's only a party," said Annie looking at her reflected in the mirror.

But Beth could see Annie's eyes shining and her hand was shaking a bit.

"Well I hope you have a lovely time," smiled Beth back at her. "Just be home for midnight and don't turn into a pumpkin."

When the pizza arrived just after seven, they were all sitting in the front room watching a Saturday evening quiz programme. Phil answered the door and paid the delivery boy before taking the boxes into the front room. He handed them out to each of his family and sat down again to eat his pizza.

As soon as Annie had finished hers, she jumped up and put her empty box on the table.

"I'm going to finish getting ready now," she said as she left the room.

"Can we watch our other DVD now?" asked James.

They had put Christina's choice on as soon as they had returned with their dad from the video shop.

'Yes when this programme has finished," said their mother. "I want to see who wins."

Twenty minutes later the door opened and Annie poked her head round.

"I'm off now – back by midnight," she promised.

Beth and Phil both got to their feet.

"I'll see you out," Beth said as she followed Annie and Phil to the front door. "Now I'm not going to nag you, but just be careful and don't drink anything you are not sure of," said Beth as Annie pulled the front door open.

"I'm not stupid," said Annie. "But I know what you're saying and I'll be careful – I promise."

"I know you will but mums have to repeat these things all the time to make sure they're doing their job properly," joked Beth as she kissed her daughter's cheek.

"Goodbye and have a great time' said Beth as she watched them both walk down the path.

She closed the door and went back inside. The quiz had finished now and she had missed the end anyway. She went into the front room and collected all the empty boxes as James was pushing the DVD into the machine.

"Enjoy your film," she said as she carried the rubbish out of the room. "Dad and I will sit in the conservatory for a bit when he gets back."

Beth piled the boxes by the back door ready for the recycling bin and went into the conservatory. She put the radiator on as it was getting quite chilly. Looking out across the gardens she could see an array of lights in the house she thought would be where Annie was going. She had never taken much notice of her neighbours apart from those living next door. Mrs Hall was on one side and the Parkers on the other. Life was too busy these days for chatting and getting to know folk who lived close by, she mused.

Beth was glad she had a week off work to relax and enjoy. She enjoyed her part time job, working for a local firm of accountants, but it would be nice not to have to get up and rush about for a few mornings. She mostly took time off during the school holidays but sometimes went in for a couple of hours in the mornings to keep her work up to date. On these occasions, her parents would come around and keep an eye on the children. As they were all getting older now this might not be so necessary, thought Beth. But her

father in particular enjoyed his role as a granddad and liked to spend time with the children. They too loved his visits as he always gave them his full attention – something parents often did not, or could not, do.

Beth sat on the settee and leant back into the soft cushions. Phil would be back in a minute and would join her, probably bringing a bottle of wine and two glasses for them to share. She must not drink so much tonight, she thought, remembering the slight headache she had experienced that morning, just stick to one glass.

Chapter Three

*T*en o'clock on Monday morning saw Beth filling the washing machine and thinking about the previous weekend. Annie had enjoyed her party and been brought home by Ben just before midnight.

Phil and Beth had been in bed when they heard her key in the door. She had quietly gone to her bedroom without calling out goodnight in case she woke them.

Sunday had been the usual type of day with everyone getting up late. Annie had told them about the party, or the bits she wanted them to know, and said she was going to Ben's house again on Monday afternoon to watch a DVD with him.

Christina and James had teased Annie a bit about her 'new boyfriend Ben' until Beth had put a stop to it.

Phil and James had left for the under-14 football match which kicked off at two o'clock and Beth had promised to go and watch for a while. She had arrived just as James had saved a promising header by a very tall striker from the opposing team. He looked as if he should be playing for the under 18s! She clapped and cheered with the other parents as James threw the ball out into the field again. There was more clapping and cheering from the locals when their team won by four goals to two. All was well with the world but not for Beth.

Annie and Christina had stayed home to finish their homework. Annie had also promised to peel the potatoes ready for the meal that evening. Beth usually cooked a roast dinner on Sundays although they did occasionally go to the local Toby Inn if they had had a busy weekend.

As Beth finished filling the washing machine and turning it to the correct programme for its load, the dishwasher completed its cycle of cleaning the weekend's dishes.

Beth stood up and picked up her mobile phone from the table. She rang Amanda's number and put the phone to her ear.

"Hiya," came Amanda's voice. "What time are you coming over then?"

"About three o'clock if that's ok with you," replied Beth. "Mum and Dad are going to take the kids to the boating lake and Annie is going to a friend's house this afternoon. So I could actually make the call here but I think if I come to you I will be more likely to go through with it,'" she explained.

"That's fine with me, "Amanda replied encouragingly. "Paul is going to a friend's house as well this afternoon and Claire has a friend coming to us. So it's worked out well. You

can make your plan and phone call in peace. I won't even bother you but I will want to know what happens. Ok?"

"Oh, of course" agreed Beth. "I'll probably need to talk to you about it anyway."

She heard Christina coming down the stairs and quickly said goodbye to Amanda.

"What time are Grandma and Grandad coming to take us boating?" asked Christina.

"At two o'clock," replied her mother. "We'll have a quick lunch at about twelve thirty and then you'll be ready in time."

Christina was always worrying about being late or people forgetting treats she had been promised. Beth didn't know why she had this in-built fear as she had never been let down. Well, certainly not on a regular basis. Everyone forgets things sometimes, even promises made to little girls. Beth hoped that Christina would grow out of this worry before she became interested in dating boys as she would surely have to suffer their lateness and

being 'stood up' at least once. Everyone did!

"Let's walk down to the shops as I've got some dry cleaning to take in and could do with some more fruit and veg for tonight's dinner," said Beth. "Go and get James and ask Annie if she wants to come or stay here. Oh and pick up the plastic bag with your dad's jacket in from the spare room too please," she added.

Christina ran out of the room happy now she had been reassured that her grandparents would not forget their promise.Beth gathered her handbag and put on her jacket from the coat pegs in the hallway.

James and Christina ran downstairs and Annie peered over the banister rail.

"I'll stay here if you don't mind," she said.

"Yes that's fine," replied Beth, opening the front door. "We won't be long anyway."

She took the plastic bag from Christina and rolled it up to carry under her arm.

"Come on then let's go," she said to the younger children.

The rest of the morning passed quickly and it was soon time for Vera and Jack to collect the children. Beth waved them off in the car and went back indoors. She collected her handbag and car keys and went out of the front door, banging it hard behind her.

She drove the short distance to Amanda's house and parked outside. A little apprehensively Beth glanced up at the large detached house and saw Amanda looking out of her bedroom window. She waved and got out of the car, automatically locking the door behind her.

Amanda was opening the front door as Beth arrived and they hugged briefly, not saying anything. They went into the front room and shut the door.

"How do you feel?," Amanda asked.

"Okay I think," replied Beth. "I've tried not to think about it too much since I saw you on Saturday. Not sure if that is a good thing though, as I don't feel very well prepared. I'll have to sit and think for a few minutes and write something down, like I said."

"I'll leave you to it then," said Amanda getting up from her chair.

"What time do you think I should come back in?"

"Give me half an hour and then see if I've made the call by then," said Beth.

Amanda left the room and Beth took out her pen and a notebook she had brought with her. She opened the note book and prepared to write down her thoughts. Her mind suddenly went blank. What was she going to say? What would the person who answered the phone say? She chewed the end of her pen thoughtfully.

If Lisa answered the phone she would pretend to be asking questions for a market research company that had got her name from a listing. Beth wrote that down in her notebook.

If someone else answered the phone, she would ask for Lisa. If they said Lisa was there, she would carry on as above. If not, she would ask if she was at work. If she was at work she would ask for the number or name of the firm – it could be the same as Phil's if that was how they knew each other.

Beth scribbled down her notes quickly as she thought of them.

What if it was none of the above? Well, she would have to deal with that as it happened. She couldn't write down every eventuality could she?

She put the pen down next to the notebook on the table and leaned back in the chair. Taking a deep breath she looked at the hands-free phone Amanda had placed in readiness for her call.

After several more deep breaths, Beth took her purse out of her handbag and extracted the small piece of paper containing the phone number. She opened it up and re-read the message again.

"Come on, just get on with it," she said out loud to herself. "You can't keep putting it off. Deal with it!"

So saying, she picked up the receiver of the phone and carefully pressed the numbers.

She put the phone to her ear and waited. The phone rang six times and was then answered by a man's voice who stated the phone number.

"H-hello?" said Beth. "C-c-c-can I speak to Lisa please?"

"Lisa's not here at the moment, who's calling?" asked the voice.

"I'm just ringing on behalf of a market research company asking about…tea,"

stuttered Beth. "Brands of tea, and coffee. Is she at work?"

"Yes I think so' said the voice becoming slightly impatient. "Can you ring back later?"

"Er, yes I suppose so," said Beth. "Where does she work? Can I ring her there?" she probed.

"She works for the local council and they don't like personal calls in working hours," the man's voice informed her.

"Oh no, I suppose they don't," replied Beth. She wanted to continue the conversation now she had started it and try to find out more about Lisa.

"Does Lisa drink tea – or coffee?" she asked.

"Yes of course," replied the voice getting impatient again. "Now I really don't have time for this. If you want information from Lisa you had better ring back after six. I think she'll be in by then, but I don't always know for sure these days," he said ominously.

"Oh, why's that?" blurted out Beth. "Does she work late sometimes?"

"Yes she does, but I don't know why that's any of your business," was his reply.

"Oh, no, of course not," said Beth. "Do you know anyone called Phil?" she suddenly asked recklessly.

"What the – who are you?" he demanded, his voice becoming angry. "Phil – huh? I don't know Phil but Lisa sure as hell does!"

Beth nearly dropped the phone as his voice spat the words down the line to her. Her worst nightmare was coming true.

"What do you mean?" she asked shakily.

"I mean it's this fellow Phil who has caused all my problems. Who are you, why are you ringing and asking these questions?" he asked.

"I'm ringing to find out who Lisa is," said Beth, recovering slightly from the shock. "Who are you then? Are you Lisa's boyfriend or husband?"

"Yes, I'm her husband. Well I am at the moment but how long for I don't yet know," he said. 'Are you related to Phil? His wife maybe?"

"Yes I am," she admitted. "What's going on – do you know?"

"Well I hate to have to be the one to tell you but I think they are having some sort of an affair. I only found out on Friday when I heard her talking to him on the phone. I asked who she was talking to and she wouldn't tell me. I kept on at her, asking if it was someone from work, until she eventually said that she had been seeing him for about three months and that was why…well we then talked about some personal stuff."

His tone changed as he suddenly reminded himself that he was telling a complete stranger all about his private life.

Beth found it difficult to breathe trying to take in what the man at the other end of the phone was telling her. How could Phil be the person that he was talking about? Surely there must be a mistake.

"How did they meet if they don't work together?" she asked suddenly.

"At a pub during a lunch time office party for one of Lisa's friends. I think your husband was at the same place for the same type of thing.

29

I don't know all the gory details, and I don't want to. It's bad enough finding out your wife has been lying and cheating – and now you know it's with your husband. Did you not guess before?'

'No," said Beth. "I knew our marriage was a bit, well, stale I suppose. Not exactly rocky as we don't argue or anything very much. Just a bit boring, I suppose' she continued trying to think back over the past few months.

"Well it's going to get rocky now isn't it," he said unsympathetically. "What are you going to do?"

"I don't know," replied Beth. "I've not had time to think about that. It's just such a shock. I knew it might be something like this, but to talk to you and find out what's happened, it's just awful."

"Yes I know," said the man speaking more quietly now. "I was shocked too. Our marriage was a bit, what did you say – rocky? We were arguing over a few problems we were having. I suppose we were both staying out of each other's way a bit to save the arguments. She was working later in the evenings, or so she said, and I stayed away a few nights more than normal with my job."

Beth found she was rocking backwards and forwards and had her arm folded across her stomach. A sort of protection against the shock of finding out that Phil had been unfaithful.

"Well what do we do now?" she asked.

"I've told Lisa that she must stop seeing him and she said she would. I don't know yet whether I believe her, but I'll have to wait and see what happens in the next few days. If she still works late or wants to go out on her own, then I'll know if she meant it or not."

"Do you think I should tell Phil I know and get him to stop seeing her too?" asked Beth.

"It's up to you. I don't know. Maybe it isn't your Phil?"

"Oh it is," affirmed Beth. "I found a piece of paper in his suit pocket with your telephone number and Lisa's name inside a drawing of a heart. There's no doubt."

"Well, you have to decide if you confront him or leave it and hope they stop seeing each other. I can't tell you what to do."

Beth found tears welling in her eyes and she caught her breath in her throat as she realised that her life might be on the point of changing forever. She managed a kind of sobbing sound down the phone and the man cleared his throat.

Chapter Three

"Are you alright?" he asked in a concerned way. "I'm sorry it's all come out like this, it must be a big shock for you. Are you ok?"

Beth tried to speak but her body would not co-operate. Her tongue felt dry and unable to move, her brain would not work properly and her eyes were stinging as she tried to stop the flow of tears.

"Can I do anything to help you?" asked the man again as no sound came from Beth. "Where are you? Are you at home? Is anyone with you?" He sent out a barrage of questions all of which Beth was incapable of answering.

"I-I-I-m at m-my friend's house," she managed after swallowing deeply and taking a breath. "I'll be alright in a minute, just a shock. I'll be ok."

"Well, I don't know what to say to help you. I am just as shocked as you are. I wonder if we should keep in touch and let each other know if we find out anything," he suggested.

Beth realised that this was a good idea as it gave her somebody else to connect with who was dealing with the same problem. She found his voice vaguely reassuring even when he was brusque.

"Yes that's a good idea," she said. "Shall we swap mobile numbers?"

Beth picked up her pen ready to write down his number which she did before telling him her mobile number.

"Are you going to be alright?" asked the man again. "You said you were at your friend's house, is she there with you?"

"She's not in the room but she will come back in a minute," Beth replied. "I'll tell her

what's happened and get her advice too. I hope we can keep in touch just to make sure that they don't keep seeing each other."

"Yes that's fine, but I hope we won't need to and they will end their...affair' he responded, hesitating before using the last word, almost as if he was reluctantly admitted some flaw in himself.

"'Bye then and thanks for talking to me," said Beth standing up. "I'll ring or text you if I have any news, please do the same."

"I will," affirmed the man as he prepared to end the call. "Goodbye... and good luck."

Beth clicked the phone off just as Amanda returned to the room. Beth paused in her tracks,

looked at her and managed a small smile.

"Well, what's happened?" asked Amanda, continuing to cross the room to Beth.

"Did you manage to speak to someone?"

"Oh yes," said Beth. "I spoke to the man whose wife is having an affair with Phil," she announced loudly.

"No!" Said Amanda, wide-eyes as she sank into one of the armchairs. "Are you sure?"

"Oh yes," said Beth, sitting down again. "He has had it out with his wife as he found her talking to Phil on the phone on Friday. But I can't think when he would have phoned her, we were in all night, unless it was before he got home from work'.

She remembered seeing Phil joking with Mrs Hall next door and he had seemed quite exuberant coming in and racing up the stairs.

"What are you going to do?" asked Amanda, coming straight to the point.

"I don't know yet," said Beth. "I don't know whether to just ask him outright or to wait and see if I see any signs of him meeting this Lisa. The other man said Lisa promised not to see Phil again. I suppose they are going to try and stay together, he didn't say anything about leaving her or divorce."

"You have to decide what's right for you though, Beth. Can you keep living with Phil knowing that he has been seeing someone else?" asked Amanda.

"Yes I know but it's still such a shock. I really had no idea that Phil wasn't happy with me. It probably sounds stupid and it's always the wife who's last to hear," Beth managed to joke.

"I must admit I can't believe it either," agreed Amanda. "You always seemed such a happy couple and you don't argue much do you?"

"Perhaps that's the problem." Beth wondered. "Maybe we just don't care enough about each other to argue."

"Rubbish," said Amanda. "That's not true. Lots of people stay happily married without always rowing and shouting. John and I don't argue and I hope we are happy together…oh sorry, I don't mean to sound smug," she apologised looking slightly embarrassed in case she had upset Beth.

"No, no, don't worry. We can't spend all the time worrying about saying the wrong thing' said Beth, smiling at her friend.

"I'll go and make a cup of tea and leave you to think for a few minutes. You need a clear head to deal with something like this."

Amanda got up and went out to the kitchen. Beth heard her clinking cups and spoons and sat back in the chair. She crossed her legs and closed her eyes. If only this had not happened. If only she could have carried on with her life as it was. What was she going to do?

When Amanda came back into the room carrying a tray of tea and biscuits, Beth was no nearer making a decision.

They sat and drank their tea, neither of them feeling like indulging in the chocolate biscuits Amanda had placed on a plate. Eventually Beth put her cup down and sat up straight.

"I can't go on as if nothing has happened," she said decisively. "But I don't want to ruin our marriage if he will get over this Lisa. I think I will see what happens this week – he'll be home a bit more as he has taken some days off for half term. If we are together for a while, and I know what's been going on, I am sure I will see some signs. If he gives up this girl I may be able to get over it and try to forget,"

Amanda looked at Beth for a few seconds before saying, "Are you sure? It's a big thing he has done by cheating on you. Can you really forgive and forget?"

"I didn't say forgive," said Beth. "I may be able to forget, or at least put it to the back of my mind, but, like you say. he has cheated on me. I've never wanted to be with another man, and still don't,"

Amanda was not sure that Beth would be able to forget but maybe she could move on and live with what had happened. Amanda knew that, if it were her, she would have to confront her husband with this sort of news and sort it out between the two of them. But Beth obviously wanted to keep quiet about her discovery and see what happened.

Beth stood up and picked up her bag and coat.

"'I'd better get back now," she said to her friend. "You've been so kind, letting me come here to deal with this. I'll see what happens this week with Phil, and I'll keep you up to date."

She moved towards the door and Amanda stood up to follow her.

"You know where I am if you need me," she reassured Beth. "Just call and I'll be there – sounds like a song doesn't it?" she tried to make Beth smile.

Beth responded with a small smile to show her appreciation of her friend's help and then pulled open the front door and stepped outside.

"I'll see you soon. Hope you enjoy half term," she said.

"You too," agreed Amanda as she waved Beth off. "Don't forget to ring me if you need to."

"I won't," nodded Beth getting into her car. She started the engine and put on her seatbelt before waving again to Amanda and driving off.

The rest of half term passed quickly as they were fully occupied most of the time. Phil and Beth took the children swimming, walking in the woods, they went to the cinema one rainy afternoon and generally did things that were not possible when school and work got in the way.

Beth managed to keep an eye on Phil without him realising he was under surveillance. They spent most of the week together apart from one morning when he went into work. Beth quizzed him when he returned about what he had been doing, but he casually mentioned a meeting with a prospective client and a long chat with a colleague which must have taken up most of the time he was away.

Whilst they were passing the shop, Beth had collected the dry cleaning items and asked Phil to return his own suit to the wardrobe. He had not shown any realisation that the piece of paper might have been found or even washed away! She kept trying to talk herself into thinking that it might not be true, may not be her Phil, but she always came back to her conversation with the stranger on the telephone.

Annie had met Ben most days during the holiday, much to her siblings' delight as they were able to tease her. Beth stepped in as much as possible to save Annie's blushes and embarrassment.

On the Friday of half term, they met Verity, John, Sam and Lucy at Pizza Hut and had a riotous couple of hours with everyone's imagination running riot as they spent the lottery win several times over.

Verity had quietly told Beth that she was planning to buy presents for everyone but had not said what or when. John had paid for the outing as his treat!

So the week passed and soon they were all back into their normal routine. Beth returned to her job on the following Monday morning at 9.30 and managed to catch up on the past week's backlog of work by the end of the day. It was not a busy time for the accountancy firm and nobody else was on holiday that particular week so there were no extra jobs involved in covering other people's work.

Beth had rung Amanda once during the last weekend before she returned to work and just told her briefly that nothing had happened. They had agreed to meet up again one afternoon the following week when they were both free.

The Wednesday night before this meeting, Beth was upstairs getting ready for bed when she remembered that she had left her purse in the kitchen. She ran lightly back down the stairs but stopped when she heard Phil's voice speaking in the utility room. She stopped and tried to hear what he was saying.

However he was talking too quietly for her to hear the exact words but it was obvious he was not talking to a client. What client would ring at this time of night anyway? She glanced through the open door at the kitchen clock and saw it was just coming up to half past eleven.

Beth quietly moved backwards towards the stairs again and stepped up each one carefully so as not to make a noise. As she trod on the stair third from the top, it gave out its usual squeak. She immediately ran back down making a lot of noise.

"Just getting my purse from the kitchen," she called out. As she went through the door she heard Phil say 'Got to go – bye' and then he came out of the utility room.

"Who was that on the phone?" She asked as she picked up her purse.

"Oh, it was a wrong number. I asked the bloke what number he wanted and he had mis-dialled by one digit," Phil said, not looking at Beth. He waited for her to start back up the stairs, for the third time that night, and switched off the downstairs lights.

"What were you doing in the utility room?" persisted Beth.

"Oh, just checking the door was locked' he quickly replied.

Beth went into the en suite and shut the door behind her. As she brushed her teeth and took off her make up she realised that she had nearly caught him out. There had been no wrong number ringing his phone. He had been speaking to Lisa.

How could she get into bed with him and pretend nothing was wrong? On the other hand she did not want to start an argument at this time of night and risk waking their children. She opened the door and went back into the bedroom.

Phil was undressing and waiting for his turn in the shower room. They did not speak until they were both in bed and Phil turned off his bedside light.

"Night," he said. "Sleep well."

"Same to you," she responded but knew she wouldn't.

Beth lay there well into the early hours of the next morning listening to Phil breathing easily as he slept. How could he? He obviously had no conscience about what he was doing and also did not realise that Beth had any suspicions at all. Eventually she must have fallen asleep as the alarm clock burst into life and woke her as usual at seven o'clock.

Beth's heart dropped as she woke up and remembered what had happened late last night. Phil was slowly getting out of bed and he lumbered towards the shower room to wash and shave.

Beth lay in bed for a few minutes as her body felt as heavy as lead. She took some deep breaths to calm herself and then sat up. She forced her legs out of bed and began to get dressed.

The routine of the early morning rush hour overtook her and it was not until everyone had left for work and school that she sat at the kitchen table with a cup of coffee to think. The tears flooded her eyes but she dabbed them and regained control.

She only had half an hour before she needed to leave for work. Luckily it was a short working day for Beth and she would finish at one o'clock. Amanda was meeting her again at the café in Morrisons' supermarket.

Beth struggled through the few hours at work before driving to the supermarket car park. Again she bought the coffees and sat at a table by the window to look out for her friend's arrival.

Five minutes later, Amanda drove into the car park and parked next to Beth's car. She glanced over to the café windows and waved as she saw Beth was there. After Amanda had settled herself in a chair and taken a welcoming sip of her drink she looked closely at Beth.

"Something's happened hasn't it?" she asked.

"Yes it has," replied Beth. "I caught Phil on the phone last night, in the utility room at half past eleven. He said goodbye to someone. When I asked who it was he said it was a wrong number. But I know it wasn't. It was his tone of voice while I was listening in the hallway. He was definitely talking to someone he knows – someone he knows very well."

"Did you take it any further than just accepting it was a wrong number?" asked Amanda.

"No, it was too late to start questioning him and I didn't want a row with the children asleep in bed," said Beth.

'Yeah I understand that. Do you know what are you going to do now?" Amanda asked.

"Oh I don't know," Beth replied crossly. "I'm so fed up with this, not knowing what's going on, not knowing what to do about it, not knowing what is going to happen…" Beth frowned as she looked out of the window, not seeing the cars and shoppers, just staring into the distance.

Amanda gave her a minute's silence to think and then said, "You've got to speak to Phil and ask him what's going on."

Beth looked across the table at her friend and sighed. "I might ring that man again and see if he has found anything out since we spoke. I don't know why but that just seems the right thing to do. After all, I don't even know really for sure that Phil is having an affair with Lisa. I know it all points towards it, but I still have that small element of doubt in my mind."

"Are you sure you aren't just clutching at straws?" Amanda suggested. "I know it would be great if it wasn't Phil, but surely there are too many coincidences."

"Yes I know there are," Beth agreed. "But I still need to be one hundred per cent sure in my mind before I speak to Phil. I don't want to accuse him wrongly and I don't want to break up our marriage if I don't have to."

"Ok then, so when are you going to ring this man again? Do you want to come to my house so you're not interrupted?'

"No it's ok but thanks. I'll do this one on my own. I'll go out in the car and ring his mobile like he said I could. If he thinks they are still seeing each other than I will probably face up to it and ask Phil. I think I am gradually coming to terms and realising that he is having an affair with Lisa. I'm definitely over the first shock of finding out. But why am I not really upset? I had the start of some tears earlier but I only seem to be on a mission to find out what's happening and it doesn't seem real." Beth shook her head as if to shake out the answer to these questions.

"It's your mind protecting you," said Amanda wisely. "I don't know much about psychology or anything like that, but I seem to have read somewhere there is a syndrome to make you come to terms with a shock by getting on and dealing with the more practical side of it. I suppose it will hit you sometime that Phil has done this," she tapered off a bit not wanting to say anything hurtful to Beth.

"Yes," agreed Beth, nodding her head slowly. "That's what it is. It's a shock, a big shock. But I don't feel sad or hurt, just curious for answers. I can't even begin to think what it will mean for the children if we split up or something."

"Do you still love Phil?"

"I don't know,"Beth replied thoughtfully. "I think so. But I'm also confused as to why he has done this. We are reasonably happy together, I would have thought. We're not all lovey-dovey any more, maybe that's the problem. We don't hold hands or kiss much nowadays. We don't even, you know, make love very often." she added with difficulty.

"Oh you keep reading about the 'average' twice a week nooky but everyone's different. And you can't be the same all the time: there are lots of things to change that average, like illness, working away, kids playing up, work stuff and just general tiredness' said Amanda knowledgeably.

"Well I do feel a bit put out that Phil obviously doesn't fancy me any more and has found someone else," said Beth as the realisation hit her probably for the first time. "It's not very nice knowing your husband has gone off you!"

"You don't know that's the reason. It could just be the opportunity presented itself to him – he is only a man after all," said Amanda trying to inject a bit of humour into the situation.

"What, you mean she threw herself at him," said Beth smiling a bit. ""Well what man could resist that? Maybe she's always having affairs and decided that Phil would be the next one."

"Could be," agreed Amanda a little dubiously. "But maybe he should also have put up

some resistance to that situation."

"Oh I know," Beth acknowledged. "I am not exonerating him from blame at all, just exploring possibilities."

They finished their coffees and sat lost in their separate thoughts for a few minutes.

"I'll have to go now 'cos I said I'd pop into the garden centre for a few bulbs for Mrs Ashton next door," said Amanda eventually. "Shall we meet up again in a couple of days – will you have phoned this man by then?"

"Yes," said Beth with determination, getting to her feet. "I'm not delaying this at all. I might

ring before the kids get home from school."

"Let me know what happens then and what you're going to do."

Amanda stood up too and they collected their bags and coats before leaving the store.

They hugged briefly by the cars and then drove off in their opposite directions.

When Beth arrived home she went straight inside to the kitchen. She glanced at the clock. It was nearly quarter to three and if she was going to call this man she didn't have much time. She ran upstairs to get out of her work clothes and try to collect her thoughts for the conversation. Again, she didn't know how she would react to his comments, whatever they were.

She went back downstairs and took her mobile phone out of her handbag, flipped it open and went to the number she had put in under the heading 'man'.

Beth took a deep breath and pressed to dial the number. It rang four times before the voice answered with a "Good afternoon, Dave speaking."

"Oh hello Dave," she stuttered taken unawares that she knew his name now. "It's…well it's the…I'm the woman who rang you last week about……well about Lisa…and Phil."

There was silence for a few seconds before Dave replied: "Oh yes, hello. I've been expecting a call from you. You know they're still seeing each other, don't you?"

Beth sat down on the nearest chair with a thud. "Er, well I suppose I did," she said. "I caught Phil on the phone last night at eleven thirty talking to someone. That's why I've rung you to find out if you think they are still seeing each other. And now you've told me."

"I'm sorry I broke it to you like that but I thought that's why you were ringing me, because you knew it was still going on," explained Dave.

"Well yes I did really, I suppose," she admitted. "But I wanted to know if you thought they were still seeing each other," she said again.

"I don't know if they've actually seen each other again. Lisa has only been working normal hours and she's not been out in the evenings or last weekend. But I did hear her on the phone yesterday morning before she left for work. It was about half past eight and I'd left for work five minutes earlier, but forgotten a file. I went back into the house and she was on the phone in the hallway as she was putting on her boots. She noticed me come in the

back door and quickly ended the call. She was red in the face when I got closer to her and I said 'was that him?' She tried to deny it but I could see that it was him she'd been speaking to."

"I asked if she had seen him again and she said 'no because she had said she wouldn't'. I said that if she carried on with him it would be the end of our marriage."

'What are we going to do?" asked Beth linking them together on the same side. "Should we confront them or talk to them, I just don't know what's the best thing."

"Well I'm not going to put up with my wife seeing someone else," Dave said loudly down the phone. "I would rather she left our house and ended our marriage. I'm so angry about this and I'd like to punch them both," he finished emphatically.

"I know how you feel," Beth agreed. "I don't feel sad or anything, just confused and now angry as well. Do you think we should try and confront them both sometime and get it over with?"

"I don't know." The voice on the phone suddenly sounded weary. "I really don't know. I think I still love Lisa but she has really tried my patience over the last few weeks. I told her not to see him again, but they are obviously still in contact with each other."

Beth felt sympathy towards Dave as he shared his feelings with her and understood the confusion and bewilderment he was going through. The same as she was.

"Why don't we meet up and discuss this face to face," she suggested suddenly, surprising even herself. "Maybe we will come up with a solution if we meet each other and talk."

"Do you think so?" asked Dave. "I don't know what good that will do, although it would be nice to put a face to your voice."

"Yes, let's meet," insisted Beth. "We can talk better about what we should do. I don't think either of us wants to end our marriages yet, certainly not if there is some hope that they will end their relationship – whatever it is. I definitely think we should meet."

"Ok then, where and when?" asked Dave. "I can make anytime within reason during the day as long as it is somewhere near my office."

"Ok, where is your office?" asked Beth.

"It's next to St Mark's Church in Leonard Street. Number twelve, above the dental practice." said Dave.

"Oh I know. I don't go to that dentist but I know where you mean. Isn't there a coffee shop just round the corner. It's painted cream and white I think. It always reminds me of a cup of coffee. In fact it's even called 'The Coffee Cup'. I could meet you any day after three o'clock when I finish work. I'll just have to get my parents to watch the kids for an hour when they get in from school. But that's ok, they're used to helping me out sometimes. I'll say I'm doing overtime."

'It's all sounding like we're having an affair," joked Dave as he listened to Beth's plans.

"Oh, no, I didn't mean it at all like that," Beth said quickly. "I was just trying to make arrangements so…"

"I know," he reassured her. "I'm only joking. Just trying to find the funny side of this sad situation – if there is one."

Beth realised she had over-reacted and tried a small laugh. It came out as a bit of a gulp and she hoped he didn't think she had just burped down the phone.

"Ok let's meet tomorrow at three o'clock at the coffee shop round the corner from my office," confirmed Dave. "Will that be alright?"

"Yes fine," said Beth composing herself. "How will we recognise each other? Please don't say you will wear a flower in your buttonhole,"she almost joked.

Dave managed a proper laugh and said he would wait outside carrying a newspaper under his arm, which still sounded like a cliché to her.

They finished the call and Beth returned the mobile to her handbag. It was nearly time for the children to return from school so she went into the kitchen to get organised for their homecoming.

As usual, James and Christina bounced through the door first, full of their day's activities. Annie followed shortly afterwards having said her goodbyes to Ben. She was allowed to see him on a Friday evening and at weekends due to studying for her GCSEs and apparently Ben's parents were happy with this arrangement too.

Beth listened to their chatter as they settled at the table before making a start on their homework. She tried to join in and ask her usual questions but her mind was elsewhere. Were Phil and Lisa together now? Surely not during work time but Beth could not be sure. They were not schoolchildren and restricted to certain hours or days for their meetings. A visit to a client or some other legitimate reason could be their way of leaving work early. Her mind could play all sorts of tricks and provide many different scenarios, all of which may or may not be true. Would she ever know? She hoped this meeting with Dave tomorrow would help provide some of the answers, or at least a way forward.

Chapter Four

--ooOoo--

*T*he next day Beth left work and collected her car from the side street where she parked. She drove to the multi-storey car park near to the café where she was to meet Dave.

Walking along the tree-lined road towards the Coffee Cup café she tried to decide what to say. It was difficult meeting someone for the first time and having to talk about a very personal and painful problem. At least it was a problem they both had and he had sounded quite reasonable on the phone. If he had shouted and sworn and sounded as if he was violent, she would not have agreed to meet him. She certainly would not have suggested the meeting.

She rounded the corner and looked ahead to see if he was waiting outside. There was a man standing by the window of the next shop, looking at his watch. Was he carrying a newspaper? As he turned round and looked towards her, Beth saw that he was indeed.

She smiled and walked quickly up to him. He was a slim man with brown floppy hair, a few inches taller than Beth, and she noticed the twinkle in his eye as she stopped in front of him. She felt she already knew him but that was ridiculous just from a couple of phone calls.

"Hi are you Dave?" she asked bravely.

"Yes I am," he answered looking her up and down. "You must be Beth. Pleased to meet you." He offered her his hand and they shook hands formally.

"Shall we go inside and get a drink?" he suggested.

"Ok," agreed Beth walking towards the door of the cafe. "We'd better sit at the back so no-one sees us."

They walked to the back of the half-filled café and stopped by a table laid for four. Beth slipped her jacket off and put it on the back of her chair. Dave sat down and picked up a menu.

"What would you like?" he asked. "Tea or coffee or a cold drink?"

"Coffee please," she said settling in her chair and placing her handbag on the one next to her.

The waitress came over and took their order. When she had gone, Dave sat forward and looked directly at Beth.

"How do you feel about all this now?" he asked seriously. "Have you still not spoken to your husband?"

"No I haven't yet. I want to know it's definitely him before I say anything. I know really that it is, but I just seem to need some sort of proof," Beth said.

"I know what you mean," Dave responded. "I think it is something to do with acceptance of
what they have done. I didn't want to believe it at first either."

"I can't believe Phil could do this and still come home and act normally," said Beth shaking her head. "I know I couldn't act like nothing was going on."

"I know," agreed Dave. "I'm sure I would say or do something that would give the game away. But then I suppose they have in a way, as we've both found out now what's going on."

"Yes that's true," said Beth thoughtfully. "Does Lisa still think you are suspicious of her?"

"I don't know. I've not said anything since I told her to finish with him or we would have to split up. As you phoned me and we arranged this meeting I thought I'd wait and see what we agreed to do before I say anything else."

"What can we do?" asked Beth.

At that moment the waitress brought their drinks and put them on the table in front of them but the wrong way round. After she had left, Dave picked up the cups and saucers and swapped them round. He sighed and said, "I don't know what we can do."

"Maybe we should talk to them at home, you talk to Lisa and I talk to Phil?" suggested Beth.

"Ok," said Dave "What do we say? Are you having an affair? They are hardly going to admit it, are they?"

"I just don't know," said Beth wearily picking up her cup and taking a sip. "'I really wish I knew what to do."

"Maybe we should try and catch them together, you know, catch them out," said Dave. "We could find out where they are going to meet and be there to confront them."

'Well yes, that sounds like a good idea but how do we find out where they are meeting?" asked Beth reasonably

"We could set them up. Arrange a meeting for them. Pretend to take arrangements and pass them on." Dave was thinking aloud.

"It all sounds a bit dramatic, like something on television," said Beth. She tried not to giggle. She didn't know Dave and he might not like her laughing at what he said. Also he might not approve of her finding humour in this situation. He had sounded much grimmer and more serious on the phone and might revert to that if she said the wrong thing.

"Yes I suppose it does," admitted Dave, smiling at her. "I'm getting carried away with the situation."

"Not necessarily," said Beth slowly as she began to think. "Maybe there is some way we can arrange for them to meet and for us to be there."

"But are you prepared to do that? Can you cope with confronting them?" asked Dave. "I know that I will be able to deal with it as I've already told Lisa that I'm not prepared to carry on with her if she is still seeing…Phil," he finished the sentence hesitantly.

Beth pondered for a moment and then said, "I think I would be Ok because I would be prepared. We could plan where we want to do this, obviously it will have to be somewhere that we can all talk and where they can't storm off somewhere else."

They drank their coffee in silence for a few minutes, each thinking about how they could plan the meeting. Eventually Dave put his cup down and sat back in his chair.

"It's not going to be easy, arranging a meeting without them becoming suspicious. Could we both say we had taken a phone call from a customer, or someone from work, and say they wanted to meet Lisa, or Phil, at a time and place?" he said.

"Yes I was thinking along the same lines about a message – maybe from someone at work. What does Lisa do?" Beth asked.

"She works for an architect, drawing plans and things. So sometimes she does go out and meet clients on her own," replied Dave.

"That's good, Phil is the same. He often goes to meet clients outside the office so it wouldn't be that difficult. But I don't get phone calls about his meetings. I would have to say someone from work rang with the message but the meeting would have to be straight away so he didn't check at the office."

"Mmmm, yes the timing could be difficult as they would find out that no-one from their offices had made the appointments. Is there any other way of doing it? Could they be meeting anyone else?" asked Dave.

"Well we could just say someone had rung and left a message to meet up with them. We could pretend we thought it was someone from work but that might not be realistic so maybe we'd better be more precise," Beth suggested.

"And we'd have to make the meeting pretty much straight away so they didn't have time to check," agreed Dave.

"Yes, maybe a message in the morning to meet in an hour's time, or something like that."'

"Right when shall we do it?" asked Dave enthusiastically. Beth did not feel quite the same hurry to get things moving but realised it would be silly to delay too long.

"How about next weekend? We could get them to meet here at midday or whatever is convenient for you," said Dave. "We could wait on the other side of the road and then follow them in."

"Do you really think this is the best place to confront our partners and ask if they are having an affair?" queried Beth, looking around the café somewhat incredulously. "I imagined a quieter place with no-one else around."

"Well that would be Ok but how can we arrange a business meeting in the middle of a field?" asked Dave reasonably. "I don't think they would fall for that one!"

"Oh no I suppose not," agreed Beth "What a shame. Well if you think this will be the best place. We will have to say that the other person…oh will they need a name do you think?" She suddenly realised.

"'We will have to make up a name and hope they just think it is a new client they will be meeting. Does Phil do that sometimes?" asked Dave.

"Yes I think so, although most of his meetings are arranged through the tele-sales department at his office. I'll have to be convincing and say that it is a last-minute thing and the person is desperate to meet him," said Beth.

"I'll do the same for Lisa. She often meets new clients and her boss arranges the meeting. He likes her to get all the basic information before he gets involved because a lot of them cancel before it gets to the detailed planning stage. So I'll say he has rung and asked her to meet him here just to have a quick chat about what 'he' plans to do with his factory or warehouse or something."

"What do we do when we catch them?" asked Beth thinking ahead. "Do you think there will be a lot of shouting? They might try to run away." Again her sense of humour got the better of her and she giggled.

"We'll be outside – over there across the road," said Dave pointing out of the window. "We can come in here or wait until they leave, what do you think is best"'

"I don't know," Beth answered as she thought about it. "I suppose we had better come in here in case they leave separately. We are hoping to find them together aren't we?"

"Of course, that's the whole point of the exercise. So we're going to arrange for a meeting at about midday next Saturday, here at this café. You and I can meet over the road at about half past eleven. Is that going to be alright with your arrangements with children, and things?' he tailed off slightly, realising he was sounding very organising. But Beth needed organising and agreed with him by nodding her head.

"Ok, we'd better be in contact by mobile during the morning until we meet up," said Dave.

"It sounds like we need to synchronise watches and wear disguises and other things that spies always seem to do in films," said Beth, only half joking. Dave looked sharply at her to see if she was taking the situation seriously and she quickly continued realising she might cause offence, "Oh it's Ok I'm only joking. I'm just a bit wound up about this whole thing. It's a weird situation to be in, talking to you when you're a stranger. And I don't want to be trapping my husband into meeting another woman to prove he's having an affair."

Beth's voice had risen slightly and the two women on the next table looked over at her.

"Now look what I've done," said Beth blushing. "Now everybody knows what's happening."

"No they don't' smiled Dave reassuringly. "No-one really knows what we are talking about. It could be anyone we're talking about – we could even be practising for a play."

"Huh, I wish it was a play and not reality," Beth ruefully replied, shrugging her shoulders

"Are we done then?" asked Dave. "Do we need to decide anything else at this stage?"

"I just want to know what we are going to do when we come in on them. Are we just going to sit down at their table – or at the next table? What will they do when they see us? Phil doesn't know you and I don't know Lisa. It's going to be awkward explaining why we are here too – they'll know they've been set up."

"Yes I realise that, but I thought our aim was to catch them out so we can address the situation and move on from there," said Dave slightly pompously.

"Move on where?" demanded Beth reasonably. "'Where do you think we are going to move on to – the divorce court?"

She realised her voice was becoming shrill as she digested the reality of the situation and tried to come to terms with the scenario to be played out on Saturday.

"I've already told Lisa that we are finished if she is still seeing this man. Phil," Dave said briefly.

"Ok that's fine for you, but what am I going to do? Phil doesn't know that I know what's going on. It will be a big shock for him." Beth almost sounded sorry for her husband!

"He needs a big shock!" Dave quickly responded. "He's having an affair with my wife and cheating on you!"

They sat in silence for a few minutes digesting what Dave had just said. Eventually Beth sighed and sat back in her chair. She knew that Dave had spoken true words and she had to come to terms with the situation. Her marriage to Phil was probably over. She did not want it to be over, but could she forgive and forget what he had done? Phil was not the philandering type, never even really flirted much with her friends or colleague's wives. Well, certainly not in front of her.

Beth suddenly realised that perhaps this fling with Lisa was not just a casual affair. Maybe he was deeply in love with her. Perhaps he was planning to leave Beth and the children at some stage, either in the near or distant future.

Beth felt glad now that she had found out about this liaison during the past few weeks. If Phil had just announced he was leaving one day, it would have been such a shock for her.

"I'm Ok',"she announced to Dave. "I'm just still adjusting to the fact that my marriage could be finished. It's not an easy thing to accept. I didn't know Phil could do this to me and the children." She finished slightly unsteadily.

"I know," Dave said softly, reaching across to take her hand. "It's a horrible shock and you've got to deal with it. Are you sure you want to go ahead with our plan for Saturday?"

"Oh yes," Beth nodded her head firmly. "I don't want to be messing about, not knowing, I'd rather just get it over with and, like you said, move on."

"Are we set for Saturday then?" Dave repeated. "We'll tell them to meet their client here

at midday and we'll be waiting over the road for them. Then, when they realise what's happened, we'll come over and confront them. See what they've got to say."

"Ok and we'll keep in contact on Saturday morning by text message," confirmed Beth. She stood up and pushed the chair back behind her. Dave stood up too and took his wallet out of his jacket pocket. Beth reached for her handbag and took out her purse.

"No, it's Ok, I'll pay," said Dave, taking a note out of his wallet. "You can pay next time," he joked smiling at her.

Beth pulled on her coat and smiled back. "I don't know why I'm not in floods of tears. I suppose it still doesn't feel real. But come Saturday, when we are lurking about across the road, that will feel real."

They walked to the till and Dave paid for their drinks. He pulled the cafe door open and allowed Beth to walk out first.

"What a gentleman," she teased as she smiled up at him. "Not many left these days."

"Oh I know I'm such a gentleman," he agreed ruefully. "Not playing to the Queensbury rules at the weekend, though are we?"

"Like you said – they started it," said Beth as they set off towards the multi-storey car park.

They stopped at the entrance and Beth said, "I'm on the second floor, where are you parked?"

"Here by the gate," Dave pointed to his silver Mercedes waiting patiently for his return. He put out his right hand and they solemnly looked at each other as their hands joined together.

"We'll get through this,don't you worry," Dave said releasing her hand and swinging his keys ready for action. "Ring me before Saturday if you need to. If I don't answer straight away, I'll text you and get back to you when I can."

"Ok thanks," Beth said. "Same for you too – if you need to ring me. If not, I'll let you know when I'm on my way next Saturday."

"Right – see you then." said Dave giving her another smile and then turning towards his car. "Take care," he added.

"Yes, and you too," replied Beth as she went towards the stairs. She heard him open the car door and start the engine before she had reached the top of the stairs to walk towards her own car.

She drove out of the car park but instead of indicating left, she turned right and drove along the road. It would be a good idea to find another parking place, she thought. Phil would be bound to use the multi-storey car park next Saturday so she'd better not park there too. She drove slowly along looking for a side road. Just past the café on the left hand side was a road leading to a car park behind the supermarket. She turned left and drove into the car park. It was free for two hours parking but would probably be quite busy next Saturday morning. She would have to make sure she was here in good time to find a space.

Beth drove out of the car park again and headed for home. Her parents had said they would stay at her house until she got back as she had told them she needed to work some overtime. She shook her head at the lies she needed to tell and decided she would speak to them after the Saturday meeting.

It was only fair that they knew the situation as she would probably need their help more if Phil moved out of the house. As she drove along she tried to imagine life without him on a day-to-day basis. Most of the household chores fell to her as she only worked part time and Phil often visited clients in the evenings. She was used to managing on her own, but there was still the comfort of another adult to rely on when necessary.

The children's routine would carry on, with school and homework and their various hobbies. Annie attended modern and jazz dancing lessons twice a week. She did not take it seriously by sitting exams but just enjoyed learning new routines. Christine loved animals and helped at the local sanctuary at the weekends, walking dogs and cleaning out cages. James was wholly devoted to football, both playing and watching, and obviously he would miss Phil's presence most of all.

Luckily her parents had always been close to the family, both physically and emotionally. They helped out during school holidays and at times like these when she needed to work extra hours. Except that of course she hadn't been working extra hours!

'It's hard work living a double life,' she thought wryly to herself. 'I don't think I am really cut out for it.'

Beth drove smartly into the drive in front of her home and parked next to Jack's pride and joy – a brand new silver Range Rover. He had always wanted a 4x4 and had recently managed to scrape enough money together to buy his dream. He knew it was expensive to run on his pension but it certainly helped with transporting the children when necessary.

She went into the house and called out, "I'm back – anyone in?"

"Of course we are," shouted Christine. "We're in the kitchen."

Beth smiled at her enthusiasm and went into the kitchen to find them all sat around the table with mugs of drinks in front of them.

"We've been to the park again and collected conkers," said Christine, showing her mum a big box full. "Grandad is going to put some of them on string so we can have a competition."

The other two children looked at their mother sheepishly as they rather felt they were too old to display all this enthusiasm for a childish game.

Beth smiled at her parents and said, "I hope they haven't been too much for you? Sorry I'm later than I thought I would be."

"That's Ok dear," her mum said, getting up to switch the kettle on. "And no, they are never too much for us, we are not in our dotage yet, you know!"

Beth took her jacket off and put it on the back of the spare chair. She sat down and waited for her mum to prepare her a cup of tea. She felt that she was a child again, waiting for her drink, but the illusion did not last long as she looked around the table at her own three children.

"Verity is inviting us all to her house on Friday night for a bit of a party," Vera said as she placed the steaming mug of tea in front of Beth. "I think she's going to talk about the money they've won and their plans for it."

"Oh right, I thought they'd gone a bit quiet recently," Beth replied. "We saw them at half term and I don't think I've spoken to her since."

"No, I've not heard from her during the last few days," said her mother, sitting down again. "I expect they've had a lot to talk about before they tell us their plans. It's really exciting and I hope they're going to treat themselves to a good holiday. They deserve it, working as hard as they both do."

"Yes they do," agreed Beth. She was glad her sister had some good luck, it counter-balanced her own feelings at the situation she found herself in.

"Homework time?" she questioned the children.

"Ok," they reluctantly chorused. They got up from the table and went upstairs.

"They're very good children." said Jack when they had gone out of hearing. "You've done a great job bringing them up. All the things you read in the papers and see on television these days, there's so much that could go wrong for youngsters. Let's hope they stay on the straight and narrow."

Beth looked at her dad and smiled. "Yes they are good but they're still only quite young still, even Annie. She is seeing a boy who lives in the next road but he seems to be quite sensible. I expect she's told you?"

"She has mentioned a lad called Ben," her mum said. "We've not said too much in front of the others in case they tease her."

"Yes they do tend to but she puts them in their place," laughed Beth. "'She can be quite firm with them when she needs to!"

Her parents got up from the table and made to leave.

"We'll see you on Friday at Verity's then," said her mum as she put her coat on.

"I'll ring Verity and find out what time and if she wants me to help prepare some food," said Beth as she followed her parents down the hallway to the front door. "And thanks, thanks ever so much for helping me out this evening."

She kissed them both goodbye and waved as they drove off.

Beth carried on with the normal routine of the evening: preparing dinner, cleaning out sandwich boxes, sorting the washing out of the machine and into the drier. All the usual chores. But her mind was elsewhere. She was planning how to get Phil to the café on Saturday. Obviously she would have to pretend that a telephone call had come through from the office and that he needed to meet the 'client' on an urgent basis. Could she be

convincing?

She would also need to arrange to leave the house herself, on her own, and she would have to be outside the café before Phil arrived.

None of the children needed to be anywhere at that time on a Saturday, although Annie had a dancing lesson at four. She could leave Annie in charge for a couple of hours quite safely.

There was a lot to think about. She heard Phil arrive home and he entered the kitchen first.

"Can't stop for dinner tonight," he said in a rush. "Got to meet the Johnsons in half an hour. Hope to be able to sign them up tonight," He didn't look at her as he was speaking and she realised he might be inventing an excuse to go out.

"Where are you meeting them?" she asked.

"At their house which is the other side of town. It shouldn't take too long as we've already gone through the paperwork. They just wanted a few days to make their minds up. And now they have." He grabbed an apple from the fruit bowl and made to go out of the kitchen.

"Ok," said Beth. "Can you ask the kids to come down 'cos dinner's ready."

The children chattered away as they sat and ate their meal but Beth just pushed her food around the plate.

"Aren't you hungry Mum?"asked Christine, quite concerned. "Don't you want your dinner tonight?"

They all looked at her plate and Beth pushed it away from her.

"No I'm not really hungry. You can finish it if you want," she said to them. "I think I'll go up and have a bath. James, it's your turn to fill the dishwasher and then make sure you've all done your homework before you watch television."

She left the room and went upstairs. She would ring Amanda from her bedroom where she would be undisturbed for a while.

Beth shut the door firmly behind her and dialled Amanda's number on her phone. Amanda picked up almost immediately and said, "Well, what's happened?"

"Oh you are so impatient," laughed Beth.

"Come on, just get on with it. I've been thinking about you all day."

"Ok. Well, we're going to get them to go on a false appointment and meet at the café we, that's me and Dave, were at today. Then we are going to be across the road and we'll walk in on them," explained Beth quietly down the phone.

"Then what?" asked Amanda still impatient. "What are you going to do then?"

"Don't quite know yet. We'll have to play it by ear and see what their reactions are. But I know that Dave will not be taking any excuses from them. I just don't know how Phil is going to react," said Beth.

"Blow Phil!" exclaimed Amanda. "What about you? How are you going to react? Have you thought about that yet for goodness sake?"

"I still don't really know. I know it sounds pathetic, but I'm still not accepting this, well, situation I suppose you'd call it. I think I am getting to the angry stage though. Phil walked in tonight and said he was going straight out to visit some clients the other side of town, but that he wouldn't be long. I'm sure he is going to meet…her."

Beth's voice became stronger as she realised what had happened that evening.

"Good on you girl. You get angry – you deserve it. What a rat! You give him 'what-for' on Saturday. Now, do you need to meet up and talk about it, or are you coping alright?'

"I'm Ok actually," confirmed Beth. "The man, Dave is his name, he's quite a reliable and sensible type. We are going to phone or text each other if we have any problems. We're meeting outside the café, lurking on the other side of the road – if you please!"

"Sounds a bit like cloak and dagger stuff. Do you think you're up to it?" asked Amanda.

"Yes I thought that too, but there seems no alternative. I would rather confront both of them together than have a big scene here with Phil. He can't deny it if we catch them together," Beth reasoned.

"Yes I see the sense in that. Just be careful and get yourself fully prepared for any eventuality," advised Amanda. "Sorry I'll have to go now, we've got friends coming and I think they have just arrived."

"Oh sorry to keep you. I'll ring you again later in the week before

Saturday, if you don't mind."

"Course I don't mind,"' said Amanda firmly to her friend. "You ring me whenever you need to – that's what friends are for," she sang.

They said their goodbyes and Beth closed the phone. She sat on the bed for a few more minutes before getting up and walking to the door. She would go and have a good hot soak in the bath and try to forget her problems for an hour or so.

Chapter Five

--ooOoo--

*F*riday evening saw Beth and Annie in the kitchen frantically baking sausage rolls and vol-au-vents.

"I don't know," said Beth wiping her hot face with a floury hand. "Your aunt decides to throw a party and look at us – working away in a hot kitchen after a full day at work and school."

"I don't mind," said Annie as she rolled out dough for the sausage rolls. "It's going to be fun finding out what they are going to spend the money on."

"Yes I suppose so. I hope they're going to have some fun with it, not just pay off the mortgage and any loans or debts they have. I think they should all go on a round the world trip, go to Australia or spend a month in Florida, or…just get away from it all."

Beth looked up at the clock as she thought about her dream holidays.

"I'd like to go round the world. Maybe I'll have a gap year after A levels and go to Australia and find a job there. Marilyn said she'd like to as well, we could go together' said Annie to her mum.

Beth looked at her daughter and thought, 'Yikes! That's only two years away. She could be off and gone around the world. Wish I'd had the chance when I was a teenager!'

They continued rolling and stuffing and baking until there were 36 sausage rolls and 24 vol-au-vents ready for Verity and John's party. Then, as they piled all the utensils into the dishwasher and wiped the table clean Beth said, "I hope the boys and Christina are ready so we can use the bathroom. You go up and see, Annie, and get started."

When Beth was alone in the kitchen finishing the clearing up, she thought about her plans for Saturday morning. She had not contacted Dave again but probably would in the morning after she had told Phil about his 'meeting'.

She gave a final swipe of the dishcloth over the surfaces round the kitchen and pushed all the chairs back under the table. The party food was packed into three tins which stood by the kitchen door so they were not forgotten.

Beth left the kitchen and ran upstairs to get ready for the party. She could hear the children getting dressed and yelling to each other from their bedrooms. It was nice for them all to be getting dressed up and going out together. Beth briefly wondered if they would ever do this again.

Phil was combing his hair as she entered their bedroom and stood up from where he was sat on the edge of the bed.

"I'm ready, I'll go and wait downstairs," he said putting his comb in the back pocket of his trousers. Beth watched him as he left the room and then turned towards the en suite to start the shower.

She was showered, dressed and make up applied within twenty minutes and joined the rest of her family who were assembled in the kitchen.

"Right, take a tin each please," Beth said to her children as Phil was checking the back doors were locked. "Just be careful not to shake them about too much – remember we have to eat the food inside," she warned them.

They trooped out of the house and into Phil's car. The children chattered excitedly in the back seat of the car but Phil and Beth did not speak until they arrived at John and Verity's house.

"Everybody out," said Phil as he parked the car on the drive behind Beth's parents' vehicle. "Let's go and have some fun!"

They pushed the front door open and went inside the house. It felt felt warm and all the rooms were lit up brightly with extra Christmas tree lights hung around the walls. There was the sound of excited voices coming from all directions interspersed with bursts of laughter.

Beth and her family made their way to the kitchen at the back of the house. The children placed their tins on the table next to several cling-filmed plates of food. Verity was stood by the hob stirring some pasta and she looked flushed but happy.

'Oh, Hi. You've arrived at last. Everyone is here now and we can start the food," she said giving the pan one last stir. "Come on Beth, help me get the food ready for everyone. Can you put your offerings on those plates by the sink and take the cling film off these others please. I'll dish up this pasta and the sauce and then everyone can come and help themselves. I was going to do a sit down meal, but thought it would be nicer for everyone to help themselves to whatever they want." She chattered as she moved about the kitchen.

Beth did as she was told and then went to the door and yelled, "Come on everyone, the food is ready. Verity says come and help yourselves."

She moved further into the room towards her parents who were talking to John's father by the window.

"Hi mum," she said as she kissed her check and then turned to her father and did the same. "How are you both? Isn't this great all the family being together for a celebration."

Her mother looked sharply at her as if to ask a question but Beth had turned away and gone back into the kitchen.

Everyone moved towards the food and helped themselves. Besides Verity, Beth and their families, both of John's parents were present as well as his sister, Isobel, and Keith, his brother, with their partners and children.

Once everyone had a plate piled with food they settled down to eat. Even Verity perched on the side of an armchair with her plate and managed to swallow a few mouthfuls. John's latest acquisition, a new CD player standing in the corner of the room, was quietly playing a soulful tune.

As they all finished eating, Sam, Lucy, Christina and James were asked to collect the plates and put them in the kitchen. When they returned and sat down again, John stood up and tinkled a spoon against the side of his glass.

"We have gathered you all here this evening, not just to eat and have a good time, but to tell you what we plan to do with our winnings," he started.

Everyone cheered and clapped and then burst into laughter.

"Obviously some of the money has to be spent on boring things like mortgages and debts." John paused to look at his children, who groaned. "But we want to spend most of it on something more exciting.

"Verity and I have talked about this now for several days – well since we found out we had won – and we want to use the money to give us a different lifestyle. We think most people would want to do this if they suddenly came into a lot of money. We don't know if our winnings are actually enough to do what we want, but we can always come back or find jobs out there, or something," he continued looking around at everyone.

"Well where are you going?" asked his father. "Are you moving abroad?"

"Oh no, don't say you are going to move to another country," his mother said sounding distraught. "You know I don't like flying. When will I ever see you again?"

"It's Ok, don't panic," said John, smiling reassuringly at his parents. "I don't mean we are moving away as in abroad – just into the country."

"Into the country?" echoed his father. "What do you mean?"

"If you give me a chance to explain, then I'll tell you. What Verity and I, and Sam and Lucy too, what we want to do is to move to the country and buy some land where we can become market gardeners. We have looked into it and even got some property details. Most of the best places to buy are either in Cornwall or Kent. That's why we would be moving away. But we both feel we can offer a better lifestyle to the children and we will be happier working for ourselves than slaving away for other people' explained John.

"We are so excited by this," said Verity, standing up and grinning around at everyone looking at her. "It's something we have never talked about or even considered. We thought we'd be in this house forever and have to work at our jobs until we retired. Neither of us like our jobs, they are just a means of producing money. I feel we are so lucky to be given this chance to do something exciting, different and…" She shrugged her shoulders as she searched for the right words.

"Entrepreuneurial," said James suddenly. Everyone looked at him and he blushed. "It's just a word we talked about at school this week. It means that you are adventurous and can form a business for yourself' he explained.

Everyone laughed and James blushed a deeper red.

"That's a great word, James," said Verity. "Exactly the one I would have chosen if I'd managed to think of it myself." She smiled at James who subsided back into his chair, still blushing.

"But that's not all," John began again. "Obviously we are not so insensitive that we would not want to treat everyone in this room to a little present."

"'Yes," confirmed Verity. "We have made a list of what we would like to give you all,"

"But first, tell us a bit more about your plans for this market gardening," Jack asked. 'Have you decided where to buy, what are you going to grow,? Will it be a money-making business?"

"Yes to all three questions," said John. "We think we'd like to buy in Cornwall because one of the things we'd like to grow would be daffodils. But we'll also grow vegetables and maybe keep hens and goats. We really do need to do a bit more research into the most viable crops and products. And yes, we are certainly hoping it will be money-making because this lottery win won't last forever."

Silence descended on the room as everyone digested the future plans for the Simkins family. John and Verity looked round at their relatives to try and gauge their reactions. Beth stood up and walked over to Verity before putting her arm around her shoulders and giving her a big hug.

"Well I think it's great. I wish you all the very best of luck. Like you say, it's not every day you get a chance to change your lifestyle, especially to make your dreams come true." She sounded quite wistful and her mother looked at her again that evening, noticing the slight panic in her eyes. She made a resolve to try and get a quiet word with her eldest daughter before the end of the party.

"Thanks, Sis," Verity squeezed her sister's hand and looked up at her.

"Now come on, let's get the puddings out shall we?"

The children all stood up and unusually obediently went into the kitchen with Verity. Once
everyone had a bowl and spoon in their hand, John again stood up and asked if they wanted to know about the list of presents.

"Oh yes," said most of the children at the same time. The adults laughed at their enthusiasm and John pulled a sheet of paper from his top pocket.

"Right, let's start with Jack and Vera. We'd like to buy them a new greenhouse for their garden as they are always complaining the one they have is too small. Would you like that?' he asked them.

"Oh no lad, you don't have to do that," said Jack. "You keep the money for yourselves."

"Now come on dad don't spoil our pleasure in treating you all," said Verity. "We really want to buy everyone something. That's why we're having this party."

"Well thank you very much. That's all I can say," said Vera. "We would be delighted to accept a new greehouse and it will certainly give us lots of pleasure." She stood up and kissed her daughter and son in law. Jack also stood up and shook John's hand before kissing his youngest daughter's cheek.

"Yes, thank you both very much," he said gruffly as he sat down again.

"Ok, now my mum and dad would like a new suite for their sitting room and I'm going to arrange for the room to be fully decorated, with new curtains and carpet as well," John smiled as he looked at his parents' faces which both showed their shock and surprise.

"For Isobel and Keith's families I would like to pay for them all to go on a trip to Disneyland in Florida. I know you've been saving up to go there and now you can just go and book at the travel agents.

"For Beth and Phil, we'd like to give you some money towards landscaping your garden. You've been talking about that for about five years now and never got round to it." Everyone laughed as Beth and Phil looked astounded. They did not realise their habit of saying occasionally that they must get round to 'doing something with the garden' had been taken on board by John and Verity.

"Oh great, that's wonderful," said Beth, planning ahead and envisaging a beautiful, work-free area at the back of her house. "I must get some ideas from Amanda and she may know the best person for the job."

"For Annie, Christina and James we'd like to treat them to a holiday at Woodlands next year. We thought they could go during the Easter holidays when the garden is being landscaped," suggested Verity.

"What's Woodlands?" asked Isobel. "I've never heard of it."

"Oh you will when your children get a bit older. It's a holiday camp type place for teenagers based in Somerset. They can indulge in all their hobbies and interests. They sleep in mini-dormitories and they can do lots of exciting activities like scuba diving, jet ski-ing, abseiling, rock climbing, horse riding and all that sort of thing.

But there are also lots of indoor activities like aerobics, badminton, computer and IT stuff. It's a teenager's dream. We'll book them in for a week at the beginning of April, during the school holidays if you like," said Verity looking to Beth for her approval.

"Oh, wow!" shouted Christina bouncing up and down in her chair. "My friend Sarah went this year with her sister and she said it was the greatest ever. Wait till I tell her I'm going too."

James looked excited too at the prospect of a week at Woodlands. Annie however did not look quite so thrilled and Beth decided to speak to her before Verity and John booked her place. She may not want to go to a teen-park which was really aimed at the younger age group. Of course, she was also probably thinking about being away from Ben for a week, too.

"I think we've covered everyone now," said John, raising his voice over everyone's excited chatter. "So let's have another drink and toast to our new lifestyle and to all of you too."

They raised their glasses.

"To John, Verity, Sam and Lucy," said Phil standing up quickly before anyone else had a chance to offer the toast. "We all wish them the very best for the future and hope their new plans come to fruition – literally."

"To John, Verity, Sam and Lucy," everyone echoed standing up and raising their glasses.

"And thanks for this lovely party too," said Jack. "Maybe the next one will be in Cornwall and we'll all come to visit you," he added laughing.

Everyone raised their glasses again before John moved to the CD player and turned the music up a notch.

"Let's enjoy the rest of the evening – help yourselves to drink and any food that's still around. Have a great time," he said loudly above the voice of James Blunt.

Beth's mother moved towards her and put her arm out to her daughter. "Is there anything the matter darling?" she asked.

"What do you mean?" Beth responded, looking quickly at Phil as he went into the kitchen to replenish his glass. "Why should anything be the matter?"

"Because you look anxious, not quite yourself. Have you been working too hard or is there a problem?"

Beth looked at her mother and swallowed. "No mum, don't worry. There's nothing wrong. If there is...I mean if there was, I'd tell you. Everything's fine," she said firmly as she tried to reassure herself as much as her mother.

"Well what is it then?" her mother persisted.

"Nothing. I'm probably just tired. Don't worry," repeated Beth. "Look, it's great news about your getting a new greenhouse isn't it? I had no idea they planned a big surprise for us all like this, did you? I thought they would just tell us what they are planning to do with the money. I can't believe they're going to move away though."

The thought of not living close to her sister suddenly hit her and she felt quite tearful.

'I know, it is a bit of a shock. Verity had actually told me they planned something which might mean them moving but I didn't know exactly what. But don't worry, we can visit them and you email each other anyway don't you?'

"Yes I know but it's not the same as having them living in the same town, just a few minutes drive away is it?" asked Beth.

"No but they have to be able to follow their dream," clichéd her mother. "I'm sure we'll still see plenty of them and it will be marvellous for holidays in Cornwall. You can take your caravan and stay somewhere near them. Even go and help out on the farm."

"It's not going to be a farm,"said Verity, coming up behind them. "It's a smallholding. We will actually start quite small and hopefully build up to the daffodil growing which obviously needs big fields. I can't believe we have both had the same type of dream all this time but only just talked about it."

"It's great for you all. But what about Sam and Lucy? Are they happy to be leaving their friends behind?" asked Beth.

"Well not really but they both want to move to the country. Lucy would like a pony and Sam would like a quad bike. They know that they can't have these things living here but would be able to if we had more room."

"Christina would love a pony too. She so enjoys her time at the animal sanctuary at the weekends. I keep saying she can have some riding lessons but we never seem to get round to booking them. Maybe I'll do something this weekend," Beth said thoughtfully, almost to herself.

"Yes that would be good for her," agreed Beth's mother. "Anyway, I think your father and I should make a move now. It's getting quite late and your father doesn't really like driving in the dark."

Vera and Jack said their goodbyes and then John's parents decided to leave as well.

When all the farewells had been said, everyone remaining returned to the sitting room and John turned the music up a little more.

"Come on everyone – let's dance shall we?' suggested Verity grabbing Sam and swinging him round.

John pushed back some of the chairs to make some space and all the children, apart from Annie, began dancing to the latest chart topping CD.

Annie went into the kitchen and poured herself a drink. Beth noticed and followed her in.

"I saw that you didn't look quite delighted with the offer of the holiday from John and Verity – do you not want to go?" she asked.

"Well not really." replied Annie. "It's a bit young for me really 'cos it's mostly for under sixteens. I'll go if you want me to look after the other two but don't forget I'll be taking my GCSE's after Easter."

"Yes I know, I hadn't forgotten. I think James and Christina will be alright to go on their own. There will be lots of things they want to do and they won't have time to miss us," Beth reassured her – and herself.

"Ok but will you tell Aunt Verity and Uncle John 'cos I wouldn't like them to think I was throwing their present back at them," Annie said worriedly.

"Of course I'll tell them and they'll quite understand. Don't you worry." Beth said.

"What will I understand?' asked Verity as she came into the kitchen huffing and puffing after the exertion of dancing.

"It's just that Annie will be studying for her GCSE's next Easter and it's probably not a good idea for her to go away when she should be revising," said Beth.

"Oh yes of course, I had quite forgotten," Verity looked at her niece. "Well I tell you what – why don't we give you some spending money while the other two are away and you can buy yourself some nice new clothes to wear after you have finished your exams."

"Oh Aunty Verity that would be marvellous," Annie threw her arms round her aunt and kissed her. "Thank you so much – I would so love that."

Verity laughed as she staggered under Annie's excited embrace.

"I may let Sam and Lucy go with your two for the week too' Verity said to Beth, getting her breath back as Annie left the kitchen. "I think they would enjoy all the activities and it may

coincide with us moving. It will give them something else to look forward to. Oh, by the way, who was the handsome man you were leaving the Coffee Cup with one afternoon this week?' she suddenly turned to Beth and asked.

Beth jumped and nearly dropped her glass.

"Handsome man?" she asked, stalling for time. "When was that?"

"Oh it must have been Wednesday afternoon. I'd been to the dentist and saw you across the road. You both came out of the café and then walked towards the multi storey car park'."

"Oh, er, that must have been a client I had to meet for Allan, my boss. He couldn't make the meeting so he asked me to go instead," Beth improvised quickly.

"Lucky you then – he looked quite a dish," said Verity turning to the sink and turning on the hot tap.

Beth made her excuses to go to the bathroom and ran quickly up the stairs. Her face felt as if it was burning at the lie she had come out with so swiftly to her sister. She went into the bathroom and locked the door. She turned the cold tap on and put her hands underneath the cool water. She splashed her face and dried it on the towel laid next to the basin.

Beth turned round and looked at herself in the mirror. Her cheeks were still flushed from the unexpectedness of being found out. But found out doing what? she asked her reflection reasonably. What had she done wrong? Nothing. Just following up the possibility that her husband was having an affair. He had certainly been quiet that evening, not his usual self as normally he would crack jokes and join in with everyone's banter.

She heard footsteps running up the stairs and quickly flushed the toilet and opened the door. Isobel was outside and they exchanged pleasantries before Beth went back downstairs.

The children were still dancing to some of the latest pop tunes and Phil and John were chatting quietly with Keith. Verity was in the kitchen, loading the dishwasher and washing some of the saucepans. Beth went back out and picked up a dishcloth to help her sister.

"When do you plan to move?" she asked Verity.

"Don't really know yet – we have to find somewhere we like enough to buy. But we have got two viewings next weekend, both in Cornwall. They are already run as market gardens but both present owners are ready to retire. It would help us to take over an already running business but we don't mind if we just buy a small farm and start up by ourselves," Verity explained.

"I shall really miss you when you live the other side of the country," Beth told her sister.

"Yes I'll miss you too but we can visit. And you can certainly come to stay with us for holidays. We don't really see each other a lot nowadays anyway, what with work, school, kids and all the other things we do' Verity said.

"I know we don't but we know we can if we need to. But this will mean a proper trip for at least a couple of nights stop over whether we come to you or you come back here' Beth said.

"Please don't make me feel guilty," said Verity, turning to her sister. "It's been hard making this decision but John and I really want to give it a go. If we don't do something now while we have the money, we never will."

"I'm sorry, I know I'm being selfish," Beth said putting her hand on her sister's arm. "I'm just feeling a bit weird at the moment. Probably the time of the month or the kids getting older. I just don't feel that I can cope with changes."

"You'll be alright, you're a strong person Beth," said Verity. "We all have to accept changes sometimes. Lots of people move away from their families with promotions or whatever. Look what happened when dad changed his work – we all moved and it was ok. It was probably harder for mum but she just looked forward to the new challenge."

"Yes you're right I know. You're quite clever for a younger sister," Beth smiled at Verity. 'We'll all look forward to visiting you and seeing your new project. Mum and dad will certainly enjoy holidays in Cornwall and knowing dad he'll want to help out too," she continued.

The party continued until about midnight when Isobel and Keith collected their various partners and children together and left. Beth and Phil agreed to one last cup of coffee if the five remaining children settled down and were quiet for half an hour. On hearing this they all immediately ran upstairs to Sam's room to try and prolong their evening out

as long as possible.

The four adults sat with their coffees and reflected on the evening.

"I hope our mums and dads are ok with us going to live away," said Verity as she snuggled up to John on the sofa. "They all seemed to be delighted for us but when reality hits and they realise we won't just be across town for them to visit any more, I hope they are still pleased for us."

Beth looked at her sister and wished she had not spoken of her own reservations about the projected move.

"I'm sure everyone will be fine once they get used to the idea," she reassured her sister. "You'll probably have a constant stream of visitors, especially in the summer months."

"Yes that's right," agreed John squeezing Verity's shoulders and smiling at her. "They'll all get used to us living away. Don't forget we haven't definitely decided on Cornwall yet. We still need to look around before we decide."

"Oh I know. I can't wait to get there this weekend and have a look but I know we should look at other places too before making a decision. I just like the idea of Cornwall, it sounds like an all-year holiday," she laughed.

John also laughed before he told Verity in no uncertain terms that they were not going to live in Cornwall for an all-year holiday but to work for their livings.

Beth and Verity exchanged glances across the room. They both knew that John would let Verity do exactly what she wanted although he would work very hard to ensure the family had a good living.

Phil stood up and placed his cup on the table. "Come on then," he said. "We'd better round up the kids and go. It's getting late. Although of course we haven't got to get up for work in the morning."

Beth stood up too smiling wryly to herself. She knew that he would actually have some work in the morning after she received the 'phone call' from the office.

They left and drove home through the cold night air. Christina was almost asleep when they arrived home and all three children went straight upstairs to bed.

Phil and Beth followed shortly afterwards having made sure all lights were turned off and doors locked securely.

Beth lay in bed thinking about the events planned for the next morning when her life could be changed forever. Maybe this was the last night she would lay in bed and listen to Phil snoring quietly beside her. Strangely enough this thought did not fill her with the dread she expected but more with a feeling of anticipation. Her life was very predicable and had been for a long time, probably since the birth of the children.

Once she had settled into the change of lifestyle that resulted from having babies and toddlers, the school year kept her to a continuous routine and she almost looked forward to the possibility of changing her pattern of life. But would this change be for the better? Might it not mean she was still stuck in a routine but had the added problem of money worries? She tossed and turned for a while before finally succumbing to tiredness and falling asleep.

Chapter Six

--ooOoo--

*T*he next morning dawned with a clear blue sky and the sun shining brightly. Beth woke up to find that she was alone in bed. She turned over to look at the bedside clock and noticed the hands pointing to nine o'clock.

'Yikes!' she thought, jumping out of bed and slipping her feet into her slippers. She hurried into the en-suite and then got dressed as quickly as possible before running downstairs where she found Phil in the kitchen making tea. There was no sign of the three children.

"Morning," he said turning round to look at her as she stopped and stood in the doorway.

"Tea?"

"Oh, yes please," Beth replied as she sat on one of the kitchen chairs. "How long have you been up?"

"Only about ten or fifteen minutes." he said. "How are you feeling? Any sign of a hangover?"

"No I'm fine.," Beth said. "What about you?"

"Ok I think, just a bit tired," Phil moved to the fridge and opened the door before exclaiming, "Oh no, we've got no milk. I'll have to go down to the shop and get some."

Beth realised this was the perfect opportunity she needed for her phone call.

"Ok, can you get some bread as well please?" she said, racking her brain to think of anything else to prolong his shopping trip. "Oh and maybe some bacon, orange squash and…er…some washing up liquid."

"Hey aren't you going shopping at the supermarket today?" laughed Phil as he reached for his jacket. "Can't you get all that there?"

"I don't know if I've got time to shop," improvised Beth. "I've got quite a lot on today." If he only knew!

"Alright, I'll get milk, bread, bacon, squash and what was the other thing?"

"Washing up liquid."

"Right," said Phil as he left the kitchen. "Back in a few minutes."

Beth listened to him shut the front door, start the car and drive away.

She thought to herself, 'Office has rung, need you to meet a client, meeting at The Coffee Cup, can't get there any other time. Meet at 11.30. Only time available to meet'.

It seemed she had her thoughts in the right order and that it also seemed quite plausible. She just had to hope that Phil thought so too.

Beth sat waiting for Phil's return and hoped the children did not come down before she had told him of his proposed meeting. Although the general mayhem would probably help, she did not want to be distracted and say the wrong thing.

Luckily Phil arrived back with his bag of shopping before the children had emerged from their beds. He put the shopping on the table and Beth stood up to put it away.

She turned her back on Phil and opened the fridge door as she said, "Oh the office has just rung and they want you to meet a client this morning. Apparently this man has telephoned and requested a meeting at 11.30 this morning. It sounded very urgent and she said this was the only time he was available. The meeting is to be at the Coffee Pot café. Do you know where that is?'

She turned round to Phil as she finished speaking. He looked quite surprised at her words but replied quite quickly.

"Who rang from the office," he asked first.

"I think it was Nicola," replied Beth.

"Oh, ok I didn't know she was working today. So did she say anything else about this client or have I to ring her back for the details?"

"Oh no," Beth said quickly. "She was just leaving the office so she won't be there now. She just said to meet this man and get some details and see what he wants."

Phil finished making the tea and sat down at the table with Beth.

"It seems very strange that Nicola has rung and I have to meet a client at such short notice. Normally we have to prepare quotations so we know what we are talking about. Still, I suppose if this bloke wants to meet me it must be urgent," mused Phil staring into his mug of tea.

"Yes," agreed Beth. "Nicola sounded quite definite that he would be there then so you'll need to leave before eleven o'clock won't you so you get there on time?"

Phil looked up at the kitchen clock and nodded.

"Yes, that gives me just under an hour to have some breakfast, get changed and go."

They sat quietly for a few minutes with their drinks, both lost in their separate thoughts. When Beth had finished her cup of tea she stood up and began reaching for the bowls, the spoons, the boxes of cereal and put them on the table ready for breakfast.

Sounds were heard from upstairs and soon the children joined them in the kitchen. They all sat round the table and ate their breakfast whilst planning their day's activities.

When Phil had finished his cereal and a second cup of tea he went upstairs to change into his suit in readiness for the meeting.

Beth told the children that she needed to pop out for an hour to finish some work at her office and that Annie could be in charge until she returned. Christina still looked tired from the late night and Beth suggested they all sat down in front of a DVD for a while to recover.

Beth cleared the table and loaded the dishwasher. She heard Phil coming back down the stairs and turned towards him.

'I'll get off now. It may be difficult to park this time of day, although there is a multi-storey nearby if I remember correctly," Phil told Beth as he picked up his car keys.

"I don't know what time I'll be back. Are you going out?" he asked.

"Yes," said Beth. "I'm just going to pop in to the office for an hour to finish off something I've just remembered. I'm leaving Annie in charge but they're all watching a DVD which won't end for a while. When I get back I'll take them in to town before Annie's dancing lesson."

"Ok I'll see you later then. I'll let you know when I've finished with this chap. Oh, did Nicola tell you his name? Or how I will recognise him?' asked Phil.

"Er, she said he would wait inside the café and he will be on his own. I can't remember if she gave me a name. I didn't have a pen so I couldn't write anything down – sorry," Beth said.

"I'm sure I'll find him. Won't be many men out there on their own on a Saturday morning, most will be shopping with wives and children, or just with children if they're having their weekly access time," Phil joked.

Beth looked at him and felt surprised he expected her to laugh about separated families. Maybe he didn't think it could happen to them.

"See you later," called Phil as he passed the front room. "Enjoy your film."

"We will," chorused James and Christina.

Beth went upstairs quickly to get ready and was soon leaving the house with her bag and coat swinging behind her. She jumped into the car and drove swiftly out of the drive. She encountered the usual amount of traffic for a Saturday morning but managed to park easily behind the supermarket.

After locking the car and putting the keys into her bag she pulled out her mobile and sent a text message to Dave. He replied within seconds and told her he could see her and was waiting by the entrance. She spotted him and made her way to join him.

"Hi," she said nervously. "Everything worked out ok for you?"

"Yes, Lisa's already in the café. What time will Phil be here?" asked Dave.

"I'm surprised he's not already. He left before me. I hope he hasn't gone into the office first to get something or check on the man's name who he's supposed to be meeting. I couldn't think of a name on the spur of the moment and had forgotten to have one planned," she explained to Dave.

"Let's wait here until we see him go in and then we'll give them a few minutes before we join them," suggested Dave.

It was difficult to lurk surreptitiously in the doorway of the supermarket with so many people pushing trolleys in and out. After having his shins bashed a couple of times, Dave suggested they move across the path and stand behind the recycling bins that were situated there.

Of course, they were still in everyone's way as bottles and

newspapers were hurled into the large plastic containers. Dave and Beth kept dodging about whilst trying to keep an eye out for Phil.

"Is that him there," said Dave to Beth.

"No," Beth said peering across the road to look at a tall, distinguished gentleman who was going into the café on his own.

"Phil is shorter and has lighter coloured hair," she described her husband to Dave.

"What if he doesn't turn up?" she suddenly asked. "I can't think why he wouldn't, unless he has been in to the office first and found out there was no appointment."

Dave looked at his watch.

"It's twenty five to twelve now so he's definitely late."

"We couldn't have missed him, could we? Maybe he was in there before you arrived. They could be in there together now' said Beth.

Dave looked doubtful. "I was here at eleven fifteen. Surely he wouldn't have got here earlier than that, would he?"

"No, he only left just before eleven. It would take him longer than twenty minutes to drive here, park and get into the café' Beth seemed reassured.

They watched and waited for another five minutes in silence.

As Dave looked at his watch again, Beth glanced idly at the café. She noticed the entrance door, people sat at tables looking out of the window and her eyes moved upwards towards the name above the shop.

"OH MY LIFE!" she suddenly blurted out.

"What's wrong?" asked Dave as he and several passers-by looked at her in astonishment.

Beth stood there with her hand over her mouth looking at the sign which stated 'The Coffee Cup'. She then looked at Dave, took her hand away and said," You'll never guess what I've done! I've only told him the wrong name for the café. I said The Coffee Pot and this is The Coffee Cup. I can't believe I've been so stupid."

Dave looked at her for a few seconds before bursting out laughing.

"Well a fine couple of spies we are!" he spluttered. "I don't think MI5 will be adding us to their payroll."

Beth was so relieved that he had taken her announcement so well that she joined in his laughter. When they had finished annoying the passers by with their amusement, Beth asked, "What do we do now?

Lisa is in there waiting for someone, and Phil is somewhere else waiting for someone else."

Dave thought for a few seconds and then made a suggestion.

"How about if I follow Lisa when she comes out of here and you go over to the Coffee Pot and see if you can follow Phil. When their meetings are aborted they may make arrangements to meet up as they have some spare time on their hands."

"Oh what a brilliant idea," agreed Beth. "I'll drive to the Coffee Pot now. It's only about five minutes in the car, but I might have trouble parking. I'll ring you when I get there."

She turned round and started to run back to her car. Dave watched her from his hiding place and waved as she drove out the exit.

Beth drove as quickly as the traffic allowed to the multi storey car park near the Coffee Pot café. It was a large car park and the chances of parking near her husband's car were quite remote. She drove purposefully to the top level and easily found a space.

She locked the car and ran towards the stairs. Most people seemed to be coming back up the staircase so it was quite a battle to reach the pavement level.

As she ran out into the fresh air, Beth took some deep breaths. Now she was having to 'spy' on her own. It had all happened so quickly and she hadn't realised the implications.

She strode along the pavement towards The Coffee Pot which was located just inside the precinct.

As she neared the café her steps grew slower and she looked around to find a suitable place to conceal herself. A convenient mobile display unit gave her the cover she needed to be able to watch the doorway of the café but not be seen by anyone coming out. Well, she certainly wouldn't be spotted by anyone not expecting to see her.

So began her wait to find out what happened when her husband left.

She stood there for about ten minutes before he finally opened the door and came out into the precinct. He did look up and down, searching the crowd, but luckily did not spot her hiding behind the AA sign. He strode off away from the car park entrance so obviously he was not intending to go straight back to his car.

Beth dialled Dave's mobile number and put the phone to her ear.

'Hi it's me,' she said when he answered. "What's happened your end? Dave has just left the café and is walking into the precinct."

"Hi, Lisa left a few minutes ago and I'm following her in my car. It looks like she might be going towards the precinct. I'm trying to keep far enough back so that she doesn't spot me in her mirror, but I do know she doesn't use it very often anyway – apart from putting on lipstick."

"Oh, ha ha – let's joke about women drivers," said Beth as she followed her husband through the crowded shopping centre.

"I wasn't joking about all women drivers, just my wife," said Dave. 'I'll ring you back in a minute when I've parked."

Beth put her phone into her pocket and concentrated on following Phil. He walked out of the precinct at the other end and continued across the road and into the park opposite.

Beth dodged the traffic whilst keeping her distance. They walked through the centre of the park, one unaware he had a follower and the other trying to keep up but ready to hide behind a tree if she had to.

When he reached the bandstand in the middle of the park, Phil turned right towards the river and headed for an empty bench. He sat down and looked at his watch.

Beth stayed by the bandstand, hidden from his view by a large leafless bush. Her phone rang and she answered Dave immediately.

"I'm coming through the park towards the bandstand," he said. "Where are you?"

"I'm already at the bandstand and Phil is sitting on a bench by the river. You'd better come and find me' she said looking around.

A few minutes later she spotted a dark haired girl walking purposefully along the other path. She turned left before she reached the bandstand and headed towards the bench where Phil was waiting.

Beth looked further down the path and saw Dave jogging towards her. He ran across the grass and joined Beth by the bandstand.

"I can't believe it," he said as he got his breath back. "Their clients didn't show up and now they've arranged this meeting."

Beth and Dave looked over towards the bench where Phil had stood up and put his arms around Lisa. They kissed passionately before sitting down with Phil's arm still around her shoulders.

Beth and Dave just stared at the scene before them. Beth felt her heart and stomach lurch downwards towards her feet and she stumbled backwards slightly. Dave put his arm out to catch her before she fell and she grabbed his hand.

"Oh no, it's all true then," she moaned. "That's all the proof we need, isn't it?" she said looking up at Dave.

'Yes I'm afraid so," he agreed gently. "But we knew all along really, didn't we.This just confirms our suspicions."

"Yes I know but it doesn't make it any easier. I didn't really want it to be true. I thought Phil and I were happy together, so why has he had to go and find someone else?" asked Beth.

"I don't know. Why does this type of thing ever happen? Because it does, you know. It is not just happening to the two of us, there are plenty more people out there who are unhappy," Dave said earnestly to Beth.

"Well it only feels like it is happening to me at the moment. I'm sorry if that sounds selfish but that's how I feel," said Beth as leant back against the wall of the bandstand. "What are we going to do now?" she asked Dave.

"We could go over there and confront them as we were going to in the café," suggested Dave.

"I don't know if I can now," said Beth. "It would have been different if they had been sat at a table in the café with other people about."

"I thought you wanted this meeting to happen without an audience," said Dave.

"Yes but now it's reality, it's different. I don't know what I want to do."

Beth glanced over to the bench again and noticed Phil and Lisa were snuggled up together watching the ducks swimming on the river.

"They look so cosy together, it would be a shame to spoil it," she said sarcastically, anger getting a hold of her. "Why don't we just leave them to it and hope they don't bother to come home to us?"

She began walking away from the scene of the two lovers and continued: "But I don't think we'll be that lucky. I think they will go home and expect to carry on as if nothing has happened. They won't know we have been here watching them in the park and they'll just think that life will continue. They get the best of both their worlds. But I don't know why they don't just leave us and get a new life together if they are so passionate about each

other."

Beth spat out the last sentence.

Dave followed Beth around the bandstand and they walked slowly along another path.

"Are you going to tell Phil you've seen him?," he asked Beth. "'Cos to be honest I don't think I can go on much longer knowing that Lisa is still seeing him. I did tell her to finish it and we'd try to stay together, but now I don't want to be with her at all. She's just a liar and a cheat and he's welcome to her."

Dave shoved his hands in his coat pockets and kicked leaves along the path showing his distress.

Beth stopped and turned to him.

"It's awful that we've been put in this position," she agreed. "I don't want to stay with Phil either now. I'm feeling so hurt and angry seeing him with someone else and then pretending at home that nothing's wrong. It's just so difficult to deal with the situation. It feels like a betrayal. I've got the kids to think of too. They're going to be hurt as well. But I agree with you – they're welcome to each other."

They smiled sadly at each other before continuing along the pathway. Neither knew where they were heading but just kept walking. Eventually they arrived at a park gate and stopped. Dave rubbed his face with his hand and Beth stood there staring at the ground.

"We'd better go home then, I suppose," she said. "I need to get back. I'm going to talk to Phil tonight and tell him that I know about Lisa. I'll ask him if he is going to leave me or if he intends to finish with her. Either way, I'm going to ask him to move out for a bit. We both obviously need some breathing space."

"Wow you're being very decisive," said Dave admiringly. "In that case I will speak to Lisa again. I'll tell her that she can either leave tonight and go to Phil, or that we have to move away so she never sees him again. I've not told you yet but I applied for a job last week in Barnstaple which is in North Devon. I've got an interview on Thursday and I'll probably take the job, whatever happens.'

"Yes that makes sense," agreed Beth. "We both seem to know what we are going to do but we just need to stick to our decisions now. Can I ring you later this evening?"

"Of course. If I can't answer straight away, I'll definitely call you back. We can then find out what's happened to each other," said Dave.

"I must go then," Beth said and went to walk towards the car park where she had left her car. "I'll call you later – good luck."

"You too. Take care and we'll speak soon." Dave turned and walked the other way to where his car had been left parked on double yellow lines in his haste to follow Lisa.

Beth was amazed she wasn't crying as she sped back homeward. She knew she had a difficult time ahead of her and must not shirk from what she had to do.

The children were still watching their DVD when she arrived home so she ran upstairs and washed her face with cold water. When she went downstairs again, the film had finished so she told the children to get ready to go out. She would take them for a late lunch at the

local garden centre and then over to visit their grandparents for the afternoon.

If she was busy for the next few hours, and kept out of Phil's way, maybe she could arrange some time alone with him so they could discuss his morning's tete-a-tete with Lisa.

Chapter Seven

--ooOoo--

*A*s Beth drove home from her parents' house she felt very alone. She had left the children with Jack and Vera who had promised to bring them back about nine o'clock. They loved to spend time with her children and Beth hoped that Verity's offspring did not feel neglected. Jack and Vera seemed to give the lion's share of their attention to Annie, James and Christina.

Beth reached home just after five o'clock and saw that Phil's car was already parked in the drive. She stopped the car, took the keys out of the ignition and slumped back in the seat, taking a deep breath.

'This is it then.' she thought as she stared ahead at the front door. 'I've got to go in there and ask Phil whether our marriage is ended.'

She took several more deep breaths before getting out of the car and locking the door. She slowly and a little nervously walked towards the house and opened the front door with her key.

Closing the door behind her she stopped in the hallway to gauge Phil's whereabouts. The television was obviously switched on in the front room so Beth slipped her coat off and walked in. Phil was slumped in a chair with a can of beer on the table next to him. He was watching the sports results and did not look up as she entered the room.

"Phil, I need to talk to you. Can we turn the television off please?" she asked.

"Just wait a moment until it finishes. It's only on for another ten minutes. Can't it wait?" asked Phil still not looking at Beth.

She walked across to the television and switched it off.

"Hey, what's so important that I can't finish watching the footy results?" he asked, abruptly sitting up in the chair.

"I'll tell you what's so important and can't wait for the football results, shall I?" It was not really a question and Beth did not wait for an answer. "Who is Lisa and why have you been meeting her?"

Phil looked astounded and slumped backwards into his chair.

"W-W-What did you say?" he blustered, obviously playing for time.

"I said, who is Lisa?" demanded Beth.

"Er, how do you know about Lisa?" Phil responded with another question.

"I know about Lisa because I saw you with her today, down by the river in the park," explained Beth patiently but firmly. "Now come on, tell me about her – now."

Phil stood up so he was on the same level as Beth.

"Where are the children?" he asked looking around as if he would suddenly spy them in the room.

"I've left them with mum and dad. Obviously I didn't want them to hear this conversation," Beth responded. "Now answer my question please."

"Well, Lisa is someone I've met and I was going to tell you about her soon. We've been meeting for a few weeks. I don't think that you and I are very happy together any more. I know we've got the children but that's all there seems to be between us these days."

Phil spoke accusingly at Beth.

'Well of course we've got the children, they're ours and we made them together. I would have thought that most couples went through dull or boring times in their marriages. That doesn't mean that you have to find someone else though. Couldn't we have tried to improve things, maybe by talking to each other?" asked Beth.

"I suppose so but you never seemed bothered. You appear to be happy enough with your job, the kids and their things, your family and friends, but you never wanted to go out with me in the evenings or get a babysitter," Phil continued.

"But you never said anything," Beth spoke sharply. "Why couldn't you tell me that you wanted to do things together instead of going off and finding someone else."

"I didn't go off and find someone else," Phil said. "I just happened to meet Lisa and we got on well together. I didn't plan to meet her again, we just bumped into each other and went for a drink one evening after work. It's a long time since I've connected with someone so quickly and easily and it felt good. Lisa wasn't particularly unhappy with her husband, but again they never seemed to do anything together or go anywhere. He's very wrapped up

in his work, she says."

"And how far has this relationship gone – are you sleeping with her?" asked Beth looking straight at Phil.

She realised from his response that the answer was yes. He couldn't meet her eye and turned away from her, moving towards the window.

"Yes I am sleeping with her," he finally answered. "She actually enjoys sex and does not just endure it like you do."

He turned with his accusation hanging in the air between them.

"Oh right, that's it now then," Beth responded, her temperature rising. "I should have guessed that sex would be the reason. How can you expect us to still be lovey-dovey when we've been married this long? Surely the contentment and comfort we give each other is what to expect in marriages after this time?"

"Maybe according to your magazines or television dramas, but I want to make love to someone who shows a bit of life and actually joins in. And anyway, it's not just about sex," he finished.

'Well what else is it about then?"' she yelled at him as she became more frustrated and angry with his responses.

"It's about the enjoyment of being with someone. The excitement of being together. Don't you understand that – can't you see?" he asked, wildly running his hands through his hair.

"No I can't see that. I would have thought that our marriage and the children would have meant enough to you to resist excitement and enjoyment with someone else!" she shouted.

"Well obviously it doesn't!" he shouted back. "I can't help what's happened. I don't know what to do. I think I love Lisa. But I also love my family."

"Well guess what Phil, you're going to have to grow up make up your mind now what you want. I'm not waiting about while you decide if you want me or her. If you choose her you can pack your bags and go now. If you decide you want to stay with me, then you'll have to promise never to see her again and you'll also have to make me believe that you still care about me."

Beth sank down in a chair after giving Phil the ultimatum. He stood looking at her for a while and then sat back in his chair.

"I don't know what to do. I don't think I can give up seeing Lisa. I talked to her this afternoon about what we were going to do and we both agreed that I would probably tell you and she would tell her husband that we want to be together."

Phil spoke quietly as he dropped the bombshell on Beth.Beth put her head in her hands and began to cry. Phil did not get up to comfort her but sat quietly watching. Eventually

her sobs lessened and she was able to speak again.

"That's your decision made then," she said, her voice wavering slightly. "You'd better go and pack some things and leave. I don't want to spend any more time with you if you want to be with somebody else. 'll tell the children you've been called away by work and maybe we'll tell them the truth tomorrow. When I'm more able to cope."

Phil sighed and then stood up and walked towards the door.

"I am very sorry that we are finishing our marriage like this," he said. "I wanted to be able to tell you in my own way. I know there is no best time to hear something like this, but you're right, there's no point trying to carry on with our lives together if we're unhappy."

"But I wasn't unhappy," Beth blurted out, twisting round in her chair to look at him in the doorway. "I didn't realise there was anything wrong with our relationship."

Phil looked at her sadly.

"Maybe that's the problem then, we both want different things from our marriage. You seem to be quite content with a boring job, looking after the children and living in a rut. I'm not. Maybe I've changed recently. I just know I don't want to live like this any longer. Of course I'll want to see the children, this has nothing to do with them. I still want to be their father."

"Yes I know. I won't stop you seeing them. They are going to be devastated though, I hope you realise that," she spoke accusingly.

"I know they will be. We'll have to do what we can to keep it right for them. You'll all stay here, of course. Well, at least until we get something else sorted out."

Phil turned and went up the stairs. Beth wondered what he meant by that last cryptic comment. What did he have in mind to sort out? Was he planning to move in here with Lisa? No, surely not. She and the children would need the house. He wouldn't turn them out in the street, would he? Of course she might have to get a full time job now. Maybe she could increase her hours with the accountancy firm. She would need to speak to her boss on Monday.

Tears formed in her eyes again and she sobbed quietly into a tissue she had taken from the pocket of her coat which was slung on the back of the chair. She could hear Phil opening doors and stomping around above her.

She glanced at the clock on the mantelpiece and was surprised it was only six o'clock. It felt that a life time had passed since she had arrived home.At least the children wouldn't be back for a few hours so she could get herself together. She would ring Amanda when Phil had gone and maybe ask if she could call round for an hour. Obviously Amanda might already have plans for the evening but Beth did not feel inclined at this moment to phone

her sister.

Eventually Phil came back downstairs carrying a couple of suitcases and with a back pack slung over his shoulder.

"I've got quite a lot of stuff here but I'll come back tomorrow for the rest. Do you want me to come back and tell the children with you?" he asked Beth.

"Yes I think that's best. Come in the afternoon and I'll make sure we're all here," said Beth not looking round at him. She did not want to watch him leave the house.

"I'm going to book in at the travel lodge," he informed her. "Just in case you want me."

"I don't really care" said Beth somewhat petulantly. "I can ring your mobile if I need you for anything."

"Ok I'll go now. See you tomorrow afternoon." Phil spoke as if he was just leaving for the office on a weekday. Beth felt as if her whole life was crashing around her and couldn't understand how he could act as if everything was normal.

"Bye," she managed.

He picked up his bags and manoeuvred his way out of the front door. Beth sat there listening to the banging of the car doors and the engine starting before he drove away.

She continued to sit in the dark for several minutes, just thinking about the events of the last few hours. Eventually she shook herself, both mentally and physically, and stood up.

After drawing the curtains across the windows and picking up the half empty beer can, she walked through the room and went into the kitchen. The beer can was dropped into the bin with a flourish before Beth turned towards her handbag which she had left in the hallway.

Amanda's number was easy to find on her mobile phone and Beth was pleased to hear her friend's voice.

"Hi Beth. How are you? What are you doing?" she asked brightly.

"Oh Amanda. I'm so glad you're in. Are you busy tonight?' asked Beth, getting straight to the point.

"We are going out later, probably about nine o'clock. Just next door to watch a film they've managed to get hold of which we all want to see. Why do you ask? Is there anything wrong?"

"Yes there's lots wrong. Do you think you could come over for half an hour just so I can tell you. I need someone to talk to and I've got no-one else."

Beth started to sob as she realised the truth of the words she'd just spoken.

"Oh my darling, of course I'll come over. I'll leave now and be there in two ticks. Just hold on till I get there. Go and make us a nice hot, strong cup of tea and then you can tell me all about it," soothed Amanda. "Go on Beth, into the kitchen and I'll be there soon."

The phone went dead as Amanda cut the connection ready for her mercy dash.

Beth put the phone down and went to grab some more tissues. She was obviously going to need them while she told Amanda the whole sorry story. She did as she was told and went into the kitchen to make some tea.

By the time Amanda's car pulled up on the drive, Beth had the hot steaming mugs placed on the table and went to open the front door. Amanda rushed over to her and put her arms around her friend. She hugged Beth tight as the tears spilled out from her weeping eyes.

"Come on lovey let's get inside. Don't want the neighbours spying you crying on your doorstep." Amanda managed to gently guide Beth inside the hall so she could push the door shut behind her.

"Let's go and find this tea you've made, shall we?" She gave Beth a further hug and pulled away. "Then you can tell me all about it."

Beth mopped up her face with an already soggy tissue and went into the front room. They sat down on the sofa together and Amanda shrugged out of her jacket.

"What's happened to upset you so much? Is it Phil?" she asked.

"Yes it's Phil. I found him kissing this Lisa woman in the park today. I had arranged to meet Dave, Lisa's husband, and we went to see if they were together. But I gave the wrong café name and then we followed them and they met up and were kissing and talking."

Beth saw that Amanda was getting confused and tried again.

"We had set Phil and Lisa up with pretend business meetings. They were supposed to meet in a café but I gave Phil the wrong name. So Dave and I followed each of them separately and they ended up together in the park by the river. They were kissing and hugging and talking. Then Dave and I went home and I took the children to mum's for the afternoon. When I got back here I confronted Phil and he admitted that he wants to be with Lisa. Says our marriage is boring and wants to 'connect' with someone. So he's gone to a hotel for the night and is coming back here tomorrow so we can tell Annie, James and Christina that we are splitting up."

Beth dissolved into uncontrollable sobbing again.

Amanda now understood what had happened and handed Beth some dry tissues from the box nearby. She waited until Beth had calmed down slightly before handing her the mug of tea.

"Come on chicken, drink some of this and calm down a bit," she said soothingly. "Are you sure Phil has left for good or are you just having some breathing space?" she asked.

"No I think he's gone for good. He didn't seem to hold out much hope that we had anything left between us. There's so much about our relationship that he doesn't like. I just can't believe that I didn't know, didn't realise, that he felt like that."

"Would you have done something differently then if you had known?" asked Amanda.

"I don't know what I could have done. I've always been a faithful and supporting wife. I know we are not desperately in love any more but I thought that the other things, like friendship and company, meant just as much in a marriage," said Beth.

"Of course they do," agreed Amanda. "But you can't take each other for granted. I know it's difficult when there are so many other things going on, like work, family, and being busy all the time. It is difficult to make time for each other. I understand too that when you have older children it's hard to get time alone because they always seem to be there. When they're babies and toddlers you can put them to bed early and have an evening to share

together. You can't do that with teenagers!"

"I know but I thought he was happy enough with our lives. Why did I not realise he wasn't?" asked Beth.

"Sometimes we don't see what is going on beneath our noses. It's hard to be objective about our own lives. Now tell me, do you want Phil back or don't you know yet?"

"Want him back?" repeated Beth, thinking about the question Amanda had just asked. "I don't know really, but I'm so hurt and angry about what's happened that I don't think I do want him back. I told him to choose between me and her and he's obviously chosen her. I said if he chose me he would have to make me believe he really wanted to stay here."

"But he's coming back tomorrow to talk to you and the children?" asked Amanda.

"Yes, tomorrow afternoon. He's coming here to explain the situation to them. So that must mean he doesn't want to come back, I suppose. What am I going to do?" Beth began to panic.

Amanda put her arm around her friend again and squeezed her. "You've got to keep some sort of normality going for the children. What time are they due back?"

"Nine o'clock. Shall I tell my mum and dad tonight, do you think?" asked Beth.

"I don't know. Maybe you should leave telling anyone about this until tomorrow. Sleep on it. You might feel clearer in your mind about what you want tomorrow." advised Amanda.

"Yes that's right," agreed Beth. "I'll try and behave normally until tomorrow afternoon."

"And then what happens – you'll behave abnormally?" Amanda asked with a twinkle in her eye.

Beth managed a smile at Amanda's attempt at a joke.

"I'll be ok now. I just needed to tell someone what had happened so I don't feel quite so alone. You know now as well and that helps me," she reassured Amanda.

"I had better go now if you're sure you'll be alright. It's not long till the children come back and you should get yourself something to eat. Have you got something nice in the kitchen you can have?"

"Yes there's a pizza in the fridge and a bar of chocolate in the cupboard which I'll have before the kids get back," Beth stood up.

"Good, some comfort food is just what you need," agreed Amanda also standing up and reaching for her jacket.

"Are you really sure you'll be ok though. I don't want to leave you if you are still feeling desperate."

"No don't worry I'll be fine. I've got to get used to being on my own now, haven't I?" Beth said with a bright smile.

"Don't be like that," said Amanda. "Anyway I bet you won't be on your own for very long. Good looking girl like you!"

"Huh don't try and set me up with any man, not ever," Beth said vehemently. "I'll never trust anyone again."

"We'll see," Amanda said. "Anyway you have to get over this first before you can move on to pastures new."

"There won't be any pastures new I can assure you," said Beth.

"If you need to ring me I'll only be with the next door neighbours. I'll tell Brian what's happened, if you don't mind. But I'll keep it from the children for now."

"Yes, tell Brian, that's fine. I'm going to ring Dave and find out what happened and whether Lisa has gone. I'll cook my pizza and finish the chocolate and then the children will be back home."

"Well just ring me if you need me. I'll come and stay the night if you want, just let me know." Amanda jangled her keys as she walked towards the front door.

"I'll ring you tomorrow after Phil has been. I might need some moral support after he's been here."

"'Bye then, chin up and try not to cry – it makes your eyes go red and blotchy," Amanda kissed Beth's cheek and gave her another hug.

"Thanks so much for coming round to cheer me up a bit," said Beth. "I'll ring you tomorrow and please don't worry about me, I'll be fine. And I won't cry too much, I don't want red and blotchy eyes."

They smiled at each other and Amanda walked towards her car.

"'Bye," she called as she got into the driver's seat.

"'Bye," repeated Beth waving her off.

She closed the front door and went determinedly into the kitchen to prepare her meal. She put the pizza in the oven, took out a plate and some cutlery and reached in the cupboard for the bar of chocolate.

Luckily it was still there, nobody else had found it. She placed it on the table and went back out to find her mobile phone.

Beth came back into the kitchen and sat at the table dialling Dave's number quickly on her phone.

He answered straight away.

"What's happened? Have you spoken to Phil?" he asked.

"Yes and he's left. He's left me because he wants to be with Lisa. Is she still there with you or has she gone too?"Beth held her breath as she waited for his answer.

"Yes she's gone. We had a huge row and she has packed some things and left. Don't know when or if she'll come back but she didn't take much with her, so I suppose I'll have to see her again some time," Dave told her.

"It's awful isn't it?" Beth sighed before she continued. "I can't believe this has happened in such a short time. It's unbelievable that I sat here at the kitchen table this morning with my world still relatively normal and now I've got no husband and my whole life has turned upside down. I really don't know how I'm managing to speak, let alone think."

"It's absolutely crazy," agreed Dave. "I just hope they both realise the chaos they've caused to all our lives. It's alright for them I suppose, they've got each other. But you've got your children to deal with and I've got no-one."

Beth thought that he sounded as if he might start to cry down the phone and realised that if he did, she would probably join him. She couldn't think of anything to say to cheer him up or give him some hope.

They sat in silence holding their phones and thinking of their altered lives.

"What are you going to do?" Beth eventually asked quietly. "Have you made any plans, apart from the job interview you have next week?"

She suddenly thought this might give him something to look forward to.

"Oh yes, the sooner I can move away from here the better, I think. There are too many memories in this house. I'll never forgive Lisa for letting me think we had survived her earlier affair with your husband, but was actually still meeting him behind my back. What about you, will you stay in your home?"

"I certainly hope so. I don't see why the children and I should be uprooted because of Phil's desertion. I will probably have to work full time to afford the mortgage and bills, but I suppose he will also have to give us some money, maintenance or whatever it's called these days," Beth said.

"When is he coming to see you?" asked Dave.

"Tomorrow afternoon. We are going to tell the children together. I'm pretending that he has been called away with work tonight but I don't think they will believe it. It's never happened before and I don't think I am a very good liar," she answered.

"Shall we meet again sometime?" Dave asked suddenly. "If you'd like to, that is. I don't know why because there's nothing else we can do now but I think I'd like to see you again."

"That would be nice," agreed Beth sitting up straighter on the chair. "When shall we meet – next week sometime?"

"Whenever you like. Wait until you've made a few plans if you like and after I've had my interview then we'll have something else to talk about rather than doom and gloom," he said.

"I'll give you a ring next Friday when you get back from your interview and perhaps we could meet the following week," suggested Beth standing up and switching off the oven. Her pizza was ready.

"Great," said Dave. "That has given me something to look forward to. Sorry if that sounds pathetic, I mean, I hardly know you do I?"

"'It doesn't sound pathetic at all. We are in the same position so it's natural we can comfort each other a bit." said Beth. She then realised that her words could sound a bit like a 'come on'. "Well I only mean comfort in the sense of helping each other." she tried to qualify her statement.

"Yes I know what you mean." She heard Dave laugh slightly and was pleased that he seemed to be overcoming his earlier emotions. He continued, "Ring me on Friday then and we'll make arrangements to meet. I hope things are not too difficult for you tomorrow. Do you think there's any chance you might get back together again?"

"I don't think so," Beth replied, remembering the conversation with Phil in the front room earlier. "Phil seemed pretty definite he wanted to be with Lisa. Anyway, I'm not sure I want him back now after all that's happened."

"I know, I feel the same," agreed Dave. "This is the second time with Lisa and I don't think I can ever trust her again. In fact, I don't know if I'll ever trust any woman again."

"I don't think I ever want to be with a man again either," Beth said emphatically.

"On that note I'll go then," said Dave. "I'll ring you Friday and we can compare notes then. 'Bye for now."

"'Bye," said Beth closing the phone and opening the oven door. She took her pizza out of the oven and sat down to try and eat as much of it as she could manage before taking her tea and chocolate into the front room.

She sat on the chair that Phil had occupied earlier. Glancing at the clock she saw she only had half an hour before her parents brought the children back home. Beth had already decided not to tell her parents about the events of the day. She wanted to talk to the children first. Sitting back in the chair with her eyes closed, Beth tried to relax and think about something other than Phil and Lisa.

At the sound of her parent's car arriving on the drive, Beth woke with a start. She must have dozed off for a few minutes. She looked at the clock as she stood up and noticed that she had slept for half an hour.

Beth walked into the hallway and opened the front door. The children were chattering excitedly as they walked towards the house with Jack and Vera following behind them.

"Hi Mum," said James. "Where's dad's car?"

Of course it would be James who first noticed that his dad was missing.

"He's had to go out to see some clients. They live quite a way from here and he's gone to stay overnight because they need to see him first thing in the morning. He'll be back tomorrow afternoon," Beth explained.

Her mother looked surprised but didn't say anything. They all piled into the house and took off their coats.

"Cup of tea?" Beth asked her parents, leading the way to the kitchen.

"Oh yes please that would be nice." said her dad. "Now come on James you were going to show me that magazine article about the Premiership. Is it upstairs?"

"Yes, come on up and have a look." said James, racing up the stairs.

"'Ok, I'll be back in a minute for my cup of tea," promised Jack as he followed James to his bedroom.

"Right we'll have a chat in the kitchen then," said her mother. "You girls can find something to do for a bit can't you?"

Beth and her mother stood in the kitchen and looked at each other.

"Now come on I can see something's wrong Beth. What is it then? Has Phil really gone away with work or have you had a row?" asked her mother.

Beth turned away to make the tea. She didn't answer straight away as she fought to stop herself blurting everything out to her mother. She didn't want to tell her parents yet and she wanted to spare their worries.

"'No nothing's wrong. I haven't had a row with Phil. He's gone to stay in a hotel tonight as he has to meet someone early tomorrow morning." Beth thought that sounded near enough the truth anyway.

"Ok, but I know something is wrong with you. I've always known when you are hiding something you know, Lizzie B." Her mother used the pet name from when she was a child.

"Oh mum don't worry. There's nothing wrong. I'm probably just tired or a bit fed up with the humdrum of everyday life. You know how it is?" Beth tried not to break down at the use of her childhood name.

"I expect Verity's news hasn't helped either, has it? We'd all like to be able to give up our job or boring lifestyle and live out our dreams."

"Yes, that's probably right,'" agreed Beth, placing the mugs of tea on the table. They chatted about everyday things until Jack came back downstairs for his tea.

"That boy knows a lot about football. Phil has taught him well," he joked as he picked up his mug. "Are you going to watch his match tomorrow?"

"No not tomorrow," said Beth. "It's an away match and the team are travelling on a minibus. I think it kicks off at about eleven o'clock. James is being picked up at ten by one of his friend's dad to go to where the bus is collecting them all for the journey."

"Maybe I'll go and watch him next week then. It's a while since I saw him play," Jack said. "Right. we'd better make a move now Vera, can't have you staying out late two nights running, you might get a taste for it!"

"Huh not much chance of that with you, is there? You're such a stay-at-home these days. Gone are the days you used to whisk me off dancing or to a nice restaurant," Vera grumbled as she stood up.

Jack laughed as he couldn't remember the last time they had done either of those things.

"Maybe we should go out more but it's not very inviting this time of year with the dark and cold. What about tomorrow? shall we go out for Sunday lunch?" he offered as they were putting their coats on in the hallway.

"Oh really!" exclaimed his wife as she turned to him. "Do you mean that Jack? It would be lovely not to have to cook tomorrow. Let's go to the restaurant near the park shall we?"

Beth winced as the park was mentioned and she recalled her visit there during the afternoon.

"That's a good idea for you both," she agreed ushering them out after they had called quick goodbyes to the children. "Go and have a lovely Sunday lunch together. You don't always need a special occasion to enjoy yourselves."

"Thanks dear," Vera kissed Beth quickly "You should also think about going out a bit sometimes. You and Phil rarely have any time to yourselves these days, do you?"

"Yes, take our lead and do the same. You know we'll always come and stay with the children for you," Jack hugged his daughter and waved at Christina who was looking through the curtains watching their departure.

"Ok thanks Mum and Dad. I'll call you tomorrow. Enjoy your lunch out. 'Bye." Beth waved as they drove away and then shut and locked the front door.

"Did you have a good time with grandma and granddad?" she asked, walking into the front room where the children were sitting. "You had some tea or are you still hungry?"

"I'm still hungry," said James. "But we did have some tea. Beans and bacon on toast with bananas and custard for pudding. Yummee."

"I've got some pizza in the fridge and I could quickly put some potatoes in the microwave if you like?" offered Beth.

"Oh yes please," they all accepted.

Beth busied herself in the kitchen preparing supper for the children.

She didn't really want to send them to bed too early as they were a distraction from her thoughts.

When the food was ready she took it to them in the front room. They had settled down in front of the television and she joined them with a cup of tea and a biscuit.

"Don't you want any of this?" asked Christina. "Have you had your tea Mum?"

Beth smiled at her daughter who always needed to make sure that everybody was happy.

"I'm Ok thanks, darling. I had some pizza earlier so I'm not hungry now."

They watched the programme on the television until it finished at ten thirty, when Beth told them it was time for bed and nobody argued. Christina was half asleep, still catching up from her previous late night.

Annie said she was just going to ring Ben and have a quick chat as she hadn't seen him that day. They were going to meet tomorrow afternoon for a while. Beth asked Annie if she could meet him in the evening instead as Phil would be returning after lunch.

"Okay, maybe I could meet him later, at about four or five o'clock." she asked her mum.

"'Yes that's alright as long as you are either here or at his house. I don't want you going out in the dark. And I want you here when your dad gets back," finished Beth.

Beth clattered about in the kitchen whilst Annie made her phone call before calling out "Good night!" to her mum and going upstairs.

When she had finished clearing the plates away, Beth wandered back into the front room. She sat down and tried to find something to watch on the television. Nothing seemed to interest her so she picked up a magazine. This failed to keep her attention either so she decided to go to bed. She checked the back and front doors, switched off all the downstairs lights and made her way up to her bedroom.

As she got into bed she realised that, apart from a few nights away due to business courses or events, she had not slept apart from Phil for many years. Beth lay in the dark, tossing and turning, trying to get herself comfortable.

She was not bothered about being alone, because she wasn't. The children were sleeping only a few feet away from her. Her mind just wouldn't play its part and shut down so she could drift away to sleep. It kept asking questions.

What am I going to do? How will I manage? What will it be like, being a single parent?

Eventually Beth got out of bed and stood at the window. She pulled the curtain back so she could look out. It wasn't that late so some of her neighbours were watching television with lights still on downstairs in their houses. She looked up above the houses and into the sky. Stars were twinkling and she tried to make out the Plough. There was a moving light but after looking at it for a while she realised it was a plane. She tried to imagine the people on board, jetting off on holiday or going to visit friends and relatives in far away countries.

After a while she realised her feet were getting cold. She pulled the curtains back and got into bed again. This time she organised her thoughts and began to plan what she would do if she won a million pounds.

She had just spent the first few thousand when she fell asleep.

Chapter Eight

--ooOoo--

*B*eth waved James off to his football match at ten o'clock the next morning and turned back into the house. The girls were upstairs. Loud music was blaring out from Annie's room and they had to shout to each other to be heard.

"Turn the music down a bit please," Beth yelled up the stairs.

"What did you say?" shouted Christina leaning over the banister rail.

"I said turn the music down a bit," repeated Beth. "It's far too loud."

"OK," Christina turned away into Annie's room and the music was turned down just a few decibels.

Beth shrugged her shoulders and gave up. Let them have their fun. Christina was not going to the animal sanctuary that day. She usually helped them one day each weekend but Beth had said she couldn't manage to take her out there either day. She had promised that Christina could go both days on the following weekend which had placated her.

Beth went into the kitchen to peel some potatoes ready to make lunch. She decided that they would all sit down and eat together and then they would tell the children. This would also give Phil a bit of extra time to make sure he was still of the same mind. Beth supposed to herself that she was clutching at straws but didn't care. Although she felt angry at Phil for what he had done, if he appeared contrite and apologised at this stage, she thought she might be able to forgive him.

After preparing the vegetables and putting the meat into the oven, Beth made herself a cup of coffee and went to sit in the conservatory.

Her phone beeped to tell her she had received a message and she looked to see who had sent her a text. It was Phil. The message just said he would be back at two o'clock to talk to the children and collect some more of his things.

Well, there didn't seem to be any more straws to clutch, she thought as she sipped her coffee. Looks like he's made his decision.

"I'll have to come to terms with this now and deal with it. It's no good breaking down in front of the children. I've got to be strong. He's leaving me for another woman. But I can cope. I'll sort my life out and move on. That's what we have to do these days, move on," Beth told herself firmly. "No tears, no tantrums, just cope."

It was easy to tell yourself to do these logical and sensible things, but would she be able to cope when Christina was crying, James upset and Annie worried? As far as she knew, they had no idea that their parents were on the brink of separating. There had been no massive rows or disagreements, no storming out of rooms and slamming doors, nothing to give them a clue that their whole world was about to disintegrate around them.

Beth hoped that Phil would tell them gently and with some sensitivity. It never occurred to her that she could tell them, either before he arrived or when they were gathered around the kitchen table. It just seemed right that Phil should break the news to them – he was

the man of the house and it was because of him that this was happening.

Beth sighed and stood up to go back into the kitchen to finish preparing the lunch. She would make a nice pudding – an apple crumble with custard and ice cream. She knew that food was not the answer, but it might seem more normal if they all ate a good meal together.

Just after one o'clock she heard James shouting goodbye to his friend before he came running around to the back door swinging his kit bag.

"We won three nil. We beat them. I didn't let a single goal in today, Isn't that great?" he shouted as he took off his trainers and left everything in a pile by the back door.

"Oh, well done James. That's good news. Did you get man of the match?" Beth asked.

"No. Ben got that because he scored two of the goals. But I don't mind 'cos I kept a clean sheet," he grinned.

"Brilliant," agreed Beth. "Now go on upstairs and tell the girls before you have a shower. Your dad should be here soon and dinner's almost ready."

James ran upstairs and she heard him shouting his news above the music still dominating the sound waves.

Beth made the final touches to the meal and laid the table. The food was ready and keeping warm in the oven. The apple crumble was on the side with the custard ready to be made at the last minute. The ice cream was waiting unsuspecting in the freezer.

The children came downstairs and Annie asked when her dad would be back.

"Any time now." said Beth glancing at the clock."Get your drinks ready and sit down. He'll be here in a few minutes I'm sure."

The children prepared their drinks and sat at the table. Beth sat down too.

"Why did dad have to go away last night?" asked Christina eventually. "I can't remember what you said."

"It was something to do with work," Beth told her. "He had to meet someone very early this morning and it seemed more sense to drive over there and be ready for the appointment'.

"Oh, right," said Christina digesting this information. "He's never done this before though has he?"

"No, never. He'll tell you all about it when he gets here," said Beth."He's sent me a text message to say he is on his way back, so we shouldn't have to wait too long."

"Did I tell you that Ben is going to come over at six tonight for an hour or so?' asked Annie as if she sensed that a change of topic was needed. "We're going to finish some homework for science and then listen to the new CD he bought yesterday. That's Ok isn't it?"

"Yes that's fine," agreed Beth, relieved to have a change of subject. "'What about you two, do you want to do anything later this afternoon?"

"Yes, let's go bowling," suggested James. "'We'd have time for two games if we left early enough, wouldn't we?"

"Oh yes, bowling would be great," said Christina bouncing up and down on her chair.

"Would you and Ben like to come too?" she asked Annie. "Or would you rather stay here?"

"I think we'll stay here and finish this homework. It's due to be handed in tomorrow. We haven't got much to do, but Ben's quite good at science and he said he'd help me a bit," explained Annie.

"Ok then, we'll go bowling but probably only have one game," promised Beth getting up to check the dinner was not burning. She glanced at the clock. It was quarter past two. Where was Phil? Surely this wasn't the sign of things to come – being late and letting down the children?

She sat down again. She needed another diversion.

"Are you looking forward to your holiday at Woodlands?" she asked James and Christina.

"Oh yes, it'll be cool," said Christina excitedly. "I can't wait to tell my friends I'm going. They'll be so jealous. It's really nice of Aunty Verity and Uncle John to pay for us to go."

"Do they do football there?" asked James.

"Yes I think so. There are lots of outdoor and indoor activities so you'll be able to try new things as well. You know Annie is not going, don't you? It's too near her exams," Beth told them.

"Oh that's alright, we're old enough to go on our own," James assured her.

Christina did not look quite so sure but Beth thought she'd be happier when she knew that Verity was sending her two children as well.

"That sounds like Dad's car," James said. "At last, I'm starving."

Beth stood up to begin dishing out the food and heard Phil come in through the front door.

"Hiya kids," he said as he entered the kitchen. "Are you having dinner?"

"Yes come on we've starving," said James. "Guess what? We won three nil this morning. So that's put us back up the league table. Isn't that great?"

"Oh well done. Shame I missed the match. I'll come and watch next week," Phil promised.

"Sit down – there's dinner for everyone," said Beth as she handed plates to James and Annie.

"Oh right. Thanks." Phil sat at the far end of the table.

Luckily the children didn't pick up on the strained conversation between their parents. Time enough for that when they had finished eating. The children spent most of the meal telling Phil what they had been doing since they last saw him on Saturday morning. They didn't ask where he had been.

Beth sat and ate her meal quietly, allowing the chatter to wash around her, mostly unheard.

She collected the dinner plates and served the pudding to everyone before taking her place again. She pushed the crumble around her bowl, unable to finish it. When the others had finished their pudding and were preparing to leave the table Phil cleared his throat and said, "Hang on a minute kids. Just wait at the table for a few minutes."

They looked at him surprised but did as he said.

"We, that is your mum and I, have something we must tell you," he began. "First, you all have to realise that we love each and every one of you very much," he continued, looking at them all in turn.

The children looked slightly bewildered at him as he was not usually the type of dad who kept telling his children that he loved them.

"But unfortunately your mother and I have not been getting on too well lately. We don't argue or shout at each other but we seem to have grown apart," he explained.

"Are you getting a divorce?," asked Christina with tears welling up in her eyes."Please don't say you are. I don't want you to break up and not be able to live here, in this house, any more."

Beth stood up and went over to hug her youngest daughter.

"Now don't worry Christina. You won't have to move anywhere. This is your home," She looked accusingly at Phil challenging him to say something different.

Christina started to cry and wrapped her arms tightly around Beth's waist. James looked as if he might join in with her.

"What do you mean?" asked Annie. "What's happening?"

Phil cleared his throat again.

"What I mean is that I will not be living here for a while. I'm going to live somewhere else for a bit. But I'll still see you lots. I'll come over here and visit you and you can come to me too."

"What about football – will you still help with the team?" asked James.

"Of course I will. I'll still be involved with your football, I wouldn't miss that for the world," Phil reassured James. "Nothing much will change for you three except I won't be sleeping here at night and I won't be here first thing in the morning. I'll still be your dad and love you, though."

"But not mummy," said Christina through her tears. "Why don't you love Mum? What has she done wrong?"

Beth looked at Phil over her daughter's head and thought, 'Yes what have I done wrong?'

"She's done nothing wrong," said Phil looking as if he'd been cornered. "It's just one of those things that happen sometimes."

"But why is it happening to us?," asked James. "What have we done wrong? Is it us?"

"No, it's not you," said Phil loudly. "It isn't anyone's fault. I'm still going to be a big part of your lives. I'll come to parents' evenings at school, I'll take you out at weekends, come to football with you James, take you to the animal sanctuary Christina and you to your dancing lessons, Annie. I just won't be living here."

The room was silent as the children solemnly digested the life-changing information they had just heard from their father.

Beth hugged Christina tight again and then sat down.

"We'll have to try and keep our lives as normal as we can. You'll still see your dad lots of times. You can ring him whenever you want to speak to him. Both of us still love all of you very much," said Beth looking at each of her children as she spoke.

"Will you come bowling with us?" Christina asked suddenly. "Mum said we can go bowling later – will you come with us?"

Phil paused slightly before answering.

"Yes of course I'll come bowling. What time are you going?" he asked Beth.

"We can go now. I said we'd just go for one game though." Beth was tempted to ask if he had somewhere else he'd rather be, but didn't want to start an argument in front of the children. She realised he'd agreed to go with them in order to salve his conscience.

"Annie, will you come with us and see Ben a bit later?" asked Beth.

"Yes, I'll just ring and ask him to come round later," agreed Annie, leaving the kitchen.

"Shall we go now then? Are you all ready?" Phil asked looking round at them.

The other two children got to their feet and went to find their coats.

Obviously they were not as excited as they would have been under different circumstances!

Beth stood up too and began clearing away the remains of their meal. She clattered plates and filled the dishwasher as quickly as she could. She had never realised quite how uncomfortable she could feel in her own kitchen.

Phil stood awkwardly in the doorway and muttered something about making a phone call.

When Beth turned around he had gone out of the front door. Probably to ring Lisa and say he wouldn't be back for a while. Surely they would have realised he could not just tell the children that he was leaving and then go? Didn't they know that some reassurance would be needed?

Annie came back into the kitchen and walked over to her mother and put her arms around her.

"Oh Mum. It's so awful. Did you know about Dad leaving?" she asked.

"Not until yesterday," said Beth returning the hug. "I only found out when you were at your grand-parents' house in the afternoon. I came back here and spoke to your dad. He said he wanted to move out because we, your dad and I, were not getting on. I just didn't know he felt like that," Beth confided in her eldest daughter.

"It must be such a shock for you. I know it is for me, and the others. Christina is crying upstairs and James looks like he might cry too," Annie told her.

"I'd better go upstairs then. Can you just finish down here for me please?" Beth asked.

"Yes of course I can. We've all got to help each other now," Annie said, proving that she was growing up quickly.

Beth ran upstairs and into Christina's bedroom. They were both in there and Christina was sobbing into her pillow. Beth sat on the bed beside her and pulled James down next to her.

"Come on now. Don't cry. It will be alright, you know. We'll manage and you'll still see your dad lots of time. He doesn't want to lose you."

Beth stroked Christina's hair and held on to James' hand. Christina's sobs gradually subsided as she listened to her mother's words. She sat up and put her arms around Beth's waist.

"What have we done wrong? Why is he going away?" she asked again.

"You've done nothing wrong. He is not going away from you. It is just that sometimes grown ups don't get on together any more. Your dad will still be close to you and come and see you every day, I'm sure. You'll hardly notice he's not actually living here. Wait and see," Beth tried to reassure them.

They sat together on the bed for a few more minutes, all struggling to compose themselves.

"Come on we'd better go bowling," said James resolutely standing up. "Let's go and try to act like a normal family."

Beth thought that was a very sad statement – 'to act like a normal family.' Did this mean that they weren't a normal family any more?

"Yes come on Christina. Let's go bowling. It's what you wanted to do isn't it?" Beth pulled her up from the bed and hugged her tightly.

"Alright then, I'll be brave," said Christina seriously. "We've got to do things together sometimes, haven't we?"

"Yes that's right. Get your coat and let's go." Beth turned and went out of the room. She went into her bedroom to fetch her jacket and handbag.

She looked out of the window and noticed Phil in the front garden stood by his car, still talking into his mobile. They must have a lot to say to each other, she thought.

A few minutes later the four of them left the house and Phil ended his call as he saw them approaching the car.

They drove to the bowling alley and spent the next hour pretending to enjoy themselves. Nobody tried very hard to win the game and conversation was not easy. Annie did not seem inclined to speak to her father at all but the younger children almost reached the same camaraderie they normally enjoyed with him. But each time they seemed to have forgotten the news he had sprung on them earlier and when it suddenly came back to them and they withdrew from him again.

Beth noticed all this as she spent most of the time watching the four of them interact together.

When Phil had eventually been declared the winner, they went upstairs to the restaurant and enjoyed the usual post-game refreshments but not the post-mortem of the game. Instead, they sat in silence for most of the time.

Eventually Phil glanced at his watch and asked if they were all ready to leave. Beth and the children finished their drinks and stood up ready to go. There was no conversation in the car on the way home and when Phil drove onto the drive he made no move to get out of the car. Beth and the children stood on the drive.

"Aren't you coming in Dad?" asked James walking round the car to speak to his dad through the window.

"No not now. I'll come back tomorrow and see you after school," said his father.

Beth couldn't believe he was not going to get out of the car and give the children a hug.

She turned to the front door and put the key in.

"Come on then, let's go in," she said opening the door. Annie and James followed her in but Christina rushed to her father.

"Oh please don't go," she cried. "Please don't leave us and live somewhere else."

Phil sighed and took his seat belt off before climbing out of the car. He put his arms around Christina, who was crying with wrenching sobs. He looked helplessly at Beth over the top of her head.

"I've got to go now but I'll come back tomorrow," he promised. "It's alright Christina, don't cry. I'll see you after school."

Beth walked over to rescue him. She gently pulled Christina towards her and hugged her tight.

"Come on love, try and stop crying." she soothed. "Let's go inside and make a nice hot drink of chocolate. You'll feel better then and like your dad says, he'll be back tomorrow. That's not long to wait."

Christina allowed herself to be taken away from her father and into the house.

Beth drew them all into the hallway and looked at Phil who was still standing on the driveway. Her eyes told him: 'look what you've done!'

She closed the front door and helped Christina off with her coat.

"Let's go in the kitchen and make some hot chocolate. I think we've got some marshmallows to have with it too."

They did as Beth suggested and soon were all sat around the kitchen table with their steaming mugs. Beth put the packet of marshmallows on to a plate in the middle of the table.

"Now, we have all got to be really brave about this," she said looking around at them. "Dad has decided to go and live somewhere else for a while. This is nothing, absolutely nothing, to do with his feelings for all of you. It is because he doesn't want to live with me at the moment," she emphasised firmly. "We don't know yet when, or if, he will come back but whatever happens, he still loves you. He will still be involved in all parts of your lives. That's what he told you. I know it's a shock, it is for me too because I didn't know this was going to happen," Beth continued.

"It's ok Mum," said Annie reaching out to take hold of Beth's hand. "We are all going to be really brave and help you as much as we can." She looked at her brother and sister as she spoke and they nodded agreement.

'Thank you darlings, that's great," Beth smiled at them. "It's going to take a bit of getting used to, not having your dad here, but we will try and get on with our lives and just make the necessary adjustments."

Christina was still gulping slightly from the emotion of parting from her father. James seemed to sit up slightly in his chair and assume the role of the man of the house.

"Do you know where Dad has gone to live?" asked Christina.

"No I don't know but I'm sure he'll tell you soon. And take you there so you can see where he is living. You may be able to stay there as well if you want to. Perhaps overnight. We'll have to see," said Beth.

"Is dad still working at the same place?" asked James.

"Yes," answered his mother. "He's still working at Taylors."

She realised they needed to ask all these questions as they were still coming to terms with the changes to their lives. And these changes had happened so quickly, without any warning.

They sat for a while talking quietly about what they imagined would happen in the future. Annie did not say very much and Beth noticed her looking at the clock.

"Do you want to go and meet Ben?"' Beth asked.

"Oh yes please, if you don't mind," replied Annie standing up. "I said I'd ring him when we got back from bowling. Is it alright if he comes round for a bit?"

"Yes that's fine. Take him upstairs and finish your science project. I'll make some tea for about seven so he can stay and have some with us if he'd like."

"Thanks Mum," said Annie as she rushed out of the kitchen to ring Ben.

Beth looked at the other two.

"What would you like to do?" she asked them.

They didn't answer immediately. Then James suggested they played a game. Beth realised they wanted to do something together to try and remind themselves they were still

part of a family.

"That's a good idea," she agreed. "Let's play a game in the front room. If you go and set it up, I'll make some sandwiches ready for later and then I can play too."

"Oh great," agreed Christina standing up quickly. "Come on James let's go and get a game ready."

They left the kitchen, momentarily diverted with the thought of doing something to keep busy. Beth put the mugs in the sink and began to make some sandwiches ready for their tea.

Her thoughts turned to Phil's attitude during the afternoon. He didn't seem very remorseful for the turmoil he had caused by his actions. He hadn't even wanted to hug the children when he left them on the drive. Beth couldn't understand how he could treat his family so coldly. Maybe he was turning off from them so he did not feel so guilty or ashamed. Or perhaps he was trying not to feel sad or sorry for leaving his family.

Beth was sure he had gone to Lisa and was tempted to ring Dave to find out how he was coping. But she did not want the children to hear her speaking to him on the phone. They had no idea yet that another person was involved in Phil's decision to leave. She wondered if it would have made it easier for them to accept or whether it would just have complicated the scenario.

As she finished the sandwiches and put them in the fridge until later, she decided that she would call Dave later that evening when she could ring safely from her bedroom. The children would all be bathing and getting ready for school the next day before they went to bed, so she would have a few uninterrupted minutes to herself.

Beth went into the front room to find that a game of Monopoly had been set out on the coffee table. She could hear music coming from Annie's room and realised that Ben must have arrived without her hearing him, probably because she had been deep in thought in the kitchen.

They enjoyed their game for the next hour before Annie and Ben came downstairs.

"Can Ben stay for some tea?" Annie asked her mother.

"Yes of course," Beth smiled at the two of them standing in the doorway. "'Would you like to get it ready in the kitchen?"

"Ok," agreed Annie.

A couple of hours later when Ben had left and the children were busy with their preparations for school the next day, Beth went into the bedroom with her mobile phone to ring Dave. He answered on the third ring and said that yes, he could talk.

"I just thought I'd ring and see what's happening with you?" explained Beth.

"Well Lisa didn't come back today so she'll probably sneak in tomorrow when I'm at work and get the rest of her clothes. What about Phil? Did he turn up today?"

"Yes he did and we told the children together. Then we went bowling which was awful 'cos the kids were really upset. Then he brought us back home and upset everyone by just driving off." Beth explained.

"That does sound awful," agreed Dave. "How are your children coping?"

"Well Annie, she's the eldest, seems Ok. A bit quiet, I suppose. But she has a boy friend and he came to see her for a while earlier. She's probably told him all about it. The other two are more outwardly upset. Christina has cried quite a lot and James is suffering too. I played a game with them earlier to cheer them up. I think it will be better tomorrow when they go to school and get into their normal routine. Sundays are always strange days, especially the evenings."

"What about you?" asked Dave.

"Oh I've got to be alright, although it's still a shock and I'm still mad. In fact, getting madder all the time because Phil just doesn't seem to be able to do anything right. I was cross this afternoon with his 'don't care' attitude. I'm going to ask at work tomorrow if they can employ me full time. If not, I may have to look for another job."

'Well don't do anything rash. Take time to think before you rush into a new job," said Dave. "It may be that Phil has to give you enough money that you will be able to manage."

"How do I find out?" asked Beth. "I don't know what to do about money, Phil always took charge of paying bills."

"You'll have to ask him, of course. Not yet, take a few days to let things settle down first. Then you'll have to arrange to meet up with him and sort out all your finances," he advised.

"Yes of course. That's good advice. I also need to talk to my mum and dad as I'm probably going to need their help. I'll speak to them tomorrow. Thanks Dave," she said.

"That's alright, glad to be of assistance," said Dave.

"What about you? How are you coping? Have you made any further plans yet?" Beth asked him.

"No, I'll wait until I've had the interview on Thursday and then decide what I'm going to do. If I take the job then I'll probably arrange to move down there. It would make sense."

"Yes that does sound like a good idea. My sister and her husband are thinking of moving to Cornwall. They're the ones who have won some money on the lottery," she explained. "They plan to buy a small farm or market garden to run."

"That sounds like hard work," said Dave. "Although I do love Cornwall. Don't know if I'd want to live there all year though. Might be a bit quiet in the winter."

"Quiet sounds good at the moment," Beth said wistfully. "Anyway I'd better go now. I'll ring you on Friday and find out how you got on with your job interview."

"Yes that's great. We'll arrange to meet up and have another chat," agreed Dave.

"Bye for now and good luck on Thursday," said Beth as she closed the phone.

She sat on the bed for a few minutes and thought about Dave. He seemed a nice man. She felt he seemed vaguely familiar but could not think why. His smile and the way he pushed his hair out of his eyes reminded her of someone. Maybe she'd ask him if he felt they had met before when they get together again.

Beth stood up and went to chivvy the children towards their beds. Half an hour later, when the house was quiet, she sat downstairs in the semi darkness and thought about her future. Obviously she wanted to stay in her home with her children. She would like to keep her job but needed to work more hours. Her parents would be needed to help her a bit with after-school care.

She didn't want Phil to move too far away as she would then lose his help with taxi-ing the children around. She would have to find out about paying the bills, keeping the house in good repair, sorting out car repairs and MOTs, dealing with emergencies and even changing light bulbs. She was ashamed to admit to herself that she had never changed a

light bulb. How many Beth's did it take to change a light bulb? she wondered. Just me, she decided firmly. She would learn how to do it. Her father would show her.

Maybe she should learn how to change a washer in a tap and a wheel on the car? And what about all the other domestic emergencies that might occur? A plumbing disaster, electrical fault or gas leak. All these things might happen and how would she cope?

She took a deep breath and decided to go to bed. It was no good sitting here worrying about all the disasters that could happen. She had her father living within easy distance and she knew that he would always help her.

But what if he was away? Maybe visiting Verity in Cornwall? Her mind was determined to send her to bed with enough worries to keep her awake all night.

Beth stood up and went to check all the outside doors. She switched off the kettle at the plug and made sure all the taps were not dripping. It was no good inviting a disaster!

When she was in bed her thoughts turned to the next day. She would have to tell her parents and hope that they would be able to support her through the next few difficult weeks. Beth sighed and turned over and fell asleep.

Chapter Nine

--ooOoo--

*B*eth arrived early for work the next day and managed to find her boss on his own for a few minutes. She explained her changed circumstances and asked if there was a possibility he could offer her some extra hours.

Allan smiled at Beth across the desk and said that one of her colleagues had just asked if she could reduce her working hours after the Christmas break.

"I was not sure whether to agree to Suzie's request as we would have needed to employ someone else to cover the workload. But as you are willing to work extra hours, I think we'll manage and be able to accommodate everyone."

Beth was relieved that she did not have to look for another job. It also gave her a few weeks before she needed to start working full time which would allow her time to adjust to the longer working hours. They agreed that Beth would start working a few extra hours at the beginning of December in order to take over some of her colleague's tasks.

As Beth made her way to her desk she smiled at Suzie and stopped to tell her the good news. Suzie was relieved too as she was finding it difficult to work full time with her children needing to be transported to their various after-school activities.

"I'm going to start helping you in December," explained Beth. "And then you can become part time at the beginning of January."

When Beth stopped to take her coffee break at about 11.30, she rang her parents in order to arrange a convenient time to meet them. Luckily they had no plans for the afternoon and agreed to call on Beth when she arrived home from work, just after two o'clock.

Beth tried to keep her mind on her work but she kept thinking of the dismal faces of her children at breakfast time. Christina had already asked if her dad was coming to see them after school.

"Of course he will. He promised, didn't he?" reassured Beth.

The children had left for school in a sombre mood – and not just because it was Monday morning. Beth knew they'd be pleased to see their grandparents after school and hoped that Phil would not let them down.

She arrived home at the same time as her parents drove up outside her house.

"Hi mum, and dad' she kissed them both quickly before going to open the front door. "Come on in and let's get the kettle on."

"Is everything alright dear?" asked her mother, astute as always. "Why have you summoned us here this afternoon?"

"Let's go into the kitchen and have a cup of tea and then I'll tell you. Did you have a nice meal yesterday?" Beth tried to divert her mother's questions for the moment.

"Yes it was a lovely meal. We had a great time and went for a walk in the park afterwards. We said we'll have to go out to eat more often," said her father.

"Oh you must tell Beth about the funny incident in the car park," said Vera. She turned to Beth and continued: "Your father thought there was something dragging under the car when we arrived at the restaurant. He got out of the car and went to the front to have a look. He held on to the front of the car and slowly bent down but a young couple walking towards us thought he had collapsed and ran to help him. They grabbed him by the arms and pulled him upright again. Of course your father thought he was being attacked and starting to fight against them. I couldn't believe what I was seeing – it was so funny."

Vera began to laugh again at the memory.

"It wasn't funny for me or the two people who were trying to help me," said Jack trying not to laugh. "They were very embarrassed when they realised I was looking under the car and not in need of immediate medical attention."

Beth laughed as she placed the mugs of tea in front of her parents and sat down with her own.

"I don't think you two are safe to be out on your own," she joked.

Vera took a sip of her tea and regarded her daughter over the rim of the mug.

"Now come on then, tell us what's wrong," she asked. "I know something's bothering you, so let's have it."

"Yes you're right mum. As always, nothing get's past you! There is something wrong." Beth took a deep breath and began.

"At the weekend I found out that Phil has been seeing another woman,"

Vera and Jack both gasped as Beth's words penetrated their minds like a lance.

"What!" exclaimed Jack. "Seeing another woman? What woman?"

"Well she's a woman he met a few weeks ago at a works lunch held in a pub.They've been seeing each other since then. I found out because I discovered a note in his suit pocket. There was a phone number which I rang and I spoke to the woman's husband. We met at the weekend and followed Phil and Lisa, his wife. It was Saturday, when I asked you to look after the children," explained Beth.

"I can't believe it, I just can't believe it,'" repeated Jack rubbing his eyes. "So what's going to happen? Are you staying together or not?"

"No, not at the moment anyway. I confronted Phil on Saturday and then he left. As you know, he went to stay in a hotel. Well, I suppose he did, but I don't know for sure. He may have been with her. He says he would rather be with her although obviously he still wants to see the children. He's supposed to be coming here after work to see them. We told them yesterday and then all went bowling together. He brought us back here and then drove off, almost without even saying goodbye to them. Obviously they are all absolutely shattered and very upset. As I am too. I had no idea until a few days ago that our marriage was not alright."

Beth stopped speaking and hoped her parents could make sense of the tangled words. There was silence for a few seconds as her parents came to terms with the situation.

"We'll help you all we can darling," said her mother getting up to hug Beth hard. "Just ask and we'll do what we can to help you and the children."

"Yes that's right, of course we will," agreed Jack, putting his hand over Beth's hand and squeezing it reassuringly. "Are you going to be alright for money?"

"I've asked for some extra hours at work and I start after Christmas.

Someone else wants to cut down so I am going to take over some of her work. I suppose Phil will have to give me maintenance for the children," Beth said.

"Yes of course he should pay for his children," Vera agreed. "Would you like us to help after school and holiday times when you're still at work?"

"If you don't mind. The children are getting older now so they should be able to manage sometimes. But it would be nice to know they weren't coming home to an empty house every night. I think I will have to work until five o'clock so I should be back here before half past five. And during holiday times I won't be able to be as flexible as I have been."

"That's fine, don't worry. We are more than happy to help out as much as we can," Jack said and Vera nodded her agreement.

"Have you told Verity yet?" asked Vera.

"No I haven't told anyone apart from Amanda. She helped me when I first found the note. I'll ring Verity tonight and speak to her. It's a shame to give her this bad news just when she is looking forward to a new beginning."

"Oh she'll cope. She asked me a while ago if I thought you were happy together, you and Phil. I don't know why she asked and she didn't say that she had any reason to doubt that you were happy together. I think sometimes people get a premonition or feeling that something's not quite right," said Vera.

"Well she must have sensed something that I didn't," said Beth ruefully. "I was in blissful ignorance and didn't realise Phil was not happy. I suppose we had all reached a bit of a routine in our lives, with the children and our jobs. But I thought life was meant to be like that. You have the exciting and interesting times earlier and then settle down together in contentment,"

"Sounds a bit boring to me," said Jack. "Your mother and I have never experienced momentous events in our lives but I would not say we had no excitement or interesting times. I suppose we are settled and content in a way, but we've always tried to make sure that each other is happy'.

"Yes we have," agreed Vera smiling at her husband. "But we've always said that not everyone is like that. We often see couples sat in cafes or restaurants with barely a word spoken between them.

Whereas your dad and I are always talking to each other. I don't know what we find to say sometimes, but we've always been like that."

"You are both very lucky to have each other," Beth put her hands out and held on to each of her parents. "I suppose I have probably taken Phil for granted and been too involved with the children and their lives. It's the classic scenario isn't it?" she asked.

"Sometimes it is but you have to find some time for each other whatever else is going on in your lives. Phil too has probably immersed himself in his job and not taken enough time out for family and marital times. So it's not just one person's fault. It's an accumulation of circumstances," said Jack.

"Do you think you will be able to forgive Phil for his indiscretion or not?" asked Vera.

"At the moment, no, I can't forgive him. He is not showing any remorse or intention to want to come back to me. He is still seeing her and may even be living with her now. I don't know," said Beth quietly.

As she finished speaking the back door swung open and James and Christina entered the kitchen. They were pleased to see their grandparents and Christina went over to hug them both.

"Are you alright mum?" asked James anxiously looking at her.

"Yes thanks James, I'm ok. Are you both alright? Had a good day at school?" she asked as she stood up to make their drinks.

"Yes it was ok," said James, turning away to hide his face. "Not got any homework tonight anyway."

"I was sad at school today," Christina told them as she sat on her grandad's lap. "I told my friends what happened yesterday. They were all very sorry for me. Saskia told me what it was like for her when her dad collects her on Saturdays to take her out. He buys her lots of nice things and let's her eat whatever she wants. But she says sometimes her mum and dad have a big argument when he takes her back home afterwards. I hope dad comes round after work," she finished wistfully.

Beth gave them their drinks and asked if Annie had walked home with them.

"No, she's gone to see Ben. She said to tell you she'll be back by five," said James biting into a chocolate biscuit as he spoke.

The adults steered the conversation on to safe grounds, mostly talking about Verity and John's new project, for the next half an hour until Jack and Vera stood up ready to leave.

"I'll ring Verity later and talk to her." promised Beth as she waved to her parents at the front door. "'And I'll call you tomorrow," she added and tried to reassure them, "Please don't worry, we'll be alright."

"Of course you will," said Jack "I've got every confidence in you."

After Beth had closed the front door she put her arms around James and Christina and hugged them tight.

"We will be alright you know. We'll all get through this horrible time and things will work out somehow. Wait and see," she said.

James nodded and then broke away to head upstairs. Christina clung on to her mother and asked how things would work out.

"I don't know that at the moment but I do know that we are still a family. We may not all live together but you still have a mummy and a daddy who love you very much. You still have a sister and a brother as well as grandparents, aunties and uncles and cousins. So you have lots of people who love and care for you. Lots of families go through changes and different

things happen all the time. When I was your age my best friend's mother died. It was awful. I tried to help my friend as much as possible but nobody could replace her mum. Her dad tried hard to look after my friend and her sister and they had to become a little family together without a mum. We might have to become a family whose dad does not live here. But you still have a dad. He is still a big part of your life."

Beth hoped that her words would help Christina come to terms with the situation.

Christina thought for a few seconds and then hugged Beth. "I will try not to be upset all the time," she admitted. "I cried at school today and Saskia told me not to be silly. She told our teacher what had happened and now the whole class knows. But Miss Roberts was really nice and let me go to the toilets with Stephanie to compose myself. She told Saskia off for being insensitive. What does insensitive mean?," asked Christina.

Beth explained the meaning of the word and then suggested that Christina help her in the kitchen to prepare the dinner. They chatted happily together until Annie arrived home just after five.

"I hope you didn't mind that I went to see Ben for a while," she asked Beth.

"No of course not. I'm glad you told the others to pass on a message. It might be best for you to have a mobile phone so you can let me know if you're going to be late home. I'll speak to your dad and we'll get one for you. But you must promise to let me know if you aren't coming straight home and where you are going. And if I ask you to come home, you must do that. I might need you to be here sometimes if I have to work late," Beth told her.

"Yes that's fine. Can I choose the phone myself?" she asked.

"We'll see. It will probably be a pay-as-you-go type so we can give you some credit. But if you want to ring Ben or your friends you'll have to contribute something towards the cost."

"Most of my friends have got phones and I was going to ask for one for Christmas," said Annie. "I've used Marilyn's once or twice so I know how to work them."

"Can I have one too?" asked Christina hopefully.

"Not at the moment but when you're a bit older," promised Beth.

"Shall I start making a list for Christmas now?" persisted Christina.

"Later if you want to. You're helping me at the moment," Beth reminded her.

"I'll go and start my homework. Is dad coming round this evening?" Annie asked as she picked up her school bag to go upstairs.

"He said he would' Beth said. 'Dinner will be about half an hour. Can you tell James too please."

After they had eaten and cleared away the dishes, there was still no sign of Phil. Beth busied herself in the kitchen trying not to look at the clock every minute. Eventually she heard his car draw up on the drive. James and Christina heard it too and ran to the front door. Beth glanced at the clock and saw it was half past six.

"Hi kids!" Phil went straight into the front room with James and Christina without acknowledging Beth. Annie ran down the stairs and came into the kitchen.

"Are you coming in with us?" she asked.

"No I don't think so. I'll pop upstairs and make a couple of phone calls. You go in with your dad."

Beth went upstairs into her bedroom and closed the door. She would ring Verity while she had a few minutes on her own. She dialled the number and waited for Verity to pick up her phone.

"Hi Sis – how's it going?" Verity began. "We're all being a bit mad here on the internet – looking at properties for sale in Cornwall. We've got three appointments for the weekend to view possible places. We want to try and find one more to look at, so we have two each day. We've booked a bed and breakfast for Saturday night at a nice farmhouse."

"That sounds great Verity. I'm so pleased for you," responded Beth.

"What's up though? You sound a bit funny," asked Verity.

"Can you go somewhere private for a few minutes. I've got something to tell you," asked Beth.

"Yes of course I can. What is it? It's not mum or dad is it?," Verity's voice became strained.

"No, it's not mum or dad, or the children. Don't panic. Just something I need to tell you quietly."

"Ok I'm upstairs now, away from everyone else. What is it?"

Beth told her in a few sentences about the events of the weekend. Verity listened in silence. When Beth had finished speaking Verity asked if she wanted her to come over for the evening.

"No I'm fine. Phil is here at the moment, downstairs with the children. He may want to talk later. We haven't sorted anything out about finances or access or anything yet. I just wanted to tell you so you knew what was happening. I've told mum and dad this afternoon. They were devastated but offered any help that I might need. I'm going to work full time from January onwards so they've offered to be here after school. Look, I don't want to take

any excitement away from you with your new life. This is my problem and I'm going to do everything I can to make sure the children don't suffer. I hope that Phil is going to as well."

"You sound very brave and confident," Verity told her.

"Well I don't feel brave and confident. The phrase 'one day at a time' springs to mind. But I've had time to come to terms with this now and I'm going to cope with whatever happens. I can't forgive Phil and I don't think he wants to come back anyway. He is still with this Lisa as far as I know. I am going to meet Lisa's husband again next week. He is a nice man and it's good to have someone to talk to who knows how you are feeling."

"I'm glad you've got someone to talk to and you know you can call on me any time. I'll come round at a moment's notice if you get depressed or fed up. Or you could come here and bring the kids with you. Just let me know. Shall we arrange to meet anyway?" Verity asked.

"Yes let's meet later in the week. Perhaps take the kids to Pizza Hut or somewhere for dinner after school? What do you think?"

"They'd love that. I'll ring you Wednesday and we'll fix it for Thursday or Friday night, if that suits you too. Anyway, don't forget to call me if you want anything or just need to talk. I'm here for you – we both are. Look after yourself."

"I will and you too. Now get back to your surfing on the net and dream about surfing in Cornwall," Beth said. "See you soon."

Beth flopped back on the bed as she finished the call. It was a relief to tell people and each time the reality became clearer. She sighed deeply and thought about going downstairs. Would it be awkward or not? Surely she could not be expected to hide away in the house whenever Phil visited? No, she wouldn't do that. She must make sure that his visits were happy times for the children. She stood up and brushed herself down. She combed her hair but resisted the temptation to re-do her make up.

Beth went slowly back downstairs and into the front room. The four of them were obviously deep in conversation and nobody noticed her at first. Then Annie looked around and moved along the sofa for Beth to sit down.

Phil looked uncomfortable at Beth's arrival and glanced at his watch.

"Can't stay much longer, I've got to go and get some dinner," he said.

"Oh you could have some dinner here," offered Christina.

"I don't think that's a good idea but I will take you all out one night this week,"he offered. "Maybe Thursday would be a good time?" He looked at Beth for approval.

"I'll have to let you know later. I've just agreed to meet Verity after school one evening and that might have to be Thursday. But Thursday or Friday would be fine," she concluded nodding her head.

"Er, Friday's not very convenient for me, I'm afraid. Got to see some clients," he obviously prevaricated.

"Well I'll let you know about Thursday when I've spoken to Verity again," Beth said firmly.

The children looked from one parent to another trying to work out if they were arguing.

"Would you like a cup of tea?" asked Beth standing up. "I'm going to make one."

"Oh, ok that would be nice," said Phil. "Is there any homework you need help with tonight?" he asked the children.

"I didn't get any," said James. "But I'll have some science homework tomorrow, will you be here to help with that?"

"Yes I'll pop in again tomorrow after work, if that's alright with your mother."

"We are starting a new project up to Christmas about woodland areas in the UK," said Christina. "Will you be able to help me with that?"

Phil laughed. "Well I can't say I know a lot about woodland areas but we can certainly go on the internet and look up information to help with your project."

"Oh good. We have to do some of the work ourselves and some we'll be doing during the lessons. Guess what, mum says Annie can have a mobile phone."

Beth came back into the room with the mugs of tea and heard Christina.

"I think it will be a good idea for Annie to have a phone now she's a bit older. She can let me know if she's going to be late and I will be able to contact her if I need to,'" Beth explained.

"I agree that's a good idea," said Phil. "We'll have a look at the weekend if you like."

"I think we should all have phones," said Christina solemnly. "Then you can know where we all are at all times."

Beth laughed and ruffled Christina's hair. "Nice try," she said. "We'll see."

Beth noticed that Phil drank his tea quickly before standing up in readiness to leave.

"I'll be back tomorrow and help with your project," he promised Christina and then he turned to James. "I'll help with your science too."

"Are you coping with your homework and revision for your GCSEs?" he asked Annie.

"Yes I'm fine. Ben helps me with science and maths and I help him with English literature," Annie replied.

"Good, that sounds like a great system. Shame it won't work when taking the actual exam though!" Phil joked. Annie didn't laugh and just shrugged her shoulders.

Phil looked slightly uncomfortable again and moved towards the doorway.

"See you all tomorrow then," he said.

"Bye dad," chorused James and Christina.

"Bye," added Annie.

As the front door slammed behind him they subsided back into the chairs and looked at each other. Beth realised it would take a while for them to get used to this new arrangement.

"What shall we do now then?" she asked brightly. "Shall we play a game or watch television?"

"Play a game," agreed James and Christina.

"I've got some homework to finish and then I'll have a bath, mum. Can I ring Ben and Sheila too please. I need to ask Ben something about the science questions tonight and Sheila about a CD she wants to borrow?"

"Yes you can ring them both. Take the phone into the kitchen if you want some privacy."

James and Christina chose a game and the three of them played until James had soundly beaten off all female competition.

"Time for bed now," said Beth just before nine o'clock. "Off you go. I'll pack away and be up in about ten minutes."

Both children went without a murmur of opposition which Beth appreciated. She could hear Annie talking on the phone in the kitchen and decided to leave her for a few more minutes.

After she had tidied up the front room she went upstairs to kiss the children goodnight and turn out their bedroom lights. Christina clung around her neck for a few seconds as she whispered goodnight to her mother.

Beth went downstairs and into the kitchen and signalled to Annie to finish the phone call. She made a drink for them both and they went to sit in the front room.

"Are you coping alright?" asked Beth. "Only, you are the quietest and it's hard to tell with you sometimes"

"I'm fine mum. I've got several friends whose parents are separated or divorced and I know what it's like in the real world. It is a big shock when it happens to you but I've got over it now and I know we all have to move on."

Annie sounded very much in control as she spoke. Beth marvelled at her composure and wished she had her confidence.

"I know you are getting older and making your own life now. It's lovely that you have a boyfriend and lots of good friends at school. It's a difficult year for you though, with your exams to study for. You will still stay on at sixth form for your A levels won't you?" asked Beth anxiously.

"Oh yes mum. I have every intention of getting as many exams as possible. Then I may be able to go to university or find a really good job."

Beth was pleased that her eldest daughter was so sensible. She hoped the other two would follow in her footsteps but in reality there would probably be some hiccups along the way with at least one of them! They sat and finished their drinks in companionable silence listening to the clock in the hallway tick away the minutes.

When Beth was in bed about an hour later, she reflected on her first day as a single parent. It hadn't been so bad really. She had negotiated a full time position with her employer to ensure financial security, she had told most of her family about her altered circumstances, and they had reacted positively and offered her assistance, and she had dealt with the first 'access' visit by Phil without any arguments, upset or recriminations. It could have been worse – hopefully it won't be but.........

Chapter Ten

--ooOoo--

*T*he next few days flew past with Beth and her family adjusting to their new circumstances.

Phil continued to visit each night after work for about an hour and Beth stayed out of the way allowing him to have the children to himself. Most evenings she took the opportunity to phone either Amanda or Verity and have an uninterrupted chat for half an hour. They were both very supportive and kept offering to come round and spend an evening with her. But Beth wanted to get used to being on her own and put them off.

Verity was full of plans for her weekend in Cornwall and Beth encouraged her to talk about them for most of their phone call. It was nice to have something else to think of for a few minutes rather than worrying about paying the gas bill or hoping the car did not break down. She had never worried about these types of domestic disasters before. When she thought about it, she realised that she had probably divided tasks into 'blue' and 'pink' jobs. Blue jobs for Phil to deal with and Pink for her!

On Friday morning as she drove to work, she realised that Dave would probably contact her that day as they had arranged. Her heart gave a little lurch and she thought how much she was looking forward to the phone call. Perhaps they could arrange to meet some time during the weekend.

As Beth, Verity and the children had met for dinner on Thursday after school, Phil had
mentioned that he would take his children out on Saturday evening. Christina had reminded Beth that she was spending both days at the animal sanctuary as she had been promised the previous weekend. So

Beth would have to taxi her there for eight o'clock each morning and collect her at about five o'clock.

Annie's dancing lesson had been moved to three o'clock for a reason Beth couldn't quite remember, and James was going to a friend's house for the afternoon. If Beth could arrange for Annie to be taken to her dancing lesson, this would leave her free for most of the afternoon. She hoped that Dave would suggest a meeting – and that he would actually ring her later in the day.

When Beth left work and drove to the supermarket for the weekly shopping, she made sure her mobile phone was switched on and working properly. As she pushed the trolley around the store she kept glancing in her handbag which was perched on the front of the trolley to make sure her phone had not lit up to announce an incoming call.

'He'll probably ring just when I'm at the checkout,' thought Beth to herself. 'And I won't hear because I'll be rustling about with plastic bags. Typical!'

But the phone did not ring at the checkout, on the drive home or when she was putting the shopping away in the kitchen.

When Beth had finished and made herself a cup of tea she sat at the kitchen table with the phone in front of her.

"This is ridiculous," she told herself out loud. "I must be mad, waiting for a phone call from a man whose wife has left him for my husband. It just doesn't make sense."

She finished her tea and got up from the table. Glancing at the clock she noticed it was nearly time for the children to arrive home so she began to make their drinks. It occurred to her that this little routine would cease when she began working full time in the new year. Perhaps she should stop it before then so they did not associate the change with her longer working hours.

Of course, the children would be on their Christmas holiday so that would serve as a break. Beth felt relieved that more of a normal event would occur to change their routines.

As usual, James and Christina arrived home first. They had recovered some of their normal exuberance and came storming into the kitchen, laughing and pushing at each other.

"Is Annie with you, or is she with Ben?" asked Beth.

"Oh she's with Ben, kissing at the gate or something," giggled Christina. "Mum you haven't forgotten I'm going to Oakfield for both days this weekend, have you?" she asked anxiously.

"No, Christina, I haven't forgotten. I'll get you there at eight o'clock each morning as I promised."

Christina nodded, satisfied with her mother's response, and sat down at the table.

"I'm going to Alex's house tomorrow afternoon. Can you give me a lift there about twelve o'clock please mum?" asked James, wanting to make his weekend arrangements too.

"Yes that's fine. I'll take you there for twelve. How long are you staying and will they bring you back?" asked Beth.

"I think I'm staying till about six o'clock and his mum said she'd bring me back," replied James.

"Is dad coming tonight?" asked Christina as she had every afternoon that week.

"Yes, he said he would," replied Beth, patiently repeating her words from previous days.

Annie entered the kitchen at that moment and smiled at her mother.

"Hi mum. Have you had a good day?" she asked.

"Yes thanks Annie – and you too?" responded Beth.

Annie nodded and sat down next to James. Beth looked at all three children and felt a warm glow inside her. She was so lucky. They had coped so well during the last few days. She realised there might be some reaction from one or more of them in the future but they were such good children she was sure they would manage.

Annie especially had been a strong support to Beth, helping with chores around the house, making sure that James and Christina finished their homework and giving Beth a hug every so often. It could have been so different if Annie was a sullen or thoughtless teenager who blamed her mother for the separation.

'Maybe I've been reading too many stories in newspapers or magazines about today's youth', thought Beth. 'Perhaps there are still lots of youngsters who help and support their parents and work hard at school. They can't all be 'hoodies' with ASBOs, I suppose'.

Beth didn't quite know exactly what a hoodie or ASBO was, but imagined it to be something quite bad. It certainly did not sound like something she wanted for one of her children!

As she sat day-dreaming, her mobile phone on the table suddenly rang. She jumped up and grabbed hold of it to look at the screen.

Dave's name glowed back at her.

"Just taking this call," she gabbled at the surprised faces before her.

She ran out of the room pressing the green answer button as she went.

"Hello," she puffed into the phone as she ran upstairs. "Hello Dave."

"Hi Beth – you sound out of breath. Are you alright?" he asked.

"Yes I'm fine. Just running upstairs and I'm not as fit as I should be."

Beth reached her bedroom and shut the door behind her.

"How are you Dave? What happened at the interview?" she asked.

"I'm fine thanks and the interview was good. I think they will offer me the job but they've got a couple more people to see before they make a final decision. I've certainly decided that I'll take it and start as soon as I can. I'll have to give a month's notice though, and I've not got any holiday left so it will probably be January before I can start."

"Oh that's good," said Beth quietly. "I'm pleased for you."

"What about you? How are you doing this week? Have you sorted out your life at all?" asked Dave.

"Yes I've done a few things. Arranged more hours where I work after Christmas, told my family about…what's happened. They've been great. Phil has visited the children each night when he's finished work, and that's been ok," Beth told him. "'Where are you now?" she asked. "Are you still in Barnstaple or back here?"

"I'm on my way back now. Just stopped at a service station near Bristol and thought I'd ring you as we said. Are you free at the weekend for us to meet?" he asked.

Beth took a deep breath. This was it – the moment of change for her life pattern, a crossroad. She knew what she was going to say and was relieved to have the opportunity to say the one word required.

"Yes," she said. "I'm free tomorrow afternoon or possibly some time on Sunday. When's best for you?"

"I think tomorrow afternoon would be good. Where can we meet?" Dave asked.

"I don't know." Beth hadn't thought about where they could meet – just if they would meet.

"How about one o'clock at the new restaurant in Market Street. It used to be a shoe shop but I think it's an Italian now. Would you like that?" asked Dave.

"I'd love it and one o'clock would be perfect. At least we'll recognise each other this time we meet," she joked.

'Oh I'll probably still carry a newspaper under my arm just in case," Dave's words showed he still remembered their first meeting too.

Beth laughed before remembering why they had met before. Perhaps she shouldn't make fun of their previous meetings. Maybe Dave just wanted to meet her again to discuss their partners. She'd better play it cool and not make assumptions about their relationship.

"I'll see you tomorrow then at one o'clock," Dave shouted into the silence between them. "The traffic's getting worse here – I'd better go. Till tomorrow then, bye Beth."

"Bye," said Beth as she closed her phone. She sat on the bed holding it tightly between both hands. She raised her eyes to the mirror in front of her and saw the surprise and expectation on her face. The surprise of his contacting her and arranging another meeting and the expectation of what this could lead to. He may not want this to lead anywhere. Perhaps he only wants to meet me to find out if anything else has happened this week, or if Phil has said he would like to come back to me or if he's asked for a divorce.

This is not a date. Not really…Although it could be, came a voice from the back of her mind. He seemed quite keen to meet you and had already decided where this meeting

would take place.

Beth sat on the bed for a few more minutes before a loud knock on the door startled her.

"Yes, what is it?" she asked jumping up and straightening her hair. She opened the door and James stood there with his muddy football kit.

"Can you wash this before tomorrow please 'cos Alex and I will want to have a kick-about in the park behind his house tomorrow afternoon." He handed the dirty clothes to his mother.

'Back to reality,' thought Beth wryly as she went downstairs to start the dinner and collect more clothes for the washing machine.

Phil arrived earlier that night and caught them still eating at the kitchen table.

"That looks good," he commented, pinching a chip from James' plate.

"There's a bit left it you want it," said Beth.

"Oh, er, no, I'd better not. Going out to dinner later," he said gruffly.

"Who are you going out to dinner with?" asked Christina immediately.

"Er, just a friend. No-one you know," he ruffled her hair to divert her attention.

"Don't do that, dad. I'm not a child, you know. I'm nearly thirteen now," she told him in case he had forgotten.

"Oh I know you are nearly a teenager too! How will we cope with three teenagers in the house," he joked before realising what he had said. The children looked at him in silence.

"Yes, all those hormones zooming about," Beth tried to help ease the situation. "Do you think they will bump into each other?"

"What exactly are hormones?" asked Christina. "We haven't done anything about them at school yet, have you James?"

"Oh yes, of course we have. They are things inside you that make you who you are. They change at certain times of your life and one of those times is pubert," James seemed very knowledgeable and Beth was impressed.

"What's puberty?" asked Christina. James looked slightly out of his depth now and blushed.

"It's the time between childhood and becoming an adult," said Phil smoothly. "Teenage years."

"Oh right, I understand now," said Christina nodding.

"I'll clear away if you all want to go into the front room," said Beth as she stood up. The children finished their drinks and made their way out of the kitchen. Phil remained standing by the table and asked Beth if she would mind sitting down again for a few minutes as he had something to say.

She looked at him wondering what he was going to come out with now.

"We need to have a talk about a few things," he began. "Money and bills for a start. Have you got enough money for the moment?"

"Yes I'm alright. I assume the housekeeping money will still be paid into my bank account?" she asked.

"Yes that's fine," he agreed. "And most of the other bills are paid by direct debit so that can continue for now. However at some point in the future I will want to pay you a set amount, probably by direct debit into your bank account, for you to pay your own bills. Are you going to try and get some full time work?"

"Yes I'm starting in the new year. Allan has offered me full time hours as Suzie wants to go part time. It's all worked out well for that. But you want to make other arrangements in the future – what sort of things do you mean? Is it just finances?"

Phil looked away before he replied. "Yes, mostly just finances but obviously I will want to find a place of my own soon, somewhere the kids can come and visit me. I don't know how I'll be able to afford a house or flat unless we remortgage or sell this house and split the profit."

"WHAT! – you want to sell this house. But it's our home!' yelled Beth. She was taken completely by surprise at Phil's words.

"Sssh, don't upset the kids," said Phil getting up to shut the door.

"Upset the kids! I think it's a bit late for worrying about that," she hissed at him.

"Ok, yes I know. Look, don't worry about it now. I'll think of something. I don't want you and the children to have to move out of this house, but I will need somewhere to live. I can't stay at…a hotel forever," he said.

"Is that where you are? In a hotel," asked Beth.

Phil looked away again and nodded.

"Are you sure you're not staying with…her?" she asked bravely.

Phil looked at her in surprise. "Lisa has left her home too, you know," he told her.

"Yes I'm sure she has but don't expect me to feel sorry for her, or you either," retorted Beth.

"I don't want you to feel sorry for us. But we will need somewhere to live," Phil repeated.

"Ha ha, now we come to the truth. You want somewhere to live with her," said Beth.

Phil didn't answer and Beth knew he was ashamed to admit the truth.

"Go and spend some time with your children," she dismissed him. "I don't know what we can do about a re-mortgage but I don't want to sell this house. Let's think about it for a few days and talk to me again next week."

Phil took his cue and left the room. Beth sat at the table for a while and thought about Phil's words. He obviously had been egged-on by Lisa to start making arrangements for their new life together. It was alright for her though as she didn't have any children to worry about. Not that Beth would change that part of her life but it did have its extra responsibilities. It seemed that Phil had forgotten his share, though.

If they sold the house and split the equity, would there be enough for Beth to be able to buy a house with four bedrooms, she wondered. Probably not. Although house prices had risen quite a lot whilst they had lived in this house, it would cost a comparable amount to buy a similar property.

'I suppose we could manage with three bedrooms, maybe even two if I slept downstairs,' she mused. 'But the children are used to having their own space and it might even effect their school work if they couldn't do their homework in peace.'

Beth decided to go upstairs and ring Verity before they set off for their weekend away. Her opinion on the housing market would be useful too.

When Verity answered the phone, Beth could feel the excitement with her first words. She let Verity talk herself out before trying to catch her attention.

"Well that's all my news. What's happening with you Beth?" Verity eventually asked.

"Well Phil has told me tonight that I might have to sell this house so that he can afford to buy a place for him and…her. I can't believe he's expecting me and the children to move out. And to mention it so soon as well. I suppose I'm still thinking he might change his mind and want to come back to us. But I don't know if I really want that now anyway, not after all the distress and upset he's caused."

"He can't make you sell the house surely. Not with children under 16 still living there. I don't know for sure, but John can find out if you like," offered Verity. "Maybe you should see a solicitor. Isabel's father-in-law is a solicitor in town," Verity mentioned her sister-in-law.

"But I don't know if I would want to see someone who was related to us, however distantly. It might be too personal and embarrassing," said Beth.

"Sorry I hadn't thought of that. You're probably right. But it might be an idea to see a solicitor, especially if you are legally separating or divorcing, or is it too early to know yet?" asked Verity.

"Oh I don't know what I'm doing," Beth said crossly. "I just feel that it is all happening too fast. Last weekend he told me he was in love with someone else and this weekend I've got to move out."

"Now come on it's not that bad. He hasn't thrown you out on the street you know. He's probably being pushed by that Lisa and just blurted it out to you. He obviously hasn't thought it out properly either as he is still responsible for providing a home for his children," Verity tried to reassure Beth.

Beth sighed and tried to calm down. She felt very vulnerable and knew that she needed to get some sensible and practical advice.

"Should I go to the Citizen's Advice Bureau do you think?" she asked her sister.

"Yes, that's a very good idea. They'll know what you should do and where to go for help."

"OK, and I'll talk to Dave tomorrow when I meet him. He might be able to help."

"You're seeing Dave again then?" asked Verity. "Why are you meeting him again. Is it to talk about…them?"

"I don't know really. We agreed last weekend to meet again and he rang me earlier to make arrangements for tomorrow. I don't know if we're just going to talk about 'the situation' or…what," Beth finished uncertainly.

"Watch this space," quoted Verity. "Anyway, I'd better go now. We've got an early start tomorrow."

"Good luck and I hope you find a place you want to buy. Take care of yourselves and ring me when you get back. And thanks for talking to me when I'm all cross and grouchy," said Beth.

"Don't be silly, that's what sisters are for. Speak to you on Sunday, hopefully with some good news. Bye."

As they ended the phone call Beth could hear Phil's car starting up on the drive. She went to the window and looked out from behind the curtains to see him backing the car into the street and drive off.

She went downstairs to find the children sat gloomily in the front room.

"What's up with you all?" she said brightly.

"Dad can't see us until Monday now," said Christina. "He's going away for the weekend to stay with a friend. Do you think it's the same friend he's having dinner with tonight?"

Beth sat on the arm of the chair and put her hand on Christina's shoulder.

"It may be the same friend but don't forget, you will all be so busy at the weekend that Monday will soon be here and then your dad will come again."

"Yes mum's right," agreed Annie. "We've all got a busy weekend ahead."

"But dad won't be there for football on Sunday," said James.

"No he won't, but he will be there another week. We've never been able to go to every match, James. Maybe granddad will pop down to watch you this week. Shall I ask him?"

"Oh yes, but will you come too?" asked James.

"Yes I'll be there too." promised Beth.

"What shall we do now?" asked Christina. "Did you get any DVDs in town Mum?"

"No, I didn't have time to go to the shop today but I think there may be a film on television to watch. It starts in about ten minutes. Why don't you see if you can find the right channel and I'll make some popcorn in the microwave."

They settled down to watch the film and munched their way through a large bowl of popcorn. Afterwards, Beth sent them all to bed, either to sleep or read, as she felt like being on her own for a while.

She cleared away and made herself a hot drink before returning to the front room. She turned off the main light and lit a couple of scented candles before making herself comfortable in one of the armchairs.

As she reflected on the day's events, she thought of the two men who had affected her most during the last few hours.

Dave seemed a kind, strong and thoughtful type and she found that thinking about him gave her a rush of excitement that seemed to start in the back of her throat and then travelled through her whole body. When they had first met, the sequence of events had prevented her from seeing him as a man. He was just an accomplice while she came to terms with the awful realisation that her marriage was over. But now she had accepted Phil's defection, she found she was willing, and able, to move on in her life. Not that she was ready to find somebody else, as Amanda kept telling her she would do, but she was receptive to attractive men. She racked her brains trying to think of any other men she came into contact with and to whom she could be attracted. No-one at work, none of the neighbours, none of her children's friends' fathers, in fact nobody she could think of!

'Hmm, must just be Dave then,' she thought. He was good looking and in some way, slightly familiar. She could not pinpoint what she meant but she definitely felt that they had met before. She went through various scenarios of her life but could not think where they may have seen each other before.

Anyway, back to the other man – Phil. She didn't feel she knew him at all any more. He was her husband but he seemed like a different person now. He didn't want to talk to her apart from making arrangements for the children and sorting out their finances. He had been wearing a new shirt tonight – it was certainly one she had never ironed before! He wanted a new place to live which didn't include her or the children. He must be very much in love with this Lisa to give up his previous lifestyle and family, she thought.

She wondered whether she could ever actually get into bed with him again and found the idea repulsed her. How could that happen so quickly? It was only a few weeks ago she had her suspicions of this affair but she had not moved out of their bedroom. They had not had sex for at least three months, Beth thought back, and certainly not more than half a dozen times during the whole year.

Was it her fault that they had stopped making love? She tried to remember the last time they had enjoyed a good session rather than the perfunctory going through the paces. It must have been when they were on holiday in Portugal, two years ago! Beth shook her head. What had gone wrong between them? Had they fallen out of love and lust? Or was it life's routine and tiredness that had got to them?

Beth knew there was no turning back now. Not even for the sake of the children. The situation had gone too far for her to consider living with Phil again. She felt relieved as she made this decision. She was going to move on with her life and the thought excited her as she sat in the candlelit room.

It was a long time since she had experienced this expectant feeling, not knowing what would happen tomorrow, next week or next year.

Although plans had been made for the next day, she did not know the outcome of the arranged meeting with Dave. However, the children needed stability, she thought. She could not suddenly turn into the type of mother who lived without a routine. But maybe for the part of her life that was her's alone, she could enjoy this 'fizzy' feeling inside – wondering what lay ahead for the future.

Chapter Eleven

--ooOoo--

*A*fter ensuring that all three children were at their appointed places on Saturday afternoon, Beth pushed open the door of the restaurant only five minutes later than the time Dave had suggested. She glanced around quickly trying to spot him before walking to the reception desk.

"I think we have a table for two booked for one o'clock," Beth said tentatively to the young girl behind the desk.

"What name please?" she asked.

"Er, I don't really know. I can't remember," Beth looked around again and suddenly spotted Dave waving from a table at the back of the restaurant. "Oh, there he is – it's that table," she said.

A waiter appeared from the back room and escorted Beth to Dave's table. Dave stood up and pulled out the chair next to him.

"Sorry I'm a bit late," she said as she sat down. "Traffic was bad and it took a few minutes to find a parking space to park." Beth put her scarf and handbag on the spare chair and wriggled out of her coat.

"That's alright, don't worry. It's given me time to study the menu," Dave smiled at her. "I hope you're feeling hungry because the food looks really good."

"Oh I am. I only had a quick breakfast and have been taxi-ing the children to their various destinations as well as getting up to date with washing and ironing," Beth picked up a menu as she spoke.

"I think I'm going to have the ravioli with some garlic bread," advised Dave. 'What would you like?"

"I'd like the cannelloni please also with some garlic bread," said Beth after a slight pause while she read through the various options available.

"And we'll have a bottle of house white," said Dave passing his menu back to the waiter.

"Could we have some water too please," asked Beth.

"Of course madam," said the waiter as he collected her menu and strode off to the kitchen with their order.

"Well this is nice," Dave said as he sat forward across the table and looked straight into Beth's eyes. "I've been looking forward to this all week."

"Beth tried not to blush or read too much into his words. She had to play it cool and pretend that she was used to sitting in restaurants with men she barely knew.

"Have you heard whether they have offered you the job yet?" she asked to divert him from more personal subjects.

"No not yet. I don't think I'll get a letter until the middle of next week but I'm very hopeful. I got on well with the manager and he showed me around the offices. I don't think they would do that unless they were serious about offering me the job, do you?" Dave asked.

"No I don't think they would. I expect you'll be moving to Barnstaple very soon and starting a new life," Beth said, sounding very envious.

"What about you? Are you going to start a new life?" Dave enquired.

"Yes I am. I had some time yesterday evening to think about what's happened recently and I'm ready to move on. Phil has made it clear he is not coming back to me. Has your wife said anything to you this week?"

"Yes, she came to collect more of her things and said she wants to sell the house and split the proceeds. I think I'll ring some estate agents next week and get the house on the market. I don't want to live there any more even if I don't move away. I'll buy a flat or apartment probably, which is what I'll do if I go to Barnstaple."

"Phil spoke to me about selling the house. I don't know what to do, though I'll not get a very big mortgage even when I start full time work. Surely he'll have to provide a home for the children until they leave school?" Beth asked anxiously.

"Of course he has to provide somewhere for the children to live. I assume they are going to continue to live with you?"

"Yes of course they will. There's no question of them living with

Phil. He can visit them whenever he wants, but they'll stay with me," Beth said firmly.

There was no way she could consider an alternative arrangement but she was quite sure Phil would not object to this anyway.

The waiter arrived back at their table bearing a tray holding a bottle of wine, carafe of iced water and four glasses which he placed strategically around the table. Beth and Dave sat in silence for a few minutes while their drinks were poured.

When the waiter had finished Dave picked up his wine glass and raised it towards Beth.

"To new beginnings," he said. "A bit corny, I know, but I think it applies to both of us."

Beth raised her wine glass and touched it gently against Dave's making a sharp clinking noise. "New beginnings…corny or not," she agreed.

They took a few sips of their wine before replacing their glasses on the table.

"I think I've said before that I find you very familiar, I mean I think…well, you know." said Dave slightly flustered as he looked closely at her. "Have we ever met before do you think?"

Beth looked at him intently for a few seconds and felt some vague memory stir in the back of her mind.

"Surely not, we'd remember wouldn't we?" she asked.

"I suppose so, it's just that your laugh sounds familiar. Have you always lived around here?"

"No. I grew up in a small town just outside Southampton but my dad was made redundant and we all moved here when he managed to get another job. He was out of work for four months so he was lucky to find well-paid employment that he enjoyed. He's retired now." explained Beth.

"I've not always lived here either," said Dave. "My family lived in Manchester but I had to move here with my job too. Mine was because of promotion though. I met Lisa three years ago and we've been married for eighteen months."

"So we could only have met here and I'm sure one of us would remember where, if we had," said Beth.

"Unless we met somewhere else. What about on holiday? Where have you been on holiday?" asked Dave. He seemed determined to find out if his intuition was correct.

"Recently we've been to Portugal twice, Spain once and several holidays in a caravan in Cornwall and Wales," Beth listed, counting on her fingers.

"I've never been to Portugal or Spain, only France and Austria, so that can't be where we've met," said Dave. "What about before you were married, could we have met then?"

"I'm sure I would remember you," Beth smiled at him. "But when I was a child we used to go to Weston-Super-Mare most years as mum had an aunt who ran a guest house there. The only year we went somewhere different was the year I took my O levels and we went to Blackpool for a special treat."

"I went to Blackpool one year too with my family. It was about…1982. I think. Was that the same year for you too?' he asked.

Beth just sat there staring at him as she worked out the dates in her head.

"Well yes it must have been," she said eventually, having counted out the years. A thought suddenly struck her and she blurted out, "Dave – did you used to be called Davy?!"

"Yes, that's right. I was called Davy until I met Lisa. She didn't like it – thought it sounded childish so she insisted I was known as Dave. But how do you know that?" he asked.

"Because I used to be called Lizzy," Beth stated slowly, waiting for him to remember.

"Lizzy?…Oh, Lizzy!" repeated Dave as realisation struck him. "I don't believe it! That's amazing!"

They sat in silence staring at each other for a few minutes before both began speaking at once.

"What happened to you?……"

"So where were you on the last day?……"

They stopped and began to laugh.

"You first," said Dave. "But what happened on the last day – where were you?" he asked first anyway. "Why didn't you meet me?"

"Well what happened was that mum had a phone call early in the morning to say that grandma had been taken into hospital. So they wanted to make an early start.They wouldn't let me come and meet you as it was pouring with rain and they wanted to leave as quickly as possible," Beth spoke quickly trying to get the words out. "How long did you wait for me?"

"'My parents let me wait for half an hour and then dragged me away to go home," explained Dave. "I can't believe we didn't exchange addresses during the whole two weeks we were together. Why did we leave it until the last day?"

"Because we were young and didn't realise how easy it is to lose someone," explained Beth. "I think we were having such a good time we didn't want to think about the future. When you're young you don't plan ahead."

At that moment the waiter arrived with their meals. However, both of them had lost their appetites at the realisation of meeting their first love again. They sat and looked at each other over the hot steaming plates of food.

"We had such a good time in Blackpool, didn't we," Beth eventually said. "It was the best holiday ever."

"I did try to find out where you lived when I got back home. But I didn't know how to go about it – we didn't have the internet or mobiles so it wasn't so easy in those days," Dave told her.

"Yes, it would have been simple now wouldn't it? We would have exchanged mobile numbers and email addresses as a matter of course, which is what all the teenagers do now. How did you try to find me?" she asked.

"I rang the guest house where you stayed but they didn't answer the phone so I wrote to them, but they didn't write back. That was all I could do. I didn't know where you lived. We didn't seem to talk much about our normal everyday lives, did we?"

"No, you're right. I don't know what we did talk about though as we never seemed to be quiet. We were always rushing about – going to the fair, playing mini-golf, swimming in the sea, even building sand castles with Verity, my sister. And we used to go to that disco in the evenings – do you remember?" Beth asked as she began to remember the time they had spent together.

"Yes, that's right. I think we went to the disco about five times each week and we had to take Verity on the Saturday nights as your parents went to the ballroom dancing at the hotel next door' Dave remembered.

They suddenly realised their food was getting cold and picked up their cutlery to start eating.

"Do you remember the day we took the rowing boat out on the lake and got stuck on the island in the middle?" asked Dave.

"Oh yes, the man in charge had to come and rescue us. He wasn't very pleased because his assistant had gone to lunch and there was no-one to help other people in and out of the boats. It took him about twenty minutes to get us back to the jetty and he was very disgruntled. But it wasn't our fault the boat ran aground, was it?" Beth asked.

"Well I don't think we should have tried to get so close to the island. But you wanted to see if there were any baby birds in nests so I rowed up as close as I could, and then we were stuck in the mud," Dave told her.

"Oh yes, that's right. I should have known it wasn't the right time of year for baby birds' Beth laughed at the memory and took some more of her food.

"Do you remember when we all went for a picnic, your parents and mine, and that other family that my mum and dad had met in the same guest house. We went up a big hill and sat under the trees at the top. We had a huge picnic basket full of lovely food and we played a game of cricket afterwards. Verity got hit in the face with a ball thrown by your dad. Do you remember that?" she asked.

"Oh yes, my dad felt awful about it and never stopped apologising for the rest of the day. Poor Verity had a huge bruise, didn't she? How is she – and the rest of your family too?" asked Dave.

"Well the bruise has faded," laughed Beth. "No seriously, Mum and Dad are fine and they are being very supportive to me and the children. They often help me with babysitting and taking the kids out. And they often take them rowing on the lake in the park," Beth laughed.

"And Verity? Does she live locally?" asked Dave.

"Yes, but maybe not for much longer. Her husband won a lot of money from a lottery syndicate and they are hoping to move to Cornwall and run a market garden. They have two children, a boy and a girl," Beth told him.

"Wow, it's nice to hear of someone winning the lottery. I don't do the lottery or the football pools, but it would make a lot of difference to your lifestyle if you were lucky enough to win a large amount," Dave said as he finished his meal.

"How about your family – are they ok?" asked Beth politely. She couldn't remember Dave's mum being over-friendly to her as she seemed to resent Beth, or Lizzy as she was known then, taking their son away from them during their holiday.

'Yes mum and dad are both fine. They live in a bigger house now and are both retired. My brother is married, but I don't see him often now, as I told you before," he explained.

Beth finished her meal and placed her cutlery neatly on the plate. She picked up the glass of water and took a few refreshing mouthfuls.

"I just can't believe that we have met again after all this time. I was devastated when I couldn't come and meet you and, well, I cried most of the journey home. Mum was short-tempered with me, probably because her mother was ill. But when we got home, they had let grandma out of hospital as she seemed to have recovered. Apparently, it was only a stomach bug and she was soon back to normal. I didn't know how to get in contact with

you because I didn't know where you lived either, and I never went to the guest house where you were staying so I couldn't contact you that way," Beth explained.

The waiter arrived to clear their plates and asked if they wanted dessert. Dave looked at Beth and she shook her head.

"No dessert for me thanks, but a coffee would be nice," she said.

"Two coffees please," ordered Dave.

They settled back in their chairs to continue reminiscing about their shared past. As is always the case, they both remembered the holiday slightly differently and enjoyed reminding each other of forgotten moments and events.

The time passed quickly and Beth suddenly looked at her watch.

"It's nearly five o'clock!" she exclaimed. "I'd better go. I have to collect Annie from her dancing class and Christina from the animal sanctuary,"

She began collecting her bag and coat and Dave stood up.

"Can we meet again?" he asked. "Soon?"

Beth looked at him and laughed. "Let's make sure we don't lose contact this time," she teased him. "Let's swap phone numbers, addresses, national insurance numbers and anything else we can think of!"

Dave laughed too. "I still can't believe we have been brought back together by our partners' infidelity," he said.

Beth stopped pulling on her coat and looked at him. "You're right," she said. "What a small world it is. We must have been meant to meet up again – after all this time too." she shook her head in wonderment.

"Here's my business card and I'll write my home address on the back," said Dave getting out a pen.

"Oh okay. I've got your mobile number – do you have an email address too?" she asked.

"Yes, it's on the card. If you email me first, then I'll be able to write back to you."

"I don't email very much. That's because the children use the computer most of the time, for homework and emailing their friends. But I will send you one so you have my address." Beth promised.

"When shall we meet again?" Dave seemed eager to make a firm arrangement.

"Er...can I ring you? It's just that I don't know when I can be free apart from days like today when the children are all off doing their own thing. It's not often that I don't still have one of them at home, you see. And obviously you are working all week. I don't think I want the children to know about our meeting, and our past as well, at the moment. It is too much for them to cope with at once. You do understand, don't you?" she asked anxiously.

"Of course I do. I know I haven't got children but I can imagine how much stress they're coping with at the moment with their parents separating. I'll ring you in the evenings, if you don't mind. Then if it's convenient we can talk, and if not I'll ring later when you've got a few moments. Will that be alright with you?"

"Yes that's great. I might be able to talk best when Phil is with the children.I usually go upstairs and talk to Verity or my friend Amanda," Beth told him.

They walked towards the reception desk and Dave paid the bill.

"Thank you very much, it's been a very...interesting afternoon," said Beth as they left the restaurant.

"Interesting and amazing," said Dave. "I still cannot believe we have met again after all these years. I wonder what would have happened if we had kept in contact. Do you think we were too young when we met or maybe we might actually be together now as a couple, maybe married and with children?"

Beth stopped on the pavement outside the restaurant to consider his words. "I suppose we were too young at that time, especially to keep a relationship going when we lived so far apart. But as I said, we moved here shortly afterwards so we would have lived nearer each other then. It's difficult to say, though. We were very young and you were certainly my first love' she said thoughtfully.

"Yes, I had not had any girlfriends before I met you on holiday. I didn't have another until at least a year later. Maybe we were too young then, but we aren't now," he said looking mischievously at her.

Beth laughed as she agreed with him. "No, we're certainly not too young now. We've both been through a lot recently. But it would be nice to see you again."

She hoped she was not being too forward but Dave didn't seem to think so and again said that he hoped they could arrange another meeting soon. They set off together towards the car park and chatted companionably about their plans for the following week.

They reached Beth's car first and both stopped while she fumbled in her handbag for the keys. As she pulled them out of her bag, she thanked Dave again for the meal and promised to ring him some time the next day.

She was about to put the keys into the lock when he stepped forward and put his hands on her shoulders. He looked into her surprised eyes and bent to kiss her gently on her mouth. She felt a shudder of electric pass through her as their lips met and she closed her eyes to savour the moment. When he let go of her she staggered forward slightly before regaining

control of her senses.

"Right. Bye then. See you soon," she stammered before turning to get into her car.

Dave stood and watched as she backed out of the parking space and drove out of the car park. He waved as she glanced in the mirror before turning the corner towards the exit.

Beth's mind was in turmoil as she drove home. She still found it difficult to come to terms with having again met 'Davy' as she used to know him. As she had told him, he had been her first love and she had never forgotten him.

'Why didn't I realise it was him, though?' she wondered. Probably because you weren't expecting to see him ever again, she told herself. She couldn't wait to share her news with Amanda, who she knew would really appreciate the situation. She ran into the house and picked up the phone to dial Amanda.

"Hello Beth," came the response after three rings of the phone. "Are you okay? What are you doing?"

"Well, you are never in a million years going to guess who I've just met?" said Beth.

"The Queen, Robbie Williams or your double?" asked Amanda entering into the spirit of Beth's buoyant mood.

"No, none of those. It's Davy. Well Dave as he is now. You know, the husband of the woman that Phil is living with. It turns out that he is the boy I met on holiday in Blackpool when I was sixteen. We met on the first day of our holiday and spent the whole fortnight together. But we lost touch and never met or wrote to each other again.

"We've just had a meal at that new Italian restaurant and when we were talking it all came out. I really can't take it all in at the moment. But I'm so excited and I feel that I know him already. Which, of course, I do!"

"That's great news. I'm so pleased for you. You deserve something good to happen to you after the past few weeks. Are you going to meet him again?" asked Amanda.

"Oh yes I think so. He sounds keen and I'm so pleased to meet him again. It was a shame that we lost contact so abruptly after spending such a wonderful time together. I know we were only young, and we have agreed our relationship might not have lasted, especially as we lived so far from each other, but it's like we've been given a second chance."

"Yes it sounds like something you read about in those magazines – my husband's girlfriend is married to my ex-boyfriend," said Amanda.

Beth giggled uncontrollably and Amanda joined in as they both realised the silliness of the situation.

When they had regained control of themselves, Amanda said: 'We must meet up soon. Then you can tell me all about it. Have you kissed again yet?"

Beth blushed and sat up in the chair. "Well, yes we have actually. And it was lovely."

"Good. I'm so glad you are getting on with your life and moving on. Are you going to tell the children yet?"

"No. They've got enough to cope with at the moment. They don't know that Phil has moved in with another woman yet. I don't know when he's going to tell them. But I'm not going to be the first to tell them there's somebody else in our lives," Beth said firmly.

"I don't blame you. Phil should take the blame for the break up of your family, it's him who has left you," said Amanda.

"Thanks for reminding me – friend!' joked Beth. "It's ok, I'm only joking. I will probably just tell Verity at the moment. Mum and dad have enough to contend with too."

"Well let's meet up on Monday. Are you still finishing work at two o'clock? Do you want to come here and have some lunch?" asked Amanda.

"Yes, that's great. I'll be with you about quarter past two and I'll leave just after three to get back here in time for the children. I'm trying to keep things the same for them as much as possible because there'll be a lot of changes after Christmas," explained Beth.

"Ok see you then – enjoy the rest of the weekend, although it'll probably be all downhill after this afternoon," Amanda said to tease Beth further.

"Ok, see you on Monday," Beth ignored her friend's jibe.

It was time to meet Annie from dancing and then drive to collect Christina from the animal sanctuary. No more time for reminiscing about the past or dreaming of the future. Not until later tonight when the house was quiet and Beth had a few moments to think before she drifted off to sleep.

Chapter Twelve

--ooOoo--

Watching James standing in the goalmouth waiting for an opportunity to show off his ball catching skills, Beth huddled into her coat and pushed her hands deeper into the pockets.

Her father was standing next to her but he didn't seem to be aware of the bitingly cold wind blowing around them. is attention was on the twenty two fourteen-year-old lads racing about the pitch. Well, twenty of them were running about and two were aalmost stationary, stamping their feet and rubbing their hands, guarding their goal posts.

Ninety minutes seemed a long time and she was hoping to be able to leave soon with the excuse of having to prepare a Sunday dinner. Her father would stay till the bitter end, stomping around outside the changing rooms with the other parents and exchanging views of the match and its outcome.

If she waited until after half time James wouldn't notice her disappearance for a while. She glanced at her watch. Another ten minutes until the referee blew his whistle for the break.

"I'll just pop back to the car for our flask of tea," she told her dad. He nodded but didn't take his eyes off the ball. Beth walked quickly over to the car park and took the flask from the back seat. She heard her mobile phone bleep and took it out of her pocket. It was a message from Dave. Her heart beat faster as she read the few words he had sent her.

Hi Beth. Hope yr ok. Enjoyed yesterday. Hope we can meet again soon. Ring U later. Dave x

She took off her gloves so she could send him a reply.

Hi Dave. I enjoyed it 2. Yes lets meet soon. Ring me tonight. Bethx

She added the kiss at the end as he had with his message. It felt strange to be sending text messages to someone as she'd never really used her phone for texting. It made her feel like a teenager. She pressed the send button and put the phone back in her pocket. She could now look forward to a phone call from Dave later in the day.

Her plan worked as she hoped and an hour later Beth was in the kitchen peeling potatoes and preparing a large Sunday dinner. Her dad was collecting Vera on the way back from the football match and they would all eat together.

As she laid the table for six, she wondered how her sister was enjoying the weekend. Had they found their ideal place to buy? She hoped so because Verity got downhearted very quickly if things didn't fall into place immediately. They were looking at four farms that were for sale so surely one would meet their requirements.

Annie came downstairs and offered to help her mother.

"Shall I make the crumble topping?" she asked as she washed her hands at the sink.

"Yes please. That would be a great help. I've got some nice apples here and I'll peel them when I've finished the potatoes," said her mother.

They worked quickly together listening to the radio playing quietly on the shelf in the corner of the kitchen.

"How's Ben?" asked Beth after a while. "Are you still getting on well together?"

"Oh yes I think so," Annie blushed slightly. "We like the same music and we seem to have lots to talk about. There aren't any awkward silences when we're together. We've even started talking about the future. We both want to go to university and maybe we'll try to go to the same one."

"That would be nice, if you are still together," agreed Beth.

"Oh I know we are only young and we might break up or meet someone else in the next couple of years. But you've got to think about the future a bit haven't you?"

"Yes of course. And just because you're young doesn't mean to say your relationship won't last. It might, and it might not. That's the exciting thing about being young – so many different things may, or may not, happen to you," Beth told her.

Annie looked at her mother. "Did exciting things happen to you when you were my age?" she asked.

It was Beth's turn to blush as she wondered whether to tell Annie about Dave. No, perhaps it was too early yet. She really wanted the children to find out about Phil's new woman before she spoke to them about Dave.

"Yes, lots of exciting things happened to me. Grandad had to get a new job and we moved away from all our friends. That was exciting and scary. Luckily Verity and I, and grandma and grandad, managed to fit in to our new lifestyles quite well. Grandad had people at his new work to get to know. Grandma has always been able to make friends, wherever she is, and Verity is like her to some extent. I know that she'll be fine when they move to

Cornwall. And I was just starting work at that time so that's how I met most of my new friends. And of course your father too. I was only nineteen when I met your dad, that's only three years older than you are now."

Annie didn't speak for a few minutes and then asked her mother: "Are you ok about splitting up with dad? Only it seems to have happened so fast and we just seem to be getting on with life, almost as if nothing has happened."

Beth smiled. "Of course I'm not alright about splitting up with your dad. I had no idea that he was not happy in our marriage. But these things happen and we all have to move on. That's what you all say isn't it: move on. Your dad and I will always be your parents and love you, James and Christina. But sometimes life doesn't work out how you think it is going to. As we were saying just now, it can be exciting and scary. We have to adjust to the new situation with your dad coming to visit as often as he can. When he finds a place to live properly, you can go and visit him."

Annie grunted. "I don't know if I want to do that, especially if SHE is there."

Beth jumped and spun round to look at Annie. "What do you mean 'she'?" she asked.

"I mean that woman who he is living with, the one he left us for," said Annie.

"How do you know about this woman? Have you heard him talking to her?"

"Yes, I heard him speaking to her the day we all went bowling. I'd gone to the toilets and he was stood behind a pillar talking on his mobile. He was telling her where he was and what time he'd be back."

"Oh, I had no idea you knew...why didn't you say something before now?" asked Beth.

"I didn't want the others to know. James and Christina have enough to cope with and I thought you or dad would want to tell them," Annie told her.

'Well, that's very mature of you. I was waiting for your dad to tell you all. I don't know when he will but he's obviously waiting for the right moment. He probably thinks it is too soon yet' Beth smiled at her daughter.

"Yeah well, I know so he doesn't need to tell me, does he?" Annie spoke quite witheringly, not in her usual tone at all.

"He's probably embarrassed as well. Men don't always talk about their feelings, or difficult subjects, as easily as women," Beth wondered why she was sticking up for her ex.

"I know that mum. I often find it easier to talk to Marilyn or Sheila about things, than Ben. I know I haven't known him very long yet, but...I understand what you mean about men." She finished giving her mum a knowing look.

Beth laughed and decided to change the subject. They talked for a bit about Annie's GCSE exams and in no time at all James and his grandparents arrived at the back door.

Beth shooed James upstairs to shower and change and her parents hung their coats in the hallway.

Vera entered the kitchen and hugged both Beth and Annie.

"How are you two doing then?" she asked, accepting a glass of white wine from her daughter.

"We're just fine thanks Mum," Beth answered for them both. "Now, we are nearly ready. I'm going to put Christina's dinner on a plate and we'll get started without her. She's being brought back by one of the ladies who also helps out at the sanctuary on Sundays. Lydia often pops in to see her aunt, who lives round the corner, on her way home so she's dropped Christina off home several times before. It saves me a journey, which is helpful."

Christina arrived just as they had finished the main course. She bounded into the kitchen, just stopping in time to take off her muddy Wellington boots.

"Hi Grandma…and Grandad," she huffed as she struggled on one foot. "Is my dinner ready mum?"

"Yes it is but go upstairs first and wash your hands. Maybe you should change your clothes too," suggested Beth looking at her. Her trousers and sweater were covered with hay, wood shavings and other possibly unsavoury items.

"But I'm hungry. Can't I have my dinner first?" begged Christina looking at their empty plates.

"No darling. Get changed first please. You can't eat with dirty hands and it won't take a minute to put some clean clothes on. Put the dirty things in the washing basket," Beth said firmly.

"Go on Christina – the quicker you go, the quicker you'll be back and then I won't have to eat your dinner!" teased her grandad.

"Don't you dare!" squealed Christina as she ran out of the kitchen and raced upstairs.

Peace was restored until she returned to the kitchen a few minutes later. Beth stood up and gave Christina her plated dinner. She then began to dish out the apple crumble and custard.

Silence reigned for a few minutes as they all enjoyed their food.

When they had all finished eating, Beth suggested leaving the clearing away until later. She stood up and began to make some coffee as the others made their way into the front room. Vera stopped in the kitchen as Beth arranged mugs, sugar and some After Eight mints on the tray.

"How are you really darling?" Vera asked.

"Oh, you know. I'm fine. It's just a lot of changes happening which is a bit unsettling. And I feel I have to try and protect the children from the worst of it. I want to keep their lives as much the same as I can. t's early days yet too. I haven't even started working longer hours, which is obviously going to make a difference to all of us. I'll be more tired and have less time in the evenings and they've got to get used to me not being here when they get home from school," Beth sighed as she listed some of her worries.

"Well Jack and I will help as much as we can." her mother said firmly. "We'll be here every afternoon of the week if you want so they don't come home to an empty house. And in the school holidays – we can take them places. Just let us know what we can do to help and we will. We've talked about it over the last couple of days."

"Oh thanks Mum. You and Dad are just great and I know you'll help. It will all probably seem different in a few weeks time when more things are sorted out. It just seems like nothing is the same and never will be again."

"It's going to feel like that for a while. As you say, it will take a few weeks or months and then you'll know where you are. Are you sure that you're alright for money? Do you need any financial help?"

"No, that's fine thanks. Phil is still paying for everything at the moment. Obviously we need to sit down and sort out the finances. I just hope we can stay in this house," said Beth, looking round at the kitchen as she spoke.

"Might you not be able to stay here then?" asked her mother.

"Well obviously Phil needs a home too and he might need to take some money out of this house. We may have to sell and split the profit. I don't really know. I don't want to have to leave our home but he's already mentioned that he wants somewhere to live where the children can visit him."

"I hope you don't have to move. I don't think it will be good for you or the children, all that upheaval to cope with as well," her mother said. "Come on, let's join the others and forget our worries for a bit."

Later that evening Beth found herself running up and down the stairs on several occasions to talk on her mobile phone.

Firstly Dave rang about seven o'clock. They spoke for a few minutes about what they had been doing during the day. Then Dave said he had received a phone call that morning and had been called back for another meeting. He was returning to Barnstaple on Thursday and planned to stay overnight. It seemed the job was in the bag.

"Do you think I can see you again before I go?" he asked.

"Well, maybe I can arrange for Phil to take the kids out for dinner one evening next week. He wanted to take them last week but it didn't work out. If I can arrange that, maybe we could meet for a couple of hours – would that be ok with you?"

"Yes that sounds like a good idea. Let me know what you can

arrange and I'll make sure I'm free. I tend to work late most evenings now and then get something to eat about nine o'clock. It's not good eating that late but I don't go to bed until about midnight anyway. No point if I can't get to sleep is there?'

"No, not really. You're not sleeping too well then? Is that because of the...situation or your new job, or something?" she trailed off.

"I think it started with the problem with Lisa and now it's a mixture of everything. I feel tired but when I get to bed I'm wide awake. Absolutely ridiculous, of course." he finished.

"'You can't help it though. You're not doing it deliberately. I suppose I've been lucky as I've not had any trouble getting to sleep when I go to bed. I think I've had so much to cope with and plan for in the last few days, that my brain is exhausted and just gives up when my head hits the pillow."

"Sounds good to me," said Dave. "Anyway, better go now. I'll ring you tomorrow and you can let me know if we have a date. Take care and speak tomorrow."

"Bye Dave," she spoke quietly and clicked off the phone.

A date. It sounded quite old-fashioned. Maybe he would arrive at her front door with a flower in his hand and sweep her away in a vintage car, promising to have her home by eleven. But who would he promise to? Not her dad, nor her children. Beth smiled to herself as she fantasised. This was the real world and a date would actually mean rushing to meet Dave somewhere discreet and having one eye on the clock to make sure she was back in time for the children to be returned by her ex-husband. Not quite so romantic!

The next call was Amanda ringing to cancel their meeting the next day.

"I am sorry darling. We'll have to meet on Tuesday. The chairman of the horticultural group had her dates wrong and our meeting is tomorrow afternoon. Such a shame, I so wanted to catch up with your news. Is Tuesday alright for you?" Amanda spoke loudly down the phone.

"Yes Tuesday's alright. Don't worry, my news will keep, it's not that exciting," said Beth, holding the phone away from her ear slightly. "Same time at your place?"

"Yes, come straight after you finish work and I'll have some lunch ready for you," promised Amanda. "Sorry again, got to go now. I've got five more people to ring and tell that the date was wrongly booked for our meeting. See you Tuesday. Can't wait. Bye."

"Bye." Amanda had already rung off.

Beth managed to run downstairs again and picked up the ironing board just as her phone rung again. This time it was Verity.

"Hi Sis. Right, how long have you got? Are you busy or can we talk for a while?" she asked.

Beth looked at the pile of school shirts and blouses waiting to be ironed.

"Oh Verity – I have all the time in the world for you," she said, half joking. But her sister was already in full swing about the weekend.

"We had such a marvellous time," she enthused. "All four places were brilliant but one, on the north coast, is absolutely great. We are going to put in an offer tomorrow morning. It's just under our budget and has everything we wanted. It's close to a good school for the kids and not too far from the nearest town. It's a farm which has been used as a bed and breakfast but has plenty of land. They used to grow wheat and potatoes but haven't done

any growing for about three years. They've now decided to sell and move to a smaller place in Devon, near one of their grown up children. The house is in a good state, as it's been used for b&b, and the land is in reasonable condition. We're all really excited and hope they accept our offer."

"I'm so pleased that you've found somewhere on your first trip. If they don't accept will you offer more money or try one of the other places?"

"No, we'll offer more," Verity said determinedly. "We really want this place. It's just ideal. I can't wait for you all to see it. We're hoping to get some viewings for our house this week, as well. I'll have to have a good clean up tomorrow and get some coffee brewing to encourage the buyers," she joked.

"Shall I pop and see you tomorrow when I've finished work?" asked Beth.

"Oh that's a great idea. I'll get mum and dad to come over too and you can see the photos we took with the digital camera. We bought one specially and it's really good fun to take pictures and see them immediately. John is putting them on the computer so we can watch them like a slide show."

"Ok I'll be over just after two – looking forward to it," Beth said, ready to end the conversation.

But Verity wanted to know if Beth and the children were coping and had they had a good weekend.

"Yes we're coping alright. Still getting used to things being different and Phil has been away this weekend so he's not seen the children. James was upset he wouldn't be at the football match and they all miss him. He should call after school tomorrow night and I'll probably get him to take them out for dinner one evening," Beth told her. She decided not to mention her meeting with Dave.

"Seems like you're still having to arrange his life and make sure he sees his kids," observed Verity waspishly. "Men should get their priorities right."

"Are you having problems with John and his priorities then?" asked Beth trying to make her sister laugh.

"Of course not, you know he's a good family man. But I do hear about other men and their situations, you know."

"Of course you do," reassured Beth trying not to laugh at her sister's worldly wise words. "Thank you for your observations. I'll bear them in mind."

"Oh you!…I know you're taking the 'whatsit' out of me. I don't care though, I'll help you get through all this the best I can."

"Thanks Verity. I know you'll help me. Sorry, I don't mean to be flippant. I'll see you tomorrow for a slide show – looking forward to it. Bye."

The last phone call of the evening was Phil who rung to say he would call in to see the children after he'd finished work the next day. Beth said she had expected him too anyway and would he like to take them out for dinner one evening.

"Oh yes I would like to. I think Wednesday will be best. I've got a meeting till seven at work on Tuesday and Monday will be a busy day. Yes, Wednesday will be best. I'll collect them as usual when I've finished work and take them to the Pizza Hut."

Beth smiled to herself as she closed the phone and stood up again from the chair in the bedroom where she seemed to have spent most of the evening talking on her phone. She went downstairs and set up the ironing board in order to iron some clothes in readiness for the forthcoming week at work and school. All three children were watching a television programme in the front room and she called out that it would be bedtime soon.

"Can we just finish watching this please? It ends at quarter past nine," yelled James.

"OK, but be ready to go up then. No messing about please," she called back.

By ten o'clock the ironing was finished and the clothes hung up in their respective wardrobes, the children were in bed, either asleep or reading, and Beth was slumped in a chair with a glass of white wine in her hand. There had been just enough for her to squeeze out a glassful from the bottle she'd opened at lunch time for her mother and father.

So, she'd be seeing Dave again on Wednesday evening. She wondered whether to send him a text but then decided to tell him tomorrow evening when he phoned her. She experienced the fizzy feeling again when thinking about talking and meeting him again next week. She looked at the glass in her hand and knew this feeling was not caused by the wine. It was excitement and...what had she talked to Annie about? Scariness. That was it. Life was turning out to be quite exciting and scary. Not that today had been either, she admitted to herself. In fact, if Phil had been there nothing would have been much different. Apart from the phone calls taken in the bedroom. If Phil was still living with them, she would not have hidden herself away to talk quietly on the phone upstairs. There

would not have been secret meetings arranged or her friend trying to find out about the latest gossip. No, that was a bit harsh. Amanda was not a gossip – just a concerned friend. Her sister's call would have been taken downstairs with everyone joining in.

Beth closed her eyes and let the wine wash through her. She'd go upstairs and have a soak in the bath before going to bed. But just for a few minutes she let her senses take over and her body relax.

Chapter Thirteen

--ooOoo--

*T*he next few weeks leading up to Christmas flew past in a flurry of activity. Or so it seemed to Beth. Phil continued to visit the children for an hour or so every night during the week and even managed to see them for a short time most weekends.

He had not mentioned selling the house again, or re-structuring their finances, so Beth assumed he would leave that discussion until the new year when she started full time work.

Verity called in to see Beth almost every day, either early afternoon or during the evening. She was full of excitement and plans for their new life in Cornwall. Their offer had been accepted on the farm and their own house was being marketed by a local firm of estate agents. Despite the time of year, there had already been several viewings.

Beth and Dave met up once or twice a week, always at times when the children were busy either with Phil or their own commitments. Dave too was full of his move to the west country. He was due to start his new job in the middle of January and his house was also up for sale. He was planning to share the equity equally between himself and Lisa, so Beth was pleased to think that there would be some deposit available for the purchase of Phil's new home which might lessen the risk of having to put her own home on the market.

Jack and Vera were coping well with all the upheaval to their daughters' lives. They planned to visit Verity and John in Cornwall during the February half term and Beth was arranging to take some of her annual leave so she could be at home with her children for that week.

Beth found herself trying to keep everything the same as previous Christmas times – hanging decorations, sending cards, buying a

Christmas tree and baking lots of goodies for the holiday time. The children's enthusiasm didn't seem diminished by their change of circumstances and Beth attended the carol services and took them to their school discos as usual.

Phil had told the children he would be visiting his mother on Christmas Day but would take them out all day on Boxing Day. They seemed to accept this and even Christina didn't question him further.

Verity had promised to cook the Christmas Day lunch for everyone as it was the last Christmas they would be living locally. Vera had made a pudding and cake a few months earlier and Beth was going to help with the vegetables and provide an alternative dessert. Traditionally, they all sat down to Christmas dinner at about 3 o'clock with the Queen's speech on the television as background.

Beth found she could not quite get into her usual festive spirit, which Amanda told her was quite understandable.

"It's all different this year – and such a shock for you still. Don't worry, I'm sure it will be better next year. You'll have a new life by then – you wait and see," she reassured her friend.

Beth knew she was talking sense but still struggled to maintain a cheery manner and smiling face as everyone sat around the table on Christmas afternoon, pulling crackers.

She looked at the happy faces around her and tried to join in with their merriment as they read the cracker jokes to each other.

Annie noticed her mother trying to smile and squeezed her arm affectionately.

"Don't worry mum, we're going to have a new and brilliant year start in a few day's time. You'll soon get used to things being different," she whispered.

"Thanks darling, you are such a comfort to me. I don't know how you managed to become so mature and thoughtful, but I'm glad you did. It's obviously the way I've brought you up!' Beth tried to laugh at her attempted lightheartedness.

Verity glanced at the pair of them and jumped up suddenly. "Right, come on everyone, let's get this party going. ohn, why don't you get the bottle of champagne opened and we'll drink some toasts," she said.

"Good idea," agreed John, going out into the kitchen. A loud pop was heard followed by a fizzing noise. Then John came into the room with a dozen glasses filled with the beautiful bubbly liquid. Everyone took a glass, including the children, and John began the toasts.

"Firstly, let's toast all of us for being here today and enjoying this lovely meal prepared by our lovely women. Cheers!"

They all sipped their drinks and Beth felt the warm glow start inside her as she swallowed the golden champagne.

"Next, let's toast Verity, John, Sam and Lucy for their new life in Cornwall. We wish them all success for the future," said Jack raising his glass again.

Verity stood up and waited for silence. "I would like to toast my older sister, Beth. She has had an horrible time during the last few weeks but has shown a lot of courage in dealing with the problems. I think we all hope that next year will bring better times for her and Annie, James and Christina too. Let's drink to the Graingers."

Beth and the children looked slightly embarrassed but decided to stand up and raise their glasses too. So everyone laughed and the moment passed.

The children then took over and began toasting anything and everything and the rest of the meal finished in laughter and happiness.

When Beth drove the children home later that evening she realised she had actually enjoyed most of the day. She had been rather dreading the family get-together but everyone had acted normally and she had not felt left out of anything at all. It hadn't mattered that her husband had not been part of the celebrations.

She was in bed by eleven o'clock and began to think about the next day.

As Phil was taking the children out for the whole day, she and Dave had planned to spend the time together. She was going to his house and they would cook a meal together. As long as she was home by about nine o'clock, no-one would be any the wiser. She had told her parents and Verity that she was going to have a quiet day to herself and enjoy a pamper session with her new Christmas goodies. She didn't like to lie, or not quite tell the truth, but at the moment she had no choice. There was no way she was going to risk the children hearing about Dave, certainly not until they knew Phil had another relationship.

Maybe Lisa would turn up tomorrow and meet them for the first time, she thought. She rather hoped that would happen so the children could learn to deal with her sooner rather than later. But Phil was a bit of a coward and tended to put things off as long as possible – mostly in the hope that they would either go away or just sort themselves out.

Anyway, she didn't want any problems tomorrow, just the chance to spend some quality time with Dave and not have to watch the clock all the time.

It was nearly midday by the time Beth was in the car and on her way to Dave's house. Phil had turned up late to collect the children and said he would have them back by nine o'clock. That meant she would need to be back in the house just after eight in case he was early!

Still, she and Dave had about eight hours together to enjoy. She had sent him a text message to say she was on her way and he'd replied saying he was pouring the wine ready for her arrival.

Beth parked her car outside Dave's house and turned round to see him opening the front door.

"Hi, you found it ok then?" he asked rather unnecessarily.

"Yes, it was quite easy from your directions," she replied.

They went inside and Dave took her coat to hang on the rack.

"The wine is in the kitchen. I've started the dinner but thought we could finish it together, if that's alright," he said ushering her through to the back of the house.

"Yes that's great. Sorry I'm a bit late. Phil didn't pick the kids up until half an hour ago. I thought he'd told me ten o'clock but he said it was eleven. But he's always late anyway." She picked up her glass of wine and took a large gulp to calm herself. Dave took a mouthful as well. They both seemed quite nervous and looked at each other across the kitchen table.

"Shall we…"

"What have you…"

They both started to speak together and then stopped.

"You first," said Dave.

"I was just going to ask what have you started with the dinner?" said Beth. "What were you going to say?"

"I was going to say, shall we finish the veggies together?" he replied. "Here, you do the broccoli and carrots and I'll finish the potatoes." He handed her a knife and they set to work together at the kitchen sink.

"Did you have a nice day yesterday with your family?" Dave asked politely.

"Oh yes, it was nice. Different, of course. Everyone else seemed ok but I felt a bit weird. It felt as if I was on my own, which is ridiculous of course as my children and family were all there. I just felt alone and apart," Beth explained.

"I know what you mean. It was the same for me yesterday at my brother's annual get-together. He only invites us to his house once a year and that's for Christmas dinner. They have quite a posh house in Chester and a smart set of friends. Mum and Dad only visit him when they are invited and I've never been able to just pop in and see him. He's a few years older than me so we've never been that close. His wife works as a marketing

director for a large publishing company and they mix in cocktail circles!" Dave revealed.

"I didn't meet your brother on the holiday in Blackpool, did I?" asked Beth, cutting up carrots and putting them in the saucepan.

"No, he only came over to visit us for a day as he'd just started a new job then. It was probably the day your parents took you to visit their friends who had moved that way – do you remember?"

"Yes I do now. They owned a fish and chip shop on the corner of a road, somewhere. I can't remember exactly where. But I know they gave us fish and chips for our tea – which seemed strange to us – although probably perfectly obvious to them," said Beth as she remembered the day.

"Well, I felt a bit isolated yesterday too," Dave said reverting back to their original topic of conversation. "Mum and Dad were great of course, but Brian and Sadie just kept asking questions. How did it happen? Did I not realise she was seeing someone else? Who was this chap? Did I know him? They just went on and on. In the end dad told them to give it a rest and leave me alone to enjoy the day. Brian said they were just showing an interest but

they did stop then. I left just after six and went home to watch a couple of DVDs I'd bought on Christmas Eve when I was doing my Christmas shopping!"

"Typical man – leave it to the last minute!" joked Beth.

"Talking about presents, when would you like yours?" asked Dave turning to look at her.

"Oh, I've got one for you too. Shall we save them for after dinner?"

asked Beth. She'd bought Dave a nice pen and pair of cufflinks for his new job, as well as a CD which he'd said he would like.

"Well I think everything is bubbling and boiling nicely now. Shall we take our drinks in the other room and sit in comfort. I'll put some music on."

Dave led the way into the front room. Beth looked round the room and grudgingly admitted to herself that Lisa had taste. The room was decorated in shades of silver and lilac. The

walls were painted white but did not seem stark or cold due to the clever positioning of paintings and photographs. The curtains and carpets were lilac and the suite was a shiny grey which tinged with silver. All the electrical items were stainless steel and this added to the lightness and brightness in the room.

Dave had lit some candles and placed them around the room and the large silver framed mirror hanging above the fireplace reflected the bright little flames.

"Oh this is a lovely room," exclaimed Beth.

"Yes, Lisa has quite good taste. I wasn't sure about lilac as it seems a bit feminine and probably more suitable for a bedroom. But I have to admit, this room is nice," agreed Dave.

They sat on the three-seater and listened to the CD that Dave had put on to play. Every so often he would jump up and go into the kitchen to check on the food and stir the vegetables.

"Nearly ready," he said on returning from his fourth kitchen trip. "I'll just go and lay the

table."

Beth sat back into the cushions on the sofa and closed her eyes. How lovely this was to be sat in a gorgeous room with an attentive man cooking dinner for her.

"I don't think this has ever happened to me before," she said as Dave came back into the room. "No man has ever cooked a dinner for me, certainly not without me having to provide detailed instructions, help with an emergency overflow of boiling water or do the washing up at the end of the meal!"

Dave looked pleased with himself. "Well I am quite a good cook. I can't do lots of cordon bleu dishes but what I can do, I can manage on my own," he said. "Anyway, it's ready now – so would madam like to step this way?" He put his arm out and escorted her into the kitchen.

He had thrown a pale blue table cloth over the table and placed a silver candelabra in the middle. The crockery and cutlery were all accurately placed for two settings and the food was in matching dishes ready for serving.

"Wow it looks beautiful," exclaimed Beth. "I never do this at home. It's always dished up straight from the saucepans. You're really spoiling me." She leaned forward and kissed his cheek. "Thanks."

Dave blushed and rubbed his cheek. "Now you're embarrassing me," he said as he pulled out a chair for her to be seated. "Come on, let's eat now. Bon appetit!"

"Oooh la la, you speak French too," teased Beth as she helped herself to potatoes.

When they had finished eating Dave piled all the plates and bowls into the dishwasher and switched it on to rinse.

"Come on let's take our coffee into the other room and relax. Have a look through my CDs and put something else on if you like," he offered.

Beth knelt down by the rack of CDs and pulled a few out to look at. Eventually she chose a compilation of romantic ballards and passed it to Dave. He smiled as he read the title and placed it in the CD player. They sat back and listened to the music as they finished their coffee.

Eventually, just as Beth thought she might drift off to sleep in the warm room, Dave stood up and held his hand out to her.

"Come on, let's go for a wander around the garden. If we don't get some fresh air we'll both be asleep," he suggested.

"What a good idea. I am feeling very sleepy after that lovely meal," agreed Beth as she got to her feet, although she had wondered where he was going to suggest they go. Maybe upstairs?

They put their coats on and went out through the back door. Beth was surprised to find a large garden at the back of the house. A paved terrace with steps led down to a lawned area surrounded by flower borders, which in turn led to a raised decking area with a summer house and barbecue. Behind the decking was another small lawn, vegetable patch and a greenhouse.

"Who enjoys gardening?" asked Beth as she looked around. Even given the time of year when all gardens appear bare, she could see there were many plants ready to burst into life during the next few months.

"I'm afraid neither of us. I employ my next door neighbour who is a retired gent and enjoys growing vegetables and flowers. He comes in most weeks to weed, mow the lawn and tend to the vegetables. We share the produce between us. Lisa used to enjoy pottering around filling pots and hanging baskets, but I'm not much good at anything apart from cutting the grass," Dave said ruefully.

"I like gardening but my friend is an expert. She belongs to lots of horticultural groups and even gives talks to some of the local groups. Her name's Amanda and she's my best friend," explained Beth.

"Perhaps she knows my neighbour then. I believe he attends lots of meetings for gardening tips," said Dave as they strolled around.

"What's behind your garden – over there at the back?" asked Beth pointing to the fence.

"It's the field behind the rugby club. It's just rough ground really. The only people who use it are dog walkers and some motor bike scramblers. Shall we go back in now? Are you getting cold?" Dave asked.

Beth was really appreciating his concern and care for her. She was used to doing all the caring and looking after other people. She smiled at him.

"Yes, let's go back in now. It is quite cold but it was nice to get a breath of fresh air."

They went back inside and Dave took her coat to hang it up again. When he returned to the front room, Beth was stood in front of the fire warming her hands. She looked flushed and inviting as he caught her looking at him in the mirror. He walked over to her and put his hands on her shoulders to turn her around.

They stared into each other's eyes for a moment before he moved forward slowly to kiss her lips. He pulled her tighter towards him and she moved her hands up and down his spine. His right hand moved up to her hair and stroked her head as they continued kissing.

When they broke apart they were both breathless and stood staring at each other for a few minutes.

"Do you, would you like to, shall we…?" started Dave. "Erm, shall we go upstairs Beth?"

Beth nodded and smiled at him. This was to be their moment then. Their first time together. She walked beside him to the foot of the stairs and then followed him upwards.

Dave led her into the front bedroom. The curtains were half closed and the room was very tidy. She tried not to think about Dave and Lisa sharing the room, and the bed.

Dave took her face in his hands and kissed her again. She put her arms around him and hugged him tight. She could feel his arousal and moved her hands down to the base of his back, pulling him in towards her.

A groan escaped from his throat and he pulled away to take his shirt and jeans off. Beth kicked her shoes off and unzipped her skirt. She couldn't believe she was acting quite so brazenly.

Dave grabbed her hands and pulled her onto the bed. He covered her face and neck with kisses as his hands travelled over her body. After a few minutes they pulled the rest of their clothes off each other and began the sensual ritual of discovering each other's bodies for the first time.

Beth woke up to find Dave looking at her as he lay on his side.

"Hello beautiful," he said softly. "I hope you enjoyed that as much as I did. What a wonderful Christmas present."

Beth pulled him down and kissed him passionately.

"That's how wonderful if was," she said. "The most wonderfullest time ever."

They grinned at each other.

"So what do we do now then?" asked Dave. "I'm going to be living miles away from you again soon. It's like déjà vu, or history repeating itself."

Beth pulled herself up to sitting position against the pillows.

"I don't know what we're going to do but I don't want to lose you again," she said. "But I can't move away because of the children and you won't stay because you have a new job now. I don't know what we'll do. Perhaps we'll just have to meet at weekends and holidays for now and see what happens. But we won't lose each other again like last time. We have too much information on each other now!"

"It's such a shame though. We've found each other again and yet we still can't be together. It doesn't seem very fair!"

"Well, life isn't fair and nobody said it would be. That's what my mother has always told me and I'm sure she's right," said Beth. "But don't forget, we're both still married to other people. And those two people are actually having an affair together – it just doesn't seem possible, does it?"

"No, it's a strange situation, to be sure!" agreed Dave.

"Amanda said it was like one of those stories in women's magazines: 'my boyfriend's married to my husband's lover'. You know, you see them in shops all the time," Beth said.

"I hope you're not suggesting we sell our story to a women's magazine?" Dave opened his eyes in mock horror. "Mind you, how much do you think they'd pay for it?"

Beth whacked his arm and pretended to be outraged. "Sell our story! I should think not!"

She glanced over at the bedside clock and saw the time was nearly six o'clock. Dave saw her looking and swung his legs off the bed.

"Shall we go and have another drink?" he asked.

"I can't have any more wine, don't forget I've got to drive home yet," said Beth as she wriggled off the bed. "A cup of tea would be nice though."

"So much for the cigarette and glass of wine afterwards," Dave grimaced. "Shows our age doesn't it when a nice cup of tea follows a nice bit of sex."

"I'm glad you think it was a nice bit of sex," said Beth as she stepped into her skirt. "Very glad indeed."

"Of course it was nice – and I hope we can do it again soon," said Dave.

"Oh yes, so do I," agreed Beth promptly. She looked across at him and surprised herself by saying, "In fact, now would be quite good."

So saying she grabbed hold of Dave and pushed him back onto the bed.

The next time they surfaced the clock hands pointed to seven thirty.

"I'll have to go quite soon," Beth said. "Phil is getting the kids back about nine but he might be early. I have to look as if I've been there all day."

"Ok, you've worn me out now anyway," Dave pretended to stagger as he went towards the door of the en suite bathroom.

They went back downstairs and Dave made a cup of tea for them both. As they sat at the kitchen table drinking it, Beth tried not to keep looking at the clock.

"It's ok Beth. I know you want to get back home now and I don't mind. I'm not offended. As you said upstairs, we still have stuff to sort out before we can become a proper item. But I would like us to become a proper item and I hope you do too," said Dave.

"Oh yes Dave, I really do. Thanks for being so thoughtful and thank you for the lovely day we've had together. I'm so glad we have met up again and I'll try to get things sorted out with the kids, and Phil, and everything," Beth promised.

"It's alright. I've got things to do as well. Obviously I won't mention anything to Lisa until you've told your children and Phil too. Not that I expect to see Lisa anyway, although some of her things are still here."

Beth looked around expecting to see lots of items hanging about with Lisa's name on. She stood up and Dave went into the hallway to fetch her coat. He helped her into it and she located her bag and the car keys.

They walked into the hallway and stopped for a long, passionate kiss by the front door.

"'I'll ring you later when the kids are in bed," Beth promised.

"And we'll meet up again soon – perhaps this week?" asked Dave, hopefully.

"Yes, I will try and arrange something. It's difficult with the school holidays, but I will try. I want to see you soon too," Beth kissed him again and then opened the front door.

"Bye Beth – drive carefully. Call me soon," Dave said.

"I will. Thanks for dinner and...everything," called Beth.

It was not until she was almost home that she realised they had not exchanged their Christmas presents.

Chapter Fourteen

--ooOoo--

*I*t was New Year's Day and Beth was sat at the kitchen table late in the afternoon. She gazed out at the wintry garden as darkness fell, and shivered. She felt something was not quite right.

Up until that moment her day had been great. Phil had collected the children on time at ten thirty in the morning and Dave had arrived, also on time, at eleven thirty. They had enjoyed four happy hours together, preparing lunch and eating it in the front room whilst watching a romantic comedy on television. They had washed up the dishes together, laughing and spraying soap suds over each other. Dave had left at half past three as the children

were due back about four o'clock.

Beth had made herself a cup of hot chocolate and was indulging herself with the last few chocolates in a box she'd been given for Christmas. She sighed and glanced at the clock. It was just after four so any minute she would hear Phil's car arrive. She wondered if he would come into the house.

As she drank the last mouthful she heard his car outside the house. There were three loud bangs as the car doors were shut and a pounding of feet along the sideway to the kitchen door.

Christina burst in through the door first. Beth immediately noticed her red face and tearfulness. James followed with Annie behind him. Beth knew that something had happened and her premonition had been justified.

"What's the matter? What's happened?" she asked getting to her feet.

"Oh Mum. It's awful. Dad has got a girlfriend!" announced Christina.

"Yes' said James. "'And we've just met her. We had to have dinner with her. It was terrible."

Beth realised that Phil had sprung this upon them without prior warning.

"Oh dear, what a shock for you all. Did you not like her?" she asked, putting her arms around Christina.

"Did you know about her then?' demanded Christina looking sharply at her mother.

Beth and Annie exchanged glances.

"Er, well, yes. I'm afraid I did, darlings. But I didn't want to tell you. I thought your father would prepare you before you actually met her," said Beth.

She felt she was on trial here but didn't understand why that should be so.

"Why didn't you tell us then?" demanded Christina.

"'Because I wanted your father to tell you. It's his news. Maybe I should have said something, and I would have if I'd known this was going to happen. He should have told you before you met her. Was she in the car when he picked you up?" asked Beth.

"No, we had to go to the flat and she was there," explained Annie. "He took us in and introduced us all and then we went out for a meal. But it was so embarrassing. Christina burst into tears and James said 'what about Mum?' Dad didn't know what to say and Lisa just looked angry."

"Why does Dad have to live with her? She's not a nice lady. I don't like her at all," said Christina.

"Sit down all of you," said Beth. "Let's just talk about this sensibly for a few minutes."

The children sat down and looked at their mother as she continued. "Your Dad has decided that he wants to live with her instead of me. It isn't because he doesn't want to live with you three. You have got to realise that. Is that Ok? James?'

'Yes I understand that," said James.

"Annie?" asked Beth.

"Yes Mum, I know what you're saying." agreed Annie.

"And Christina?"

"I suppose so, Mum. But I don't think it's fair he's gone to live with another lady when he could still be here with us. And then we'd all be happy again," Christina persisted.

"But Dad obviously wasn't happy with Mum," said Annie. "That's why he's gone to live with another woman."

Beth grimaced. "Thanks Annie," she said.

"Sorry Mum," Annie looked anxious as she realised her mother didn't appreciate the comment.

"No, it's alright Annie. I'm sorry I didn't mean to be so touchy. Of course it is between me and your dad – we are the ones who have fallen out with each other. I still love all three of you very, very much – and so does your father."

There was silence in the kitchen as the children absorbed what their mother was saying.

James was the first to speak. "Will we have to see 'her' every time we go out with Dad now?" he asked.

"I don't know James. It's up to your dad. Obviously he wants you all to get on together. I suppose you'll need to give them a bit of a chance."

In her heart-of-hearts she knew she didn't really want her children to 'get on' with a rival 'mother-figure'.

"Well I think we should tell Dad we want to see him on his own," said Annie. "Surely we have that much right?"

"Of course you have darling," agreed her mother. "But just remember, we all have to adjust to this new situation. If they are living together in that flat, your dad might want you to visit him there sometimes. You can hardly make her leave her own home, can you?"

"I suppose not. But she was very pushy, kept asking us questions. I'd have thought Dad would have told her all about us," said Annie.

"She probably just wants to try to get to know you, find out what you like and that sort of thing," Beth suggested.

"Well I don't want to get to know her or what she likes," Christina asserted petulantly. "She can go away and never come back again, for all I care."

"I don't think that's likely to happen," said Beth laughing at her youngest daughter. "Come on now Christina, you are usually such a friendly person. Perhaps you ought to try for your dad's sake."

Christina scowled and James scuffed his feet on the floor under the table. Annie sighed and glanced at the clock.

"Do you mind if I ring Ben and ask him to come round for a bit," she asked her mother.

"Yes that's fine. He can stay for tea if he likes. Go and phone him."

Beth stood up as she spoke. She looked at the other two children. "Come on you two. Cheer up. Your dad is entitled to have new friends and we all have to move on!" She tried to make them smile but they didn't respond. She put her arms around them both and kissed each one on of the tips of their noses.

"Come on my little lovelies," she cooed. "Let's try and cheer up a bit. You don't want to ruin the last couple of days of your holiday, do you?"

James nodded and hugged his mum back. "Ok, I'll cheer up," he promised.

"Me too," agreed Christina. "What shall we do now?"

Annie smiled at her mother and then left the room to make her phone call and Beth went to the cupboard and took out some chocolate biscuits.

"Let's have a quick snack and see if we can find something nice to watch on television for a bit," she suggested.

She decided that they needed a diversion so they could slowly come to terms with the new woman in their father's life. Beth felt quite angry at the way Phil had handled the situation, springing it on the kids and then leaving her to mop up the mess. Typical – she thought.

She was very glad they had no inkling of her new liaison with Dave. They would have to continue to be discreet with their meetings, certainly until the children had accepted Phil's new woman as part of their lives.

Later that evening, after talking on the phone to Verity, she realised that her problem with keeping Dave a secret would not apply for much longer. It was only another two weeks until he left for the West Country. They were planning on keeping in touch but she wondered how long their relationship would really last with such a distance between them.

'I don't want to lose him for a second time,' she thought as she ironed clean shirts and blouses for school and work in two day's time. 'But what can I do? I have to stay here and he has to go to work.'

They were planning to meet up again the next evening. Jack and Vera were taking Beth and Verity's children to the pantomime as a special treat. John and Verity were making the most of one of the last baby-sitting opportunities and had booked a meal at the Italian restaurant. Beth was going to Dave's house for the evening, although she had told everyone she was visiting Amanda. Her friend had said she would provide an alibi for Beth

any time she wanted during the last couple of weeks before Dave left the area.

"I don't mind doing it for a short time, to help you out," she had said to Beth. |"But I wouldn't want it to be a long term thing. Mostly because we'd be bound to be found out by someone eventually. But two weeks should be alright."

Beth was very grateful for the support from her friend. She still had not told her parents or Verity about Dave, and didn't plan to. There would probably be no need, she thought. Dave will move away in a couple of weeks and that will probably be the end of us. He'll meet someone else near his work and we'll be ships that passed in the night, for the second time.

The thought depressed her but she was determined to enjoy the last few times they had together as much as possible.

When Phil arrived to collect the children at five o'clock on the last evening of the school holidays, she arranged that she would see him alone for a few minutes. The children were still upstairs and she ushered him into the front room and closed the door.

"So, what happened on Sunday?" she asked him.

"Sunday?" he asked. "Oh, you mean the children meeting Lisa. Yes, well, I decided it was the right time. They had to know sooner or later and it seemed like a good occasion. Were they Ok when they got back?"

"Well no, they weren't Ok when they got back," she mimicked him. "They were all very upset. Did you not think it would have been best to prepare them to meet Lisa, rather than just spring it upon them?"

"I thought they'd probably have realised I was living with someone else. They're not young children and I know they all have friends who have divorced or separated parents. I didn't know it would be such a big deal. They were very quiet and sullen all day, especially Christina. She just burst into tears when I took them into the flat and introduced them to Lisa. It took quite a while to settle her down so we could go out."

Beth marvelled at the way some men believed that things would just naturally come right. That nothing needed working at. Maybe that's where they'd gone wrong in their marriage, she wondered. Perhaps he thought we'd be deliriously happy all our lives without having to work at it. That must have been a big disappointment then. But why would he jump straight into another relationship? She shook her head trying to clear all the thoughts that were

racing about. She'd have to think about this sometime quietly.

But back to the present.

"You must be mad if you think they would just make assumptions like that. Of course they wouldn't think you were living with someone else. Why should they? They aren't mind readers" Beth finished abruptly.

"Alright, well, I got it wrong again then, didn't I," he said crossly stomping towards the door. "Are they ready yet? Can you tell them I'll wait in the car."

"That's right, walk away. When are you going to face up to the consequences of your actions?" Beth asked. "You can't just sweep all this under the carpet and hope it will turn out right. There are too many people involved whose lives have been turned upside-down by your walking out on us."

Phil stopped and turned round to face her. "Look, all I want to do is get on with my life. And I want everyone else to do the same. Our marriage is over, finished. I'm living with Lisa now. I want to see the children as often as I can and as I said before, when we have

a house they can come and stay with us. I just thought they should know about Lisa as they've had time to come to terms with the new situation now. Is that so bad?'

"No of course it isn't bad. And I agree that they should know the situation you are in. You are their father. But I just think you went about it the wrong way and caused too much upset. You should have sat them down on their own and told them about Lisa before you introduced them."

"Ok, as I said, I've obviously got it all wrong again. I'm sorry. Now can you call them so we can be off, please," he asked opening the door.

The children were already stood in the hallway with their coats on ready to leave. Beth hoped that they hadn't heard the conversation that had just taken place.

"Bye then, have a lovely time," she said as she waved them off.

Beth went back into the house and took a deep breath. She hated confrontation, but she felt she needed to let Phil know that he had caused a lot of upset with his action or maybe it was lack of action, she thought.

She picked up her mobile phone and dialled Dave's number. Usually he answered within the first couple of rings, but the machine went straight to answerphone. After leaving a quick message she ran upstairs to have a shower. She had arranged to meet Dave in a pub just outside town but wanted to check if he had left work and was on his way.

When she was dry, dressed and made up she picked up the phone again. There was no message or missed call so she phoned him again. The answerphone clicked on again but she did not leave a message this time.

What should she do? Go straight to the pub or wait until she heard from him? He could still be at work and maybe he was in a meeting which meant he could not phone her or send a message.

She sat on the bottom stair and wondered what to do. Her phone beeped to herald a message.

Cant come 2nite now. Sorry. Got problem at home. Lisa turned up 2 collect stuff. Will ring u when she gone. Love Dave xxx

Beth slumped back and felt tears pricking her eyes. She had been looking forward to seeing Dave again even though they'd spent the previous evening together. Well, there was nothing she could do. If Lisa had just turned up to collect the rest of her belongings, of course Dave would want to be there. Even just to make sure she didn't take some of his things or cause any damage. It also meant that the children had Phil to themselves which she was glad about.

She would just have to wait for his phone call. Maybe if he rang quite soon they would still be able to meet for a while. She wasn't expecting Phil to bring the children home until about nine thirty.

Beth trudged back upstairs and changed back into her jeans and sweatshirt. She hung the new black skirt and halterneck top back in the wardrobe to save for another day.

What should she do? She didn't want to ring Verity or Amanda in case Dave phoned. She'd have to go downstairs and watch television to try and take her mind off waiting for the phone to ring again.

In the kitchen, Beth made herself a drink and took a packet of Ginger Nuts through to the front room. She switched on the television and found a very interesting programme to watch about tigers in the wild. Unfortunately Beth found her mind kept wandering away from the prowling tigers as she kept glancing at the phone to see if it lit up.

She ate some biscuits and finished her drink. The tigers' story ended and a new detective serial began. She tried to immerse herself in the storyline but it failed to grip her attention.

The phone remained quiet. Nobody was dialling her number or sending a text message.

'What a sad case I am,' she thought. 'Sat here waiting for the phone to ring. I'm acting like a teenager – no probably worse. Today's teenagers don't wait for someone to phone them – they just ring up and chat away.' Annie had soon got used to having her own mobile and being able to ring her friends or Ben whenever she pleased.

'I can't sit here all evening just waiting,' she thought. 'Perhaps I should drive over to Dave's house and wait until Lisa goes.'

She stood up and turned the television off. As she took her cup and the biscuits back into the kitchen, she realised she couldn't carry out her plan. She'd be turning into a stalker.

Dave probably wouldn't appreciate having his ex-wife in his house and his new girlfriend waiting in a car outside.

As she debated whether to start some housework her phone burst into life in the front room. Beth raced in and grabbed hold of it. It was Dave.

"Hi Beth," he said as she answered the phone. "Look I'm really sorry we couldn't meet earlier tonight. I didn't know Lisa was coming round, she just turned up. She's taken the rest of her things and tried to take some of mine too!"

"Oh Dave. Has she gone now?" Beth tipped the words out as quick as she could.

"Yes, she's gone. Have we still got time to meet? What time are you expecting your children back?" asked Dave.

"They should be back about half past nine. What time is it now?" she asked.

"Er, it's nearly half past seven. We've got time if we go somewhere closer to your house. What about the Golden Goose? It's only a couple of minutes from you and I could be there in about ten minutes. Shall we meet there?" he asked.

"Yes, that's a good idea. I'll be there by quarter to eight but I'll have to leave just after nine o'clock in case Phil brings them back early," said Beth.

"Yes that's fine. See you in a few minutes. Drive carefully," warned Dave.

Beth ran back upstairs and grabbed her handbag and jacket. She wouldn't bother to change, the clothes she was wearing were fine for the Golden Goose. She just hoped they didn't bump into anyone she knew.

As Beth drove into the car park behind the Golden Goose, she saw Dave waiting by the side of his car. She waved and found a place to park. He walked over to meet her as she was locking the car door and he pulled her into his arms immediately.

They kissed passionately for several minutes until the cold air began to infiltrate their jackets.

"Let's go inside," Dave said putting his arm around her shoulders and steering her towards the door.

"What would you like to drink?" he asked when they entered and found a table in a secluded corner by a window.

"I'll have an orange juice with no ice please. I think I'm cold enough,"she said warming her hands on the radiator under the window.

"Back in a sec," Dave said and walked towards the bar.

Beth looked casually out of the window as she waited for his return. Oh no. She noticed a car driving into the car park. It was her parents' 4x4. What were they doing here? It wasn't their local and she didn't think they'd ever been in here before. She shrank down into her chair and hoped they would go into the other bar.

Dave returned with the drinks and sat down. "What's the matter?" he asked immediately.

"My parents have just driven into the car park. I don't know why, they never come here. What if they see us?" she asked.

"Well let's see. Can't we pretend to be work colleagues or something?" Dave suggested taking a sip of his pint.

"That's a good idea," agreed Beth warming to the theme. "We are just meeting to go through some things I need to know for my new job at work. Yes, that's fine. If they see us and come over we'll say that."

She sipped her drink and tried to look over Dave's shoulder to see if her parents were approaching. After a few minutes when they had not appeared, she relaxed slightly and looked at Dave. He was gazing at her with an amused expression on his face.

"This subterfuge, it doesn't really suit you, does it?" he said smiling at her fondly.

"No, you're right. It certainly doesn't. I don't like telling lies, or not telling the truth anyway. I've always had trouble with lying, even as a child. Verity and I never got away with anything when we were younger because I just couldn't cope with telling fibs."

While she had been talking she hadn't noticed Jack and Vera making their way over towards their secluded corner.

"Hello darling. I thought it was your car in the car park," her mother said as Beth jumped about a foot in the air and turned beetroot red.

"Oh, oh, er, hi Mum. Hello Dad," she stammered as she got shakily to her feet.

"Er, this is, my – my colleague from work. He's called Dave. We're here to talk about my new work."

"Good evening Dave," said Jack extending his hand to Dave. "Pleased to meet you. I hope Beth is doing well with her new duties at work."

"Oh yes, she's doing fine I can assure you. Pleased to meet you both. Why don't you join us?" Dave said, shaking Jack's hand and smiling at Vera.

"Oh I'm sure they don't want to sit with us, do you?" said Beth anxiously.

"Oh darling, of course we'd like to join you. But unfortunately we can't. We are meeting the Lacey's for a meal and we're a bit early. But we have a table booked in the restaurant for eight o'clock. We'd better go through and see if they have arrived early too. It was lovely to meet you, Dave." Vera turned to Dave.

"The pleasure was mine," Dave assured her.

Vera kissed Beth on her burning cheek and said, "We'll see you tomorrow, love. We'll make sure the kids are alright until you get home from work. I'll cook the dinner as well to help you on your first day."

"Oh thanks Mum. That would be lovely."

Beth sat down again and watched her parents make their way through the door of the restaurant. They disappeared from view and Beth breathed a sigh of relief.

"Phew, that was close," she said. "I can't believe it. I had no idea they were meeting the Laceys tonight and certainly not that they were coming here. What a shock"'

She took a deep gulp of her drink and started to choke. Dave got up and banged her on the back a couple of times.

"Are you alright?" he asked.

"Yeugh, yes I think so," she gasped for breath. "Oh how embarrassing. What an evening. I was so looking forward to a lovely romantic time with you and look how it's turned out?"

They both started to laugh as they saw the funny side of the evening's events

"It's the best laid plans – and all that stuff," said Dave. "Never mind. Did you speak to Phil about the kids meeting Lisa on Sunday?"

"Yes I did. I don't want him to do anything like that again so I thought it best to tell him that they should be told things first before putting them into a situation like on Sunday. They were all so upset, even Annie. But of course, as usual, he was defensive and tried to make it seem he had done everything for the best. But it's only the best for him!" she finished defiantly.

Dave took a swig of his beer and regarded Beth over the rim of his glass.

"I see you are quite a tigress when it comes to your children. You will defend them to the end," he joked.

Beth laughed and told him about the TV programme she had tried to watch earlier that evening.

They talked for a while about Lisa's visit to collect her belongings. Dave said he had struggled to keep his temper as Lisa picked up items and tried to make out they belonged to her.

"I had to keep telling her where I had bought them or who had given something to me as a present. It was very annoying. She knew what she was doing, too. Winding me up, I suppose," he said somewhat ruefully.

"Never mind. Let's forget them now shall we?" said Beth, putting her hands over Dave's across the table. "'We haven't got long so let's talk about something or someone else."

"Yes, but what?" asked Dave. "'We don't want to talk about my leaving the week after next, do we? Are you sure you can't think about moving? Your sister's going to live in Cornwall isn't she? Why don't you move near her – maybe somewhere in between us?"

"I can't at the moment. Annie's about to do her GCSE exams and I can't disrupt her. James and Christina both have their lives here with school, friends and activities. I can't disrupt them at the moment either. If it was just me, I'd be down there like a shot," she grinned at him.

"So what are we going to do then?" asked Dave. "Try and see each other at weekends?"

"I can't see any other way at the moment. I'm not going to tell the children about you yet anyway. They need to get over the shock of their father and Lisa first."

"Do you think I will be a big shock to them?" asked Dave, putting his head on one side and grinning at her.

"Oh yes, you are one big shock," she laughed at him.

They finished their drinks by ten to nine and left by the back door to avoid seeing Beth's parents again.

Dave drew Beth into the shadows of a large bush in the car park and pulled her towards him.

"Come here you gorgeous woman," he said. Beth put her face up to his and they kissed slowly and deeply for a few minutes.

"I'm so going to miss you," Dave said huskily as they drew apart to take a breath. "What am I going to do now I've found you – I don't want to lose you again."

"I know. I feel the same," Beth assured him. "We'll have to work something out. I'll sort it out somehow, I promise."

They kissed again and then Beth stepped backwards. "I'll have to go now. I'm sorry."

"Don't be sorry, Beth. You never have to say sorry to me – you will never do anything that you need to be sorry about. We both have our baggage and we have to accept that. Give me another kiss and then I'll let you go."

As Beth was driving back home she realised that she was falling for Dave in a very serious way. She didn't know how she was going to cope without him when he left for his new job. But what could she do? She needed to stay here for Annie's exams in the summer and even after that, could she disrupt the children?

She would have to talk to Amanda. But meeting Amanda was going to be difficult now. Every spare moment she had she wanted to spend with Dave. Starting from tomorrow, her working hours would be longer so there would be no time left in the day.

But she needed to speak with her friend who was always so full of good, commonsense. She'd have to arrange something or else leave it until after Dave had left.

She parked the car on her drive and walked wearily up the pathway. She would go to bed at the same time as the children tonight as she needed to be up bright and early the next morning ready for her first full time working day.

Phil had the children home by nine thirty and Beth shooed them off to bed straight away, almost without asking whether they'd enjoyed their evening. Christina was quite indignant and tried to instigate a long talk with her mother when she went to say goodnight. But Beth was firm and told her to go to sleep as she started back at school the next day.

"No buts…" She said firmly, pressing her finger on Christina's lips. "Goodnight and we'll talk tomorrow."

James and Annie had gone to their bedrooms so Beth called goodnight to them and went into her own room. She sent a quick message to Dave to say she had arrived home safely and was going to bed. He immediately returned with a message of love and kisses.

"What a wonderful way to go to sleep," she thought. "With somebody's love and kisses – just for me."

Chapter Fifteen

--ooOoo--

*B*eth was surprised to see how quickly everyone adapted to the change in routine. Annie especially was invaluable during the first few days of the new morning rush hour. As Beth had to go straight to work every morning after dropping the children at school, she did not have her previously taken-for-granted luxury of returning to an empty house to carry out the various household tasks. Everything needed to be done by eight thirty when they all left for the day.

She set her alarm clock to ring half an hour earlier to get a head-start on the day. She got into a routine of preparing the sandwich boxes the night before. She designated James to fill the dishwasher after breakfast and Christina to wipe the table and put away the cereal boxes. Annie was instructed in the use of the washing machine and would set a load of clothes in action before they left. Beth seemed to find innumerable jobs to do before their 8.30am deadline, none of which were the same two days running!

The children were delighted to find their grandparents at home when they arrived after school and even managed to start on their homework before Beth got in. Vera prepared a meal for them the first evening to help out as she had said, but after that Beth tried to get organised the night before as much as possible.

She had enjoyed working part time – with the best of both worlds – able to earn some money for herself and keep her brain ticking over, and having plenty of time to organise the children and the house. She knew it would take a while to get used to working full time again but then she was getting used to a lot of different things lately.

On the Friday night Beth arranged to meet Verity and her children at Pizza Hut. Verity was full of plans for their move which looked as if it would be delayed until after the end of February.

"Mum and Dad have said they'll come and stay at Easter now. So they'll still be here for the half time holiday. Will that mess up your holiday arrangements?" she asked Beth.

"Mmmm," said Beth through a mouthful of pizza. She swallowed and replied, "I'll just try and re-arrange my holiday. I'm sure they'll be pleased I can work half term so someone else can have the time off with their children."

"What's happening with Phil now? Does he still come around to see the kids?" asked Verity.

"Yes, he still turns up most evenings after work for an hour or so. It was a bit awkward the first few times after he had introduced them to his new girl-friend but they seem to be thawing a bit towards him now. They are all going out for a meal tomorrow night," Beth said.

She glanced over at the children's table to make sure they weren't listening but they were fully occupied with their pizzas and Sam was noisily explaining about the growing plans for their new farm.

"It's funny really," she continued to Verity. "But Annie seems to have taken it the hardest about Phil living with someone else. I would have thought as she has a boyfriend and is that much older than the other two, she would have accepted it quicker. She's being quite cold with her dad and I think even he is beginning to realise that she has a problem with Lisa."

Verity nodded as she thought about Beth's words. "Maybe it's because she's older and can see the hurt her dad has caused you. The younger ones are still only thinking of themselves, which is natural for children, but Annie can probably see the bigger picture."

"Yes, that's probably right. I have noticed that Annie seems to have matured quite a lot recently. She's always been a thoughtful girl but I can't believe how helpful and understanding she has been throughout this difficult few weeks. I just hope there won't be some sort of delayed reaction and she turns into a teenage nightmare."

Verity laughed at the thought of Annie changing from herself to a difficult teenager.

"I don't think there's much chance of that," she reassured Beth. "What about the other two – what's their reaction?"

"Well James is Ok as long as Phil promises to go to some of his football matches. I don't think he's too bothered about Lisa, as long as she doesn't impinge on his life. Christina also seems to be accepting her presence. But it's early days yet, they've only met her once – until tomorrow night. I don't even know if she is making an effort to get to know and befriend them, or not," Beth sighed as she looked at her three children laughing and enjoying themselves, all worries forgotten for the time being.

"I just wish I could wrap them in cotton wool and keep them away from all harmful and horrible things. I know that is a cliché and every parent's wish and we have to let them grow up and experience the nasty side of life too. But it doesn't stop the wishing, does it?" she asked her sister.

"No I agree with you. When Sam had that awful scare and we thought he had meningitis, I just don't know how we got through those days at the hospital. The relief was tremendous and I'll never forget it. I try not to take them for granted. It's difficult sometimes when they are being noisy or cheeky and I lose my temper and shout. Afterwards I usually feel guilty and try to make it up to them, without them knowing of course. They've got to learn the difference between right and wrong," Verity said.

As all the food had disappeared and the glasses were empty, it was obviously time to leave. They trooped into the car park and prepared to go their separate ways. Verity hugged Beth tight and asked if she would be alright over the weekend as the children were going out with their father.

"If you want to come over to us that's fine. We are all in tomorrow night. Ring me or just turn up," Verity assured her.

Beth smiled at her sister. "Thanks love, but I'll probably have a quiet night in. It's taking its toll a bit, all this full time work. I'll be able to enjoy a candlelit bath and a glass of wine without any interruptions. I'll be fine, don't worry."

"Oh I wasn't worrying, just concerned that's all," Verity flicked her hand at Beth and pretended she wasn't bothered.

"I'll see you later next week," called Beth out of the car window as she drove out of the car park.

"Yes – byee," shouted Verity and the occupants of her car.

"Did you enjoy yourselves?" asked Beth as they drove home.

"Yes it was great. Sam was telling us all about their farm. Can we go and visit them when they've moved?" asked James.

"They're going to have some animals. Hens and goats Lucy said," chimed in Christina.

Beth glanced at them by the rear view mirror. They were happy and smiling so she relaxed. They hadn't been discussing their own situation and the break up of their parents' marriage and telling Sam and Lucy how unhappy they were.

"Yes of course we'll go and visit. We will give them a chance to settle in and get the farm running, and buy the hens and goats. Then we'll arrange to stay with them during the school holidays – possibly the summer half term week. How does that sound?" she asked.

"That's great," agreed James and Christina enthusiastically.

"And you'll have finished your exams by then so you'll be able to relax and enjoy a bit of a holiday, wont you?" Beth asked Annie.

"Yes. Do you think I'd be able to bring Ben too? He could have a holiday as well then. Would Aunty Verity and Uncle John mind?" Annie looked anxiously at her mother.

"I'm sure they wouldn't mind. There will probably be lots of things we can help them with – maybe planting seeds, or something like that." Beth tapered off not quite knowing what jobs would be needed at that time of year in a market garden.

"We've got our trip to Woodlands first," James remembered. "Is it all booked now? Has Aunty Verity said anything more about it?"

"Oh yes, She's given me some brochures for you to look at – you can have them when we get home. It's all booked for the first week of the Easter holiday," Beth replied.

As soon as they arrived home Beth gave the leaflets to James and Christina who took them into the front room to read all about their holiday. Annie went straight to her room to finish some homework and ring Ben. Beth gathered up discarded school uniforms to wash ready for the next week.

Her mobile phone rang just as she turned the dial on the washing machine and she picked it up after checking who it might be. It was Dave. She answered and wandered out into the conservatory, pushing the door closed behind her.

"Hi Dave. How are you? Have you had a good day?" she asked.

"Hi to you too. I'm fine and had a good day – what about you?" he countered.

"We've just got back from Pizza Hut. Verity and I took the children there for dinner after school. Are we still ok for tomorrow night?" she asked anxiously.

"Yes of course we are, don't worry. I'm not ringing to cancel or anything. Where would you like to go? Have you any preference?" he asked.

"Well actually, could we stay here and I'll cook a meal for us. It's just that Phil and Lisa are taking the children out for a meal and I don't know where they're going. I don't want to be too nosey and ask and it hasn't come up in conversation. You know what will happen if we go out to a restaurant – they'll be there too. It's seems that's the way things turn out in life," Beth told him.

Dave laughed. "Yes I know what you mean about coincidence. It's always there to trip you up when you're not expecting it. As long as Phil doesn't want to cook a meal in your kitchen we should be alright," he joked.

It was Beth's turn to laugh. "I don't think that's very likely," she said. "I don't think he will expect to do anything else in this house ever again."

"Good. Then we're all in agreement over that," Dave said firmly. "What time would you like me to come over tomorrow night?"

"About seven would be fine. And you'll have to go by about ten because I don't think Phil will keep them out too late."

"Ok. Should I keep my jacket on and be ready to rush out of the back door in case he turns up early?" Dave was obviously in the mood for jokes.

"Yes – and I'll whisk your plate and glass away and pretend I was eating on my own," Beth joined in.

"What a scenario. It's like being a teenager again and having to keep listening in case your parents are going to come into the room," said Dave.

"I don't know what you are talking about," Beth said in a falsely posh voice. "That sort of thing never happened in our house." She paused. "Verity and I always went to our boyfriend's homes," she finished. laughing.

Dave joined her laughter and they said their goodbyes until tomorrow.

Phil drove up just before six thirty to collect the children. They all seemed to be happy enough to go with him although Christina had mentioned briefly she would prefer his new lady not to be there. Beth had reassured her by suggesting she should get to know Lisa a bit before making any judgements.

"You might like her a bit if you give her a chance," she said trying not to speak through gritted teeth.

"I might, I suppose," Christina considered for a moment. "But then I might not. She might not be my type of person. Not everyone is, are they?" she asked her mother.

Beth smiled. "No not everyone is. But sometimes we have to learn to get on with people even if we don't like them very much. And it would be nicer for your dad if you made a bit of an effort with her. Just try not to be rude and maybe ask her about herself. Most people like to talk about themselves," she advised her daughter.

"Everyone likes to talk about themselves," said James. "Sometimes it's hard to get a word in edgeways with some people."

"I hope you don't mean me," said Christina pushing him against the wall. "I don't talk too much about myself."

James laughed and pushed her back. "Of course I don't mean you, Sis. You just talk about rubbish all of the time."

Beth intervened before a full scale war broke out between her youngest children.

"Come on now. Get your coats ready to go. Your dad will be here in a minute."

She waved them off briefly and went back indoors to start preparing the meal for Dave and herself. She put some music on the stereo and hummed along with Robbie Williams.

Whilst the dinner was cooking she ran upstairs to brush her hair, apply some makeup and make sure she looked reasonably presentable. Satisfied in the mirror that all was as well as it could be with her appearance, she went back downstairs to wait for Dave's arrival.

Right on the dot of seven he rang the doorbell. As soon as the front door was closed behind him he pulled Beth towards him and kissed her firmly and insistently for several minutes.

When Beth drew back for air, she felt her eyes sparkling and her mouth tingling.

"I've been looking forward to that all day," Dave told her, stepping towards her to start again.

"Mmmm so have I," Beth agreed. "But come on, let's go and eat first. Well, not first, but...you know what I mean." She turned and walked quickly into the kitchen.

"First?" Dave picked up on her statement. "What can you mean, first? First before what – that's what I want to know?"

Beth picked up a glass of wine and put it into his hand. "Don't start teasing me' she told him. Her cheeks were slightly flushed from the heat of the moment. She hoped he would think it was the heat from the cooking.

"You sit here and I'll dish up. There, I told you at Christmas I am not in the habit of putting the food out for people to help themselves. I'm so used to piling it on to plates and handing it out. I'm just not very sophisticated, I suppose," she handed Dave his meal.

Dave smiled. "Do you think I act like that all the time?" he asked. "When I go home at night to my empty house, I use serving dishes for my dinner? You've got to be joking. Some nights it comes out of a takeaway dish and if I do cook it is straight from saucepan to plate. I was just trying to impress you, that's all."

"I know," said Beth sitting down with her dinner. "I'm just being silly. It seems strange you sitting here instead of my family. I just need to get used to it."

"How are you getting used to full time work?" asked Dave.

"Oh it's Ok. I'm getting to know the people at work better, which is nice. They didn't seem to bother much with me when I worked part time but more of them have stopped to speak to me this week. And I've been invited out to a skittles evening next week. I won't go, of course, but it was nice to be asked."

"Why won't you go?" Dave asked, looking at her across the table. "I would have thought it would be nice to go out and mix socially with your work colleagues."

"Well, I suppose so. But they are all taking their partners so it's not just work people. And I would have to leave the children or get my parents to come over. It's just too difficult."

"I'll come with you if you need a partner," Dave offered.

Beth looked at him. "I know. And I'd love that more than anything. It would be great to take you along and for you to meet them. But I don't want to do that yet. I need to give the children time to come to terms with Lisa's appearance into their lives. Then they can get to know you."

"But don't forget I'll be moving away at the end of this month," he reminded Beth gently.

Beth put her knife and fork down on the plate. She looked at the remains of her meal for a few seconds and then up at Dave.

"I know. I think it's really sunk in these last couple of days. It's just not fair, we've only just found each other again and now you're going to move." She got up and went to stand by the sink.

Dave laid his cutlery down and stood up. He caught hold of Beth's hands and pulled her towards him.

"I know it's hard and I wish you could come with me. I know you can't because of your children. But I've been thinking about this for the last few days too. Don't forget – we are still on the rebound. Maybe our relationship needs a bit of time out. I don't want you to rush from a long term marriage into something that's not going to last with me. It's Ok – I'm not having second thoughts about us," he read Beth's mind as her face gave away the thoughts rushing through her brain.

"I just think we should take it steady for a while," he continued. "You must get used to your new situation. See if you miss me when I've been gone a while. Maybe you should go out a bit with your work colleagues. I'll get settled in my new job and come and visit you for a couple of weekends. Then we can see whether we are just latching on to each other because we're suddenly on our own and in the right place at the right time."

Beth let his words sink in. It seemed to her he was trying to let her down gently and tell her that he didn't want to see her any more. A juddering sigh went through her. She pulled away from him.

"Are you saying you want to finish this now?," she asked, her voice shaking a little from the suppressed emotion.

"No of course not. I'm just saying that we should let each other have a bit of a breathing space. I don't want you to regret anything. I'm probably putting this badly, I know that most men do. I'd like to go on seeing you now until I move. Then, as I said, I'll come back for a couple of weekends during the next month or two, and maybe you could get away to visit me for a while. Then, when we are more sorted with our exes, jobs and lives, we will know if our relationship will work on a long term basis." Dave looked deep into her eyes and added, "Because that's what I would actually like – a long term relationship with you."

Relief at these words washed over Beth immediately. 'Phew', she thought to herself. She knew that her feelings for Dave were separate to those she'd had for Phil. But she could also see the sense in his words that they should 'cool it' for a while and get their lives on track before re-committing to someone else.

"Ok. I see your point," she agreed. "But it's going to be difficult. You've been such a rock for me during the past few weeks. It's felt that we were in this together – us against them. That probably sounds silly to you, but it's helped me a lot."

Dave pulled her back into his arms and stroked her hair. "I'll still be here for you. Well, not here – but at the end of a phone. I haven't seen you all this week have I? But we've still talked on the phone and we'll be able to do that when I've moved. We can still share our problems and talk as much as you want," he tried to reassure her.

Beth stood still enjoying the sensation of his hands on her hair for a few minutes. Then she took a deep breath and stepped backwards.

"Ok, I understand. So, when do you actually move? Have you got a date yet?" she asked.

"Yes, I am starting my new job on February 3rd. That's a Monday. So I'm going to Barnstaple this week to find a flat. I've got three appointments on Wednesday, so hopefully one of them will be alright. I'd like to move during the weekend before I start my job so the last day of January will probably be my final day here."

Beth listened to the dates he mentioned and realised that it was less than four weeks away.

"Shall we see each other as much as possible while we can?" she asked looking up into his eyes.

"Yes of course. But don't forget, that depends on your domestic arrangements, not mine," he reminded her, kissing her nose.

"I know. I'll try and get out as much as I can without anyone getting suspicious. You see, it's still like we are teenagers as you said earlier," she remarked trying to lift the atmosphere back to it's earlier high.

"Do you want to finish the food or shall we take the wine in the other room?" she asked.

"Take the wine," advised Dave.

They settled themselves on the sofa with the wine bottle on the coffee table in front.

Beth glanced at the clock to see how much time they had. It was nearly nine o'clock.

"Oh where has the time gone?" she asked in dismay. Dave followed her gaze and placed his glass back on the table before pulling her across his lap. 'Come on, we haven't much time. Let's get some action, my beautiful wench," he said just before his mouth landed on hers.

The next hour passed just as quickly as the previous few but far more enjoyably for both of them. When they noticed the time had somehow reached ten minutes past ten they both drew apart and straightened their clothes. Dave stood up ready to leave.

"Will I see you this week do you think?" he asked.

"I'll try. But you're away for a couple of days, aren't you?"

"Yes, I'll be staying overnight on Wednesday so any other evening will be fine. Just let me know. Don't forget to put the glasses and plates away, will you?" he reminded her.

"No I won't. I'll do it as soon as you've gone," she said.

"Come on then, cheer up my lovely Beth. Of course, I used to call you Lizzie didn't I? And I remember Verity loved to call you Lizzy Dripping!" He was trying to make her laugh.

"Yes. It was great when I got everyone to call me Beth – although Verity did still call me that name when she wanted to wind me up. Luckily when we moved here she managed to grow up a bit and we didn't have so many childish rows." Beth reminisced.

"Ok. I'll ring you tomorrow and then we'll arrange what night is best next week. Don't worry about what we've talked about. I love being with you and I don't want to lose that. I just want to make sure we can make it more permanent some day. Do you agree?" he asked.

"Oh yes, of course I do. And I do see the sense in what you're saying. We both need to get our lives sorted out before we make any new commitments. It's going to be difficult enough anyway, mostly because of my children."

"We'll be ok – you wait and see. Now get yourself off to bed when the children get home and we'll talk again tomorrow." Dave kissed her again and then walked into the hallway. As they opened the door they saw the flashing lights of Phil's car driving onto the front.

"Oh no, quick, they're back," said Beth slamming the door shut. "You really will have to go out the back. Where did you park your car?" she asked.

"It's ok – I left it further down the road so as not to compromise you!" Dave said as he moved quickly to the back door. "Don't worry – just get these plates away before they come in. I'll make a swift exit without anyone seeing me."

Beth watched him run out of the back door and then snatched up the plates quickly. She opened the dishwasher and rammed them in with the cutlery, putting it on to rinse.

She then ran into the front room and grabbed the wine bottle and glasses. She stuffed them quickly into the cupboard in the hallway before opening the front door. The children pushed their way inside, only James stopping to wave as his dad reversed off the drive.

"What's up?"' asked Beth seeing the expressions on the girls' faces. "What's happened? Did you not have a good time?"

"No we didn't!" stormed Christina, wrenching her coat off and chucking it over the bannister rail. "That Lisa is a right cow! I don't understand why dad likes her at all,"

"She's not that bad," Annie tried to calm her sister. "But I don't think we are ever going to get on very well with her," she added, said to her mother. "She just doesn't have a clue how we feel."

"Come in the front room and tell me all about it," soothed Beth with her arm around Christina.

"Well, she doesn't like animals very much and she didn't want to go to the restaurant that we always go with Dad. We had to go to a Chinese that she likes and she didn't care that I don't like Chinese food very much. She said I could eat something else off the menu. Well, all I could have was an omelette and it was disgusting. And there was no pudding. So we had to go to an ice cream shop so we could all have some pudding. Well, all of us except Lisa who couldn't eat any as she was watching her weight."

"It wasn't a very good evening," agreed Annie. "She doesn't seem to ant to make much effort to get to know us and she spent most of the time talking to Dad about people and things we didn't know about. I thought it was very rude of her and Dad didn't do anything to change the subject or get us to join in. We just talked about school a bit and James told Dad about his football game tomorrow, but that was about it."

"Yes, Dad said he would come and watch some of it. I've told him where we're playing tomorrow and he's going to try and get there, at least for the second half," said James.

"Oh well that's good then," agreed Beth. She looked at her daughters who didn't seem very impressed with their father's half promise.

"Maybe it will get better soon. Perhaps when she knows you more she will be able to talk to you," Beth said.

"But she doesn't want to talk to us so how can she get to know us?" Christina's logic asked.

"I don't know. But you have your dad to yourselves when he comes over in the evenings – perhaps you can ask him what she would like to talk about. Find out what music she likes or if she has a hobby or something," suggested Beth.

"Why don't you ask Dad?" asked Christina.

"Oh, I don't know if that's a good idea. He might think I was interfering," was Beth's immediate reaction.

"No he won't, why should he?" Christina asked innocently.

Beth glanced at Annie who said, 'I'll ask Dad, Christina. It's not fair to ask Mum to do it. I'll have a word with him when he comes over one day this week. Then maybe next time we go out with them both, we can find something to talk about that she'll be interested in."

"Well done Annie," said Beth, pleased again with the maturity her elder daughter was displaying.

"Right, I think it's bedtime now. James has an early start in the morning and you'll want to go to the sanctuary, won't you Christina?"

They made their way upstairs while Beth plumped cushions and checked all the doors and windows were locked. It wasn't until she was brushing her teeth that she remembered the bottle of wine and glasses still residing in the cupboard under the stairs. Oh well, she'd have to move them in the morning before they were found. What would the children think – that she was a secret drinker on the verge of becoming an alcoholic?

As she got into bed she received a text message from Dave:

Got away ok. Hope you got cleared up. Night sleep well with happy thoughts. All my love, Dave xx

She sent a quick reply:

Night you too. Love Beth xx

As she snuggled down under the duvet in the middle of the bed she tried to keep happy thoughts in her mind before drifting off to sleep.

Chapter Sixteen

--ooOoo--

*A*s Beth was driving back from the sanctuary the next morning, having dropped Christina off to spend the day with the animals, her phone bleeped to announce a message had been received. She picked up the phone as the next set of traffic lights were on red and pressed to read the message. It was from Verity. A brief message asking, **'can I come over?'**

Beth glanced at the lights which were still on red and quickly typed **'yes come now.'**

As she drove off when the lights turned green, she wondered why her sister's message sounded so urgent. They didn't usually see each other on a Sunday so it was an unusual request.

Beth went straight into the kitchen when she arrived home and put the kettle on ready for her sister's arrival. James had been collected for his football match and Annie was still upstairs, judging by the sound of music filtering through the ceiling.

Beth went into the front room to clear up and as she was pulling back the curtains she saw her sister's car arrive outside.

She went to open the front door and Verity almost ran inside.

"Hi Beth. Sorry about this. I just need someone to talk to. John won't listen and I don't want to upset the kids," she gabbled at Beth, giving her a quick kiss on the cheek.

"Ok – what's the matter? Come into the kitchen and we'll have a coffee and you can tell me what's wrong," Beth led her through and went to make the drinks.

"Oh, I don't know. I expect it's just last minute nerves but I'm getting quite worried about moving away. I know I wanted to do it but now it all seems so real, I don't know if I want to move away from

195

you, mum and dad. And my friends too. And the children's friends. It all seems so final – as if something's ending. I just can't seem to be excited any more. I tried to talk to John about it last night but he just pooh-poohed it as last minute nerves. And

that's what I keep telling myself it is, but it doesn't make the feelings go away,"

Beth sat opposite her sister and looked at her over the rim of her coffee cup as she took a sip of the hot liquid.

"You do still want to go though, don't you?" she asked.

'Well, yes, I think so. That's the problem. I can't get that feeling of starting a new adventure that I have had up until now. It's worrying me that we are making a big mistake. The others are all really excited and don't seem to have any problems with moving away from all the people they know. For Sam and Lucy, it is all the people they have ever known in their lives." Verity said solemnly.

"I think it's only natural that you have some doubts. I am sure I would. In fact I know I would. It's a bit like my life which has changed so much during the past few months. I know my change in lifestyle was thrust upon me so I had the shock to deal with as well, but it's still coping with something new and different. You must know in your heart, and in your head, that you made this decision after winning the money and being in a position to be able to change your life. Maybe you've rushed into it a bit quick, but that's because you were all so enthusiastic and wanted to do this. Perhaps you are just having second thoughts because you're not able to move as quickly as you hoped to and so things have slowed down a bit. It's given you some time to think."

Verity nodded thoughtfully and sipped her drink. "Yes, I see what you mean. I think I just got a bit panickey this morning. We were having breakfast and the kids were talking about their plans when we move. It all began to seem so much more real. I looked at John and I could see he was excited too. Of course, it means he can leave his job which he is over the moon about. But I quite like my job and the people there. I'm going to miss them. Also, I won't have any work friends on the farm – just John. Do you think we'll be able to work together, 24–7?" she asked anxiously.

"Of course you will. And you will meet new people who will become friends when you move. You'll have to make sure that you join in the village events and make the effort to talk to people. You'll have no problem with that as you're so friendly and outgoing. Sam and Lucy will soon make friends too, at school, and you'll meet the parents. I think John will be the one who could become more isolated and you may have to help him to get to know people. Perhaps he will have to become one of these men who goes to the pub for a

drink every night?' she tried to make her sister laugh.

Beth could see that her sister was beginning to calm down and relax. "Does John know you've come over here?" she asked.

"Yes, I said I was coming over to talk to you for a while. I think he understands that I need to get this off my chest and that he can't really help me. He desperately doesn't want me to change my mind about going," Verity said.

"You're not going to do that are you?" Beth asked.

"No. Of course not. Well, I don't think so." Verity sat deep in thought for a few minutes and Beth kept quiet. Eventually she said, "No, I still want to go. I am looking forward to it in

many ways. It will be lovely to live in the countryside, have a bigger house with land, be able to give the children things that they want and also be our own bosses. Of course there are worries and problems, which everyone has anyway. Our biggest will be to make sure we can make a living for ourselves. But we've worked out figures for the worst case scenario, and they seem to be alright."

"Good. So your biggest worry is leaving me and mum and dad?" Beth said.

"Yes. I'm going to miss you all so much. I know we don't see each other every day but we know we're there for each other. Like this morning. I knew I would be able to come round here and talk to you like this. What am I going to do in Cornwall when I need you?," Verity asked plaintively.

"Oh come on Sis, you're a big girl now. You know I'm always here at the end of the phone and we will all come and visit you regularly. But I think you will be so busy with your market garden, or farm, that you won't have time to think about needing to talk like this. You're going to become a farmer's wife and they are supposed to be the capable ones. People will come to you for advice!" Beth smiled encouragingly at her younger sister.

Verity laughed. "I hope you're right," she said.

"Of course I'm right – I'm your older sister. I know everything and I'm always right," Beth teased her.

"Huh, you think you do – just like you always thought you did when we were younger," retorted Verity regaining some of her spirit. "Do you remember when we went on that holiday and you met a boy called Davy? You thought you were right about him, didn't you? You thought you were going to meet him again when we went home, but you didn't, did you? I remember you were convinced you would marry him!"

Beth looked startled and asked Verity what had made her suddenly remember that incident.

"It was because we were packing up some photograph albums yesterday and I came across some pictures of the three of us. We had built a huge sandcastle and Davy bought some flags to put on the top. I must say, it looked pretty impressive in the photograph. Did we do it for a competition, can you remember?"

Beth stood up to put her cup on the sink in order to hide her burning cheeks. Why had Verity suddenly brought Dave into the conversation? Obviously she had no idea that Beth had met up with him again. It was just a coincidence. But it didn't prevent Beth from feeling guilty as if she had been caught out in a misdemeanour.

"Yes I remember the sandcastle but I don't think it was for a competition. I think we were just building it for ourselves," she mumbled into the washing up bowl just loud enough for Verity to hear.

With a conscious effort, Beth then turned round with a bright smile plastered to her lips.

"Right then. Do you feel better now?" she asked her sister brightly. "Have you fought off the misgivings?"

Verity got to her feet. "Yes, I have. And thanks Beth, you are a great sister. I'll go now and reassure John that we are still moving. He's starting on the garage today and he will want to go to the tip with all the rubbish we keep finding. It's amazing how much stuff you accumulate over the years. We're trying to be discerning and only keep the things we really feel passionate about. Unfortunately that includes most of the school work, paintings and models that Sam and Lucy have ever made since they were born. I think we could open an art gallery or museum with all their work."

"I'd be the same. I'm just hoping that we don't have to move from here. It would probably be a year's work just to sort everything out in the loft, the garage and under the stairs," As she said that, Beth suddenly remembered the empty bottle of wine and glasses that were still closeted in the hall cupboard. She must get them out when Verity went and before Annie came downstairs.

However, as they went into the hallway Annie came running down the stairs.

"Oh hello Aunty Verity. I didn't know you were here," she said.

"Hi Annie. Yes, I just came for a quick chat with your mum. Are you Ok? Doing homework or revision up there?" Verity asked.

"Yes I've just finished. I'm going over to Ben's for a bit, is that alright?" she asked her mother.

"That's fine. Let me know when you're coming back. James will be dropped off after his football match but I have to go and fetch Christina about five o'clock. We'll have dinner when I get back. Have you got your phone with you?" she asked as Annie slipped into her jacket and prepared to leave.

"Yes I've got it here all charged up and ready to go," Annie showed her phone to her mother as proof. "'Bye Aunty Verity, say Hi to Sam and Lucy. See you later mum. I'll ring you if I'm going to be later than, say, three o'clock."

"Bye love, take care," said Verity as Beth waved her daughter off down the garden path.

"So it's quite serious with this Ben then?" asked Verity.

"Oh yes, but they're only young. I don't expect it to last but he is a nice boy and if they want to spend time together, neither Phil nor I have any objections. His parents seem nice to Annie too. They often feed her if she's there at meal times, as I do for Ben too," Beth told her.

"I've got all this to come I suppose," Verity said. "Oh, I know what I meant to say. I'm sending off the last of the payment for the kids' holiday at Easter. James and Christina definitely still want to go don't they – only there's no refund once I've sent off the final cheque."

"Oh yes. They're both really looking forward to it. Counting the days!" Beth assured her sister. "I wanted to ask whether we get a list of clothes they'll need, or do we just send what we think they'll want?"

"They mostly just need outdoor sports clothes with plenty of underwear for changes. Also a swimming costume and nightwear. I think there are washing facilities but I can't see any of them using a washing machine or tumble drier, can you?"

"No, not at all." agreed Beth laughing."I've only just got Annie trained with the washing machine and that's just because I've had to because of my full time work."

"Are you enjoying it?" Verity asked, turning back and looking directly at her sister. "I mean, do you resent having to do it because of Phil leaving?"

Beth grinned. "Oh don't spare my feelings, Sis," she said. "No, seriously, of course I mind having to make unwanted changes to my life but I'm prepared to work full time if I can stay in this house with the children."

"Might you have to move then?'" asked Verity.

"Well Phil has hinted that he needs some money in order to buy a place for him and her to live in but I understand that Lisa and… her husband…are selling their house so they might have enough for the deposit. If so, hopefully we can stay here. But I still need to earn enough to pay the mortgage. Phil and I have not sorted our finances out as yet, but I'm sure once he's paying expenses for another house he will want to cut down his payments here."

"Yes but he still has to give you maintenance for the children, doesn't he? Isn't that until they are eighteen?"

"I think so. I'm hoping we can sort it out amicably without having to involve solicitors or the CSA. But it's difficult when he wants money to provide a home for himself and Lisa, but he still has to remember he has three children to pay for."

"Well if you need to talk about anything to me, please do. You've been a great shoulder for me to cry on today and I feel lots better now. Thanks Beth, you're a great sister," Verity hugged her sister tightly.

Beth returned the hug feeling slightly emotional. They had discussed so many things in a short space of time that she didn't quite know where her thoughts were going. Usually with Verity they stuck to everyday topics of conversation and emotions and feelings were not mentioned.

"You get yourself home and give John a hand in the garage. A job seems halved when there are two of you working," quoted Beth.

After Verity had driven away Beth turned back wearily into the house. Talking with Verity seemed to have drained her and she felt like going upstairs, getting under the duvet and going to sleep for the rest of the day. But she couldn't give in. She had three children to look after. Even though they weren't babies, they still needed her to be there and provide meals, clothes and all the other requirements necessary from a mother. Perhaps she'd ring Dave and have a chat with him for a few minutes. The house was empty so they wouldn't be disturbed.

She rang his number but he didn't answer and she didn't bother to leave a message on his answerphone. He would see by his missed calls that she had rung, and maybe he would call her back soon.

In the kitchen, Beth turned the radio on to blot out the silence and began to prepare vegetables for their meal. Her thoughts ran over the talk she'd had with Verity. Obviously Verity was only having a mild change of heart about moving and seemed to have recovered quite quickly after their chat. She'd be back home now, helping John and laughing with him over things they found from their past that had been stored away in the garage.

Beth wondered how she would feel if she had to go through all the things that held memories for her and Phil. Old photograph albums, birthday and anniversary cards, letters they had written to each other, presents and memorabilia from holidays. It would be very strange looking through and deciding who was to keep what. At present, Phil had only taken his clothes, books, records and a few tools from the shed. She supposed eventually he would want to share everything out.

As she was emptying the vegetable peelings into the bin, her phone rang. he grabbed a tea towel to dry her hands and picked up the phone. It was Dave.

"Hi Dave. Sorry to bother you. I just rang on a spur of the moment. Can you talk?"

"Yes of course I can talk. What's the matter, you sound a bit troubled? Did anyone see me leave last night?" he asked.

"Oh no, it's alright. You made a good, clean getaway and I managed to get the plates in the dishwasher. I just had a problem with the bottle of wine and glasses which I had to shove in the cupboards under the stairs. And I've just remembered they're still there. I'll have to get them out."

Dave laughed. "What would anyone think if they went to get a pair of shoes and found your empty bottle with TWO glasses?"

Beth laughed too and sat down on a chair, glad to be able to relax for a few minutes.

"They'd probably think I was either turning into a raging alcoholic or had ecome completely forgetful," she said.

"Or maybe both," responded Dave. "Anyway, what did you ring me for? Not that you have to ring me for anything in particular of course. But I just thought you had."

"Yes," said Beth trying to get her head round what he'd just said. "I did ring you for something. But it was just to talk really, because my sister has been here this morning. She's got herself in a bit of a state about moving away from mum, dad and me. I had to talk some sense in to her – which actually didn't take long so I think she was sorting herself out anyway."

"It probably helped though, talking to someone," said Dave. "But has it got you upset? Her moving away. Is that why you rang me?"

"No, not really. Of course I am sad she's moving but it's not that. Selfishly, it's more to do with my own life. I think I just got a bit panickey about coping by myself. Life just seems to be going ahead regardless of whether I can cope or not," she said laughing slightly at her own words.

"It's not selfish to worry about whether you can cope or not. Especially when you have other people relying on you, like your children. You are going through a very stressful time, Beth. And whether you like it or not, you are coping with it. You've got yourself a full time job to enable you to manage the finances and from what you've told me, you are sorting out your household routine to adapt. The children all seem to be settling down, again from what you've told me, and your parents are helping as much as they can. So in a short space of time, I would say you are definitely coping," he finished.

Beth took a deep breath as his words filtered into her brain. "Wow," she said. "That sounds like a different person you're talking about, but I suppose it must be me."

"Of course it's you," Dave laughed softly down the phone. "That's why I'm so glad we've met again. I want to get to know so much more about you,"

"But you're moving too," Beth almost wailed at him. "How can we get to know each other again if we live at opposite ends of the country?"

"Well I know, that's the question," agreed Dave. "But we discussed this yesterday. We don't have to rush into anything. Like I said, we are both on the rebound and have lots of things to sort out. Let's just take it steady and get to know each other again. Then we can sort out the logistics of how we can be together."

Beth sighed. "Yes I know you're right," she said. "It's just when I get this panickey feeling I don't want you to move away. It's like I'll be on my own again. I know we can talk on the phone and see each other occasionally, but it's not the same."

"That's probably how your sister feels too," Dave reminded her. "But you've reassured her, haven't you?"

"Yes, I suppose so," Beth said trying to compare the two situations. "I know you're right and I can't do anything different at the moment as I have the children to consider. I'll try and cope better with it and not keep bothering you. Sorry," she finished.

"You don't have to be sorry," Dave said firmly. "Please Beth, don't ever be sorry for letting me share problems and worries with you. That's what I want to do. Let me help you as much as I can."

"Thanks Dave. That's a great help. Perhaps now I feel like Verity did after our talk. It's great knowing there is someone on your side who you can talk to and who will help. My friend Amanda is the same for me. We've always helped each other with difficult situations, ever since we met in the maternity ward having our babies. But I don't think Amanda quite understands my situation any more because her marriage is so good and stable. They would absolutely never have any problems or split up, because they are such good friends, as well as being husband and wife," Beth explained.

"Even so, I'm glad you have a true friend who you can turn to as well as me," Dave said. Beth was glad he didn't feel put out by her telling him about the friendship between Amanda and herself. Some men would be jealous and try to interfere with their closeness.

"I'm just waiting for a couple to come and view the house. Otherwise I'd offer to meet up with you. But they didn't give me an exact time, just before five o'clock. They sounded quite keen so I don't want to miss them," Dave explained.

"No of course not. Don't worry. I've got plenty to do here getting ready for next week," Beth said quickly. "I wasn't ringing you to bother you and arrange to meet up, or anything, just to tell you what happened this morning."

"That's Ok Beth, you aren't bothering me – honestly. I couldn't answer the phone because I was tidying the shed before these people arrived and I'd left the mobile indoors," he explained. "I'll always ring you back if you don't get through to me straight away."

"Thanks Dave. You're great – and I'm so pleased we've met again. It's made such a difference to my life. I'll let you go now anyway, and finish your tidying. I'll ring you later this evening, if that's Ok?"

"Yes of course it is. I'll look forward to it. I'll let you know if these people are interested in buying my house. Take care and talk later," Dave finished.

"Bye," said Beth closing her phone.

The phone immediately rang again. "Hi Mum," said Annie. "Ben's parents have asked me to stay for dinner with them tonight. Is that alright – do you mind? I said I'd ring you first,"

Beth smiled and told Annie that it was fine but to make sure Ben brought her home by nine o'clock. After Annie reassured Beth that this was the plan, she put the mobile phone back on the table and finished preparing for dinner – which was now for three.

Just after two o'clock James arrived home from his football match. He was full of the three 'goals' he had saved and it wasn't until he had showered, changed his clothes and was tucking into a large ham sandwich that he told Beth that his father had not shown up at the match as he had promised.

Beth tried not to show her feelings as James divulged this piece of information. She glanced at her son to see if he was upset. He happened to look up from his plate at that second and she saw his eyes were bright with unshed tears.

"Oh James," she said putting her arms around her son's shoulders and sitting on the chair next to him. "I'm so sorry. Maybe something happened to prevent him from getting there. He definitely knew where the match was being played?" she asked.

"Oh yes, he knew. I told him and he's been there before. So he did know."

"Well, maybe there is some reason why he couldn't get there.

Perhaps he'll ring later. If not, you can ask him tomorrow when he comes in after work. There's probably a reasonable explanation," she tried to comfort James.

James just shrugged his shoulders, brushed the sleeve of his sweatshirt across his eyes and began to tuck into his sandwich again.

Beth stood up as she didn't want to fuss him too much and make a lot of his father's non-appearance. She continued with the ironing that she'd started just before James

arrived home. As she pressed the iron down hard on one of Christina's school shirts, she imagined Phil's face and pushed down harder.

'Stupid man,' she thought to herself. 'Stupid, stupid man upsetting his own children.'

When James had finished his snack he went upstairs to play computer games. Beth finished the ironing and put the clothes away in each bedroom. James was engrossed with his game while she was in his bedroom and she didn't bother to interrupt him. He seemed to have got over his disappointment and was munching Maltesers from a packet washed down with a can of coke.

"I've got to go and get Christina at five o'clock and Annie is staying to tea with Ben. Do you want to stay here or come with me?" was all she said to him.

"I'll stay here please. You won't be long will you?" James barely looked up from his screen.

"No, I'll only be gone about half an hour. Then we'll have dinner when we get back," Beth told him.

"Ok," was the only response she received.

Beth went back downstairs and made herself a cup of tea and took it into the front room. She sat back in a chair and closed her eyes. The next thing she knew was James was shaking her and saying in a panic-stricken voice, "Mum, mum, wake up, please wake up."

She opened her eyes and groaned slightly as her neck complained about the way she had lain asleep. She sat up and rubbed her shoulders, twisting her head to relieve the ache in her neck.

"What's the time?" she asked James. "How long have I been asleep?"

"It's alright, it's only half past four. But I came downstairs to get a drink and it looked like you were…well, dead," James told her.

Beth swallowed the laugh that formed in her throat as she realised that James had gone quite white with the shock of thinking he had found his mother dead on the sofa.

"Oh James, no I'm quite alright. Just a bit tired," she said pulling him down next to her.

"Yes I can see that now," he said. "But it didn't look like you were asleep, lying all twisted like that, with your head turned downwards."

"Yes, it must have been a shock. I just sat down to have a cup of tea and then I must have fallen asleep straight away. My neck hurts quite badly from lying in that position. I suppose I must be pretty tired," she said to herself wonderingly.

"Shall I make you another cup of tea?" James surprised her with the question.

"Oh yes please, darling. That would be lovely. Do you know how to?" she asked innocently.

"You boil the kettle, put the tea bag in the cup and pour water on it. Then put in some milk," James said as he stood up. "You know I'm not a baby Mum, I do know some things."

"I know you do, James. It's just that you don't drink tea and you've never made me a cup before so I didn't know if you knew how to make it."

"We actually have made tea and coffee in community studies at school," he informed her. "So I have made hot drinks before."

Beth sat back and her son went into the kitchen to make his mother a cup of tea – the first ever. She hoped it wouldn't be too milky or too strong but determined to drink it whatever – just to give him encouragement.

As she was waiting, Beth tried to think why she was so tired. She'd not been working full time for long enough to be worn out by the extra hours. Was it the emotional morning she'd had with Verity and then Dave on the phone? Or was it the build up of the past few months and all the shocks she had received?

She shook her head trying to clear it from the jumbled thoughts which were racing about trying to get organised in order to provide her with an answer.

James brought in the tea and sat down beside her again. They didn't talk much, Beth sipped her drink, which was surprisingly just right, and James was quiet and sat still for once. As the hands of the clock ticked around to five o'clock, Beth finished her tea and stood up.

"I'll have to go and fetch Christina now – do you want to come?" she asked.

"No, I'll stay here and finish my game upstairs," said James. "That's if you'll be alright driving?" he asked anxiously, remembering the sight of his mother earlier.

"I'll be fine. Don't you worry. I was only asleep – probably just tired after my first week of proper work," she said.

"Oh yes, of course. It probably has tired you out after always having stayed at home most of the day," said James.

Beth smiled to herself as she realised James probably thought she sat and watched daytime television all day while he was at school. As he raced up the stairs she suddenly remembered the items still hidden under the stairs. She glanced upwards, but James was already locked back into his space game. She opened the cupboard door and took out the

empty wine bottle and the two glasses she had flung in there the previous night. She carried them into the kitchen and put the glasses straight into the dishwasher and the wine bottle outside into the recycle box.

Beth sighed with relief as the evidence was taken away from the scene of the crime. But was it a crime? Surely not. She was a free agent and if she wanted to spend some time with a friend, that was allowed. But Dave was still a secret from everyone, apart from Amanda. And he had to stay that way for a while. She didn't want to upset her children, or her parents and sister, as they all seemed to have enough to contend with at the moment.

It just meant she had to suffer Dave's impending departure to the wilds of Barnstaple on her own. She could only talk about it to Amanda and, as she had said earlier to Dave, her friend did not quite understand what Beth was going through. Although she was obviously sympathetic and would help Beth all she could, there was still the 'I haven't been there' factor to be taken into consideration.

Chapter Seventeen

--ooOoo--

*T*he next few weeks sped past quickly as much as Beth tried to slow them down. She managed to spend a few hours with Dave each week, sandwiched in between her job and looking after the children. She also spent an evening with her work colleagues at the bowling alley in an attempt to build a bit of a social life for herself after Dave had left.

During the last week of January, which had turned extremely wintry with several snow storms, Beth spent two evenings with him. Phil took the children out for a meal again with Lisa and Verity had organised a party for all her children's friends prior to their departure. The first event was again a natural disaster with Annie, James and Christina arriving home disgruntled and unhappy. Luckily Phil had asked the children where they would like to eat

after the last debacle but it turned out that Lisa was not keen on pizza!

The party was a far greater success as Verity had booked a hall, a disco and a large buffet with plenty of soft drinks. There were about seventy young teenagers with half a dozen adults to ensure they all stuck to good behaviour whilst still enjoying themselves.

Beth spent both evenings at Dave's house helping him to pack up all his belongings. This took quite a long time as Dave kept sharing all his memories with her as he unearthed some of his long-forgotten treasures.

Dave's last weekend arrived and Beth arranged for her parents to have the children to stay overnight. She said she had met up with an old school friend who now lived in the next town and she'd arranged to stay overnight with her as they caught up on their gossip. This arrangement seemed to satisfy everyone, apart from Annie who wouldn't be able to see Ben that night. However, Beth promised a treat for them both the following week with some tickets for the cinema to see the latest film which had just been released. They had hinted for some time.

Jack and Vera collected the children at six o'clock on Saturday evening and promised to make sure James was at the football ground in good time the next morning, weather permitting, and that Christina would be taken to the animal sanctuary – again weather permitting.

After she had waved them off, Beth went quickly upstairs and ran a bath. She wanted Dave to remember her as sensual and desirable, wearing her most sexy clothes and smothered in a haze of expensive perfume. She slipped into a tight black skirt that came a good three inches above her knee and a new top she'd bought during her lunch hour last week. She'd had her hair trimmed during another lunch hour and as she sprayed on the

Chanel No 5 and looked at herself in the mirror, she thought she scrubbed up quite well – considering.

With all the rushing about and worry during the past few weeks, she seemed to have lost about half a stone. 'Not that I'd recommend this diet' she thought to herself looking in the mirror. 'But I suppose there's always a plus side to most things'.

She carried her black high heeled shoes and handbag downstairs and grabbed her warm coat. They were risking a restaurant tonight and were meeting in half an hour. Just time for a quick drink, she thought. But stopped herself. Better not, I'm driving she told herself. She walked about downstairs picking up magazines and glasses to take into the kitchen. She felt excited and keyed up about the evening ahead. It was like dating again although she could barely remember what that was like in her teenage years. She'd met Phil by the time she was twenty so most of her dates prior to him had been trips to the cinema and bowling alley. Teenagers don't usually go in for dinner dates!

She wandered restlessly about, glancing at the clock every few seconds, until suddenly her mobile rang. Her heart missed a beat! Surely Dave wasn't ringing to cancel? She grabbed the phone out of her handbag and looked at the screen. Phew! It was Amanda.

"Hi Amanda. How are you?" she asked in relief.

"Hi to you too. Just giving you a quick ring to make a date for next week. We don't seem to have seen each other much recently. How's Tuesday for you?" Amanda asked.

"What time of day do you mean – don't forget I'm a working girl now."

"Oh I know. Why don't you come over with the kids and have some tea here on Tuesday when you've finished your daily toil. Brian's away on business this week so we can have a nice girlie chat."

"Oh that would be lovely Amanda. I really need to talk to you, I've got so much to tell you," Beth said.

"Great – can't wait to hear it all. Come when you're all ready and I'll cook a big casserole and an apple crumble. I know everyone will eat that!"

"Ok sounds good. It will be nice not to have to rush home from work and start cooking – thanks. We'll probably be there just before six if that's alright?"

"Yes, that's fine. Look forward to seeing you then. Have a nice evening Beth and take care," Amanda finished the call.

Beth was grateful that her friend had been thoughtful enough to ask her over. Amanda knew that Dave was leaving this weekend and that Beth would feel lonely. She could look forward to having a lovely chat with Amanda and telling her all the events of the past few weeks. And, of course, discuss the possibilities for the future and whether her relationship with Dave could survive the distance.

Again she got the feeling of going back in time to days when she'd laugh and giggle with her girlfriends, discussing makeup, boys and how unreasonable parents could be. She looked at the clock again and realised it was time to leave.

The drive to the restaurant was uneventful and Beth was relieved that the stars were shining brightly in the sky which probably meant there would not be a snowfall during the night.

Dave was already there waiting for her and came straight towards her car as she got out. He kissed her briefly on the mouth and stepped back to look at her.

"My you look lovely tonight – good enough to eat," he laughed at her.

"Oh you," she pushed him playfully. "Let's go in and eat here before we get frozen to each other in this cold air."

"Can't think of anyone I'd rather be frozen to than you," he claimed gallantly.

"Oh you're full of it tonight, aren't you?" she said trying to keep the mood light.

"Just tonight? Why, I'm always full of it," he countered.

They were shown to their table and ordered a starter and main course with a bottle of red wine.

"Well, here we are then," said Dave sitting back in his chair. "This is it Beth. Our last evening together."

Beth looked at him. "What are you trying to say Dave?" she asked anxiously. "Do you mean we'll never be together again? I didn't think that's what we both wanted."

"Oh no, I'm sorry, love," Dave pulled her hands towards him over the table. "I didn't mean it like that. I just meant it's the end of this era. This is our last secret night together. When we meet again, which we will soon I promise, it won't be a secret any more. You'll have to tell your children and your parents and then it will all come out in the open and obviously our exes will find out too."

Beth sighed with relief. How many scares was she having to endure tonight?

"Oh I see what you mean. I hadn't thought of it like that. Yes, I suppose next time we meet it won't be a secret any more. I just hope the children can cope with it all. Especially the fact that you are Lisa's husband. They didn't enjoy their meal last week with Phil and Lisa, even though they got to choose where they went. I don't know what's going to happen to break the ice. Have you got any ideas?" she suddenly asked Dave.

Dave grimaced. "Me? I don't think I'm qualified to talk about Lisa's good points," he said. "I suppose she likes shopping and pampering herself. She enjoys her job, but that's quite boring to talk about with anyone who isn't in the same line of work. But apart from that, she's not got any hobbies or interests. She doesn't like a particular type of music, she doesn't read books, only magazines, and hasn't got a favourite television programme. It's difficult to know what she does with her time, really," he said thinking about the past.

"Well never mind. Maybe it will get sorted out and they'll start to get along before we have to tell them all about us. Let's just enjoy this evening," she said as their starters arrived.

After the meal they both drove their cars to Dave's house. As they entered the hallway, which was piled high with boxes ready for the move the next day, the reality hit Beth.

"Oh Dave. I'm going to miss you so much," she started to say as they went into the kitchen.

"Now come on, stop there," said Dave putting his fingers over her mouth. "Like you said, let's just enjoy this evening and worry about the future tomorrow. We'll go straight upstairs as the bedroom is the only civilised room left in this house. Here's a bottle of wine and some glasses, you go on up and I'll be there in a few minutes."

Beth took the bottle and glasses and made her way upstairs, carefully treading past all the paraphernalia piled up the side of the staircase. She put the wine and glasses down on the bedside table and slipped out of her coat. Dave must have left the heating on while they were out as it was very warm upstairs.

She tidied her hair in front of the mirror and checked her lipstick. Suddenly the door burst open and Dave arrived in the bedroom wearing only a black shiny thong and a red bow tie!

"What do you think?" he asked twirling around in front of her. "I thought I'd give you something to remember me by."

"Oh Dave – you're mad," she cried entering into the spirit and kicking her shoes off. They danced around the room until they were exhausted and collapsed on the bed.

When they had stopped laughing and got their breath back, Dave sat up and opened the wine. They drank several mouthfuls quickly, looking straight into each other's eyes, before placing the half empty glasses back down again. Dave leant forward and pulled off her top as she unzipped her skirt. They fell back on the pillows together and wriggled out of the rest of their clothes.

Beth woke up suddenly and opened her eyes. She looked around the room and then remembered where she was. She turned her head and saw that Dave was still sound asleep, lying on his back with his arms above his head. She stared at his face for several

minutes, trying to memorise every line and contour. She must remember to take a photo of him on her phone camera to remind herself of his good looks when he'd gone.

After a few minutes she realised she was getting cold. She glanced across the bedroom and noticed Dave's striped dressing gown hanging on the back of the door.

Beth slipped carefully out of bed and put it on. She opened the bedroom door quietly and pulled it closed behind her. Creeping as quietly as she could, she went downstairs to the kitchen. There wouldn't be much here as Dave would have been running down the food.

She opened the fridge and found a packet of croissants, the remains of a tub of butter and half a bottle of milk. She took them out of the fridge and arranged the croissants in the oven directly on the racks. They'd only take a couple of minutes to warm up.

She found a jar of instant coffee and took a couple of mugs out of the box in which they'd already been packed. When she was ready to go back upstairs, she thought she had quite a good offering for him.

She pushed the door open and manoeuvred her way inside with the mugs and croissants. Dave stirred as she put it all down on the bedside table next to him.

"What's up, what's going on." he muttered as he opened one eye and Beth grinned down at him.

"Hey you, I've got you some breakfast. And I found this dressing gown on the back of the door – were you going to forget it?"

"What dressing gown?" Dave asked as he grabbed Beth and pulled her down on top of him. "Oh this old thing – well to be honest I'd be glad to get rid of it."

Beth pulled herself back up and looked down at it. 'Well I don't think it's so bad, and it's lovely and warm."

"You have it then – to remember me by," said Dave.

"Ok I will then." Beth said as she sniffed the sleeve of the garment. "It smells of your aftershave anyway, so you must have used it recently."

"Yes I suppose so, probably put it on after I'd had a shower. Now what's for breakfast then?"

They snuggled in to bed together and enjoyed the croissants and coffee.

"I bought these specially for you, yesterday at the supermarket." Dave said as he looked at her knowingly. "I thought we'd both be hungry in the morning."

"Mmmm, I love croissants. Something about them is so luxurious and decadent," Beth told him.

They sipped their coffee and talked intermittently, both keeping off the subject of Dave's departure. But eventually they could put it off no longer. Beth kissed him briefly on the mouth and got out of bed to get dressed. As she was putting on her clothes she said: 'You can tell I'm not used to this. I should have brought something else to wear this morning. Fancy going home in my night-before clothes!"

Dave laughed. "Well don't start getting used to it now I'm going away," he warned.

They pulled the sheets off the bed and rammed them into a black bin liner Dave had placed ready.

"I'll dismantle the bed later and finish off the packing tonight ready for the removal men tomorrow morning. They're coming really early to get a good start," he told Beth.

"Where are you sleeping tonight then?" she asked.

"I'm going to kip on the settee downstairs in my sleeping bag. Then I've only got to roll over and get up when the men get here tomorrow."

They went downstairs to wash out the mugs and Beth looked at her mobile.

"I'll have to go soon," she said mournfully, looking over at Dave.

"I know you will. But come on, let's not get ourselves too sad. Try to remember this is a beginning, not an ending. I'm going away to work for a while and you are going to sort your life out. We can't live together at the moment but we will do some time in the future. Ring me whenever you want and if I can't answer straight away, I will call you back as soon as I can. Send me text messages and emails and even write letters to me. You've got my address haven't you?" he spoke firmly to try and give Beth some comfort.

Beth managed a watery smile.

"Yes I know all those things but it doesn't stop me feeling sad because I won't see you for a while now. I will try to be brave and I know we've both got things to get on with, especially with our work. I just hope you don't meet someone else in Barnstaple," she said.

"Why would I meet someone else? I'm not looking for anyone else, I'm quite happy with you, thanks very much," he tried to joke but Beth wasn't responding.

Dave took her in his arms and hugged her tight.

"Come on now, don't be despondent. I know you've had a lot of shocks in the last few weeks, but I won't let you down, I promise.

I'm not going to meet anyone else in Barnstaple, I shall be too busy working and talking to you on the phone. We'll arrange to meet again as soon as we can. I love you Beth, and I'm not going to ruin that," he said earnestly looking into her eyes.

Beth blushed and said, "Oh I love you too, Dave. I really do."

They held each other for several moments before kissing passionately. When they stopped to draw breath Beth managed to smile at Dave.

"I'll have to go now. I promised to go and watch James in the second half of his football match and then mum's cooking lunch for us all. Thanks for a lovely evening and night. Oh, I want to take a photo of you to put on my phone so I can see you whenever I want. Hang on a minute, where's my bag?"

She hunted around and found her handbag on a chair pushed under the kitchen table. She took out the phone and selected the camera. Dave smiled obligingly for her and she snapped him several times.

"I'll take one of you too," he said. "Hang on I'll just get my phone." He went into the hallway and pulled it out of his jacket. He glanced at the screen and noticed there were several messages and missed calls. As he walked back into the kitchen he flipped through them. They were all from Lisa.

He supposed they were going to be about the house sale but as he read them he realised that she wanted to see him to talk. He decided not to say anything to Beth who was looking at him anxiously as he was reading the messages.

"Just work stuff," he told her as he lifted the phone up to take her photograph. "Now come on,. I want a nice smile please."

She did as he asked but felt a niggle of doubt about the mobile messages he had been reading. Surely he wouldn't have received work messages on a Saturday night or Sunday morning?

Dave took four photos of her and then put the phone back down on the table. Beth picked up her bag and took the car keys out.

"Maybe it's best if I just go out of the front door on my own rather than you wave me off," she suggested.

Dave looked slightly startled. "Oh well, if that's what you want. I don't mind waving you off you know," he said.

"No but I don't know if I want you to," Beth said. "I don't think I want you to see me in floods of tears,"

"Well I certainly don't want to see you driving in floods of tears. Can't you have the tears either now before you leave, or when you get there?"

Beth managed a small laugh.

"Yes you're right. I can't be driving in that state. I'll save the tears until tonight when I'm alone in bed," she said.

Dave opened the front door and stood aside for Beth to go outside into the cold January air. They kissed again slowly and softly before Beth broke away to walk to her car. She waved as she got in to the driver's seat and again as she drove away.

As she drove towards her home she struggled to keep her composure. She must stay strong and brave. It's not as if they were splitting up or would never see each other again. This was just a temporary blip. Time would move on quickly and one day they would be together again forever.

Somehow Beth got through the rest of the day. When she arrived home she changed her clothes and raced off to watch James for the last thirty minutes in his football match. She waited in the car until he was ready and drove them to her parents' house.

They enjoyed a pleasant lunch and Verity popped over during the afternoon with the latest news on her move.

At half past four Beth stood up and said they would have to go and collect Christina. Vera pressed a portion of the food saved from lunch time into Beth's hands so she wouldn't have to cook anything for Christina and gave her a hug.

"You look a bit peaky," she observed. "Is this full time work getting you down or are you not feeling too well?"

Beth hugged her back. "No I'm alright mum. Don't worry. Work is fine and I'm getting used to it now. The people there are nice so it's not difficult being there. I just have to make sure I'm organised with shopping, cooking and washing. Annie helps a lot and so do the other two, so we've doing Ok."

Her mother didn't look too reassured but let it go. Jack hugged Annie and then Beth. "Keep strong," he whispered in her ear. "We're always here to help you, don't forget that."

Beth blinked back the tears at the words from her gruff father. He wasn't given to emotional speeches so she really appreciated his support.

They collected Christina from the animal sanctuary and she regaled them with a long story about the two hedgehogs that had been rescued the previous night. Beth told them all that they'd be going to Amanda's for tea on Tuesday which went down well.

"Oh great – I love Amanda's dinners," James said. Annie nudged him and he caught Beth's eye in the rear view mirror. "But of course not as much as Mum's cooking," he countered.

Beth laughed to herself. You just couldn't stop children saying what they thought.

Later that evening, while Annie was reading in her room and the younger two were getting ready for bed, Beth glanced at her phone. She had received a message which she'd obviously missed earlier. It was from Dave.

Just spoken to Lisa. She wants money from house asap. They have seen a house they want to buy. Thought you should know. Ring me when you can. Love Dave xxxx

Beth realised that was probably the message Dave had received on his phone when she was stood in his kitchen. She appreciated his not saying anything then. hat time was their special goodbye moments and she was glad they had not been spoilt by this news.

She sent him a message and said she'd ring him soon.

Beth went into the front room and flopped down into a chair. She didn't know why she felt shocked. Phil had said they were looking for a house. But for them to actually find one and move in – what did this mean? Would the children want to go and stay with them? No, surely not. They didn't like Lisa. But they might put up with her to be with their dad.

She didn't actually want to stop them from spending time with their dad, but she did feel bereft when they were with him. The four of them had formed a special life and probably a closer relationship together without a father figure. Beth didn't want that spoiling. He had already spoilt the nuclear family image they had had before.

After a while Beth went upstairs to make sure the younger two were in bed and that Annie was also settled for the night. She then went into her bedroom and shut the door. She rang Dave.

"What do you think of this news then?" she asked him.

"We knew they were going to get a house together, and the people buying this house are very eager to move in, so there's nothing stopping them. Just be glad you haven't got to move out of your house, Beth," advised Dave.

"Yes you're right," agreed Beth. "I am glad, very glad. It's just that every time something happens I think it's going to be for the worst. My marriage, which I thought was Ok, breaks down, I meet you then I lose you, Verity wins money and is moving away. These things don't help me to see the brighter side of life."

Dave laughed. "If your marriage hadn't broken down we wouldn't have met again anyway and Verity is going to have a wonderful new life even though she has to move away. You'll be able to visit her and it might mean you can come and see me too, in Barnstaple," he suggested.

"Oh yes I had already thought of that too," she agreed. "Sorry Dave, I don't mean to be depressing. I'm sure everything will work out for all of us – sometime."

"You sound very Gone with the Wind – tomorrow is another day, darling," Dave said in a posh actor's voice.

Beth giggled as he wanted her to.

"Right then Beth. Time to go to bed now. Don't be having your floods of tears now, as you said earlier. Just remember the good time we had yesterday. Will you promise me?" Dave asked her.

Beth swallowed and replied, "Yes Dave. I won't cry now, I promise. I hope your move goes well tomorrow and don't let the removal men forget anything will you?"

"Talking about forgetting things – you forgot to take my dressing gown. I'll keep it for now and let you have it next time we meet," Dave said.

"Oh yes. That's a shame, cos it smelt nicely of you and would have been something to cuddle up to at night."

"I tell you what. I'll put it in a black plastic bin liner, with an extra squirt of aftershave, and drop it off at your house before I leave tomorrow. Where shall I put it?" he asked.

"Oh thanks. Put it by the side gate next to the bins," Beth said.

"It won't get taken with the rubbish will it?" Dave asked. "Not that I'm bothered as I was going to get rid of it anyway. But if you want it, make sure you take it in tomorrow when you get home from work."

"I will, don't worry," Beth assured him.

"But I do worry because you're such a scatterbrain," Dave said.

"I'm not a scatterbrain," she tried to assure him.

"Well, what about that time you came out of the newsagents and tried to get into the wrong car?" he reminded her.

"Yes, but I was distracted and it was the same colour," she stuck up for herself.

"Hmm, not a mistake I would make though," Dave said.

"Well Ok, maybe that's a woman-thing. But I soon realised my mistake. My mother actually did get into the wrong car once outside the supermarket. It was another silver car but the man had a dog in the back that started barking and she started to ask why Dad had a dog in the car. She was so embarrassed and got out of the car so quickly. Luckily the man thought it was hilarious – well until his wife got back anyway!"

"At least I know where you get it from then." Dave said laughing. "Anyway, I'm off to bed now and I'll call you tomorrow when I'm settled in my new flat. Have a good day at work and try to keep busy, won't you?"

"Yes, thanks Dave. I'm sorry to be such a pain. I will try to get on with things and the time will go quickly."

"Night Beth. Love you lots," Dave said.

"Night to you too Dave. I love you," Beth said back.

She put her phone down and covered her eyes with her hands. No, she wasn't going to cry. Like Dave said, this was a beginning. But it was a beginning of their separation. No, I'm still not going to cry. It was the beginning of her being strong and brave. She had the children to consider and couldn't just give in.

Beth stood up and went into the en suite where she splashed her face with cold water.

She went back downstairs and made herself a cup of hot chocolate and took a couple of ginger biscuits out of the tin. he sat down in the front room and tried to relax. Peace and quietness enveloped her as she ate her biscuits and sipped the drink. When the hands of the clock arrived at half past ten, she made her way wearily upstairs and got into bed.

She lay there thinking about the wonderful time she had enjoyed with Dave yesterday evening, and mostly yesterday night. She was sure they would have many other wonderful times together, but not just yet. She must remember that Annie, James and Christina were her priority and she couldn't just abandon them to go and live in Barnstaple. And she wouldn't want to anyway. If she hoped and prayed enough then a solution would be found and that's the hope she had to cling on to. In the meantime, she would get on with her life and look forward to speaking to Dave on the phone and the occasional meetings that they might be able to arrange.

Of course: there was the week the younger two children would be at Woodfields. Maybe she could sort out a couple of nights away then. Annie would be in the middle of revision work and could just as easily do that at her grand-parents' house.

On this thought, Beth fell asleep only to dream about her children running out of various shops and getting into Lisa's car by mistake.

Chapter Eighteen

--ooOoo--

*B*eth gritted her teeth as she fought her way through the supermarket throng. She hated having to do the weekly shop at the same time as everyone else. In the old days, before she was a single, working mum, she'd go during the early afternoon when most people were either at work or collecting young children from school.

It was the week before half term in the middle of February, and everyone seemed to be out to restock their fridges and freezer following the 0cold spell of the past fortnight. The snow showers had now given way to a slushy mess in the streets but it didn't feel any warmer.

At last Beth reached the front of the queue and unloaded her shopping on to the conveyer belt. She glanced out of the window and noticed pale sunlight trying to flicker through the clouds. Maybe the day would turn out better than it had promised earlier that morning. Beth had been up since six thirty. She'd woken about an hour earlier and couldn't get back to sleep again. After sixty long minutes of tossing and turning and thumping her pillow,

she'd given up and gone downstairs in her dressing gown for a cup of tea.

She'd been tempted to wear Dave's old dressing gown that she'd salvaged from the black bin liner where he'd left it, but didn't want the children to catch her in it as they'd be bound to ask questions.

It was a shame to wake so early on a Saturday morning when she didn't have to jump out of the bed as soon as the alarm clock tolled at ten minutes past seven. Why could she be so awake on a Saturday morning but during the week it was such an effort to get out of bed on time?

As Beth drove home from the supermarket she thought ahead to the following week. As Verity had not moved south yet, Vera and Jack had obviously not gone to stay with them. This meant they could keep an eye on Beth's children while she continued to work all week.

Verity and John were now hoping to move at the end of March just at the beginning of the Easter holiday break. The four children would also be at Woodfields that week so that would seem to make it easier. Beth planned to work for the first week of the Easter holidays, as only Annie would be at home and she was quite capable of looking after herself. She would most probably be revising all day for her exams which started in May. Beth had arranged to take three days holiday during the second week as her parents were more than happy to help out for the other two days. Still, there was half term to get through first.

Beth had arranged for Jack and Vera to have the two younger children at their house for three days, again leaving Annie an empty house in which to study. Amanda was taking

James and Christina, along with her own two children, to the local theme park one day and Verity had offered to have Annie, James and Christina at her house on the Friday. So Beth could leave for work each day with a clear mind and conscience knowing that all three children were catered for.

Beth arrived home to an empty house as Phil had taken James to a football match, Christina was still at the animal sanctuary and Annie was at her dancing class.

She carried the bags into the kitchen and began to put everything away. Her mind wandered back to the conversation with Dave last night on the phone.

He had hoped to be making a trip back next week in order to sign the final papers for the house sale. But the couple buying the house had a last minute problem with their mortgage and the trip had been delayed for a couple of weeks. Beth was very disappointed as she had been looking forward to seeing him again. They had only managed to communicate via phone calls and text messages during the past few weeks.

She'd tried to hide her disappointment as much as possible during their conversation as she didn't want him to think she was relying on him too much. But she'd had a few quiet tears in bed before she'd finally managed to get to sleep.

Beth made herself a cup of tea and went to sit in the front room. She had just under an hour before she'd have to go and collect Christina and Annie. She sighed at the prospect of another evening in playing board games or watching rubbish television. It wasn't as though she'd had a fantastic social life with Phil, but at least she'd had another adult to talk to and share things with. It seemed to make all the difference. Obviously she loved her children and spending time with them, but sometimes…it just seemed there was something she was missing out on.

Her thoughts travelled back to Dave. She tried to work out if she'd feel better or worse if she didn't have him to think about. It was nice to feel there was someone there for you – someone who cared enough to find out what you'd been doing all day and whether you were alright. Vera rang her most days, but that wasn't quite the same. Your parents always worried about you, whatever your circumstances.

If Dave was not around, well on the horizon anyway, she'd have no-one apart from her sister and friends to talk to. And however much they might sympathise with her circumstances, they had their own lives to get on with and, especially at weekends, no-one really wanted to be bothered with anyone apart from their own families.

She'd been the same. Three years ago one of her friends had lost her husband. He'd been killed in a car crash. At first, everyone rallied round and visited Jennifer as much as possible. Beth and their other friends had invited her to dinners, barbecues, parties and any other social gathering. But after a while, she was expected to move on and manage her own life. Luckily she already had a good job with a publishing company and both her children were heavily involved with martial arts, which kept them busy most weekends and

evenings. Jennifer had coped tremendously well and not been a burden to any of her friends.

It was only now that Beth realised how lonely and sad she must have been. Much more so than her because Jennifer's husband had died. He hadn't chosen to leave his family and go to live with another woman. Beth made a mental note to ring Jennifer and find out how she was getting on. Perhaps they could meet up one evening and cheer each other up

a bit. She took her cup out to the kitchen, collected her coat and car keys and set off to collect her two daughters.

The half term week flew past just as Beth had planned. She felt slightly put out that she couldn't share it with her children but decided to take them out for a special treat the following Saturday.

She rang Verity and asked if they'd like to join her and take all the children to the water park in the next town. She'd seen it advertised on posters scattered around the shops and thought it would be nice for them all to spend some time together. But Verity had already planned to take her children shopping for new school shoes. So Beth decided to go anyway and asked Annie if she'd like to bring Ben along too.

The five of them set off mid-morning and Beth drove sedately along the motorway separating the two towns. The water park was situated on the edge of an industrial estate and was easy to find. Beth changed into her swimming costume and listened to Annie and Christina chattering away in the next cubicles. She was pleased that James got on with Ben and they had developed an easy relationship together, almost like brothers. They put their clothes into lockers and Beth took their bags and her book with her.

The first person that Beth saw as they went through into the swimming pool area, was Jennifer.

"I don't believe it!" she exclaimed in delight. "I was only thinking of you the other day and wondering how you were getting on."

They hugged each other delightedly and stood back to take stock.

"How are you? I'm so sorry I haven't rung you for ages. Are you here with the children?" asked Beth looking around.

"Yes, they're here somewhere. I'm fine. But how are you? I heard that you and Phil had split up? Is that right?" asked Jennifer.

"Er, yes. That's right. He's living with someone else now. A woman called Lisa. It happened last year. It was just out of the blue for me. I didn't realise anything was wrong – typical situation where the wife is always the last to know," Beth tried to smile.

"Oh I'm so sorry. What a shock for you. It must have been awful. How did you cope?" asked Jennifer.

Beth looked at Jennifer's worried face and marvelled how kind and generous she could be. Her husband had died and been taken from her, but she still had sympathy for Beth's somewhat different situation.

"Shall we sit down somewhere?" asked Beth. "I think all the kids have gone off to swim now."

"Ok. We're sat over there, do you want to join us?" asked Jennifer.

"That would be nice. Who else is you with?" asked Beth as they walked over to half a dozen sun loungers pushed together.

"Oh I'm with Liam," Jennifer blushed slightly and stopped. She turned and faced Beth. "I've met someone, you see. I've only know him about six months, but we get on really well. Come on, let me introduce you."

A large and friendly-looking man with thick black hair and wearing a pair of colourfully striped bathing trunks looked up as they arrived.

"I'm back Liam. And look, I've just met a friend who I've not seen for ages. Her name is Beth. And this is Liam," Jennifer carried out the introductions.

"Hi Beth. Pleased to meet you. It's always nice to meet Jenny's friends especially those who helped her through the bad time she's been through."

Beth shook the outstretched hand and smiled at him.

"Hi Liam. I'm pleased to meet you too. I'm glad that Jennifer has met someone nice. We were all so devastated when Graham died. And of course it was awful for Jennifer and the children."

"Hey, come and sit over here Beth," called Jennifer from her lounger. "Let's catch up on all the gossip and you can tell me what's been happening to you."

Beth sat down between the two of them and pushed her bag and book under the lounger. She looked around to try and catch sight of her children and saw that they had met up with Jennifer's two boys. She waved at Annie who nodded to acknowledge she'd seen her.

"Well, what's been going on in your life then Beth?" asked Jennifer.

So Beth told her about discovering the note in Phil's suit pocket and the events which followed. She didn't feel confident enough to talk about her meeting up with Dave again and skipped through the bits that he was involved in.

"Wow. I can't believe Phil and you have separated," said Jennifer wide-eyed. "I always thought you were really solid together. But it happens to lots of people doesn't it? Did you know that Simon and Faye have also split up?" She mentioned two of their other friends.

"Really! No, I didn't know. I'm not in touch with anyone much now. I think we've all grown apart a bit with our children growing older. I know I'm always rushing about somewhere taking them places. Sometimes I just feel like a taxi service," Beth said ruefully.

"I know what you mean," agreed Liam joining in the conversation. "I'm constantly driving my three kids to parties or their friends' houses. I've got two boys and a girl," he explained to Beth.

"Oh right. Do they live with you?" she asked.

"Yes, although they go to their mum's every other weekend from Friday to Sunday night. She's in another relationship and has had two more children with her new bloke. When we first broke up she took our children with her.

But I didn't want them living with another man as their father, so I managed to persuade her to let them live with me. I've got quite a big house and garden and it's nearer to their schools and friends. The children were quite happy with the arrangement, so I think I've been lucky," he said.

"Oh yes you are lucky – as a man, because not many men get their children to live with them full time after a break up," agreed Beth. "I don't think Phil would want ours to live full time with him and Lisa, or at least he's never said he would," she said thoughtfully.

"Has this Lisa got children?" asked Jennifer.

"No she hasn't. And she doesn't get on very well with my kids," said Beth. "I think she's a bit selfish and obsessed with herself, from what I can gather. Yes, I know, I'm going to be biased anyway," she admitted to them both.

"She sounds like a right bitch," said Jennifer grinning wickedly. "A typical wicked step-mother."

"Oh no, she's never going to be a step-mother," Beth said immediately. "I'm their only mother, and that's how it's going to stay."

Jennifer raised her eyebrows and looked at Beth. "I sense a few tricky emotions rising here. Are you jealous of her? Do you want Phil back?," she asked.

Beth paused before answering. She remembered Jennifer's way of getting straight to the point and always asking awkward questions.

"No," she said firmly. "I don't want him back. Not now he's left me and slept with another woman. I definitely wouldn't take him back."

"Good. That's settled then. And what about meeting someone else? Are you up for it?' Jennifer persisted.

Beth smiled slightly. "Yes, I suppose so," was all she said.

Jennifer opened her mouth for another question but Liam put his hand on her arm.

"Give the poor girl a break, Jen," he said. "Don't give her your Spanish Inquisition. Remember, you've only just met up again and I'm sure you don't want to frighten her off."

Jennifer laughed and pinched his arm. "Ok I get it. Sorry Beth, didn't mean to be quizzing you like that. I just wanted to find out if you were moving on with your life. I didn't mean to offend you."

Beth smiled at her friend. "You haven't offended me at all Jennifer. It's just still early days with me. I haven't decided what I'm going to do yet. It's been hard enough just getting work and the kids sorted out. You know what it's like when you're a mum, you always come last on the list."

"Oh I know. And I'm so lucky to have had a second chance with meeting Liam. I know when I lost Graham I thought my life had come to an end too. Of course, like you say, you have to go on for the children's sake. And you and Faye and Melissa were really good friends and helped me no end. I suppose it was nearly two years before I could even think about meeting anyone else. And Liam just popped up then. We bumped into each other, literally, in the supermarket. We were both rushing round buying food and trying to get back home in time for our kids, and we crashed trolleys. After we'd apologise and untangled ourselves, we got chatting. I don't even remember what we talked about. But we arranged to meet the next day for a coffee in the restaurant and just went from there. It just goes to show that you can meet your soul mate anywhere." She blew a kiss to Liam as she finished.

Beth felt the love between the two of them and was suddenly envious that they could be together. Her longing for Dave became quite intense and she was tempted to tell them about him. But no, she must keep him quiet for a bit longer. The children should know first.

She rummaged around in her bag and took out a bottle of water. "I'll just have a quick drink and then go for a bit of a swim," she said.

"We'll look after your stuff. And tell your kids to come over here and join us when they want a break," said Jennifer.

The afternoon passed quickly and when they'd all had enough swimming they agreed to go across the road to the pizza restaurant and continue the party.

Driving home later, Beth realised she'd enjoyed herself tremendously. Jennifer and Liam had been great and not allowed her to feel left out. Liam had taken the kids off to the huge water flume and Jennifer and Beth had continued catching up on their news. When they'd parted in the restaurant car park, they'd exchanged mobile phone numbers and email addresses to keep in touch.

James and Christina were pleased to have met up with Stephen and Andrew again and they'd all got on well with Liam's children. Beth thought she'd arrange a barbecue later in the year and invite them all over. She'd contact Faye and Melissa too and try and get the old gang together.

When Dave rang her that evening, she told him about the day. He was pleased she'd met up with an old friend and enjoyed herself. He knew she'd been disappointed that he wouldn't be travelling back this week. However, they had definitely set a date for the exchange of contracts for his house and he'd be back in two weeks time.

"Oh that's great Dave. I really can't wait to see you again," Beth enthused.

"Me too, Beth," he agreed. "You'll have to make arrangements so that we can spend a bit of time together. Will you be able to do that, do you think? Or have you had any more thoughts about telling your children about us yet?"

"Not yet Dave. I'm sorry but they're still not happy about Phil and Lisa. I don't want them to have to cope with anything else at the moment. Annie is studying like mad for her exams and needs to keep focused. James is still feeling put out because Phil doesn't get to many of his football matches. Christina is finding it hard to come to terms with her dad not living here any more. I just want to wait for the right time. I'm sorry."

"I said you don't have to say sorry to me, Beth. It's Ok, really. I can wait. I just thought it would be easier for you if you didn't have to lie or make unnecessary arrangements for them. That's all."

"Sor--- no not that word','she giggled as she nearly apologised again. "Anyway, I still can't wait to see you. I feel as if I'm about sixteen years old myself – waiting to see my boyfriend."

"That's Ok, I hope I am your boyfriend," Dave said.

Beth giggled again. "It just seems so strange at our time of life to have boy or girlfriends."

"And what time of life do you call this?" he laughed. "We're not in our dotage yet are we?'

"No, no, of course not. I only feel about twenty five anyway, apart from the bad days when I'm ninety five."

They finished their conversation and Beth agreed to make arrangements for the Friday and Saturday of the following week when Dave would be staying in his house for the last time. She needed to rack her brains as to why she could stay out overnight at least once that week.

She could always be staying with the long lost school friend who she used before. But then she'd have to take time off work to make it more viable. She didn't think she'd be lucky enough to get all three children off to sleep-overs on the same night, either! Perhaps she could have a work 'do' that entailed staying overnight somewhere. She'd been on a couple of socials with her work colleagues, once bowling and once for a meal at a local restaurant. But these would not mean staying out overnight. What about a theatre trip to London? Could she pretend that she was going either with friends from work or maybe Amanda? No, she didn't want to involve Amanda in her shenanigans. But then, help came from an unexpected quarter.

Phil asked to speak to Beth in the kitchen that week on the Thursday evening when he was visiting the children.

"I was hoping to take the children away for a couple of nights sometime soon. Mum said she'd like to see them so I thought I'd take them there, if that's Ok with you. Lisa will be going too," he explained.

Beth's brain managed to get into gear and work quickly for once.

"Oh that's nice. How about Friday week?" she asked.

Phil looked slightly startled at her positive and immediate reaction.

"Er, yes. I suppose so. That's a bit short notice, but I'm sure we can arrange it in time. Is there any reason why you want them to go then?" he asked.

"No of course not. Why should there be?" she asked crossly, turning away from him. "Do you want to take them then?"

"Yes of course. I'll ring Mum tonight and make the arrangements. Shall I tell the kids?" he asked.

"Yes that's fine. Tell them now if you want," she said, clattering the saucepans about in the sink as she washed them.

Phil went back into the front room and told the children he'd be taking them away to visit their grandmother for a couple of nights. Annie wandered into the kitchen a few minutes later.

"I'm not really sure I want to go with Dad," she said to Beth who was now drying the saucepans. "I've got to keep revising."

Beth looked at her and realised she didn't want to go without Ben.

"It's only for a night or two and you can take some books with you to look at while you are there. Your gran hasn't seen you for quite a while now and I'm sure she'll be looking forward to your visit. She'll miss you if you don't go with Christina and James."

Annie looked down at the floor and scuffed her shoe on the tiles. "I know. I feel guilty about not going, but I don't want to go with Lisa either," she admitted.

Beth crossed the room and put an arm around her shoulders.

"I know. It's hard for you all trying to get to know another woman who's with your dad. But maybe this will be a good chance for you all to get to know each other a bit better. Your gran will see the situation and will help you too. And I know you'll miss Ben, but it's only for a couple of days. Don't forget, at Easter you'll have all that time together while the kids are away and I'm at work. Lots of time for studying!" Beth squeezed her shoulders again.

"Oh alright then Mum. But what about you? Will you be alright while we're away?"

"I'll be fine. It'll give me a chance to catch up with a friend of mine in the evening. I'll be able to go out without worrying about getting back in time for your grandparents to go home. Don't worry about me." Beth turned back to the sink to hide her slightly blushing cheeks. She really hated this lying but still thought it was for the best at present.

So the next night when Dave rang, Beth told him she'd be able to spend Friday night, all day and night Saturday and Sunday morning with him.

"That's great news. Something to really look forward to," he said.

It was hard work getting everything ready for the three children so that they could set off straight from school on Friday evening. Beth made sure they had enough clothes packed for the two days and nights they'd be away as well as clean school uniform for the following Monday morning.

She drove them to school on the Friday morning with very mixed feelings. She was going to miss them while they were away and it was the first trip they'd made to Phil's mother without her. She felt slightly left out. But she had a whole weekend to spend with Dave. That made her heart lift and her stomach contract.

She got out of the car and hugged and kissed all three of them before they went into school. James did not appreciate this too much but bore it stoically in front of his mates. They all ran off and at least the two girls remembered to turn and wave to Beth as she stood by the car.

Beth swallowed down her feelings of upset and drove quickly to work. The day passed with the usual Friday-atmosphere of anticipation of the weekend to come. Even the girls in the typing pool, who Beth secretly called the Flicky Hair Brigade, were more hyper and giggly than usual.

On the stroke of five o'clock Beth closed her computer down and picked up her bag and coat ready to leave. Just as she stood up from her chair, her boss, Allan, poked his head out of his office.

"Could you pop in here a moment please Beth," he asked. Beth inwardly groaned. Now what. She went into his office and stood by the door.

"Come in Beth," he beckoned so she sat down in the chair by his desk. "I've got a bit of a problem' he started. "Some of these accounts for the Lesteridge company have been put on the filing cabinet and forgotten. They need them completing by Monday morning so I'm coming in tomorrow to try and finish them off. I was wondering if you'd be able to come in for a couple of hours and give me a hand? Of course, you'll get some overtime pay."

Beth looked at him in horror. Why now, why this weekend?

"Er, well I do actually have plans this weekend. When would you want me to come in – tomorrow morning?" she asked.

"Yes, probably between nine and twelve. Although if they take longer, perhaps you could stay until we're done?" he asked.

Beth felt her body droop. Why this weekend when Dave was here. It just wasn't fair. Obviously the extra money would come in handy but she wanted to spend all the time with Dave that she could.

"I don't know." she began. "I've made plans to see someone. Can I just ring and see if they mind?"

"Yes of course Beth. I'm sorry I didn't mean to spring this on you, but we've only just found them. It's going to be a rush job to get them ready for Monday," said Allan.

"I'll go outside and ring Da—them and come back and let you know," she said standing up and going towards the door. "Won't be a minute." She closed the office door behind her.

"Hi Dave." she said when he answered her call. "You'll never believe it but my boss has just asked me to do some overtime tomorrow. It's the first time he's asked and I don't want to let him down. But I wanted to spend all the time at the weekend with you too. What shall I do?"

"Oh Beth, that's a shame. But of course you must do the overtime. It's Ok – I've got some things to do here anyway. And I wanted to see a mate of mine for a quick chat. We'll meet up again after you've finished work. We'll have a nice takeaway and a night in. We'll be alright at your house won't we?"

"Yes, we'll be fine at my house. But are you sure you don't mind that I have to work tomorrow? I don't have to do it, you know."

"No, I know you don't have to, but it's probably best you do. Then you'll get asked again and I know you need the money. Now, what time are you coming over here tonight? Have you finished work now?"

"Oh yes, yes. I'll be leaving in a minute and I'll come straight to your house shall I?" she asked eagerly.

"Yes that's great. Can't wait to see you again. I've missed you so much. But just drive carefully and get here safely," he said.

"Oh I will. See you in a few minutes. Bye Dave." She finished the call and went in to Allan's office to confirm she would be able to work tomorrow.

"I hope I haven 't upset too many of your arrangements," he said. "Only I thought your children were pretty busy at the weekends and it wouldn't inconvenience you too much."

"No, no, that's fine. I'll be in for nine o'clock tomorrow," she gabbled edging towards the door.

"Yes, see you then," said Allan.

Dave took her to a smart new restaurant just opened on the edge of town.

"How did you know about this place?"' she asked as they took their seats.

"Oh my mate told me about it when I rang him earlier. You know, the one I'm seeing tomorrow while you're working," he explained.

They had spent a passionate two hours on Dave's sleeping bag on the living room floor confirming how much they'd missed each other. Afterwards, feeling hungry, they'd decided to go out to eat trusting they wouldn't meet anyone else they knew.

The new restaurant was very busy when they arrived but a small table for two had been found in a handy little dark corner. Just right for secret lovers, thought Beth.

While they were waiting for the food to arrive at their table, Dave told Beth about his new job and flat. He'd filled her in with most details during their phone calls, but there were still things to tell her.

As Beth gazed at him across the table she realised just how much she'd missed him. In such a short time of knowing him, he'd become a very important part of her life.

"Come on, your turn now then. Tell me all the things you've not told me already," he said.

"There's not much to tell really. My life is pretty mundane and routine. One day much like the previous one," she said. "I tell you most things on the phone each night."

Dave laughed. "I think you're feeling a tad sorry for yourself," he observed. "Now why would that be?"

She laughed with him. "I think you're right," she agreed. "I'm a bit cross that I've got to work tomorrow. It just seems so unfair that the one weekend you're here is the time they've got some overtime for me. As my boss Allan said, I would normally be free as the children are quite busy on Saturdays."

"Never mind. I'm going to see my mate and I've got a couple of things to do in town. Then we can have a lovely quiet evening at your house and indulge ourselves as we want..." Dave promised seductively.

"Mmm, that sounds good. I don't think I can wait that long though. Shall we skip pudding?"' she asked provocatively pouting at him.

"Skip pudding? Well, for a woman to offer to do that, my luck must be changing," Dave said signalling the waiter for the bill. "Come on then, let's go and find out what you've got planned for my dessert."

They left the restaurant arm-in-arm and drove back to Dave's house without any further conversation.

Early the next morning, Beth rose stiffly from the sleeping bag and made her way into the kitchen to make some coffee. She carried the two mugs back into the living room and they sat side-by-side, backs against the settee, sipping their drinks and talking quietly.

Beth got dressed in her work clothes and set off for the office just before nine o'clock. They managed to finish the work by one o'clock and she rang Dave to let him know. However, he was just meeting with his friend so he said he'd meet her at about four o'clock at her house.

She drove home and immediately switched the heating on. The weather was still cold outside and more snow was forecast overnight. She ran a hot bath and spent nearly an hour soaking and reading her book.

She dressed in a tight black skirt and some fishnet tights she'd bought. But, after looking in the mirror, changed her mind and slipped into a comfortable warm dress she'd had for years.

Dave arrived just after four o'clock and they sat in the front room as darkness fell outside. Beth had lit some candles and put some romantic music on the CD player and they drank the bottle of wine Dave had brought with him. They ordered a takeaway meal for seven o'clock and then went to bed at eight. eth felt a happiness and desire that she'd never experienced before.

Dave was everything that she'd ever wanted or hoped for – and more. She felt so lucky to have a second chance – just as Jennifer had also said.

"I'm going to miss you even more now," Dave said stroking her hair. "I hope we can live together at some point soon."

Beth felt a warm glow inside her. "Do you really mean that?" she asked.

"Of course I do," Dave told her. "I wouldn't have said it otherwise."

Beth nodded. "I know, it's just hard to believe that it is us here, together. After all the time that has passed since we very first met – and now we're finding out just how much we mean to each other. Don't you agree?" she asked anxiously looking up at his face.

"Yes my darling Beth. I do agree. But it's up to you I'm afraid. You've got to sort out your life so that we can be together. And unfortunately I don't think that will be here. You are going to have to move to Barnstaple with me. And of course the children can come too."

Beth pulled herself up. "But how can I do that? They need to be here for their school and friends. How can I move them away?"

"I don't know. I can't answer that for you. I'm not asking you to choose between us, because I'm going to be here for you anyway. But it may mean we have to live apart for a few years yet if you're not able to move until the children are grown up. Have you thought of that?" he asked her gently.

"No not really. I've put off thinking about anything in the future too much. I've just been trying to cope with the present," she told him. "But I do know that it's my situation that needs sorting out.'"

"Beth, I'm not asking you to rush into anything or do anything you don't want to do. You know that don't you?" he asked and she nodded. "I just think we have to accept that we'll have to live apart for a while, as we've discussed before."

Beth knew this was true. She had to accept that she wouldn't be able to live with him for a few months or even possibly years. She swallowed the tears away. She didn't want to cry during the few hours they had together. She took a deep breath.

"'Come on, let's just enjoy this time together. We can worry about the future later,'" she said pulling him towards her.

Chapter Nineteen

--ooOoo--

*T*he morning that James and Christina were leaving for Woodfields dawned bright and sunny. Phil was due to collect them at ten o'clock so there was much rushing about and grabbing last minute items to pack in their rucksacks.

As Beth sat drinking a cup of coffee in the kitchen, she could just see their bags stood to attention by the front door. James and Christina were still upstairs making sure they hadn't forgotten anything that would be crucial to the enjoyment of their week away.

The last few weeks had rushed past as the weather became warmer and spring broke forth. She'd missed Dave a lot since the last few days they'd spent together but looked forward to their nightly phone call. He was very busy with his new job and seldom arrived back at his flat before eight o'clock. He also found it necessary to work most weekends, although he had managed a visit to his parents last Sunday which had been Mother's Day.

James came running downstairs and thrust a last minute CD into his rucksack.

"That's it then. I'm packed," he announced, coming into the kitchen.

"Good," smiled Beth. "I hope you have a great time. I expect it will whizz past really quickly and you'll be back here before you know it!"

"'I know. I'm really looking forward to trying some different sports like abseiling and canoeing," he told her.

Beth tried not to look too alarmed as she imagined her son and heir dangling off a mountain from a rope or becoming trapped underneath a submerged canoe in the white water rapids. But she remembered that Verity and John had assured her that all the children were very well supervised and health and safety was a priority.

Christina came into the kitchen carrying the woolly lamb she always took to bed with her.

"Do you think the others will laugh at me if I take Larry with me?" she asked anxiously.

James rolled his eyes and said, "Of course they'll laugh at you. I don't expect anyone else sleeps with a toy lamb."

Christina looked upset and turned to her mother. "What do you think? Shall I take him or leave him here?" she asked.

"Well, if Larry stays here he can look after your bedroom while you're gone. But if you think you'll miss him too much, why don't you hide him in your rucksack and just get him out if you need him?" she suggested.

Christina brightened up immediately and said she'd tuck him in a pocket of her backpack as her mother suggested.

They heard a beeping sound outside. "That must be your dad," said Beth. "Now come on, let's get your bags loaded in the car."

Both children hugged her tightly when they had loaded the car and were ready to set off.

"Now be good both of you and do everything the instructors tell you. Ring me every night from the phone booth that Aunty Verity tells me is there. You've got plenty of change in your rucksacks that I've given you."

Annie came downstairs and stood outside on the drive ready to wave her sister and brother off on their big adventure.

"Have a great time," she told them. "See you next week."

Phil got back into the driver's seat and started the engine. "I'll ring you tomorrow Annie, and perhaps we can go out for a meal," he called out of the window.

Beth glanced at her daughter who looked none too pleased at the prospect of a night out with her dad and his girlfriend. But she didn't say anything.

"Bye, see you soon. Ring me when you get there," Beth called out as the car moved out of the drive and into the road. The two of them stood waving until the car disappeared round the corner and then they went back inside the house.

"Well," said Beth as she closed the door. "It's going to seem very quiet this week. And strange," she added as she felt a few tears on their way with the realisation that her youngest children had temporarily flown the nest.

Annie smiled and put an arm around her shoulders. "Come on Mum, cheer up. They won't be gone long and you've still got me here to look after. Let me make you a nice cup of tea," she offered.

Beth smiled at her eldest daughter's thoughtfulness. "Yes I know. Sorry, just a few moments of realisation hit me. I'll be Ok. And of course, I know I've still got you to look after. Although sometimes I feel as though you are all grown up now and don't need me to look after you. That is, obviously, apart from the washing, ironing, cooking and clearing up after you of course!" she joked.

Annie laughed. "Exactly Mum. I'm not that grown up. I still need you to check up on me and make sure I clean my teeth and wash behind my ears."

"I don't think I've ever done that," said Beth. "Well, certainly not since you were babies. I trust you to clean your teeth every morning and night and whatever is behind your ears is certainly your own business."

They laughed together and took their mugs of tea into the front room where the sun was streaming through the window.

"What are your plans today then?" asked Beth.

"I'm going to Ben's at eleven to finish some homework. Then, as there is no dancing lesson today, his mum is taking us to the cinema and giving us some money for a pizza afterwards. Is that Ok with you?" she asked.

"Yes that's fine. I've got lots of things to catch up on. It's nice not to have to worry about being a taxi service for one day."

Annie smiled at her mother. She knew that she'd much really rather be taking Christina to the animal sanctuary and James to a football match. And then worrying about what to give them for tea that night.

"Will you go and see Aunty Verity or Amanda?" she asked.

"Maybe. Don't worry about me. I'll be fine. I really have got lots of things to catch up on and I'll probably get a takeaway for myself tonight. What time are you coming back after the cinema? Do you want me to come and fetch you both?"

"Oh, that would be nice. Can I ring you when we're ready? We'll go to the cinema first and then for a meal, so I don't know exactly when we'll be ready to come back."

"Yes, that's fine. I'll come and get you when you ring me. I'll just try and remember not to have a glass of wine with my takeaway."

They stood up ready to go their separate ways for the rest of the day.

Beth was indeed looking forward to having a bit of time and space to herself. She was planning to go into town to choose a new dress as she had a special meal to attend with her work colleagues the following week and she'd also be able to wear it next time Dave came back and took her out.

The chance to see Dave again happened quicker than Beth anticipated.

During their nightly phone call that evening, he told her that he was coming to stay overnight the following Wednesday as he had to meet up with an old colleague on business. He suggested that they went to an out-of-town restaurant and arranged to meet her in the car park at eight o'clock.

Having made sure that Annie was settled with Ben for the evening, Beth was looking forward to this unexpected treat. She was wearing the new dress she'd bought during her shopping trip and felt happy and confident as she stepped out of her car and spotted Dave waving to her.

"Hiya sweetheart, how are you?" Dave kissed her cheek and nuzzled her ear.

Beth laughed and squirmed as he tickled her. "Hiya yourself. I'm fine – are you?"

"Yes I am now. Had a bit of a nightmare on the motorway and the journey took about an hour longer than it should have taken. But I'm here now, that's the main thing."

"When are you meeting your friend from work?" Beth asked as they walked across the car park to the door of the restaurant.

"Tomorrow morning and then I'll have to go straight back to Barnstaple as we're having a big meeting in the office at three o'clock. So I'll have to be gone by about midday. I'm afraid we won't be able to meet again tomorrow," he apologised.

"No, no that's alright. I understand and I'm just glad we've got this evening. But I won't be able to ask you back or come to your hotel tonight as Annie is expecting me home. She thinks I've gone out for a meal with someone from work," Beth explained.

"'I know, it was short notice and we'll just have to make the most of this evening,'" Dave agreed with her.

They walked through the restaurant behind the waiter who was showing them to a table right at the back. However, as they passed a table where a couple sat holding hands, Beth realised she was looking at Phil. Phil and Lisa. She stopped short and Dave nearly cannoned into her. Lisa's back was towards them so he obviously hadn't realised who they were about to pass.

Phil looked up and half rose from his seat. "Beth" he uttered, looking guilty.

Lisa turned round and stared at Beth. She then looked behind her and noticed her husband. "Oh, Dave," she said.

Neither Beth nor Dave knew what to say as they realised this was the moment when their ex-partners would realise what had happened.

Phil looked at Dave and asked, "Who's this then Beth?"

"Er, this is Dave," she answered.

"Yes." interrupted Lisa. "This is certainly Dave. My ex-husband Dave."

Phil look astounded. "What's happening?" he asked. "Why are you two here together?"

"A very good question," agreed Lisa. "What's been happening between you two then?"

The waiter stood quietly by while this interchange took place. He then stepped forward and asked if they wanted to join this couple. Nobody spoke for a moment. The possibility of sharing a table seemed horrendous to all four of them. It was Phil who eventually broke the awkward silence.

"I think it would be a very good idea if we all sat together and sorted this out," he stated.

The waiter immediately set to and placed two more chairs around the table and signalled for more cutlery and glasses to be brought over.

Eventually Beth and Dave sat down on opposite sides of the table, next to their ex-partners. They ordered drinks to get rid of the waiter and then all looked at each other.

"Well, I think an explanation is in order, don't you?" asked Phil breaking the silence. "Why are you two here together?"

"We're old friends," began Beth. "What happened was that we met up again a few weeks ago and then realised the situation," she explained, not entirely accurately.

"Yes, that's right," agreed Dave taking up the story. "We originally met years ago when we were teenagers on holiday but then we lost touch. And then, suddenly, we met each other again. And that's when we, er, realised who we were married to and what had happened," he finished.

"So why have you come to a restaurant tonight? Are you seeing each other?" asked Lisa coming straight to the point.

Beth and Dave exchanged glances but realised there was no point lying.

"Yes we are," said Dave. "It's pure coincidence and obviously slightly embarrassing. But we didn't meet each other again until after you two had left us both. I think I need to make that quite clear to you."

The waiter came back at that moment to enquire if Beth and Dave would like to order and if the others would like to delay their meals so they could all eat together.

Beth and Dave ordered their food and Phil said they would all eat together.

Again, there was silence around the table as they digested the situation in which they all found themselves.

"So, do our children know about you and...Dave?" asked Phil.

"No, they don't yet. I haven't told them because I thought they had enough to cope with at present. They still haven't got over you leaving us, let alone that you have another...well, girlfriend," Beth told him.

Phil shuffled slightly in his seat and then attacked again. "When do you propose letting them know that you are seeing Lisa's husband?"

"Obviously I'll have to tell them soon. I wasn't keeping it a secret for any other reason than to protect them," Beth felt she needed to explain.

Phil looked cynical. "I don't know why it had to be kept from them. I suppose you've had to lie and pretend to be with someone else?" he asked.

"I hardly think you are in a position to lecture me about lying," she countered hotly. "Think of all the lies I endured before you upped and left our family home."

Phil blushed and began to bluster. "Well, that was different. I wasn't pretending to be someone I'm not."

"Yes, you were. You were pretending to be a happily married family man. That was the biggest lie," she countered immediately.

"Now, come on. Let's not get into a slanging match, at least not here in public," advised Dave. "Let's try and discuss this sensibly and maturely."

Beth smiled at him across the table. "Yes, I agree. Let's talk about what we're going to do now."

"We don't have to do anything." Phil said. "It's you who needs to put the record straight."

"Ok. I'll do that. I'll tell Annie tonight and the others when they get back from their holiday. But let me tell them, Phil."

"I will. But you only have until the weekend," he said.

Their food arrived at that moment and they all made an effort to eat. Beth's appetite had certainly deserted her in the heat of the last few moments, but she forced herself and managed to clear most of her plate. Conversation was halted whilst they ate as there was certainly no small talk to be made between the four of them.

When they'd all finished and the waiter had cleared their plates they resumed the discussion.

"Have you bought a new house or flat yet" Beth asked. "Annie said you'd been looking at properties but haven't moved into one yet."

"We're still looking at the moment. But unfortunately, Lisa didn't get as much as she thought she would from the sale of their house."

"That was because I went for a quick sale," Dave said immediately. "I just wanted to get rid of the house and move as fast as I could."

"Well, anyway, whatever the reason we are a bit short of money and can't quite afford to get the house we want. So, I might need to talk to you about our house, Beth," Phil informed her.

Beth gasped. "I thought you said it was alright for me and the kids to stay there, at least until they've all finished school. That's what you said a few weeks ago."

"I know I said that then. But in reality, like I've just said, we're a bit short so we might need to talk about the house. But not here. I'll talk to you privately – some time next week when I'm visiting the kids."

Dave tried to smile reassuringly at Beth. "Don't worry, you have to have a place for the children. No-one can put you out on the street," he said.

Phil looked annoyed at this interruption. "No-one is going to put them out on the street," his voice raised as he refuted this suggestion. "We just might have to find somewhere smaller or cheaper for them to live."

Lisa smiled cattishly as she picked up her wine glass. "We all have to make sacrifices in these situations," she said smugly.

Beth turned to her and snarled, "My children are not going to make any sacrifices at all. This situation is none of their doing. You've taken away their father, surely that's enough?"

"Lisa didn't take me away. I went because I wanted to," Phil leant forward to speak directly into Beth's face. "Don't take it out on Lisa."

"Oh, I'm not taking it out on Lisa at all. What's the point? You both know what you've done and the problems you've caused. I think you can take it out on yourselves," Beth retorted.

Dave pushed his chair back and stood up. "I think this discussion is finished. Come on Beth, we'll go now and leave them to their just desserts."

Beth picked up her handbag and stood up too. "Yes Dave, we'll go now. But I don't know why you have to be so aggressive Phil. You were the one who started having an affair and left me and the children. This situation is all your doing, not mine. I'm just trying to move on and get on with my life. I will tell the children about Dave now and it is probably best to get it out in the open. I just hope they can cope. But I don't want to have to move them out of

their home. Just remember that please – both of you."

"Well, we'll have to see. But, as I said, I'll talk to you about that next week," Phil said.

Dave and Beth walked to the reception desk and paid their bill. Beth was shaking as she walked into the car park with Dave. "Come over to my car and we'll decide what to do now," he said taking her arm.

They sat in the front seats and Dave held her hand tightly until she'd calmed down.

"I can't believe they had to be in the same restaurant as us. What are the chances of that?" she asked.

"Well, it seems all of this has been a set of coincidences. Maybe that's the last one," Dave comforted her.

"I hope you're right," she smiled at him. "I suppose it's best that we have to tell everyone now. It will be much better than sneaking around and trying not to be seen by anybody. I just hope the kids cope alright."

"Do you want me to be there when you tell them?" asked Dave. "We could go back to your house and speak to Annie now?"

Beth squeezed his hand. "No, I think it's best I tell them on my own. And then we can arrange for you to meet them. I just hope they take to you more than they have to Lisa."

"Oh I'll make sure they do," laughed Dave. "I'm a much nicer person anyway. What do you want to do now? Shall we go somewhere else for a while. It's still quite early."

Beth glanced at her watch. It was only an hour and a half since they'd come into the car park. It seemed like a life time had passed!

"Yes, let's go for a drink somewhere. I told Annie I'd be back about ten so she'll be fine."

"I'll drive and we'll leave your car here for now. We can fetch it later."

Dave buckled up his seat belt and started the car.

They found a nice pub situated next to a stream and ordered their drinks. They sat together in a sheltered corner outside, on a wooden bench seat. Dave put his arm around Beth and she snuggled in to him.

"Did your sister's house move go alright last week?" Dave asked.

"Yes, they moved on Saturday, the same day the children went to their holiday adventure camp. I think that helped Verity and John, not having to worry about the kids. She's rung me a couple of times to say they are getting sorted out and John is already working outside on the land. They plan to buy a few animals too, goats and chickens I think. Mum and Dad are planning to visit them next month, but I think they'll stay in a bed and breakfast so as not to be in their way. Verity's asked if I want to take the kids there after Annie's finished her exams and school has finished. So that'll be about the end of July."

Dave nodded. "That's great because it's not too far away from Barnstaple. So, if everyone is going to know about us – we should be able to meet without any problems."

"Of course, and you'll be able to come to the farm and meet them too. Although, you've already met Verity – but ages ago," she smiled.

"Yes I only remember her as your slightly annoying younger sister," he said.

"Well, she's not changed much – she's still my slightly annoying younger sister," Beth laughed.

They enjoyed an hour sat talking together in the garden of the pub. Twinkling fairy lights lit the pathways and in the sky a large moon shone down on them.

Eventually Beth looked at her watch and said she'd have to go. Dave took her back to the restaurant and they kissed passionately before she got into her own car and drove home. Dave wished her luck in telling Annie and told her to ring him before she went to bed.

Annie and Ben were sat on the sofa watching a DVD when Beth arrived home. She greeted them and Annie said they only had another half an hour of the film to watch.

Beth closed the door and left them to it. She went into the kitchen and took their empty pizza boxes out to the bin. She made herself a cup of tea and sat down to think.

It must have been a tremendous shock for Phil, and Lisa, to realise their ex-partners were actually seeing each other! The implications would only materialise as time went by. Surely it was the type of situation that a good television drama could centre on but no-one would believe it happened in real life!

When Annie had said her goodbyes to Ben on the doorstep, Beth called her into the kitchen.

"I've got something to tell you," she started. "Sit down for a few minutes please Annie."

"What's the matter, Mum? Has anything bad happened?" Annie asked anxiously.

"No, no, don't worry. It's nothing bad. It's just something that's happened and you need to know. I'll tell the others when they get back from their holiday."

"Come on then, tell me. Don't leave me wondering," Annie said.

"Sorry, darling. Yes, I need to tell you but I just don't know where to start really." Beth found it was more difficult than she'd thought.

"Start at the beginning, Mum. Just tell me," demanded Annie.

"Yes, sorry. Well, you know your dad is going out with Lisa? And

Lisa's ex husband is called Dave. Well, it turns out that I knew Dave years ago. I met him on holiday when I was about your age. I think I've told you before. But we lost contact. And now, we've met each other again. But, he is Lisa's husband. Or ex-husband," Beth finished looking anxiously at her daughter.

"Ok. So you've met an old boyfriend again who happens to be Lisa's husband. Or ex-husband. So what?"

"Well, it turns out we're still quite attracted to each other," Beth said.

"Oh, you mean you want to go out together again? You want him to be your boyfriend?" asked Annie.

"Er, yes. Well, I suppose it's probably already happened. You see, I have actually been seeing him a bit. Just once or twice," Beth explained.

"When have you seen him? I don't remember you saying you were meeting anyone called Dave," Annie said.

Beth blushed a bit. "Well, I've not actually told anyone yet. I didn't want to cause any problems for you and James and Christina. I thought you had enough to cope with, knowing your dad is seeing Lisa. I wanted to keep Dave quiet for a bit. Just for your sakes," she said reassuringly.

Annie nodded. "Oh, I see." She thought about this for a few minutes. "So have you seen him when you've told us you've been somewhere else?" she asked straight to the point.

Beth nodded, slightly ashamed of herself now. It didn't now seem that it had been such a good idea to keep her meetings with Dave a secret.

"Yes, I'm sorry darling. I really thought it was for the best. I didn't want to worry you with your exams coming up. I was going to tell you soon, though."

"So why are you telling me tonight?" Annie asked.

"Er, because we met your father and Lisa in a restaurant and we all had a chat together," Beth explained.

"Oh, that was tonight was it? You weren't really meeting someone from work then?" Annie seemed to be the parent asking all the awkward questions.

"Yes it was tonight. And I've come straight back home to tell you. And I shall tell James and Christina on Saturday night when they're back home. I'm not telling them on the phone, though," Beth tried to regain control of the conversation.

Annie was quiet for a few minutes and then she smiled across at her mother.

"Oh, Mum. I'm glad you're getting on with your life. It's a bit strange that he's Lisa's husband, but at least you knew him first!"

Beth hadn't thought of it from this angle and realised it was somehow comforting to her.

"Yes, that's right. You're right darling. I hadn't though of that before. I knew him first," she giggled slightly to herself. "Thanks, Annie."

"That's Ok," Annie said. "I think it's fine, Mum. But you shouldn't have been worried about telling me. I'm older than the others and know a bit more about things. I can cope better with grown up stuff, you know."

Beth smiled and put her hand across the table to her daughter. "I know you can. I was just worried about upsetting you, especially with your exams coming up. I know you've been acting very maturely since your dad…well, left. And you've been a great help and comfort to me. I'm very proud of you and I'm glad you've got a nice boyfriend in Ben. He's a good lad," she finished.

"Yes he is nice. Sometimes I think he is too nice, though. Do you know what he's offered to do?" she asked.

"No, what's that?"

"He's helping Melissa with her science revision. When I went round to his house yesterday, she was already there. And she wouldn't go until I said we were going out. She's a real pain and keeps flirting with him. But he doesn't seem to notice and just keeps talking nicely to her. When I asked him about her, he just said he felt sorry for her because she was struggling with the last project we did in the Chemistry syllabus and that's why he offered to help her. But I think she's planned it and pretending not to understand just so she can go round to his house. Do you think that might be right?"

Beth considered Annie's dilemma. "Well, you can't really know if someone is struggling with a subject or not. Only the exam results will tell. But it's only a few weeks until you take the exams anyway and after that she won't have an excuse to go to Ben's house. And remember, it's you he's going out with – regardless of who he helps with their revision."

"Yeah, you're right. I shouldn't get so paranoid. But Melissa is just a bit annoying, especially if she's trying to get off with Ben when she knows he's going out with me."

"Oh, you'll find plenty of girls like that in the world," advised Beth. "You have to get used to unscrupulous people, both men and women – remember all's fair in love and war. Have you used that quote in English?"

"Yes, it's Shakespeare isn't it?"

"So, just try to be nice and act cool. Don't let Ben know you're getting jealous or paranoid. Men don't like that sort of thing. But also, don't be used as a doormat or be taken for granted. Try and distance yourself a bit from the situation and enjoy the time you and Ben spend together," advised Beth.

"Yes and most of all – I won't let them be alone together," laughed Annie. "Then there's no temptation!"

They laughed and then gave each other a big hug.

"Come on, let's go to bed now. I've got to ring Dave and tell him that you'll be happy to meet him. And you can send Ben a nice text message too," Beth stood up and went to lock the back door.

Annie put the cups into the sink and they both went upstairs to their separate rooms. Beth rang Dave and told him that Annie had accepted that her mother had a new boyfriend, but had found all the coincidences rather freaky! They laughed quietly together and Dave said he'd ring her tomorrow night when he was back in Barnstaple.

"Good night my love. I'm glad we've gone public now. I'm sure it will be so much easier" Dave said.

Beth wasn't so sure. She still had James and Christina to tell, not to mention the rest of her family. She just hoped the older members would be pleased for her and the younger ones would be able to accept that she needed to have the chance of a life of her own.

Chapter Twenty

--ooOoo--

"*H*i Mum, we're back!" yelled James, rushing into the kitchen through the open back door. "Have you missed us?"

Beth turned around quickly from emptying the dishwasher as her son noisily announced his arrival home.

"Oh James, I didn't hear the car outside. You made me jump," she caught her breath and grabbed hold of him in a fierce hug.

"Hi Mum, I'm back too," said Christina throwing her rucksack down on the floor. "Phew, that's heavy."

Beth pulled her into the hug and squeezed them both tightly. "Oh I've missed you both – loads and loads," she said.

Annie wandered into the kitchen carrying a glass and plate. "Hi kids. Have you had a good time?" she asked.

"Oh it was wicked," said James.

"Yes we've had a great time," said Christina at the same time.

"Come on then and tell us what you've been doing. Mum said you'd tried surfing and canoeing, James. And you've been horse riding every day. I bet you're sore," Annie laughed.

"Here are some cold drinks I made earlier," announced Beth in her best Blue Peter mode. "Come on, sit down at the table and tell us all about your adventures."

They sat around the table and both younger children took a deep gulp of strawberry milk shake from their glasses. Beth and Annie waited patiently until they were ready to speak.

"Well, I've been riding every day. And it's the best thing ever. Mum, do you think I can have some lessons now so I can learn to do it properly. Aunty Verity is taking Lucy to riding lessons when she gets home and I said I'd ask if I can go too. Do you think we can afford it?" she asked anxiously looking at her mother.

Beth sighed. "Well, I'll have to find out how much it costs. And then probably speak to your father too. He may be able to help out. But when will you go? You're at the animal sanctuary most weekends and it will be difficult after school as I work until five o'clock."

Christina's face fell as she saw her dream of learning to ride disappear before it had started.Beth tried to console her. "However," she started and Christina looked hopeful. "The nights are lighter for a few months now and maybe we'll be able to find somewhere that isn't too expensive. Do any of your friends at school have riding lessons?"

"Yes they do. I'll ring Laura 'cos she's always talking about horses. I think she helps out at a stables too, so maybe I'd be able to do that to pay for my lessons," Christina nodded satisfied that she could help the situation.

"Anyway," burst in James impatiently. "I've been surfing all the time and I really, really love that. But I don't suppose there's anywhere around here where I'll be able to do it, is there?"'

Beth looked doubtful. "Well I think you need to be near the sea, James. But perhaps you'll be able to have another go when we visit Aunty Verity and Uncle John in the school holidays."

James looked slightly mollified at the prospect of more surfing. Annie looked at her mother wondering if she was going to speak to the children about Dave. Beth caught her look and cleared her throat.

"I'm glad you've both had such a good time. I hope you remembered to thank Aunty Verity and Uncle John when they brought you home?" she asked.

"Yes we did," James assured her. "They've gone round to Grandma and Grandad's house now but said they'll meet us at four o'clock at the big pub down the road for something to eat before they go back home."

"Yes, Aunty Verity mentioned that on the phone last night. What's the time now?" she asked, turning round to look at the clock. "Oh, it's only just after two now so I've time to start some washing," she said as she got up from her chair.

"Mum," said Annie. "I think you can tell them now."

Beth looked at her across the table. "Oh do you think so?" she asked vaguely and sat down again.

"Tell us what?" demanded Christina. "Have you got some exciting news for us?"

"No, not exactly exciting. But I want to tell you about someone I've met who I knew a long time ago."

"Oh, who is it?" asked James.

"His name is Dave. I met him years ago when I was about Annie's age. We were on holiday at the seaside and I suppose he was my first real boyfriend." Beth flushed slightly.

"Ooh," said Christina resting her head on her hands with her elbows on the table. "Did you kiss him?" she asked.

"Er, well, yes I suppose I did," admitted Beth.

"Yeuch," said James.

"Anyway, the thing is, we met each other again recently. And we like each other. But he's moved away to Barnstaple, which is near where you were staying at the adventure holiday," explained Beth.

"Ok, so is he your boyfriend?" asked James getting straight to the point.

"Well, I suppose he might be. But there's another complication."

"What's that then?" asked James.

"He happens to be Lisa's husband," said Beth.

James and Christina looked at her as they tried to work out the relationship and how it would affect themselves.

"So he's married to Lisa, who is Dad's girlfriend. But you knew him ages ago when you were younger," James said.

"'Yes, darling. That's about it," Beth agreed.

"So, if he's living in Barnster-whatever, how can he be your boyfriend?" asked the ever-practical Christina.

"Well, he's only just moved there. He had to take another job and sell the house that he and Lisa lived in. We've just met a few times before he left and once or twice when he's been back. He came back for a couple of days while you were away and we went to a restaurant for a meal. Your dad and Lisa happened to be there too, so we all sat together at the same table," explained Beth.

Again James and Christina were silent as they digested this information.

"That must have been a bit difficult," said James as he thought about it.

"Well, yes it was a bit awkward at first. But then everyone realised what had happened and it got a bit easier."

"Is he still going to be your boyfriend?" asked Christina.

"Well, I hope so. I really like him and I hope you all do too," said Beth looking at the three of them.

"So when can we meet him then? When is he coming back again?" Annie asked.

"Er, I don't know exactly when. Sometimes he just comes back without much notice. I think he has to meet people who he used to work with. Anyway, I'll try to find out when we can all get together and you can start to get to know him," Beth said.

James nodded his head. "That's Ok Mum. I'm cool with it. I know you've got to have someone now that Dad's got Lisa."

"Thanks James. That's very grown up of you," she tousled his hair and smiled at him.

"I don't mind either," said Christina after a short pause. "Cos it will be nice for you to have a boyfriend – even though he is older than a boy. Maybe he'd be able to help pay for my riding lessons," she said thoughtfully.

Beth laughed. "No Christina. You must not expect anyone else to give you money for things. It is up to me and your dad to pay for anything you need. Please remember that, and don't ask Dave or Lisa or anyone else."

"Ok Mum, I won't," agreed Christina.

"Right then, now that's all sorted let's get ourselves ready to go and meet Aunty Verity and everyone. If you two take your rucksacks upstairs and empty them, I'll come and collect the washing in a few minutes. Then you can both have a shower and put on some clean clothes. Have you finished your homework Annie?" she asked.

"Nearly. I probably need another half an hour then I'll be done."

"OK, you go and finish and then have a shower. We'll be ready to leave at half past three."

They went their separate ways and Beth cleared away the empty glasses. She planned to tell her parents and sister about Dave this afternoon, hopefully while the children were busy between themselves.

At half past three they were all ready to leave and the second load of washing was churning away in the machine. Beth drove to the large family pub and parked neatly by the front door. As they got out of the car they could see Jack and Vera already sat at a large table in the conservatory.

"Hi darlings," her mother greeted them as they arrived at the table. "Have you two had a lovely time at the adventure park?" she kissed each one of them in turn.

"Oh yes, Grandma. It was ace," said James."Where's Sam and Lucy?" he asked looking around.

"Oh they stopped on the way here to get petrol and sweets for the journey home. They want to be on the road by six so they get most of the way back in the light," said Jack. "Now, what would you all like to drink?"

As they were giving their drink orders the others arrived. Verity and Beth hugged each other and John kissed his sister-in-law on the cheek.

"Come on then James and Sam, you can help me and your dad to carry the drinks," organised their grandfather.

The three girls said they were going outside to sit by the ornamental fish pond and would be back to order their food in a few minutes. Vera, Verity and Beth sat down with relief. It was nice to know that everyone was catered for and they could relax. They chatted quietly about the children's holiday and Verity's new home.

When the men arrived back with the drinks the girls came back inside to order some food. This took a while and in the end John organised a list which he wrote on a spare piece of paper Beth found in her handbag. The younger ones went outside again and Beth decided this would be a good time to broach the subject of Dave.

When John and Verity had finished telling an amusing story about a mix up with an order for seed that had been incorrectly delivered, and they had all finished laughing, she sat forward in her seat and put her glass firmly down on the table.

"I've got something to tell you," she started. She looked across at her mother who was looking slightly worried. "Oh, no, it's alright it's nothing bad," Beth continued. "Well, I don't think it's bad anyway. Don't worry Mum," she tried to reassure Vera. "It's just that I've met someone who I knew a long time ago. Well, it's the boy from that seaside holiday we were talking about the other day, Verity. Dave. Although he was called Davy then. Well, we've met again and found that we like each other."

"Oh that's great news, Sis," said Verity. "How did you meet him again? Does he live near here?"

"Well, he used to but he's just moved to Barnstaple. He changed his job."

"Oh, what does he do?" asked John. "What did you say his name was?"

"It's Dave Evans and he used to work for Adlers but now he's working in Barnstaple for another company,'" Beth said.

"So how did you meet him again and how did you recognise each other?" asked Verity.

"'Well, this is where it gets a bit complicated," said Beth looking down at the table and twiddling with a beer mat. "He's actually married to Lisa, the woman that Phil is now living with."

There was silence around the table. "What?" Jack exclaimed eventually. "Are you sure?"

"I know it's hard to take in, Dad," Beth said looking at her father. "But it's just one of those coincidences that happen in life from time to time. I didn't know he was Davy at first but when we got talking, we realised we knew each other from years ago."

"Yes I remember the lad. He was a nice, polite boy, although his parents were a bit old-fashioned, I think. We didn't really get to know them very well, did we dear?" Vera asked her daughter.

"No, that's right Mum. But we did go on a picnic with them one day. And there was an incident with a cricket ball, wasn't there Verity?" Beth turned to her sister with a smile.

"Oh, yes I got hit on the nose by his dad," Verity turned to John. "It really hurt and his dad was ever so embarrassed."

"So what's going on between the two of you then," asked Jack turning back to Beth.

"Well, we've been seeing each other for a few weeks but then he moved to Barnstaple. He's been back here a couple of times to meet his ex-colleagues from work and we've met up then too. He came back last Wednesday and took me to a restaurant in the evening. Unfortunately Phil and Lisa were there too, and we all ended up sat together. It was quite embarrassing and I think Phil was a bit put out. Anyway, I promised I would tell the children and you too. The kids have been quite good and accepted what I've told them. But they haven't met him yet. I just hope they like him better than they like Lisa," Beth finished.

"When will you see him again?" asked Verity.

"I don't know at the moment. I hope he can come back this way soon so the kids can meet him and get to know him before their dad says anything or they form the wrong opinion. Or even change their mind about approving of our relationship."

At this moment the waiters brought their food to the table and John went outside to bring the children in to eat. So all talk of Dave was suspended while everyone made short work of their meals.

Verity and John talked about the move and how they were settling in to their new lifestyle. Sam and Lucy also added their comments and how they were looking forward to getting back home later that evening. Verity and Beth smiled at each other across the table as this confirmed that all was well with the younger generation who had adapted to the house move better than had been expected.

"We're going to visit them at the beginning of June for the half term week," Vera told Beth. "And I understand you'll be going for a while during the school holidays in the summer?"

"Yes, that's right. If it's still Ok with you?" asked Beth.

"Of course it's alright with us, isn't it John?"

"Yes, I'll need plenty of hands on the decks in August. Lots of things to be picked and sorted and washed ready for selling," John said.

"Do you think you can come for a fortnight?"asked Verity. "Only you won't be going anywhere else, will you?"

"Actually I was hoping to arrange to have three weeks off from work. I was going to ask for an extra week as unpaid leave and I'd like to get the first three weeks of August if possible. Would that be convenient for you?" she asked.

"Yes that's fine. We're not going anywhere. And I don't think we've got any other bookings at the moment! I think your sister wanted to come for a few days,didn't she John?"

"Yes, but I think she'd like to come towards the end of the school holidays. They're going camping in France for three weeks as soon as they break up from school in July."

"That's settled then. And you'll be able to do lots of surfing James. Sam's told me how much you enjoyed it last week. We've got a good beach less than a mile away and they do tuition as well. Perhaps you can both go together, boys," Verity said.

James looked absolutely delighted. Well, as delighted any fourteen year old boy can manage who wants to remain 'cool'.

"Wicked." He said, short and to the point.

"Will we be able to go riding, Aunty Verity?" asked Christina.

Verity looked over to her own daughter. "Well, actually we've got a surprise for Lucy," she announced. "I was going to keep it a secret until we arrived home, but I think I'll tell you now. For her birthday next week, we've got a pony for Lucy from the farm next door."

Lucy shrieked with surprise. "Oh Mum, that's brilliant. It's just what I wanted, a pony. Oh, now I really can't wait to get home. What colour is he, or she? How old is he? How big is he?" she questioned.

Verity laughed. "He is a he called Toby. He's 14.2hh and black with a white star on his face. He's fourteen years old and the children on the farm next door have outgrown him. I've promised to give him back to them if we don't want him any more."

"Not want him!" exclaimed Lucy. "Of course I want him. I'll never let him go. And you can ride him too, Christina," she added generously to her cousin. "We'll have such fun when you come to stay."

Christina looked as if she would burst with happiness. "Now I'll really need some riding lessons," she said to her mother.

Beth smiled and hugged her daughter. "I know you will, and we'll get something arranged, I promise. Now finish your ice cream and then you can go outside for a while until we go home'.

The children finished their sweets and raced outside, forgetting their teenage dignity in their excitement.

"Well, fancy buying Lucy a pony for her birthday. Every little girl's dream," said Jack.

"We haven't actually bought Toby. We've got him on loan which means that we pay for everything, like his food and vet's bills, but we don't own him. And, like I said, if Lucy outgrows him or doesn't want him any more, we give him back to his owners next door,'" explained Verity.

"Sounds like a great arrangement," said Jack nodding his head slowly. "But it looks as if Christina's going to want one too, Beth. Where will you keep a horse – in the back garden?" he laughed.

Beth rolled her eyes and said, "Yes, what have you started, Verity. Getting Lucy a pony! How am I to keep Christina from wanting one too?"

"Well you won't be able to stop her wanting one. So you'll have to move into the countryside, near us of course, and get her a pony too," joked Verity.

"Oh yes, and what about James and Annie? They're not going to be too pleased if they had to move away from their friends. And I'm sure Phil would have something to say too," she added.

"You can please some of the people some of the time, but not all the people all of the time," misquoted her father. "Now would anyone like another drink?"

As they stood in the car park half an hour later waving goodbye to Verity, John, Sam and Lucy, Beth shivered slightly in the cool evening air.

"Are you alright darling?" her mother asked. "Have you gone cold?"

"No, I think it's all this talk of moving and holidays. It's a bit unsettling," Beth told her quietly as the others walked towards the cars. "I'll be alright. Don't worry."

"I won't worry. I know you've had a lot to cope with today, telling everyone about Dave. Just don't let your heart rule your head. Try and keep a bit of distance and don't rush into anything," she advised her daughter.

Beth laughed. "There's actually quite a lot of distance involved at the moment," she said. "Although I think that Barnstaple is quite close to where Verity has moved. I'll have to have a good look at a map."

"Yes, it would be nice if you could meet Dave a few times when you're staying at Verity's in the summer. But do you think we might get to meet him soon? Well, meet him again, I should say."

"I'll be speaking to him later this evening. I'll tell him that everyone knows now and ask when we can all meet up. But I don't want a big thing made of it. I'm not a teenager bringing her first boyfriend home for approval from parents," she warned her mother with a smile.

"I know that, darling. But it is important that the children meet him. And probably soon too. You don't want Phil to plant any nasty thoughts in their minds, do you?" she said.

"Yes, I'd thought of that too. He was a bit sarcastic when we met by accident in that restaurant. I just hope he's got over it now. I mean, it was him who met somebody else first anyway. So how can he judge?"

"Men. It's just their way. They won't admit it, but it's one rule for them and another for their wife. Not that your father is like that, of course, but I've seen it in other relationships. You know my friend Dorothy, well her husband is quite happy to go to the pub any night of the week he likes but when she enrolled in some evening classes last year, he hit the roof. It's Ok now as she explained to him that she's going to classes to learn how to speak Spanish to help with their holidays abroad. So while Phil is quite happy with his relationship he's not quite so pleased to see you with another man. Double standards," finished Vera with a flourish.

They arrived at the cars and everyone kissed and hugged before setting off to their homes.

"What a lucky girl Lucy is," said Beth. "Being given a pony for her birthday."

She glanced in the rear view mirror to gauge Christina's reaction.

"Yes, she's very lucky. But we couldn't have one in the town and we've not got a big enough garden anyway. I suppose I could have a pony and keep it somewhere else," Christina began to fantasise.

Beth jumped in quickly. "Well I think you'd better have some lessons and learn how to ride and look after a horse first. You might not like all the work that goes with having a pony."

"'Course she will," said James. "She spends all her weekends with those smelly dogs and other animals at the sanctuary. So she's not going to be worried by a horse,"

"Thanks James," Beth squinted her eyes at him and laughed. "You're a great help, I must say."

"Why is he a great help?" asked Christina.

Annie and Beth laughed and James and Christina exchanged glances which suggested their mother and sister were both mad.

Later that evening, Beth went upstairs to make her nightly phone call to Dave. She told him what had happened during the day and he said he was pleased that everyone now knew about them.

"When do you think you will be this way again," she asked.

"I'm hoping to come and see my parents in a few weeks. It's Mum's birthday and I usually take them out for a meal. Perhaps you could come too and I'll introduce, or re-introduce, you to them. I did mention to Mum on the phone last night that I'd re-met the girl from my first holiday romance. She was amazed and intrigued and is looking forward to seeing you again. Do you think you might be able to come for a meal with them?"

"I'd love to," Beth said immediately. "I'll arrange someone to be here with the kids that evening, or do we need to stay overnight?"

"It's probably best if we stay in a hotel and I'd like to stay for two nights if you can arrange that. It saves having to rush back and means we can both have a glass of wine with the meal. If you can come, I'll book a hotel room for us. I'd rather that than stay with my parents – give us a bit of privacy."

"Ok, what nights will it be?" she asked, giggling slightly.

"It's the second Friday in May. I'll take a couple of days off work and come and meet your family first and then we can leave on Friday and be back on the Sunday afternoon. Will that fit in with all your arrangements?"

"Yes, I'll take Friday off work too then. If you want to stay here on the Thursday night, I'm sure that will be alright," she offered.

"OK, as long as your kids are alright about it. Don't want to put them off before they've even met me."

"No, I hope Phil doesn't try to do that – or Lisa. I had a text message earlier today from Phil saying he needs to talk to me. I don't know what that's about. But I'm not going to ring him now. He can wait till Monday when he comes over to see the kids."

"Yes, don't blame you. No point getting upset this time of night. What are you doing tomorrow?" he asked.

"Not much. Christina wants to go to the animal sanctuary so I said she could, although I'm sure she'll be tired after the week she's just had. But it's still the Easter holidays so she hasn't got school again for another week. I'm sure James will want to meet up with some of his mates and Annie is going to spend the day with Ben. So actually, I've got quite a free day – apart from some taxi-ing, of course. What about you?'

"I've got a report to finish which should take about three hours and then Mike from work has asked me over to lunch with his family. They've got four boys aged between three and twelve, so that should be fun! I think they've taken pity on me as I'm all on my own here."

"Well, as long as they don't try to set you up with the local single lasses," teased Beth. "You'll have to tell them you're spoken for!"

Dave laughed. "I'll make sure I tell them tomorrow. But I won't say too much and it will give them some good gossip for the week at work. There are five girls in the admin department who thrive on gossip, including Mike's wife who works there part time!"

"And are the other four girls single or married," asked Beth trying to sound disinterested.

Dave laughed again. "They're all either married or engaged. I think that's why they like to gossip – to add a bit of colour to their otherwise possibly boring lives."

Beth laughed too. "No, it's just women. We all like to gossip whether we've got boring or colourful lives of our own. It's just that women like to know about everything and everyone, all the time' she explained.

"Oh right, now I understand,"Dave said. "Anyway, I'll tell you all about my 'family day' tomorrow when I ring you. Hope you get the chance to relax a bit tomorrow – in between the driving! And I'll make arrangements for Mum's birthday meal and our overnight stay. You can tell everyone that they'll meet me that week. I'll come over on Thursday morning and we should have three or four days, and nights, together," he promised.

"Oh that will be wonderful. Can't wait. Also, Verity has asked us to stay with them in August so we should be able to meet then as well. I'm going to try and book three weeks holiday although one will be unpaid. I'll look on the map and find out how close their house is to you in Barnstaple. But I'll have the car anyway, so I'll be able to drive over to you, or you can come over to the farm."

"Great. Let's just hope our families like each other next month. I must say I'm getting a bit nervous about meeting your children."

"Oh, don't be. They don't bite, you know. I'm sure it will be fine. Maybe we'll go out and you can meet them at a neutral place. A MacDonalds or Pizza Hut are usually good bets for keeping them sweet!"

Dave laughed. "Sounds good. I'll look forward to it then, as long as you keep them well fed."

Beth laughed again too. "You make them sound like animals from the zoo."

"Well I thought that's what teenagers are like these days – all fangs, claws and flying fur."

"Yes, well, that's not all the time. They do have their moments, of course.as I'm sure we did in our time."

"Not me," said Dave. "I was a model teenager and student. Never put a foot wrong. Although my brother might say different after I put glue in his briefcase the first day he started work."

"Why did you do that?" asked Beth.

"Because he told my Dad that I'd been talking to next door's au pair over the garden fence. He made out that we were having a raging affair. But I was only fifteen and interested in Swedish politics."

"Yeah right, as James would say," said Beth disbelievingly. "And obviously your dad didn't believe you either?"

"No. Strange that. He grounded me for a fortnight so I thought I'd teach my goody-goody brother a lesson. It was four pounds well spent for a tube of extra-strength glue."

"So did you get into trouble for that as well?" asked Beth.

"Yes, of course I did. Another fortnight locked up chez-Evans and by the time I was released from my incarceration Anika had gone back home to Sweden, so that was the end of that!"

They both laughed and then said their goodbyes to each other until the following night.

As Beth got ready for bed that night, she wondered why Phil had sent the text message about needing to talk to her. She hoped it wasn't going to be anything too life-changing and decided that possibly she'd contact him tomorrow to find out what he wanted.

Chapter Twenty One

--ooOoo--

*B*eth let herself back into the house again just before midday the next morning. She had already taken Christina to the animal sanctuary where she would be cleaning cages and sweeping up until about four o'clock that afternoon. ames had just been deposited at his best friend's house where he was no doubt regaling his mates with tales of surfing and canoeing. Annie had left for Ben's about half an hour ago.

She made herself a cup of coffee and took it into the conservatory where she sat on one of the comfortable sofas and sighed contentedly as the warm sunshine filtered into the room and relaxed her.

However, after a few minutes she remembered the text message received from Phil the previous day.

'I suppose I ought to ring him,' she thought and retrieved her phone from under the newspaper she'd brought with her to read while drinking her coffee. She dialled his number and waited for him to answer.

"Morning Beth," he said in a gruff voice.

"Oh, hello Phil. You sent me a message yesterday that we needed to talk so I thought I'd ring you. Is it convenient to talk now?" she asked.

"Er, yes. Hang on a moment I'll just go downstairs," he said amidst shuffling noises and whispered sounds.

'Oh, er, spare me the details,' thought Beth grimacing into her cup.

"Right, Ok. I'm downstairs now," Phil said unnecessarily. "I didn't think you were going to ring back so I was going to talk to you tomorrow when I came over to see the kids. Are they Ok? Did they get back from their adventure camp yesterday?"

"Yes of course they did. I'd have rung you otherwise. I thought you might have rung yourself yesterday to talk to them, but you didn't," she accused.

"No, I was working yesterday and then I thought I'd be seeing them tomorrow anyway," he defended himself.

"What did you want to talk to me about?" she asked.

"Well, do you remember I said I might need some equity to be released from our property in order to finance my next purchase?" he asked pompously.

"Yes of course I do. I was worried we might have to move. Why, what's happened? Do you need some money from this house then?" she asked quickly.

"Yes I think I will need to reconsider our finances. The housing market has slumped recently and Lisa didn't get quite as much from her sale as she'd hoped – as you probably know already."

"So are you saying we need to sell this house?" asked Beth, ignoring his last statement. "Just tell me straight without all the fancy words."

"Yes we might have to sell the house. Obviously I will make sure you and the kids have somewhere to live. I'm not going to leave you all homeless. However, Lisa and I need to buy a place too but we need more deposit. I thought if we sold our house and you had three quarters of the equity, which should be about £100,000, and I had the rest, then we'd both be able to manage. Obviously you'll have to take out a small mortgage but you should
be able to arrange that now you are working full time."

"Why can't you buy a smaller place that you can afford? After all, there's only you and her?" asked Beth.

"We want to buy a four bedroomed house so there are rooms for the kids when they come to stay. Also Lisa wants to be able to invite her family and friends to visit. She likes entertaining at weekends."

"I'm sure she does!" Beth said. "I am sure entertaining is one of Lisa's fortes."

"Now there's no need to be like that," Phil replied. "Let's try and keep this civilised."

"Civilised! How can it be civilised when you want to make us move from the family home we've brought our children up in for the last ten years?" asked Beth.

"Well, things have changed now haven't they? Can't you move in with Dave?" Phil asked nastily.

Beth gasped. "Don't be stupid!" she retorted hotly. "Things have changed becuse you changed them! And, I've only known him a short time and he's moved away to Barnstaple anyway. The kids haven't even met him yet. Don't talk rubbish!"

"Alright, keep your hair on," he came back with. "But we really do need to sort out our finances. I'm sure your lawyer or solicitor will be arranging some maintenance for me to pay and then we'll need to get a divorce too."

Beth couldn't believe her ears. Again, all this seemed to be happening so quickly. Phil hadn't mentioned divorce before. She supposed he wanted to marry Lisa!

"Look, I'll have to think about all this," she said. "I haven't even got a lawyer or solicitor and this is the first I've heard about divorce."

"Well we can't stay married can we?" he rhetorically asked. "We've both got new partners now. I suggest we get on with it all as quickly as possible. Lisa's quite happy to be cited as the guilty party for our divorce and I'll do the same for her's. Have you got a problem with that?"

"You've obviously both got this all nicely sorted out between you. I've got no problem with it: it's just the kids I worry about. Not that I think they imagine there's any chance of us getting back together again but it's a final step and it just seems to be happening very fast. I probably need a bit more time to get my head round it too."

"Well you have a think about it all and find a solicitor to act for you. I'll bring mine's details over to you tomorrow and they can fight it out between them. But you'll also have to put the house up for sale quite soon. We'd like to be in our new home before the end of this year, preferably about October time. I'll talk to you again tomorrow when I'm there. Is that Ok? Was there anything else you wanted to talk about?"

"No, it was you who wanted to talk to me if you remember, not the other way around. I keep hearing what you want without any thought about anyone else. Well, I have to think about it from every point of view and I'll speak to you tomorrow." she finished in a small but firm voice.

Well that conversation had certainly ruined her quiet and indulgent day, she thought. She closed her eyes and tried to imagine living somewhere else. What an upheaval, having to move, especially as she'd have to buy a smaller house. The girls would probably have to share a bedroom and all their furniture wouldn't fit into a smaller house. Phil would want some of it anyway, she supposed.

She decided she needed to talk about her problem to someone and picked up her phone to ring Amanda.

"Hi Amanda. How are you? We don't seem to have spoken recently," she began.

"Oh hi to you too. No, I've been rushed off my feet this week with some displays that I had to prepare for the exhibition at the library. They wanted them in time for the re-opening of the children's section after the refurbishment. You must have seen it in the paper?" Amanda responded.

"Oh, yes, that's right. I did see it and I meant to ring you. The flowers looked fabulous in the photos," Beth said.

"Thanks. The Council thought so too and they've commissioned me to do all the arrangements for their annual banquet in October."

"That's great. You must be really pleased to be getting well known now,'" Beth was delighted with her friend's success.

"Yes I am. It's taken a while but I feel that I'm getting somewhere at last. Now what's up with you Beth? You sound a bit fraught," Amanda asked.

"Oh Amanda. You know I told you Phil had mentioned that we might have to sell the house? Well, I've just spoken to him again and he's determined to make us move. It seems he and Lisa want to buy a four bedroomed property and he needs some equity from this house to help pay for it. It just doesn't seem fair that he can chuck us out of our home and make us move into a pokey three bedroomed house. The girls will have to share a bedroom and they'll probably argue all the time. And I don't expect all my

furniture will fit into a smaller house either," she finished.

"Oh Beth, don't get upset," Amanda said. 'You need to find out whether he can do this first. I know he has to provide a home for the three children until they are eighteen, or leave school, or some such time. Let's find out from a solicitor first before you jump to conclusions."

"Oh I certainly need a solicitor," Beth continued. "He's also told me that we are getting a divorce and to find myself a lawyer."

Amanda was quiet for a few seconds. "Well, you'd better find one then. I'm sure you can also apply for legal aid. I think, if you are earning below a certain amount, you are entitled to free legals. You may qualify, Beth," advised Amanda.

"Yes I need to find out. I think I'll go and see someone from Manton's tomorrow. They're the solicitor firm next door to where I work," she informed Amanda.

"There's also the Citizen's Advice Bureau. They give help to people in your situation. I don't think they're open all day though, it might be best to ring them first."

"Ok thanks, I will. I need all the help I can get," Beth said.

"Have you told Dave about all this yet?" asked Amanda.

"No, I rang you first. I'll speak to him later. But I'm sure he'll be able to help me too. It's just a shame that he's so far away now. I feel like I've lost him again," Beth said.

"He's very supportive though, isn't he? Perhaps he'll make a special trip to see you this week and give you some help," Amanda said.

"I don't think so. He's very busy at work at the moment. But he's coming to meet the family soon and we're going to a birthday dinner at his parent's that same weekend. I'll ring him later and tell him what's happened. I just needed to talk to someone straight away before I went into a depressed mood worrying about what might happen to us. I was sat here picturing a small, dark house in which I was trying to fit all my furniture, with the kids

arguing all the time, no garden and miles to drive to work and school," Beth

shuddered as she put her thoughts into words.

"Oh, I expect it was falling down, with rotten window frames and an old mattress dumped in the garden too, wasn't it?" teased Amanda.

Beth laughed. "I know I've been over-dramatising but it's difficult not to when you fear the worst."

"It might not be the worst. You might find a lovely four bedroomed house that you can afford, or you might discover that the girls have always wanted to share a bedroom together," Amanda said.

Beth giggled again. "I don't think so. They do get on well most of the time but Annie is so well organised and tidy I don't think she would be happy sharing with Christina and her collection of soft toy

271

animals and dolls. And I don't think I'll find a four bedroomed house within my price range. I suppose I could always share a bedroom with one of them."

It was Amanda's turn to laugh. "Yes that's really going to work. Maybe you could put in bunk beds for you and Christina. Imagine being jolted about all night with a healthy teenager turning over and wriggling about all the time. You'd never get any sleep!"

As usual, Amanda managed to make Beth feel better about the situation. She was great at turning a 'worst case scenario' into a hopeless joke.

"Anyway, I'd better go if you're feeling a bit better. Brian's probably finished loading the dishwasher now and this afternoon we're going to that new garden centre that's just opened up on the other side of Nottingham. Make sure you speak to Dave soon and go and see a solicitor tomorrow, Beth. Don't put it off," she advised.

"No, I will go and see someone tomorrow, I promise. Have a nice time at the garden centre, and I'll ring you tomorrow night," Beth said.

Beth closed her eyes and laid back in the chair. Her coffee had gone cold and she didn't feel like reading the paper. It would only be more bad news and depressing stories of what other people were currently enduring. Beth felt she had enough on her plate without taking on any more misery!

She suddenly woke with a jolt and realised she must have nodded off. She opened her eyes and glanced at the clock in the kitchen through the doorway. Oh, what a relief. It was only ten minutes after she'd finished talking to Amanda.

She stood up and stretched her arms up as high as they would reach. Her back felt released from the position she'd been wedged in on the chair whilst she dozed.

Beth picked up the paper and the cup and took them into the kitchen. She decided it was too nice a day to stay indoors and that she would take a walk along by the canal. When the children were young, she would take them for long walks in the pram or pushchair along the bank of the canal. The children enjoyed watching the boats drifting along and always waved at the people on board.

She left the house by the front door and set off at a good pace, realising that it was quite a long time since she'd walked anywhere from her home. Everywhere they went seemed to involve a car journey! It would be nice to have a dog, she thought as she reached the gap in the hedge which she squeezed through to reach the towpath.

The trees seemed taller and the undergrowth thicker than she remembered. There were several boats moored further up, near the canal-side pub. Two boats were being driven towards her and the large man wearing a navy blue cap waved as he steered past her.

She walked along trying to keep her thoughts away from the problems Phil had inflicted upon her. But it was no use. What else would she think about anyway?

Beth walked for about half an hour before she realised she was tiring and saw a handy bench which provide a brief rest. She wished she'd brought a drink or flask with her. But she'd left in such a hurry, just wanting to get away from the home that she might have to leave in the near future. A few tears trickled down her cheek and she put up her hand to brush them away.

"'It's no good sitting here feeling sorry for yourself," she said out loud. "You'll just have to get on with it – whatever happens. If Phil wants the house sold, then we'll have to find somewhere else to live. It's not the end of the world," she spoke sternly to herself.

After a few more sniffs and a wipe across her face with the back of her hand, she sat up straight and told herself to get a grip. She stood up and set off back towards home, and as she reached the gap in the hedge, the peace and tranquillity surrounding her eventually had its effect and she decided that she did feel slightly more optimistic and able to cope than she had earlier.

A little later in her kitchen as she was drinking a cup of tea and deciding whether to indulge

herself with a third chocolate biscuit, Annie returned home.

"Hi darling. Are you Ok? Did you have a nice time at Ben's," she asked.

Annie slumped down in a chair and reached for the biscuit tin.

"It was alright. That Melissa was there again. She's a right pain. She even asked Ben, in front of me, if he wanted to go to a party tonight. She made it obvious that I wasn't invited."

Beth shook her head. "That doesn't seem very fair. She knows you are a couple and she should ask you both. How does Ben react?"

"Typical boy – just pretends it was a mistake. When I asked him about her after she'd gone, he still says she's only there to get help with her homework. I hope she doesn't go round to his house when I'm not there, but he says she doesn't," Annie replied.

"Well that's Ok then. He probably doesn't want to be alone with her and prefers you to be there too," reassured Beth.

"Yes, I suppose so. At least when the exams are over she'll have no excuse to keep going to his house. Anyway, I'm going back to Ben's later, if that's alright. We've got the house to ourselves as his parents are going out to dinner."

"Yes, that's fine. Just be home by ten. Are you having a take away or do you want some dinner before you go?"

"His mum is ordering us a Chinese before they leave. I'll go and have a shower now." Annie got up and went upstairs.

Beth glanced at the clock. It was an hour before she needed to collect Christina so she decided to go upstairs too and indulge herself with a nice hot bubble bath.

Later that evening, Beth was upstairs ready to speak to Dave when her mobile rung. It was Dave.

"Oh I was just going to ring you," she said immediately into the phone.

"Well I got to you first," he countered.

"Great. I wish you could get to me,'" Beth teased him.

Dave groaned. "Don't tempt me please – not when I'm so far away from you," he said.

"When do you think you will be able to come here again?" she asked.

"Probably not until the weekend of Mum's birthday party. I'm absolutely snowed under here. I can't believe the amount of work there is at the moment. Are you alright? Has anything happened?" he enquired.

"Well, yes, I suppose it has. I had a message from Phil yesterday and I rang him back today to find out what he wanted. He still wants me to sell this house as they need more money to be able to afford a big house themselves. Apparently they need four bedrooms so they can have the children to stay and also Lisa's family want to visit. So he wants me to put the house up for sale and start looking for another home for us – and I will have to get a mortgage too. He also wants me to get a solicitor or lawyer so we can get divorced. He said that Lisa is prepared to be cited in our divorce and he will do it for your's" Beth blurted it all out.

"Wow, that's a lot to think about. Lisa had sent me a text about the divorce – can you imagine ending a marriage with a text message?" he asked.

"Seems incredible," agreed Beth.

"So I knew about that part of it. I'm sorry you'll have to sell your house. Are you sure he can insist on that, with the children I mean?" Dave asked.

"I don't know. I'm going to the Citizen's Advice Bureau and to find a solicitor tomorrow in my lunch hour. There is a firm of solicitor's next door to my office, so I'll pop in there for an appointment," she told him.

"You certainly need to find out what your rights are," Dave said. "Make sure you claim legal aid too, if you are entitled"

"Yes, that's what Amanda said. I rang her earlier, just after I'd spoken to Phil. I didn't know if you'd be working so I thought I'd talk to you tonight," Beth said.

"I didn't finish until just after six o'clock and I've got to go back in for a few hours tomorrow too. I'll be glad when we have this new system up and running," he told her.

"When do you think that will be?" she asked.

"Probably about the end of July. That's what we are aiming for. We've got a big job starting in September so we need to know what we're doing by then. So when are you going to see a solicitor?" he asked.

"I'll try and get an appointment tomorrow," she told him again. "I don't know if you can just get in and see someone or if you have to book. And Amanda said to ring the Citizen's Advice Bureau as well for some help. I'm going to be busy tomorrow," she said.

"Sounds like it. I'm sorry I'm not there to be more of a support to you. What will you do about selling the house? Are you going to put it up for sale now?"

"No, not yet. I'll find out what my rights are first and then how much I can borrow with a mortgage just in my name. I'll look in the local paper this week and get an idea of house prices. I'm quite shocked by all this although I suppose I should have seen it coming. Phil and Lisa obviously want to get married and buy a nice, big house

for themselves. It is just so amazing how quickly Phil seems to have forgotten our life together, and even his own
   children."

Dave was silent for a few seconds. "Do you want me to take some holiday and come and help you?" he offered.

"Oh Dave. That's so nice of you, but I'll be alright. You've got too much to do with your new job and it's not your responsibility anyway," she said.

"I want it to be my responsibility, though," he responded. "I know I've not met your kids yet, but I just feel as if I should be helping you get through all these difficult decisions and situations. It's not our fault this has happened – we were the innocent parties in both our marriages. But it seems that Lisa and Phil having a much easier time than we are."

"I know, I agree with you. But I'm glad I've got the children with me. It serves him right if he loses their love and respect. I know they are all a bit disillusioned with him at the moment, mostly because of what's happened but also because, I'm afraid, they don't like Lisa."

"That makes five of us then, doesn't it?" joked Dave.

Beth laughed. "I suppose it does. But I would prefer them to just get on a bit with her so that they look forward to being with their dad. I'm not such a nice person that I want her to be a second mum to them, or anything like that. But I don't like them being upset when they come back from an outing with their dad and her."

They spoke for a few more minutes about how they'd spent the day and then Dave wished Beth luck for her appointments the next day.

"Ring me as soon as you want tomorrow – even if it's during the day," he told her. "I'll try and answer but if not I'll ring you back as soon as I can."

"Thanks Dave. I'll speak to you tomorrow then. Love you lots," she said as they finished their telephone conversation.

The next day Beth rang the Citizen's Advice Bureau and arranged to see someone at one o'clock. They advised her to see a solicitor as the divorce and settlement would all be tied together as children were involved. So Beth called in at the solicitor's offices on her way back to work and made an appointment with a Mr Walker for the next day during her lunch break.

Just before she left work for the day, her boss told everyone to be in promptly the next morning as he had an announcement to make. He added that no-one need be worried, they were not closing down or making redundancies, but he needed to speak to everyone at nine fifteen to make them aware of some changes that would be taking place. He went back into his own office and shut the door making it clear that no further news would be

imparted that night.

Obviously, as they were leaving, everyone began to speculate as to what the announcement would be. Beth felt she had enough to deal with at the moment, without having to worry about her job, especially if she needed to get a mortgage to buy her own house.

When Phil arrived for his usual nightly visit, he called out briefly to the children before breezing through the hallway to the kitchen where Beth was loading the dishwasher with the dinner plates. He shut the door behind him and pulled out a chair from under the table.

"Well, have you seen a solicitor yet?" he asked, sitting down and placing a piece of paper in front of him on the table.

Beth stood up and turned round to face him.

"No, not yet but I have made an appointment for tomorrow. I went to the Citizen's Advice Bureau and they said that a solicitor would deal with the divorce, settlement and child maintenance all together. It seems that I will probably be entitled to legal aid too," she told him.

"Good. Right. Shall we put the house up for sale this week, then?" he asked.

"Er, no I don't think so," she said firmly. "I want to wait until I know whether I can stay here with the children, or at least until they are all eighteen or have left school."

"I think I only have to provide a home for them. I don't think you will just be entitled to stay here without my consent too," he informed her.

"Well we'll have to wait and see. I'm seeing a Mr Walker tomorrow at one o'clock and I'll let you know after that. Also I need to talk to you about half term. Mum and Dad are visiting Verity and John at their new farm for the week and I can't have any time off work. So you'll have to help out with looking after Christina and James. Annie will be alright, she'll have finished most of her exams by then, but I don't want to leave her all week responsible for the other two," she said.

Phil looked slightly surprised. "Well, it's a bit late to arrange holiday now, but I'll see what I can do. I may not be able to have the whole week off though."

"Just get as many days as you can then. Also, I've booked three weeks off work for the beginning of August when we are going to stay with Verity. Do you want to take the children away during the holidays?" she asked.

Phil looked away from Beth. "Well, I hadn't planned to. Lisa and I are going away for a fortnight at the end of August. But I'll probably be able to take a few days off to help out, if you like."

"If I like? Well, yes, I do like. And you can let me know what days you are able to have the kids, and then Mum and Dad will probably help out for the rest of the school holidays. But I do think it would be a good idea for you to take them out for a few days and treat them. Take them to a theme park or the seaside, or somewhere. Preferably just you too, if…Lisa…is working," she advised.

Phil nodded as he listened to Beth's words. "Yes, I heard what you're saying. I'll try and take a couple of days off each week between your holiday and mine. Maybe I'll take them to visit my parents again too."

"Yes that's a good idea," Beth agreed. "Now go and spend some time with your children."

The next day, Beth walked into the office at ten minutes to nine. She wanted to finish off some figures before the meeting Allan had called. By nine fifteen everyone was stood about holding cups of coffee and shifting about uneasily. They talked quietly in small groups and when Allan entered the room, all conversations ended immediately.

"Good morning everyone. Now I don't want to keep you long but I need to let you know what's going on. I've been having talks with the directors from Mitchells during the past few weeks. You may have seen them visiting the offices last week. They have suggested a merger between our two companies. I've thought long and hard about this and decided that it would be good for this firm.

"We would move into a larger building and all departments will integrate with Mitchell's. It means we will be able to tender for bigger and better accounts and I've been assured there will be no job losses. However, I am prepared to offer voluntary redundancy to anyone who does not want to continue working for the two companies."

Chapter Twenty One

"When are we moving and where to?" asked one of the senior accountants.

"The move will be at the beginning of September and we are going to lease one of the new office blocks on the new business park just behind Tesco's. We would have needed new premises anyway as the landlord wants this building back for redevelopment purposes," Allan told them. "It's a few months before the move and I will speak individually to everyone during the next few weeks. If you all think about whether you wish to continue working for us or if you'd rather take the redundancy package and let me know during the interview. Are there any other questions?' he asked, looking round at everyone.

"Will our salaries or promotion prospects be affected?" came a voice from the back.

"Salaries will be held at their present level but obviously promotion possibilities may alter as there will be more staff. However, if we expand as we hope to, then there will actually be more chances for promotion," Allan responded.

"When are we going to be interviewed?" asked one of the secretaries.

"As I said, I'll arrange to see every one of you individually. This will probably be next month. So that gives you plenty of time to think about your futures. That's all I can really tell you at present. If you have any other questions that are really pressing, email me and I'll try to answer you. Right, back to work everyone," Allan smiled round and turned to go back into his office.

Beth slumped down on her chair. This was awful. The business park was right across town and she'd have to negotiate busy rush hour traffic in the morning and evening which was bound to effect her routines. It meant that she'd have to leave home earlier in the morning and would arrive back later every evening.

It seemed that her whole life was changing and she just didn't seem able to cope. Obviously there was no way she could accept redundancy, she'd only been working full time a matter of months. And she didn't fancy looking around for another job. Her confidence was pretty low and, apart from Dave's arrival in her life, she felt everything was going wrong. Even Dave had been snatched away from her after just a few weeks!

At one o'clock she went next door to her appointment with Mr

Walker. She walked into the reception area and gave her name to the receptionist, feeling quite intimidated. She'd never been to a solicitor before and didn't quite know what to expect. She was given a form to complete while she waited to be seen.

After a few minutes the receptionist called her name and pointed to a staircase. "Go up the stairs and Mr Walker is in the third office on the right," she said.

Beth climbed the stairs slowly, clutching her form, and reached the top just slightly out of breath. She counted the doors on the right and knocked on the one marked Mr I Walker.

"Come in," she heard.

She opened the door and stepped inside, pushing it closed behind her.

"Good afternoon. Beth Grainger – nice to meet you," said Mr Walker as he stood up and stretched out his hand. Beth stepped up to the desk and took his hand. 'Hello Mr Walker. It's good of you to see me at short notice," she said.

"Not at all. Now, sit down please," he indicated a chair and she obediently sat down. "Now, it's a divorce and maintenance case, isn't it?" he asked looking through some papers in front of him.

"Yes, that's right. My husband wants me to sell the house but I don't know if I'm entitled to stay there until the children are grown up," she said.

"Right, well let's see. Have you filled in the form with all your details?" he asked.

Beth handed him the completed document and he looked through it quickly.

"Mmm, three children all under eighteen. All in full time education?" he asked looking at her.

"Yes, that's right. Although Annie takes her GCSEs next month and she's staying on to do her A levels," Beth told him.

"Mmmm" Mr Walker didn't seem particularly interested in Annie's future plans! He asked Beth several pertinent questions all of which she managed to answer without stuttering or repeating herself. He took out some documents from the filing cabinet behind his desk and began to fill them in.

"I need you to look through these and then sign and date where indicated," he informed Beth. She did as she was asked and Mr

Walker glanced through the paperwork to make sure she'd signed in all the necessary places. When he'd checked to his satisfaction, he looked across the desk at Beth.

"Well, I think we should go for maximum maintenance payments. Mr Grainger left you and committed adultery with another woman. This he does not contest. We shall need to work out the exact amount of assets and liabilities of the marriage and then come to an agreed arrangement as to how this is distributed between you both. You are correct, however, and you and the children cannot be made homeless. However, Mr Grainer will probably be entitled to retrieve some equity from the house and, if you cannot remortgage and remain there, you may need to sell. You should brace yourself for this possibility," he informed her.

Beth nodded. She had already braced herself for this news so it did not come as too big a shock.

"Do I need to put the house up for sale now, this week?" she asked. "Only Phil – Mr Grainger – told me that he wanted to sell the house as quickly as possible."

"No, I don't think you need to put the house on the market yet. We need to enter into negotiations with Mr Grainger's solicitors in the first place. Do you have their details?" he asked.

Beth opened her handbag and took out the piece of paper Phil had given her yesterday.

"These are his solicitors," she said as she handed it to Mr Walker.

He glanced at it. "Oh, right. This firm of solicitors are quite hostile in many cases like these," he said.

Beth felt this was hardly reassuring and did not seem to bode too well for her.

"What happens now?" she asked.

"I'll arrange to communicate with this Ms Forbes your husband has instructed and then I'll write to you setting out our terms of business. You will need to sign and return the acceptance form to me and then we'll arrange another appointment. Are there any problems with access?" he asked.

"No, not really. Phil comes round most evenings after he's finished work to see the children. He also takes them out sometimes at weekends or in the evenings," Beth said.

"That's fine then. No problems there," he said writing this down on one of the forms in front of him. "I'll be in touch with you this week Mrs Grainger and I'll see you again when I have something to impart to you."

Mr Walker stood up and put out his hand again. Beth also stood up and dropped her still open handbag. She scrabbled around under the chair trying to reach for her lipstick, purse and cheque book which seemed to have wedged themselves in an inaccessible place. After retrieving them she rammed them into her handbag and pushed her hair back from around her red face. She was not making a good impression!

"Thanks Mr Walker. I'll see you again soon," she managed as she shook his still outstretched hand.

Outside in the street, Beth took several steadying breaths before walking back to the office. What a nightmare, she thought as she sat behind her desk again. What shall I worry about most? My job, my home, my kids or just my life!

Chapter Twenty Two

--ooOoo--

*B*y the second week in May, Annie had sat most of her GCSEs. Beth noticed how quiet and tense she seemed and hoped it was only the pressure of the exams that was causing this. She thought she'd wait until later in the month to confront Annie if she didn't seem to have improved by then.

Dave was due to arrive at about eight o'clock on the Thursday night. Beth had organised a makeshift bed in the dining room with a camp bed and a sleeping bag. She didn't want to cause any problems with sleeping arrangements during this first meeting. She told Dave he would be sleeping downstairs and he'd quite understood.

"We've got two nights together at the hotel near my parents, so I can wait until then," he assured her. Jack and Vera were moving in for the weekend and would taxi the children to their various destinations on Saturday.

Beth left work early on Friday so they could get a good start up the motorway during the afternoon. She was looking forward to meeting Dave's parents again even though she could barely remember them from the holiday long ago.

Just before eight o'clock, Beth ran upstairs to comb her hair and touch up her make up before Dave arrived. The children were all downstairs watching Eastenders and she knew they were slightly apprehensive about meeting their mother's new boyfriend. Relations hadn't improved at all between them and Lisa and Beth supposed they imagined Dave might be a similar person and they wouldn't get on with him either. She hoped the evening went well and they all liked each other.

As the closing music to the TV programme finished, Dave arrived at their front door. Beth hadn't heard his car which he parked on the street in front of the house. She'd been in the kitchen checking the lasagne she'd cooked for their supper.

"He's here," yelled James. "'Are you going to the door mum?"

"Yes, I'll go," Beth said as she hurried into the hallway. She opened the door and stepped back in surprise as she could hardly see Dave behind all the parcels and the large bouquet of flowers he was holding.

"Oh, are you there Dave?" she asked, standing on tip toe to see the top of his head. "Come in, if you can. Do you want me to take something?"

"No, it's alright, I'll manage," Dave replied as he tentatively stepped inside the hall and
stood there getting his bearings.

The children came out of the front room and stared at the apparition in front of them.

"Is this Dave?" asked Christina. "Why have you got all those presents? Are they for us?"

"Christina!" said her mother. "Don't be so nosy. Now come on Dave, let me help you."

"Ok," he agreed. "Now take the flowers Beth – they're for you. Christina, the square blue package is for you, the big red one for James and the two green parcels are for Annie."

As Dave spoke Beth and the children unloaded him.

"'Oh. Wow!" said James as he clutched a huge box covered in red shiny paper. "What's this then?"

"I should open it and find out," said Dave flexing his arms now they were released from his burdens.

The children started opening their parcels in the hallway and Beth stood holding her flowers. Christina got inside hers first and found a large hamster cage complete with bedding, food and water bottle.

"There's no hamster in there yet," said Dave "But I thought you might like another one. Your mother said your last hamster died last year and I thought it was time you found another furry friend."

"Oh yes. Twinkles died ages ago and I lent his cage to one of my friends who has got some pet rats. Oh, Mum, is it alright if I have another hamster? I really would like one again, please," she pleaded, turning to her mother.

"Yes Christina, you can have another hamster. I know you missed

Twinkles when he died and I think you've had time to grieve now. Maybe you can go with Grandma and Grandad at the weekend and buy one," she suggested.

"Oh ace. Thank you so much...Dave," Christina turned to him and beamed full of gratitude. "I really love animals and I help out at an animal sanctuary at the weekend but they're not my own," she explained.

"Yes your mum told me. I think you do a great job helping animals," Dave said smiling at her.

"Whey, look at this," James managed to get a word in. "Oh Dave, this is great, just what I really wanted."

Somehow Dave had managed to wrap up a surf board without the paper tearing. Beth didn't think she'd have been able to manage such a good job with a large and awkward shape.

"Oh Dave," she said. "You shouldn't have bought all these presents for them."

"Of course I should," he contradicted her, winking over their heads. "Kids love presents – don't you?"

"Yes of course," shouted Christina. "We really, really love presents. Thank you very much. Now I'll have to think of a name to call my hamster when I get him."

Annie had sat herself down on the stairs to open her parcels. In one was a beautiful wooden jewellery box. The lid was inlaid with gold and silver stars and moons and inside were six silky spaces for necklaces, bracelets and rings. The other parcel held an MP3 player.

"Oh Dave. Thank you so much. The jewellery box is lovely and thank you for the MP3 player too. It's a great colour," Annie said looking up at him.

Dave smiled. "I'm glad you like it. I expect you have an MP3 player already but I didn't know what else to buy you."

"And thank you very much for these beautiful flowers. I'd better put them in water," Beth leant over and planted a kiss on Dave's lips. James pulled a face and Annie looked away.

"Shall I bring my bag in now?" he asked, to recover from the awkward moment.

"If you like. I've only got to dish up the lasagne but I can put the flowers in a vase first. I've put you in here, in the dining room, on a camp bed. Let me know if you want any more pillows or anything,"

Beth pointed to his sleeping corner.

"Now do you kids want any more to eat or have you had enough?" asked Beth walking into the kitchen.

"I'd like some please Mum," said James.

In the end they all sat round the kitchen table and finished off the lasagne and garlic bread that Beth had prepared. Conversation flowed naturally and all three of the children seemed to accept Dave. He made them laugh on several occasions and she was glad to just sit and take a back seat.

Later that evening Beth and Dave were alone in the front room finishing off the bottle of wine they'd opened.

"Well I think that went quite well, don't you?" Dave whispered quietly into Beth's right ear.

She looked round to make sure they were alone. "Yes I think so too. But you didn't have to spend all that money on presents for them. Not that I'm not grateful, of course."

"I thought it would break the ice. I didn't do it to buy their affection, or anything. I just wanted to get on with them right from the start," Dave explained.

Beth squeezed his hand and kissed him lovingly on his mouth.

"Mmm, I do love you so much, Dave. I've missed you these past few weeks. It's been really difficult coping with everything." She hadn't meant to blurt out her feelings so early but he didn't seem to mind.

"I know you've had a lot to cope with and I think you've done really well. What are you going to do about your job?" he asked.

"I don't know. I haven't really coped with anything at all," she said. "I've just not made any decisions. I haven't put the house up for sale, haven't decided what to do about my job and I haven't been back to see the solicitor about the divorce either," she confessed.

Dave laughed. "'Well it doesn't matter. There's plenty of time for all that. You've got to

take time, you know, so that you make the right decision. It's no good rushing into something and then regretting it later."

Beth rested her head on his shoulder and closed her eyes. It was lovely to have somebody else to lean on. She knew she mustn't get used to it as he would be going back to Barnstaple on Sunday night, but she could just pretend and revel in being taken care of for a short time. She didn't think she'd ever felt like this with Phil. They had just got on with their lives and not had to cope with any great upheavals that caused worry and stress.

Obviously they'd had problems to deal with, but nothing momentous or life changing.

The next day, Dave and Beth set off for Wales. Jack and Vera had arrived just after lunch and Beth introduced them to Dave. Vera shook his hand warmly and said she could just about remember the young man he'd been during that seaside holiday. Jack looked at him keenly but seemed satisfied that he was a decent chap and wouldn't mess about with his daughter's emotions.

Beth reminded them how to work the television, washing machine and dishwasher. She'd written down the timings for taking Christina to the animal sanctuary, James was playing cricket for the school team on Saturday afternoon and Annie had her weekly dancing lesson.

Beth waved goodbye to her family and then sat back in the passenger seat ready for the journey.

"Are you Ok then?" Dave asked as he drove towards the motorway.

"Yes, I'm fine. I'm looking forward to meeting your parents again. I hope they'll like me," she added.

Dave smiled. "What is there not to like?" he asked.

"Hmm, lots. Ask Phil," Beth said grimly.

"Not a good judge. No, we'll ask everybody else who knows you instead," Dave said.

Beth smiled. Dave always seemed to cheer her up and find something amusing to say about everything.

"Are you sure you slept alright on that camp bed?" she asked again.

"Yes, I was fine. I can usually sleep anywhere," he reassured her. "Not that it was uncomfortable or anything, but I'm a good sleeper."

"What time will we arrive?" she asked. "It's nearly four o'clock now, does it take two or three hours to get there?"

"Usually about two, but the traffic will probably be bad so I would say nearer three. I think we'll check in at the hotel first and then go to Mum and Dad's. We should be there about seven o'clock. Mum is cooking for us so I said we'd eat at eight. Can you wait that long or do you want me to stop at a service station for a snack?" he asked considerately.

"No, I'll be fine. And I've bought some biscuits if we do get hungry on the journey. You get into that sort of mode when you've got hungry teenagers to feed," she said.

"That's probably something I'll never find out," Dave said ruefully. Beth looked at him. He looked somewhat regretful.

"Do you want to have children?" she asked suddenly.

"Yes I do. That's partly why there were problems with Lisa because she didn't want to start a family. I was prepared to live without children though, until I found out she was being unfaithful," Dave explained.

"Well, I don't think I will have any more children," Beth started to say. 'Oh, but if you want children, don't you think you should find someone to have them with?'

"Oh Beth. What a strange place to have a conversation like this – on the motorway going to my parents' house. I don't know what I want any more. I had got used to the idea of not having any children but I suppose it has entered my head again, since I split up with Lisa. But most of that time, I've been getting to know you again. And I'd rather be with you and not have children, than the alternative. Does that make sense?"

Beth put her hand on his knee. "Of course it does. I know what you're saying. But I suppose, if you really wanted a child, we could have one. All my bits are still in working order, you know."

Dave laughed. "And hopefully so are mine. But shall we leave this conversation for a more appropriate time. I don't think either of us are really in the right state of mind to be making any more life changing decisions. You especially, have several more to make quite soon," he reminded her.

Beth sighed.

"Yes, I know you're right. But I won't definitely say that I will not have any more children. I'm still just the right side of forty but I think if we do decide to have a baby, we'd better be quick about it."

Dave shook his head and laughed again. "I don't know Beth. Here we are doing just over seventy miles an hour on the motorway talking about our reproductive organs."

"Oh I wouldn't put it quite like that," she countered. "I was talking about my biological clock ticking away and the fact that we should have sex, sex and more sex very soon."

"Well you'll have to wait until we get to the hotel, my dear," Dave joked. "Then I'll try to oblige."

They passed the journey in good spirits and arrived at the hotel just after seven o'clock. They checked in and took their bags up the two flights of stairs to their room. Dave rang his parents to say they'd arrived and would be over in about half an hour. They unpacked their suitcases and drew the curtains.

Beth went into the bathroom and washed her face before applying some make up. She changed into a red linen sleeveless dress and pulled on her high heeled shoes. After pulling a comb through her hair and sending a text message to Annie, she picked up her handbag and jacket.

"Are you ready then?" she asked Dave who was just coming out of the en suite bathroom.

"Yes I'm ready. You're not nervous, are you Beth?" he asked looking at her closely.

"Of course I am. Weren't you nervous yesterday meeting Annie, James and Christina?" she asked.

Dave admitted that he had been.

"Can we stop somewhere to get some flowers for your mum?" she asked Dave as they left the hotel.

"Yes, there's a shop on the way that should still be open. That's a nice thought, Beth," Dave said.

When they turned into the road where Dave's parents lived, Beth was surprised that the houses were so big. Each property looked as if it had at least five bedrooms and an acre of garden.

"I didn't realise your parents had such a large house," she said.

Dave shrugged his shoulders. "I suppose I've just taken it for granted and of course I've never lived here. Dad was promoted to quite a good job during his last years before retiring and mum inherited a lot of money from an aunt who died about twenty years ago. So they bought this house supposedly as an investment. But they love the space. We grew up in a small three bedroom semi so they've revelled in the extra rooms and big garden. Mum loves gardening and dad enjoys painting. He's got one of the back bedrooms as a studio. It is particularly good for the light, apparently. So they both keep busy with their hobbies and the other two bedrooms are guest rooms. They have some friends in Scotland and Mum's sister who lives in Kent and they come to stay about three times a year. And of course my brother and his family stay occasionally."

Beth didn't ask if he and Lisa had stayed there because they obviously had.

Dave drove the car through some ornate wrought iron gates, up a sweeping drive and stopped the car outside the front door. His parents immediately opened the door and came out down the steps to greet their son and Beth.

"Hello Beth. Dave has told us about meeting up with you again. It's so nice to meet you although, of course, we have met before, but it seems such a long time ago now," his mother took Beth's hands in her's and warmly kissed her cheek.

"Oh it's lovely to meet you again too. I know what you mean, it does seem years ago that we were enjoying that holiday. So much has happened since then."

Beth smiled at the older woman. She turned and reached into the car to pick up the bouquet of flowers she'd bought after leaving the hotel. She handed to Frances.

"Oh Beth. They're lovely but you shouldn't have. Thank you," Frances said turning to her husband. "Darling, look at the lovely flowers Beth has bought us.'

"Well, well, my dear. Very nice of you Beth and it's good to meet you. Now come in to the house and let's get some drinks organised." Dave's father took hold of Beth's arm and marched back into his home. They went into a large room at the back of the house and Beth could sell the delicious scent of a dinner cooking in the kitchen.

She realised she was starving and hoped they didn't have to wait too long before dinner was served.

"Now, do call me Frances, dear, and Dave's Dad – Roger," advised Dave's mum handing her a glass of sherry.

"Thank you, Frances," Beth said obediently, sipping her drink.

"Cheers then everyone," said Roger holding his glass aloft. "Bottoms up is what I say!"

"Cheers," they all agreed. "Happy birthday Mum – tomorrow," added Dave.

"Thank you dear. Now dinner is just about ready. I'll just put these lovely flowers in water and then we can go through to the dining room," Frances said to Beth's relief.

They sat at a huge oak dining table which was set with four places but would have easily held a dinner party of twenty four. The food was hot and delicious and, while she ate, Beth listened to Dave talking with his parents about people and events she did not know.

Eventually they turned to her and began to ask questions about her children, her home and her job. She answered briefly each time and felt like a teenager again, being asked what subjects she was studying for exams.

Beth especially enjoyed the dessert of strawberry tart that Frances had made that afternoon. "I'd love to have the recipe," she said.

"Of course. The children would like it, wouldn't they. Dave and his brother always loved their puddings. Now, shall we go back into the drawing room for coffee?"

Dave and his dad had a small brandy with their coffee and Frances opened a box of mint chocolates which she placed on the small table in front of them.

"So what have you planned for tomorrow," Dave asked.

"Well, I thought we could go down to the boat house and see if we can get the Sally-Anne out on the lake. Do you like boating?" Roger asked Beth.

"Well, I really haven't done much of it. Although I do like walking by the canal and watching the boats go by," she said.

"Hmm, well, not quite the same. Anyway, I thought we'd take a trip out and you could make up a picnic, Fran. We could stop on the island if you like?"

"That sounds like a lovely idea. I checked the weather forecast earlier and it seems to be a good day tomorrow. I'll make a picnic and we'll leave about eleven o'clock. Will that fit in with your plans, Dave?" his mother asked.

"Your plans are our plans, Mum. It's your birthday weekend. We'll do whatever you would like. We'll be here about ten thirty. Don't forget we're taking you out for a meal at the Regency Hotel in the evening. The table is booked for eight o'clock, so we'll have to be back in time to get ready. Beth has bought a new dress specially, haven't you?"

"Er, yes I have. I hope it's alright for the Regency'."

"I'm sure it will be lovely," Frances reassured her. "Now do you two think you should be getting back to the hotel before it's too late. You don't want to get locked out, do you?"

"I hardly think that's likely to happen, Mum. It's only ten o'clock.

But you're right. We're pretty tired so we'll get an early night. Are you ready Beth?"

Beth stood up and turned to Frances and Roger.

"Thank you so much for the lovely meal. It was delicious. I'm really looking forward to tomorrow and spending the day with you."

"Oh we are too, my dear," said Frances stepping forward to kiss goodnight to Beth and then Dave.

"Here's your jacket, m'dear," Roger held it for her as she slipped her arms into the sleeves. "See you both tomorrow."

"Well what did you think?" Dave asked as they drove back to the hotel. "Do you reckon you'll like my mum and dad?"

"Oh, of course I will. They're lovely. I meant what I said about looking forward to spending the day with them," Beth said.

"Well, let's enjoy the night before first," Dave said.

Which they did!!

Chapter Twenty Three

--ooOoo--

*A*s they drove back on Sunday afternoon, Beth and Dave talked about the weekend.

"I so enjoyed the trip on the boat," Beth said. "I'd love to do that again sometime. And the kids would enjoy it too."

Dave nodded. "Well, sometime soon, we'll take them to meet Mum and Dad and we'll go out in the boat. What did you really think of the Regency?" he asked.

Beth laughed. "Well, it was a little old-fashioned wasn't it? The waiters looked like they'd been serving food for about a hundred years. And the maitre'd – he was amazing – so stiff and starchy! But actually I enjoyed the evening very much. It was nice to go somewhere so posh and be thoroughly spoiled. Shame your brother and his wife couldn't get there."

"Yes. They went last year but their two children didn't behave particularly well. I think they were a bit bored. It's not quite the place for children, is it?"

"No. I don't think James and Christina would cope very well with all that formality and cutlery. Annie would probably be Ok, but she's a bit older."

"I expect they prefer pizza and fast food places, don't' they?" Dave asked.

Beth nodded. "Yes, they certainly do. But I try not to take them there too often. A bit of home cooking is best. Although working full time is not conducive to preparing lots of meals from basics and I have resorted to frozen food more just recently."

"Mum and Dad always enjoy going to the Regency. I think it gives them a bit of a blast from the past. They've always enjoyed formal dinner dances and the chance to entertain at home in their dining room."

"Have they ever used the whole table?" Beth asked wonderingly.

"Oh, yes. At Christmas time and for a few other large family gatherings. Also Mum used to entertain some of Dad's work colleagues before he retired. She enjoys cooking but I think she finds it rather tiring now. It's the same with the garden. I sometimes wonder if they shouldn't downsize now," Dave said.

"Have you spoken to them about that?" Beth asked.

"No, not yet. I thought I'd talk to my brother first and see if he thinks the same. I don't want to interfere with their lives when they are obviously so happy. If I start putting doubt into their minds as to whether they can cope, it might precipitate their moving."

"Yes, I know what you mean. I look at my mum and dad sometimes and hope they're not getting too tired helping with the kids after school. I know they enjoy it but with me working it is a big commitment for them. They can't really let me down one day if they feel tired or off-colour," Beth said.

"Well it's not going to be forever. All the children are growing up, aren't they?" Dave reasoned.

"Yes, that's true," Beth realised that it would probably only be a year or two until they could manage on their own for the hour or so before she arrived home from work. That made her feel a bit better about her parents' commitment.

When they arrived at Beth's house, it was obvious that no-one was in. Dave pulled Beth's case out of the back of the car as she opened the front door.

"Anyone in?" she called. There was no response.

"There's no-one in at the moment. Let's go and get a nice cool drink," she suggested.

"Where are they likely to be?" asked Dave as he sat down in a comfortable chair in the conservatory.

"I'm not sure. Annie may be at Ben's house, just across the back there. Mum and Dad might have taken the other two out somewhere nice for the afternoon. I'm sure they'll all turn up eventually," she said.

They sat for nearly an hour, quietly talking and enjoying their last few moments together before Dave had to set off on his journey back to Barnstaple.

"'When will I see you again?" Beth had to ask.

"I'm hoping to get away for a few days next month," he said. "I need to talk to Donald about something technical for the new computer programme. I won't bore you with the details! Donald is someone I used to work with and he's a particular genius when it comes to anything connected with computers," Dave explained.

"Oh great. Not too long then. I'm taking two weeks off work at the beginning of August to stay with Verity and John. They don't live too far from you so hopefully we should be able to get together a few times, if you'd like."

"Of course I would like. That sounds wonderful. Shall I try and get some holiday booked for when you're there?" he asked.

"Yes, then we can spend some time together without always rushing about so much and looking at the clock." she said.

At these words, Dave glanced at his watch and finished his drink before standing up ready to leave.

"It's a shame you've got to go before they get back," Beth said, carrying both glasses back into the kitchen.

"Will you be alright on your own?" Dave asked, suddenly concerned.

"Oh, of course I will. I didn't mean that. It would just have been nice to have everyone here to wave you off. No, I'm fine on my own, don't worry about me," she reassured him.

They hugged and kissed for a few minutes in the hallway, as they whispered their goodbyes to each other.

"I'll ring you when I get back and it won't be long till we're together again," Dave promised.

Beth waved him off with a forced smile and a few tears gathering in her eyes. She didn't want him to remember her as a red-eyed blubbering wreck, so she kept hold of herself until she went back indoors. She sat on the stairs and put her face in her hands. She didn't cry but felt all her worries and problems come tumbling back on to her shoulders. Work, house, Phil, kids and Dave living what seemed like a million miles away. She sat there for a few minutes before mentally shaking herself back to full control again.

As she stood up she heard a key turn in the front door and Annie came in. It was immediately obvious that she too had been crying and Beth went straight over and put her arms around her daughter's heaving shoulders.

"What on earth's the matter Annie?" she asked.

"Oh, Mum. It's not fair," she managed between sobs. "I've just broken up with Ben."

"Oh darling. That's awful. What happened?"

"That Melissa. It's all her fault. She turned up again at Ben's house about an hour ago and started making comments about me. Horrible comments about broken families and how it affects teenagers and makes them go bad. She pretended it was all to do with research for her English essay, but I knew she was just trying to upset me."

"Well what has that to do with you and Ben?" asked Beth.

"After she'd gone I told Ben I was fed up with her coming round all the time. But he said he didn't mind. So I said that I did mind and he'd better choose between her and me and which one of us he wanted to have as a girlfriend. He said that he thought perhaps he didn't want a girlfriend at all at the moment. He wanted to keep his options open and didn't want to be tied down to one person. I said that I thought he liked me and he said he did, but didn't want to get seriously into a relationship."

"Well you are both very young still," Beth said gently as she steered Annie into the front room.

"I know and I didn't think we'd necessarily last forever or get married or anything like that," Annie said, sitting down and subsiding to just a few sniffs. "But I thought we had something special together, and he's been so supportive and helped me when Dad left us. I can't believe he didn't stand up for me when Melissa started going on. When I asked why he hadn't, he just said he didn't think she meant to get at me. I mean, how stupid can anyone be?" Annie ended on a belligerent note as she looked to her mother for an answer.

Beth shook her head. "I know it's hard, darling, but it happens to all of us sometime. There are not many people who go through life without breaking up with someone they think is special. I remember your Aunt Verity was devastated when she was about nineteen and her boyfriend dumped her after they'd been together for about two years. She wouldn't go out or do anything for six months afterwards." She glanced at Annie and continued, "'But of course, you're not going to do that, Annie. You must pick yourself up and carry on, especially at the moment when you're in the middle of your exams. Are you sure it's not just exam worry that has got to Ben?" she asked.

Annie shook her head. "No Mum, I'm sure it's not that. We just don't seem to have a laugh any more and it seems he'd rather go out with his friends than be with me. Haven't you noticed I haven't been over to his house much during the last two weeks?"

Beth was ashamed to admit that she hadn't noticed. She'd been too preoccupied with her own problems, and then looking forward to her weekend away with Dave which had taken up all her thoughts recently.

"I'm sorry Annie. All I know is that you've been closeted upstairs studying for your exams every evening. I just thought you and Ben had decided to revise separately while you were taking your GCSEs."

"It's going to seem weird not being Ben's girlfriend any more," mused Annie. "I've been seeing him for about eight months now. I've got to get used to being single again. Like you did, Mum."

"Oh yes, thanks for reminding me! Anyway, I'm practically still single with Dave living at the other end of the country," Beth said, with a short laugh.

"Oh, how was your weekend? Sorry Mum, I forgot to ask," Annie said.

"That's all right, darling. You had other things on your mind. But yes, we had a lovely weekend. We went out in a boat on a lake on Saturday and took a picnic to an island. It was lovely. So peaceful. And Dave's parents are very nice. They live in a large house which they rattle around in together."

Annie laughed which brought a bit of colour back into her pale cheeks.

"Dave says we'll all go there one weekend and go out in the boat again. That will be nice won't it?," she asked.

Annie nodded. "Yes it will. I'll try and get over Ben as quickly as I can but I feel so sad and angry all at once. I'm angry that Melissa has caused this problem between us and I'm sad that Ben doesn't want to go out with me any more."

"Maybe he'll change his mind when he realises he's going to miss you," Beth said.

"Maybe," Annie said quietly. "But somehow I don't think so. He's got big plans for the summer holidays and they don't include me. He's going camping with some of his friends and then on to a fishing holiday with his dad and brother for two weeks. By the time we've been to stay at Aunty Verity's, there wouldn't be much time left for us."

"Do you think you're going to be able to concentrate on the rest of your exams?" Beth asked anxiously.

"Oh, yes Mum. Don't worry. I still want to get good grades in my GCSEs. Although I don't know if I really want to go back to school now to do A levels. Marilyn and Sheila are both going to college to study art and Linda is doing to do a secretarial course. So all my best friends are going somewhere else."

"What would you like to do then? Have you any ideas?" Beth asked.

This was the first she'd heard that Annie didn't want to stay on at school and take more exams. This was another worrying niggle for the back of her head and here she was, dealing with it on her own.

"Have you told your father any of this yet?" she asked.

"No, I've only just realised it myself really. Breaking up with Ben has made me think of what job I want to do in the future. And I don't know what I want to be at the moment. I'm not good at anything particularly, not like Sheila and Marilyn who both know what they want to do after leaving art college. Even Linda is planning to become a PA after her secretarial course. I hadn't even decided which A levels to take, I was going to wait for the GCSE results."

"Well, perhaps that's still the best option. Wait until we get your results in August and then decide if you want to go on and take A levels, or do something else. I suppose you could even get a job," Beth said dubiously.

Annie laughed. "Yes Mum, I could get a job. But doing what? Anything worthwhile needs qualifications or experience, or both. And I've got neither. No, I'll have to take some sort of course but the difficult thing is choosing what I want to do."

"I suppose you don't have to go back to school. You could go to the college and take a course there. But, as you said, you need to know what you want to do. You'll have to go and get some careers advice from the library. When we get back from Aunt Verity's, we'll go together," Beth said.

"Thanks Mum. That's great. I don't have to worry about it yet, then. I'll wait for the exam results and decide then," Annie sighed with relief.

Beth was very glad she'd had this talk with Annie and seemed to have put her mind at rest. It would take her a few days, or maybe even weeks, to get over her first boyfriend. But as she'd said, it happened to most people and you just had to move on.

"Where do you think Grandma and Granddad have taken James and Christina?" Beth asked, looking at her watch.

"They said they were going to that new garden centre. Do you remember, the one you said Amanda had been to recently?" Annie told her.

"Oh, right." Beth couldn't imagine James being remotely interested in garden centres and wondered why they'd been gone so long. He was not good at hiding his boredom and she thought his grandparents would have brought him back long before this. As Beth stood up and looked out of the window she noticed Jack drive his car onto the drive.

"Oh, they're back," she said with some relief. She went to the front door and opened it to greet them all.

"Hi Mum. Guess what? We've been to the garden centre and it was ace," yelled Christina climbing out of the back of the car. She was clutching a small box with holes in the top.

"Look what we've bought. A hamster! There was a pet's corner and they sell some of the animals. We think it's a girl and I'm going to call her Tinkerbell. Grandad said she looked like a little fairy'.

"I hope you don't mind," Beth's father said as he came towards the house. "But we thought it would be nice to put a hamster in that lovely cage that Dave bought Christina. You did say she could have one, didn't you?" he asked anxiously.

"Oh, of course dad. That's fine. Don't worry. Thanks for going to buy one. How much was it? I'll just get my purse," Beth said.

"No, no, that's alright. We've bought Tinkerbell for Christina," her mother said as she stepped into the hallway.

"Look, Mum," Christina opened the box slightly to show off her new pet.

Beth peeped inside and saw a small pale brown coloured hamster hiding as best she could in the shavings at the bottom of the box.

"Oh, she's lovely," Beth agreed. "Now take her upstairs and settle her into her new home. Don't forget to give her some water, will you?"

Christina didn't need telling twice and carried the box carefully upstairs.

"Cup of tea?" offered Beth looking closely at her parents to gauge if they were exhausted after their weekend.

"Yes darling, that would be nice. And then we'll take you all out for dinner tonight. Dad's booked a table at the Old Well for six thirty. He thought you'd be too tired for cooking after your weekend away, and it's a treat for us too."

"Have they worn you out Mum?" Beth asked quietly as they stood in the kitchen waiting for the kettle to boil.

"What? Oh no, of course not dear. They mostly just get on with their own things, don't they? As you said, we were just a taxi service yesterday and today Annie went to Ben's house about midday so we took the others to the garden centre for a snack and a look round. It was amazing – James actually seemed to enjoy himself there. He got quite interested in some of the plants. He said they were studying cacti in biology and got talking to one of the garden centre staff who seemed to be very knowledgeable. Then we found the pet's corner and you know the rest."

"I did wonder what was holding James' interest for so long," Beth admitted. "He's not one for keeping quiet when he's bored or not interested."

They took the tea into the conservatory and joined Jack and James who were discussing the next England cricket match. Annie had gone upstairs with Christina to help with Tinkerbell.

"Christina says that she's going to start some horse riding lessons," Jack said. "Can you afford to pay for them Beth?"

Beth nodded. "Yes Dad, Phil has agreed to go halves with me and she's only having half an hour a week at present, on a Wednesday evening starting this week."

"Verity says that Lucy loves the little pony they have borrowed for her. Apparently the girl from the next door farm gives her a riding lesson once or twice a week. So Christina will be able to share the pony when you visit in August."

"Yes. I must admit, I'm so looking forward to going away. It seems that's all I'm working towards at the moment."

"Are you still having problems at work?" Vera asked.

"Well, only that I haven't decided whether I want to keep my job.

It is such a long way to travel through the rush hour traffic and will probably add about an hour to my journey time each day. But the only alternative is to find another job. I've been looking in the paper, but there's not much about at the moment. Apart from temporary holiday jobs, of course. I think it's probably something else I'll leave until after I've been away in August."

"Oh, what else are you leaving until after you've been away?" Vera immediately wanted to know.

"Er, well. Just the usual type of problems, you know," Beth didn't want to tell her parents about having to put the house up for sale, or Phil's request for a divorce, until it was absolutely necessary.

"Are you sure that's all?" asked her father.

"Yes, I'm sure. As I said, I'm just looking forward to getting away for a few weeks," she responded.

"When will you be seeing Dave again? It's a shame we missed him this afternoon. He seems a very nice, polite young man," her mother said.

"Yes, Mum. He is a nice man. I think he's coming back this way again in June as he's got to meet an ex-colleague. And he doesn't live too far from Verity and John so I should be able to see him at the beginning of August," Beth told her.

"Why did he move away so soon after you'd met? Was it something you said, Beth?" her father said, smiling at her.

"Oh, ha ha – very funny! He wanted to move away from this area after his marriage broke down and so he applied for jobs in other parts of the country. It just happened that he was offered the one in Barnstaple. They certainly needed him as he's been so busy there since joining, although he says it should settle down a bit when they have their new systems in place. He said he'll try and take a few days holiday when we're in Cornwall so we can spend some time together."

"Well, we're certainly looking forward to staying with Verity next month. It's so peaceful in that part of the world. It would be an ideal place to retire to, I suppose," mused Jack.

Vera looked at him. "Well, we can't move at the moment Jack, we've got to help Beth and the children."

"Oh, I know that, dear. I was only thinking aloud. Of course we won't be moving, certainly until the children are older and Beth doesn't need us so much," Jack replied.

Beth felt a twinge of guilt inside her. Were her parents thinking of retiring to Cornwall? Was it only the fact that she needed their help that was keeping them here?

She was about to ask them when Vera rose to her feet and said that she thought they'd pop home first to freshen up and then meet Beth and the children at the Old Well at six thirty.

"'James, go upstairs please and tell the girls that Grandma and Grandad are going," said Beth also standing up.

As James ran upstairs, Beth turned to her parents intending to ask if they were finding it too difficult and tiring helping with the children. But Vera forestalled her and put her hand on Beth's arm.

"Don't take any notice of us," she said. "We love keeping an eye on Annie, James and Christina and it's no bother. We really enjoy taking them out and spending time with them. So you are not to worry about us, Beth."

"Of course I worry about you, Mum. I don't want to impose on you both. But it won't be forever. As Dave said to me earlier today, the children are growing up and they'll be able to manage on their own quite soon."

"Exactly," agreed her father giving her a hug. "In the meantime, as your mother said, we love taking them out and about. So don't worry. And we'll be here in the summer holidays while you're at work. We'll try and make sure they don't get bored."

The children came into the room and, to Beth's pleasure and pride, thanked their grandparents for the weekend without having to be told.

As Beth shut the front door, having waved them off, Christina grabbed her hand and said, "Come upstairs and see Tinkerbell, Mum. She's all settled in her new home now. Come and look."

Beth allowed herself to be dragged upstairs and duly admired Tinkerbell's living quarters.

When she came back onto the landing she noticed that Annie had gone back into her own bedroom. Beth knocked quietly and opened the door.

"Are you alright, Annie?" she asked.

"Yes, Mum. Don't worry. I'll get ready to go out with Grandma and Grandad," Annie said.

Beth went into her own bedroom and opened the weekend case she'd left on the bed. She sorted out the washing and put her toiletries back in the en suite shower room. She just had time for a quick shower and change of clothes.

When they arrived at the restaurant, Jack and Vera were already enjoying their drinks at a table by the window. As he spotted them hovering by the door, Jack stood up and waved.

"Over here," he called.

Beth led the way to the table and Jack took orders for drinks. He went to the bar with James and Beth looked round the busy restaurant. She noticed half a dozen people sat at a table in the far corner. As she glanced at them she realised that Phil and Lisa were part of the group who were making a lot of noise and had obviously been drinking.

Beth immediately turned away and pulled her hair around her face. What should she do? She didn't want the children to see their father making a spectacle of himself but also didn't see why their plans for a quiet meal together should be disrupted. She just hoped the group had nearly finished and would be leaving soon before one of the children spotted their dad.

Jack and James arrived with the drinks and menus. After a few minutes the waitress arrived to take their orders. Beth glanced surreptitiously over to the corner of the room. She saw a waiter arriving with a tray of coffees. Good. That meant they would be leaving soon. Vera was asking Christina about her riding lessons and Jack and James were discussing cricket again. Beth began to talk to Annie about the last two exams she had to take during the next week. She hoped that the noisy group would leave through the back exit and not have to pass by their table. She couldn't look round in case Annie followed her gaze and the minutes ticked slowly past as she waited for their food to arrive to create another small diversion.

After what seemed an age, the waitress arrived back at their table carrying three plates of food. Another waiter accompanied her with the remaining meals and Beth breathed a sigh of relief as she noticed Phil and Lisa standing up ready to leave. She hoped that no-one in her party would see them as they'd be too busy eating to look round.

Just as she took the first mouthful of her lasagne, she heard his voice.

"Oh, look who's here!" came Phil's loud comment as he stopped by their table.

"Hi kids. I didn't know you were coming here today," he slurred slightly.

"Oh Dad, hi," James said.

"Good evening, Phil," Jack said immediately noticing that Phil was slightly worse for wear. "We're just having a quiet meal and it looks like you've finished yours?"

"Yes, Jack. That's right. We've just finished ours. We were sitting over there," Phil pointed to the corner of the restaurant where their friends still sat.

"But we've finished now." He looked at Beth. "So, where's lover boy today, then?" he asked.

Beth looked up at him ready with a sharp comment. But Vera interrupted and put her hand on Beth's arm.

"We're just having a quiet family meal, Phil. Perhaps you should go now as you've finished yours. I'm sure you'll be seeing the children again tomorrow," she suggested.

"Yes, come on Phil," said Lisa pulling his arm. "Let's go now."

"I hope he's not going to be driving," Jack asked.

"No, of course not. We're in my car," Lisa informed him snootily. "We're quite well aware of the drink driving laws."

"I'm sure you are, my dear," said Jack patronisingly. "Anyway, our food is getting cold so we'll bid you good day," he ended, dismissing them.

Phil looked at his father-in-law and said, somewhat belligerently. "I'm just speaking to my children. That is allowed, you know. I have every right…"

"We'll see you tomorrow, Dad, after you've finished work," Annie suddenly interrupted. "Why don't you go home with…Lisa…now."

Phil looked at his eldest daughter. "Yes Annie. I'll see you tomorrow, after work," he repeated obediently. "Bye then" and he stumbled around the table to kiss each of his children on the top of their heads. He followed Lisa out of the restaurant, stumbling again as he went through the doorway.

Jack and Vera picked up their cutlery and resumed their meal. The children looked at Beth and she smiled reassuringly at them, also picking up her knife and fork.

"Don't worry now. Your father has just had a few drinks. He's obviously been celebrating with his friends. It's nothing to worry about. He'll be back to normal again tomorrow," she said. James and Christina nodded and Annie smiled at her mother.

"So what are you hoping to do at half term then?" Jack asked the children in an attempt to lighten the atmosphere.

As James and Christina immediately began to list everything they wanted to cram in to the week's holiday, Beth managed to relax enough to enjoy the rest of her dinner. However, she did notice that Annie didn't eat a lot and just pushed the food around the plate trying to hide some of it.

When they'd finished their meal with either coffee or ice cream, depending on their age, Jack went to pay the bill and they all walked out to the car park. Vera took Beth's arm to hold her back from the others.

"Phil wasn't very pleasant in there. He's not abusive or anything when he comes round to see the children, is he?" she asked anxiously.

Beth smiled. "No, Mum. Honestly, that's just what he's like when he's had too much to drink. It's always made him a bit, well, aggressive, I suppose. But he's not violent or abusive. Just a bit bolshie, I suppose you'd call it."

Vera nodded. "That's alright then. I wouldn't like to think you or the children are exposed to any possible violence or bullying from him. He was starting to be pretty rude to you though, wasn't he?

"Yes, but that's the first time he's spoken to me like that. I still think it was the drink talking, though. He's been quite reasonable really, for someone who just upped and left their wife and family," Beth finished ruefully.

"Well, just let us know if you have any problems. It seems obvious there's no hope for a reconciliation between the two of you now. You've both found new partners already. It's just amazing that they are married to each other, as well."

Beth hugged her mother as they reached the car. "Don't worry, everything's fine," she said, wishing she could believe that too.

Jack hugged his daughter and repeated his wife's words about letting them know if Beth had any problems.

Beth and the children waved to Jack and Vera and then set off back to their own home.

The children were quiet in the car and Beth realised they were trying to make sense of their father's erratic behaviour. Phil had never allowed himself to become drunk in front of the children and had only indulged in moderate amounts of alcohol since they were born. Obviously his behaviour was altering now he was free from family responsibilities.

Chapter Twenty Four

--ooOoo--

*A*t the beginning of June, the week of half term passed smoothly. Annie's exams were over and she was coming to terms with her split from Ben. James had finished his SATs and Christina was ecstatic with her weekly riding lessons on Wednesday evenings.

Phil had three days off work and took the children out somewhere different each day. Lisa accompanied them once when they went to a theme park and seemed to make a big effort to join in with them, riding on some of the biggest and scariest rides with James and Phil.

Amanda volunteered to take all five children out for a picnic on the Friday and so the week was covered without Beth needing any more time off work. Her interview with her boss was scheduled for the following Tuesday and she was still undecided whether to take the redundancy option or try and cope with the extra travelling.

After showing himself up at the restaurant in front of the children, Phil had apologised to them the next day. He'd said that they'd been celebrating two of Lisa's friends becoming engaged and that he didn't usually go out and get drunk. They accepted this and Beth was glad he'd been up front with them instead of trying to make excuses.

She'd received the forms from the solicitor and had signed and returned them the next day. Phil didn't speak to her very much during his visits to see the children, which were now reduced to about four times a week. He hadn't mentioned putting the house up for sale again and she hoped this would last for a few more weeks. Every time she tried to reach a decision about one of her problems, another would enter her head and distract her.

Dave was making arrangements to see his ex-colleague for the last week of June. He said he'd be able to stay for three nights and that he'd booked some holiday during the first two weeks of August to coincide with Beth's visit to Verity and John. So Beth just tried to keep going with their routine of work, school and weekends.

Annie had started a part time job in a local nursing home where she made cups of tea and read newspapers to the elderly folk during the afternoons. Amanda had found this job for Annie as her mother was one of the residents.

As the days became hotter and longer, Beth seemed to become more and more dissatisfied with her life. She resented being at work all day with the sun shining outside and her children arriving home before she did. She worried about losing her home and how she'd be able to afford a mortgage, however small, with the possibility of having to change her job. Most of her colleagues were excited about the changes and were looking forward to working in a brand new office. However, one or two were applying for other jobs but were experiencing difficulty finding something suitable.

When it came to her interview with Allan, she told him she was still undecided about whether to take redundancy or not. She explained that she would like to wait until she returned from her holiday in Cornwall to make her final decision.

Allan agreed that she needed more time to make her mind up. He said that he'd be away on holiday until the end of August and that he'd wait for her decision until then. She was glad she'd always got on well with her boss and that he was agreeable to take into account her mixed feelings.

Jack and Vera returned from their week in Cornwall full of enthusiasm for all Verity and John's plans.

"They want to grow several acres of daffodils and strawberries," Jack told Beth. "Although these are seasonal, they think they can manage the harvesting without having to buy too much heavy equipment at this stage. They may make some of the strawberry fields pick your own. They've bought some hens, ducks and goats and have rented a stall at the local market to sell the eggs and milk. They've really adapted to their new life and Sam and Lucy seem so happy and love being out doors all the time. Verity never has to ask them to do something twice."

"Has Sam already had lots of surfing lessons?" asked James. He was looking forward to using the new board that Dave had given him.

"'Yes, he has a lesson every Saturday afternoon. But they are going to book you in for a week's lessons when you go in August," his grandfather reassured him.

"And how's Toby?" Christina wanted to know.

"Oh, he's lovely," said Vera. "I don't know much about horses but Lucy seems to ride him very well. She's always out there, mucking about, or whatever it is."

"Oh Grandma – it's called mucking out," Christina told her as they all laughed.

Dave arrived on her doorstep on the Wednesday evening just after they'd arrived back from Christina's riding lesson.

"Oh, hi. I wasn't expecting you for another hour," Beth said as she opened the door to him. "We've only just got back. How are you – did you have a good journey? she asked.

Dave lifted his two cases into the hallway and put them down at his feet.

"Yes, I'm fine and it was a good journey – that's why I'm here so early. Now come here, my lovely Beth, and give me a kiss," he pulled her to him and kissed her soundly.

"Yeuch, do you have to do that," James said as he came down the stairs.

"Hiya mate. How's tricks?" Dave said as he let Beth go.

"Fine thanks, Dave. How long are you staying?"

"Trying to get rid of me already? Huh, I know I'm not welcome here then!"

"No, I didn't mean that," said James looking worried.

"I know you didn't, mate. Only joking," Dave said grinning at him. "It's just my weird sense of humour."

James laughed and went into the kitchen.

"Come on, let's get your stuff in the dining room where I've set your bed up again. Hope that's alright," she added looking at him anxiously.

He nodded and winked at her. "That's fine, Beth. I didn't expect anything else," he reassured her.

They organised his clothes and he took his toiletries up to the bathroom. When he came down again, Beth had made some sandwiches for everyone.

"Can you shout the girls please," she asked James.

They all sat around the kitchen table and made short work of the sandwiches, crisps, sausage rolls and a fruit salad Annie had made earlier.

"That was great," said Dave, patting his stomach. "Just what I needed after that long journey."

"You must come upstairs and see my new hamster," Christina said.

"Grandma and Grandad bought her for me at the garden centre and I've called her Tinkerbell."

"I'd love to come and see Tinkerbell," said Dave getting up. "Shall we go and look at her now?"

Beth was pleased that Dave seemed to get on well with all her children. She tidied up the kitchen and made some coffee which she took into the front room, where she waited for Dave to return downstairs.

"Well, that's a fine looking wee beastie upstairs," he said as he sat on the sofa next to Beth. She giggled.

"Don't bother with the Scottish accent," she said digging him in the ribs with her elbow. "It's nae tha good."

Dave took a sip of his coffee and then turned to Beth.

"Now then, have you come to any decisions yet?" he asked.

"What about?"

"You know what about. Your job, your house, your divorce. All those minor issues of life!"

"Well no I haven't," she admitted. "I have decided, though, that I'm going to wait until after our holiday to make the decisions. I'm hoping that the peace and tranquility of country life in Cornwall will help my decisive powers."

Dave sat back into the settee. "Well if you think that's wise. But I'm not sure you shouldn't just get on and face up to things. After all, what's going to change when you're in Cornwall?"

"I don't know, really. It's just a feeling I've got. I don't seem to have the energy to confront things at the moment. The last blow was having to decide about moving to another office the other side of town or whether to take redundancy. I just don't know what's best at the moment. I'm sorry," she ended.

"You don't have to be sorry, Beth," Dave said immediately, turning to her and kissing her cheek. "My love, it's your life and therefore your decisions. They mostly won't affect anyone else, I suppose, apart from the children. And they're very adaptable, so they say. I mean, if you had to move to another house the kids probably wouldn't mind that much. It's you who wants to stay here, isn't it?"

Beth thought about it. "Yes, you're probably right," she agreed. "It's me who wants to stay here. And I think that's because I don't want any more changes in my life than because of memories and stuff like that."

"Well, do as you said and leave the decision-making until after your holiday. If you don't pressure yourself too much the answers will probably just occur to you anyway," Dave said wisely.

"Mmm, that's what I thought," agreed Beth snuggling up to him. "Now, shall we watch something or would you rather listen to music?"

They found a film on one of the Sky channels and within twenty minutes all three children had come downstairs to watch it with them. It was a romantic comedy that did include several very funny moments and even James was able to watch the whole film without a murmur of criticism.

The next day everyone was up early and ready for work and school. Apart from Annie, of course, who was free to stay in bed all morning now her school days had ended. She'd told Beth that she was looking forward to the school prom next Friday evening, although she was a bit worried how she'd react watching Ben dance with other girls. One of her friend's fathers had booked a stretch limousine to take six of them to the hotel where the prom was to be held.

Beth had taken Annie shopping to buy a beautiful plum-coloured dress and had booked a hair appointment for five o'clock when she finished her shift at the nursing home.

James and Christina, Beth and Dave all left the house at the same time and called their goodbyes out to Annie.

"I'll see you back here by six o'clock," Dave promised as he walked over to his car. "We'll go mad and have a takeaway, shall we?""

"Oh, yes, can we have pizza?" Christina yelled out of the back window of Beth's car.

"No, let's have a Chinese," James said. "I like all those crispy bits and noodles."

"We'll sort it out tonight, you two," Beth said as she waved to Dave. "Now, seat belts on and close the windows, please."

The three days of Dave's visit flew past for Beth. They took the children out for a meal on the Friday and Vera cooked for them all on Saturday evening. Jack and Dave found they were in agreement about football teams and England's cricketers with James joining in their conversations too.

After lunch on Sunday afternoon, Dave packed all his belongings into his cases and piled them on the back seat of his car. He turned to give Beth a last hug.

"Come on now, don't get upset. It's not long until you'll be in the west country and we can enjoy some days exploring the coastline. You know I've not had much time to get out and about so it will be great to do it together," he said and then kissed her long and lingeringly.

"Bye Dave!" called Christina from the front doorway. "See you soon."

Beth pulled away and managed a watery smile. "I know it's not long now. 'm really looking forward to getting away. I just can't bear the thought of coming back to deal with all my problems. Maybe they'll disappear if I'm not here," she said.

"Maybe," Dave said pulling her back towards him. "But remember Beth, I'm here to help you. I don't want to take over and make any decisions for you, but if you want to talk things over, just call me. We'll still have our nightly telephone conversations anyway. I'll ring you when I get back. Just try and relax and chill out a bit, as James might say."

"Ha, you're picking up the teenage lingo too," Beth laughed. "It doesn't take long before everything is wicked or ace or cool."

They laughed together and Dave got into the car. Beth waved until he'd driven out of sight. She took a deep breath and turned to go back into the house.

Christina was still stood in the doorway. "Come on Mum, cheer up. It's not long till you see Dave again. And you've still got us, you know."

"I know, darling. Thank you. I just get a bit sad when he drives away. I'll be alright in a few minutes. And I know I've got you – I wouldn't be without any of you."

Christina wrapped her arms around Beth's waist and squeezed her tight for a few seconds.

Annie and James appeared from the front room and Beth opened her arms to them too. Annie came straight over but James hesitated slightly before giving up and joining in with the group hug.

"Ok, that's it. Let's cheer ourselves up a bit. What shall we do for the rest of the day?" Beth asked as they all drew apart.

"Let's go out somewhere," suggested James.

"Where?" asked Christina.

"What about swimming?" asked Beth. "Shall we go to the pool?"

"'Yes, let's. It will be warm enough to swim outside," agreed Christina.

"You'll come, won't you Annie?" Beth turned to her eldest daughter.

Annie nodded. "Yes, Mum. I'll come. It will be nice to swim in the outdoor pool."

They all went upstairs and packed swimming costumes and towels into their sports bags and set off for the pool.

Later that evening, Dave rang to say he'd just arrived back at his flat. The roads had been quite busy so the journey had taken nearly an hour longer than usual. Beth had been worrying for the last half an hour or so, as he hadn't rung to confirm he'd got back safely.

"What did you do after I left?" asked Dave.

"We went swimming at the local pool. It was nice. There weren't many people there and I managed to swim for about twenty minutes in the outdoor pool. One of James's friends was there too, so he was happy and the girls swam a bit and then we sunbathed outside. I'd forgotten how relaxing and therapeutic swimming is. I'll have to go more often!" she said.

"I'm pleased you found something nice to take your mind off my departure," Dave said. "Have you got anything planned for this week, or is it just work, work, work?" he asked.

"I'm going out for a meal with some of the girls from my department on Tuesday evening. It's straight from work so Mum and Dad are going to cook tea here that night. Apart from that, you're right, it's just work, work, work. Same for you?"

"Yes, same for me. I've got to put all the ideas Doug gave me into practice so I'll probably have to work late most nights this week. I think I'll be like you and ready for our break at the beginning of August."

They said their goodbyes and Beth spent the rest of the evening tidying up the house and preparing for the next week at work.

The week passed quickly and it was soon Friday evening and the night of the prom. Beth collected Annie from the nursing home after work and took her to the hairdressing salon. She'd also booked an appointment for a trim and they enjoyed an hour's pampering.

Jack and Vera had prepared tea and Annie managed to eat a small portion before rushing upstairs to have a careful bath to avoid messing up her hairstyle.

Beth went upstairs half an hour later and found Annie sat at her dressing table in her underwear applying mascara. She waited until she'd finished before offering to help her into the beautiful dress hanging on the back of the door.

As Beth pulled up the zip in the side of the dress they both looked at Annie's reflection in the long full length mirror.

'Wow!" said Annie, disbelievingly. Her hair was piled on the top of her head with a few curls hanging artfully down. The colouring of the dress suited Annie's complexion and a pair of sparkly sandals completed the outfit.

"Yes, wow," agreed Beth. "What a stunner. You're going to turn some heads tonight, Annie. Now let's take some photographs in the garden before it's time for you to go. And your Dad should be here in a few minutes," she said looking at her watch.

As Beth was taking some photographs of Annie stood in front of the lavender bushes in the back garden, Phil arrived out through the conservatory door.

"Oh Annie. You look beautiful," he said immediately. Beth was pleased that he voiced his approval so quickly.

Annie blushed slightly and smiled at her father. "Thanks Dad," she said.

Beth realised this was probably the first positive reaction she'd given her dad for many months.

He must have noticed too as he went straight over and kissed Annie.

"You will be the belle of the ball," he said. "Won't she Beth?"

"Oh certainly she will," agreed Beth. "But come on, let's go inside and wait for the car to collect you. It's nearly eight o'clock and it will be here in a minute."

The pink stretched limousine arrived exactly at eight o'clock and parked outside. The back door was opened by the uniformed chauffeur and Annie was ushered into the car to join her friends.

Beth, Phil, James and Christina watched and waved as Annie was taken to her school prom in style.

"Can I have a pink car for my school prom too?" Christina asked as they went back into the house.

"Of course you can," Phil immediately said. "And James can have one too!"

They all laughed apart from James who immediately said he didn't want to ride in a pink car.

"Anyway, I'll have to go now. I only came over to see Annie in her ball dress," Phil said without thinking.

James and Christina looked crushed.

"I'm sure you wanted to see James and Christina too, didn't you?" Beth stated firmly.

"Oh, of course I did. Sorry kids, didn't mean it quite like that. I've had a bad week at work, lots of things on my mind," Phil apologised as he realised what he'd said.

"Anyway, I'll come over tomorrow afternoon for an hour, if that's alright Beth?" he looked at her and she nodded. "I'll take you all into town and you can each buy a CD, if you'd like?" he added to James and Christina.

Both children looked slightly mollified and waved to their father from the doorway.

Beth went into the kitchen, shaking her head. She couldn't believe some of the things Phil came out with. He seemed to have lost the plot somewhat, she thought to herself.

She rang Dave just before ten o'clock. The younger children had just gone to bed and Annie was not due back until midnight.

"I've only just got home," he said, yawning down the phone. "I went for a drink with two of the other blokes from my department. We've spent all week working closely together trying to get the systems operating and we managed it late this afternoon. So we thought we'd go out and celebrate."

"Oh, that's nice. Where did you go?" Beth asked.

"To a pub down the road. They do meals as well so we soaked up some of the beer. I left my car at work and got a taxi home, so I'll have to go and pick it up tomorrow. I'll probably cycle to work and do a couple of hours catching up with the paperwork that's been left this week. What time is Annie due back?"

"About midnight. She looked gorgeous in her lovely ball dress. I've taken lots of photos so I'll email you a couple."

"Great. I'm off to bed now. I'll ring you again tomorrow. Love you lots, Beth," Dave said.

Beth said her goodbyes and closed the phone. He sounded weary, she thought, although that could be as a result of the alcohol that he was not used to as much as the extra hours at work he'd done that week.

She was almost asleep in the chair downstairs when she heard the car draw up outside. Beth pulled herself up and staggered into the hallway. She opened the door as Annie was walking up the pathway. Her friends were waving to her from the car window as the chauffeur drove off.

"Hi Mum," Annie said. "I've had such a good time. It was brilliant. I'll never forget it and there was an official photographer taking photos of us all. I'm in about six. One on my own and the rest with Linda, Sheila, Marilyn and some with others too. The car was great too. There were sweets and drinks in there for the journey."

"Not alcoholic drinks I hope," Beth said quickly.

"No, Mum. Relax. Just Pepsi and lemonade. We had a lovely fruit punch at the prom – and that had no alcohol in either, so don't worry."

Beth laughed. "Ok, I won't worry. I'm pleased that you have a lovely time. It will certainly be a night to remember."

Annie twirled around in the middle of the room and hummed a tune to herself.

"Did you dance with anyone nice?" Beth couldn't resist asking.

Annie laughed as she stopped and looked at her mother.

"Yes, I danced with Ben a couple of times and with two of his friends. Also with a boy from another class who I've not really seen before. His name was Clive. I think he likes me a bit, but I'm not really bothered. It was more of an evening to spend with your mates that you've spent all these years with at school. That's what made it so much fun. Just having a laugh with Sheila, Linda and Marilyn."

Beth nodded approvingly. Plenty of time for romance later. Annie had been through the experience of loving and losing, now was the time to just have some fun.

"Come on then, let's get you out of that lovely dress and into bed. Your Dad is coming over tomorrow afternoon to take you all out into town. I think he wants to buy you a CD each. The others seemed pleased."

Annie nodded and they went upstairs together. Outside Annie's bedroom door she kissed her mother's cheek and said, "Thanks mum for all the help and for this lovely dress."

Beth smiled and kissed her back. "That's alright. It was a pleasure to see you so happy. Goodnight Annie."

When she was in bed, Beth breathed a sigh of happiness. She realised she had much to look forward to in the next few months. And mostly she was happy to let life slip by for a while. She wanted to enjoy the summer months without worrying about mortgages, jobs, houses and their future.

Chapter Twenty Five

--ooOoo--

*A*s Beth closed the last file on her desk and placed it in her out tray, she glanced up at the clock. It was quarter past five. Only a few more minutes and she'd be packing up to leave for her three week vacation.

At home, there were six suitcases standing in the hallway, packed and carried downstairs late last night. Hopefully, Jack and Vera would be supervising the children with their last minute activities. She planned to drive home after work, have a quick sandwich and shower and then be on the road for six thirty. It was a good four-hour drive to Verity and John's farmhouse and she was sure it would take at least another hour due to all the other cars that would be on the road travelling in a south westerly direction.

As the hands of the clock moved slowly downwards, Beth stood up and picked up her handbag. Allan came out of his office and wished her a happy holiday.

"See you at the end of August when we're all back," he promised.

She drove home feeling as if it was the last day of the school term, which it had been for James and Christina. Vera had made a large plate of sandwiches which the children had just started on as Beth arrived home.

"Hi everyone. Ready for holiday time?" she called slinging her keys and handbag on the stairs.

"Oh yes!" shouted Christina with her mouth full.

"We're in the kitchen," her mother called unnecessarily.

Beth joined them around the kitchen table and took a couple of sandwiches.

"You are sure you can drive all the way to Verity's after a full day's work?" her mother asked anxiously.

"Oh yes Mum. I'll be fine. The roads are easy as it's all motorway until the last bit. Then I've written down the directions that John sent me so that Annie can read them to me when we get closer. Don't worry, we'll be fine. I'll ring you when we arrive,"' Beth promised.

"Verity rang about half an hour ago and I told her you'd be leaving about six thirty. She said she'll have some supper ready for when you get there and you'd all go to bed late so you'll have time to recover from the journey," Jack said.

"Oh great," said Christina. "I love staying up late. Will I be able to go out and meet Toby when we get there?"

"Toby?" asked Beth munching her sandwich.

"Yes, Toby. Lucy's horse,"Christina reminded her.

"Oh, yes of course. I don't know. I suppose so. It depends what Verity says," Beth said putting the decision on to her sister.

"Shall I load up the car for you Beth?" her father asked.

"Oh, thanks Dad. Would you mind. Just be careful though, some of those cases are quite heavy," Beth said.

"Yes be careful Jack.You don't want to aggravate your back, do you?" Vera reminded him.

"No, of course not. I'll be careful. Come on James, you can give me a hand."

James finished his drink and grabbed another sandwich on the way out.

"I'll put the rest of the sandwiches in a bag for you in case you get hungry on the journey," Vera said standing up.

"Thanks Mum. There are some bottles of drink in the fridge to take too," Beth said. "I'll just go and have a quick shower and change and then we'll be off. Have you said goodbye to Tinkerbell?" she asked Christina.

"Yes I have. And I've written down the instructions for Grandma and Grandad to follow. You will ring me if she misses me, won't you?" she asked Vera.

"Of course I will, love. Now don't you worry. We'll look after Tinkerbell for you and she'll be good as new when you come back," Vera assured her.

Christina seemed satisfied and went into the hallway where

Tinkerbell was waiting in her cage to be taken to her temporary new home.

Beth showered and changed into a loose pair of cotton trousers and a T-shirt. She took a fleece out of the drawer in case the end of the journey got colder. She wanted to be comfortable for the long journey. She hadn't done a lot of long distance driving, but didn't mind going on the motorway.

Vera had finished clearing away in the kitchen and the suitcases were packed in Beth's car when she went back downstairs.

"Have you all got your hand luggage?"' she asked.

"Yes Mum," they assured her.

Beth checked that the doors and windows were locked, all taps and appliances were switched off and all luggage had been stowed away in the car.

"We'll wave you off and then go home with Tinkerbell," Vera said.

The children kissed Jack and Vera as Beth locked the front door. They climbed into the car and Beth gave a last minute hug to each of her parents.

"I'll ring you when we get there. Now don't worry, we'll be fine. See you when we get back," she said.

"Bye darling. Drive carefully," called Vera.

"Take care all of you and have a lovely holiday," Jack waved from the driveway.

Beth eased the car out on to the road and waved to her parents.

"Here we go, then. Off on our holidays," she said gaily.

The children cheered and settled down for the journey.

Beth stopped at the last service station on the M5 and allowed the children time to stretch their legs and visit the facilities. They ate some of the sandwiches Vera had made and finished off the drinks. She'd made slightly better time than she'd thought as there was not as much traffic on the motorway as she'd anticipated. Maybe most people had left before her, she thought as they pulled out of the motorway service station.

When they left the motorway Annie began to read the instructions for the rest of the journey. John had done a good job and they arrived at the farmhouse just before eleven o'clock.

Beth climbed stiffly out from behind the wheel and stretched her arms into the air. She looked around. The driveway leading to the house from the road was rutted with patches of gravel. It swept in a large arc in front of the house and then back out of another set of gates.

'Pretty impressive' thought Beth.

She looked up at the house. It was a typical Cornish stone farmhouse with six large upper windows and four on the ground floor, two each side of the front porch.

As she stood there, Lucy and Sam came racing from the side of the house.

"You're here!" they cried.

The children began to chatter excitedly to each other and Beth smiled at their enthusiasm. She felt in need of a strong drink of some sort – maybe only tea though!

"Hi Beth. Oh, it's lovely to see you. Come on in," Verity arrived and enveloped her sister in a big hug.

"Shall I bring the cases in now?" Beth asked when she was set free.

"No, leave them for now. Just bring your handbag or whatever. I've made a big dish of lasagne and garlic bread. Thought you'd probably be hungry after your long journey. Come on, this way,"

Verity led them around the back of the house and into a large stone floor kitchen. There was a huge shiny range along one wall with cupboards and shelves surrounding it. The sink was located under the window which Beth was sure would provide wonderful views whilst you were washing up. A huge wooden table with ten chairs was placed in the middle of the kitchen and this was laid ready for eight people to eat.

"What a wonderful kitchen," Beth said as she looked round. "Wow, Verity, it's fantastic."

Verity stood up, flushed from the oven, and grinned.

"Yes, it is great isn't it? A dream come true, really."

John entered the kitchen wiping his hands on a towel.

"Oh, hi Beth. Hi kids," he said going over to give Beth a kiss.

"Hi John. Your directions were spot on. Annie and I had no problems getting here at all, did we?" Beth said.

"Well it's quite easy really. Only a few junctions and turnings to negotiate. Even women drivers can manage," he joked, ducking out of the way before Annie, Beth or Verity took reprisals.

They sat at the table and Verity passed round plates piled high with steaming lasagne. Two wicker baskets contained the garlic bread and a casserole dish was heaped with salad.

"This looks delicious," Beth said picking up her cutlery. "You must have been busy, Verity."

"Well I think I've adapted quite well to being a farmer's wife," Verity said, grinning at John. 'You just have to get organised and do all the jobs as they come up. It's that simple. I must admit, I don't get so het up and stressed as I used to before we moved here. There must be something in the air, I think."

"I can't wait to have a good look round tomorrow. I suppose it's too late tonight, isn't it?" Beth said.

"Well, it's dark out there now so better wait until the morning."

Christina looked disappointed and said she'd hoped to be able to meet Toby that night.

"He's out in the paddock behind the hen houses. I think you should wait until tomorrow and see him properly," Verity said. Beth was relieved she'd had the decision taken away from her.

"You've still got to see your bedrooms where you'll be staying, anyway," Verity said trying to cheer Christina up a bit.

"Oh, yes. Am I near Lucy?" Christina asked.

"Yes, I've put you in the same room. We've put a camp bed in Lucy's bedroom and made some space in her wardrobe and cupboard so you can sleep together. James is in the small room next to Sam and Annie – we've cleared a room at the end of the corridor for you. You can get some peace and quiet if you need it – or play your music loud and not disturb anyone," Verity told them.

"Where's Mum going to sleep?" asked Christina.

"Oh your mum has got the special guest room. It has its own en suite, which she's used to, and overlooks the back garden and paddock. I hope you like it," Verity turned to Beth and smiled.

"It sounds perfect," Beth said, stifling a yawn.

"Come on then, let's get cleared away and we'll show everyone where they're sleeping," Verity said standing up and collecting the plates.

"Is there no pudding, Mum?" asked Sam.

"Are you still hungry?" his mother asked.

"Well, no I suppose not really, but we always have pudding," Sam insisted.

"Not at this time of night we don't, young man," his father intervened. "Now take James upstairs and show him his room."

The children all left the kitchen and were heard running up the staircase towards their sleeping quarters. Verity stacked the plates in the sink and turned to Beth.

"Come on then. I'll show you where you're sleeping. If you give your keys to John he'll empty the car for you, won't you darling?"

"Are you sure? I don't mind carrying the cases upstairs," Beth asked as she rummaged in her handbag for the car keys.

"I'll get the boys to help me, don't you worry," John said.

The next half hour was spent getting everyone organised upstairs. Beth was pleased with her bedroom for the next three weeks. The large double bed had a pale blue duvet with matching pillow cases and dark blue curtains hung at the windows. She tried to see outside but, with no street lights or shining moon, it was pitch black. The en suite contained a white shiny bath and basin, both with gold coloured taps.

She could hear the others settling in to their bedrooms and the boys and John huffed and puffed upstairs with the suitcases. Beth made sure the cases went into the correct rooms and began some unpacking. She placed her toiletries in the en suite and her nightdress, dressing gown and slippers on the bed.

Verity came in and asked if there was anything else she needed that night.

"No, I'm fine thanks Verity. Just tired now. I'll make sure the kids settle down and then I'm ready for bed, if that's alright," Beth yawned behind her hand.

"That's fine. Don't worry, I'll go and settle everyone – you just get yourself off to bed. It doesn't matter what time you get up in the morning, we've nothing on and nobody is coming round. The kids can get up when they want and Sam and Lucy will make sure they get some breakfast. John and I are going to have a bit of a lie in too, just this once."

"Oh I haven't rung Mum and Dad. I promised I'd let them know we were here," Beth suddenly remembered.

"It's alright, don't worry. I've just rung them and said you were going to bed as you were tired from the journey. I said you'd speak to them tomorrow. Now, off to bed, Beth. See you in the morning."

Beth smiled and kissed her sister on her cheek.

"Thanks Verity. It's been lovely getting here and being spoiled. But you must let me help if you have things I can do."

Verity laughed. "Yes, Beth. I'm sure I'll find something for you to do, otherwise you might get bored, anyway! Now go to sleep."

Beth was more than happy to comply with her sister's instructions.

When she woke the next morning the sun was streaming through the gap in the curtains.

She lay quietly for a few minutes remembering the long car journey and the welcoming meal Verity had prepared for their arrival. Her two suitcases stood by the wall waiting to be unpacked but Beth refused to be rushed and remained in bed, looking around the room.

After a few minutes, however, she decided she needed the loo. She swung her legs out of bed, pushed her feet into her slippers and went into the en suite.

When she returned to the bedroom she walked over to the window and pulled the curtains open. She gasped in surprise. The view was breathtaking. Large green fields stretched out before her, interspersed with a few huge trees and surrounded by hedges. Directly below the window was the garden which was a mass of colourful flowers and shrubs. Someone obviously worked long and hard to keep it looking so beautiful.

To the right were several small sheds which Beth realised were the hen houses. Behind them was a paddock which was empty. The girls must have got up early and she wondered if they were riding or grooming Toby. To the left of the house was the lane she'd driven along last night. It meandered round several corners and into the distance towards a church she could just see on the horizon.

There was no-one in sight and Beth realised she couldn't hear anybody moving about either. She took her phone out of her bag and looked to see the time. It was half past ten!! She couldn't believe it. She hadn't slept in that late since, well probably since she was a teenager.

After having quickly got dressed, she opened her bedroom door and peeped out. Still no sound of anyone else. She moved quietly towards the staircase and crept downstairs.As she entered the kitchen, Verity came in through the back door.

"Oh good morning, Beth. We left you to sleep. It seemed you needed it. Are you alright?'

"Oh yes, thanks Verity. I can't believe I've slept so late. Where is everybody?" she asked, looking round.

"Well John has taken the boys to the surf school to book their lessons. Lucy and Christina are out in the stables with the horses. Annie is helping me to clean out the chicken runs. Now, what would you like for breakfast?"

"Er, chicken runs?' asked Beth bemusedly. "Annie? Cleaning out chicken runs?"

"Yes. She offered to help me and I think she's enjoying it. Apart from the smell, of course," Verity said.

Beth shook her head. Well, this country air must be affecting them all.

"Horses?" she said, realising what else Verity had said. "I thought you just had the one pony called Toby."

Verity smiled secretively. "Well, what I didn't tell Christina last night when she wanted to visit Toby, was that we had borrowed another pony for the fortnight called Silver. He's a quiet little old gentleman, also from the farm next door. He's 26 years old and semi retired but they said that Christina could borrow him as long as she didn't gallop or jump him. And I don't think she's quite ready to do that, anyway."

"Oh Verity. How am I ever going to get Christina to go back home if you've given her a pony – even if it is only on loan?" Beth laughed and sat down at the table.

Verity laughed too. "Anyway, what would you like? Toast, cereal, bacon and eggs? Tea or coffee?"

"Some tea and toast would be nice," Beth said. "But can't I get it if you are cleaning out the chickens?"

"We've nearly finished now. I've just left Annie to put out the straw beds and fill up the water containers and then she'll be back here. I'll make a big pot of tea cos I think I've just heard John's car coming up the drive. He'll be wanting another cup by now, too."

"Have you both settled here well then?" asked Beth.

"Oh, yes Beth. It's wonderful. None of us would change anything now. Our new lifestyle is so peaceful and it seems like we can just do as we like. That's not quite true, of course. We've got animals that need looking after every day and crops in the field, but it doesn't seem like work."

Beth sipped her cup of tea and tried not to envy her sister. She seemed to have landed on her feet and didn't appear to have any problems at all.

'Not like me!' thought Beth. 'That's all I've got – problems'.

But she was happy for her sister. And she was determined to make the most of the three weeks ahead that she would spend in this lovely farm house.

After breakfast, Beth went back up to her bedroom to unpack. As she was hanging her clothes in the wardrobe, her mobile phone rang. She picked it up and saw it was Dave calling.

"Hi Dave. Sorry, I should have rung you last night to let you know we'd arrived safely. I was just so tired and Verity had prepared a huge meal for us. When we'd finished I just collapsed in bed. I was going to ring you soon."

"That's alright. I was just a bit concerned that I didn't receive a quick text or something to let me know you were safe," Dave sounded a bit hurt that she'd forgotten to speak to him.

"Sorry Dave. I really am. When do you think you can come over?," asked Beth trying to get him to forgive her forgetfulness.

"Well, I could come over tomorrow. I'm at work now just trying to get finished before I start my holiday. I've also got to come in for a meeting on Wednesday morning next week, so I've cancelled that as holiday. I'll probably have another day during your second week. But I could come over tomorrow, if that suits you." he said.

"Yes, tomorrow would be great. We are still unpacking and getting settled. I haven't even seen any of the kids yet. I slept until half past ten and by then they were all off doing things. James has gone surfing with his new board, Christina is with the ponies and Annie is cleaning out the chicken runs."

Dave laughed. "Sounds like they've adapted to the country life very easily. How are you going to prise Christina away from the animals? She's only got a small hamster to go back to?"

"I know. That's what I said to Verity," laughed Beth. "I'm not going to worry about that now, I'm just going to enjoy the next two weeks and forget everything back home."

"Very wise. It will do you good. What time shall I come over and can you give me the postcode to put in the sat nav?" he asked.

When she'd made the necessary arrangements and remembered to tell Dave that she loved him, she finished her unpacking and then went into the girls' bedroom to make sure Christina was settled. She was amazed to find Christina's clothes hanging or neatly folded in the cupboards and drawers, and even more bewildered to see that James had unpacked his suitcase too.

When she arrived back downstairs in the kitchen, Verity was peeling potatoes ready for lunch.

"I can't believe the kids have got themselves organised so well. They've unpacked and hung up their clothes without being asked," she said.

"Well, there may have been some bribery mentioned at breakfast," Verity admitted. "Something about no surfing or riding until they'd organised their bedrooms."

Beth laughed, relieved that her children hadn't been kidnapped and swapped for aliens.

"Oh I see. That's alright then. Now I understand. Can I help you Verity?" she asked wandering over to the window and looking outside.

Verity put the lid on the saucepan of potatoes and placed it on the Aga. She turned to Beth and said: "No, I'm fine. You go outside and explore a bit. You'll probably find Lucy and Christina grooming the ponies, Annie is sitting on a deck chair in the garden reading a book I've lent her and John is mending something in the shed. Tell them all lunch will be about an hour. John will go and fetch the boys in about ten minutes as their lesson will be

finished by now. Are you happy enough for James to be learning to surf?" she asked.

"Yes. He has been looking forward to learning more about surfing, and I think he may even prefer it to football. He's a good, strong swimmer and loves being in the water. It took me ages to get him out of the pool the other day when we went swimming."

"Have you rung Dave yet?" Verity asked.

"Yes, I've just spoken to him. I think he was a bit put out as I hadn't let him know we were here. But he's going to come over tomorrow afternoon, if you don't mind?"

"Course I don't mind. You treat this house as your home, Beth. Make the most of your holiday. Are you going to spend some time with Dave?"

"Yes, I'd like to. He's taken some holiday next week and we

thought we'd explore the countryside and coast a bit. He's not had a chance since he moved here. I'll take the kids out of your way too, if you like?"

"I don't mind either way. They're no trouble here, in fact they'll probably be a help. Although I've actually got something in mind for Annie to keep her from getting too bored. The people who live in the cottage across the field there are having to move to Truro with his job. They want to go house hunting but they've got three young children, two girls of five and three and a boy aged ten months. I said that Annie could probably look after them for a couple of afternoons next week so they can get out on their own to view some

properties. Do you think Annie would like to do that and is she capable? She'll get paid," Verity told Beth.

Beth thought about it. She knew that Annie was patient with the elderly folk at the nursing home where she'd been working for a few weeks. Surely she'd be as good with children too? "Best thing is to ask her. I don't mind if she's happy. The children will be in their own home so it shouldn't be too difficult. And we'll only be here if she needs some help. She can always ring us on her mobile," Beth said.

When they were all sat around the table enjoying the lunch that Verity had prepared, Beth asked Annie if she'd like to do the babysitting.

"It would only mean playing with the children for a couple or three hours and maybe preparing them some drinks. I am sure Janine will leave some food ready if they need to eat. She's said she'll pay you too, if you're interested," added Verity.

Annie quickly decided that she'd like the opportunity to earn some money and that she'd love to look after some little children.

"It will be the opposite end of the scale to what I'm used to," she said.

Beth and Verity laughed and agreed with her.

"So how did you get on at the surf school, James?" asked Beth.

"It was ace. They are so cool, the instructors. Two of the men have got pony tails and they are so good out on the waves. I want to go every day so I can get as good as them," James said, waving his fork about.

"And I want to go riding every day on lovely Silver. He is such a sweet pony and he loves to be groomed. We're going to ride around

329

the big field this afternoon, Lucy says. She's done it several times, so it's alright Mum," Christina assured Beth.

Beth looked at Verity for confirmation of this statement.

"Yes, it's fine. There is a nice lane running around the field. It's all fenced in, nowhere near a road. Ideal for them to get used to hacking out on the ponies," Verity said.

"Hacking out?" said Beth. "That sounds very technical and equestrian."

"Well, you soon get to learn the language of horsey people," Verity laughed. "I might even have a go myself one day."

"Yes, we were never really interested in horse riding as children, were we? I suppose we had our music and dancing lessons on Saturday mornings and that was it. There weren't so many opportunities as there are nowadays," she told the children solemnly.

"What? Do you mean in the old days?" James said straight-faced.

"Hmmm, yes I suppose it is the old days to you, young man," said his uncle. "But you should count yourself lucky that you have so many chances of trying different things. I would have loved to learn to surf if I'd had the chance."

"Why don't you try it then, Dad?" asked Sam. "There are some old, I ean older, people learning in the class after ours."

'I might just do that." said John. "If I've got the time, of course."

The rest of the day was spent out in the garden. John disappeared to finish off his repair work and the two girls went riding. Verity, Beth and Annie took books and magazines outside and arranged sun loungers strategically to catch the rays. James and Sam also lounged about in the garden, arguing good naturedly about football teams and players for the new season.

Dave arrived at the farm just before two o'clock. He parked his car next to Beth's and got out just as she came over to greet him. They hugged and kissed passionately before Dave reached into the car and pulled out a large pot plant.

Beth laughed at the sight of it. "What's this then, Dave?" she asked.

He looked slightly put out. "t's a present for Verity. A pot plant. I called in at a garden centre yesterday afternoon when I'd finished work.

"Why? What's wrong with it?" he asked, looking closely at the foliage.

"Oh, nothing. It just seems strange to pull a large pot plant out of the back of your car. I'm sure Verity will love it," Beth tried to keep a straight face, but spluttered slightly at the effort.

Hmmm, well I thought it was nice' Dave said locking his car.

"Oh it is nice, Dave. I'm sorry. It's a lovely thought. You are always buying presents for people – that's so generous and thoughtful'.

She put her arm through his and led him round to the back of the house where Verity was just taking off her Wellington boots by the door.

"Hi Dave. It's nice to meet you again," she said offering him her hand to shake.

He held out the pot plant and said, "Hello Verity. This is for you. I bought it yesterday and I hope you like it"

Verity took hold of the pot in both hands and looked slightly bemused.

'Well thank you Dave" she said. "You didn't have to buy me anything. But thanks, it's lovely."

Dave smiled triumphantly at Beth who had to hide her grin. She knew that Verity was not keen on watering house plants and this would probably be dried up and dead by the end of the month.

"Let's go inside." Verity suggested holding the pot in front of her and putting it down on the first available surface. "Unless you'd rather sit outside? It is lovely this afternoon,"

"Yes, let's sit outside," agreed Beth. "It's a shame to waste the sunshine."

They settled on the sun loungers and Verity brought a tray of tea and scones outside.

"Hey, when did you make these?" asked Beth.

"First thing this morning," Verity said handing round cups of tea. "I told you, I am much more organised these days than I ever was before."

"You must be," said Beth. "I can't imagine getting up at the crack of dawn to bake."

"Oh, you would if you got used to a different lifestyle. I don't have to get up and dash off to work for nine o'clock any more. As I said, I can arrange my own day how I want, within reason. And I've found that I seem to have more energy that I've ever had before. Certainly at this time of year, it's lovely to get up early and make the most of the day."

They sat in the garden all afternoon, chatting and enjoying the sun and warmth. Lucy and Christina arrived back just after four o'clock, having enjoyed their ride and put the ponies back in the paddock. Verity sent them upstairs to wash and change before she allowed them any refreshments.

"I'll take Annie over to meet the children after tea." she said. "Janine said they'd be in at about seven o'clock. I think she'd like to go into Truro tomorrow afternoon to visit some estate agents and then make some appointments for viewings later in the week, if that's fine with you Annie."

"Yes, I don't mind. Have the children got lots of toys or do I have to make up games for them?" she asked.

"Oh they've got all the usual toys. And they've got a paddling pool and sand in the garden, as well as a swing and a slide. I think they're quite good children and the girls play nicely together. I looked after them one afternoon recently when she went to visit her mother in hospital. They were no trouble at all. The little boy has a sleep just after lunch for an hour or two. I wouldn't have said you'd do it if they were naughty or difficult children," Verity reassured her.

"Shall we go out for the day tomorrow then?" Dave asked Beth.

"Yes, we can do," Beth said looking round at her family. "What about you James and Christina, do you want to come with us?"

"Oh, no thanks." said Christina. "Lucy and I are going riding again and we've got lots of work to do in the stables as well."

"I've got my surfing lesson and we might be able to stay after and practice on our own. The instructor said he'd keep an eye on us as they have two more lessons following ours," James said.

"Oh, well, it's just you and me then," Beth said. "Where shall we go?"

Dave turned to Verity. "Where would you recommend? Have you found any nice places yet?"

She looked a bit embarrassed and told them that they'd not had much of a chance to explore themselves as they'd been busy on the farm and in the house.

"Oh that's quite understandable. Why would you want to leave a lovely place like this anyway?" Dave said looking round. "It's just beautiful here and so peaceful and quiet."

"We'll just go and do our own exploring and report back to you," suggested Beth.

"That sounds like a good idea. Now, I'm going in to get tea ready. You can stay, can't you Dave?' Verity said standing up and collecting the tea things on to her tray.

"If you don't mind, I'd love to stay for tea. Thank you Verity," said Dave.

"That's settled then. Come on girls, you can help me set the table and put out the food."

Beth and Dave were left on their own in the garden to enjoy the early evening sunshine.

Beth lay back in her chair and felt at peace with everyone and everything. This was the life – shame it had to come to an end. But she didn't have to think about that yet.

Chapter Twenty Six

--ooOoo--

*T*he first fortnight of their holiday flew past. Christina and James fitted in with everything that Lucy and Sam did. The girls groomed and rode the ponies every day, and then helped Verity with the other animals, and the boys enjoyed surfing in the mornings and either worked in the fields with John or played table tennis, which had been set up in one of the old barns.

Verity had introduced Annie to Janine and her three young children and she agreed to look after them four afternoons that week. This meant Janine and her husband could go house hunting on their own. Annie found she enjoyed playing with the children and even changing the little boy's nappies was not as bad as she'd thought it would be.

Janine also employed a young girl from the village who came three times a week to do the ironing and some cleaning. Annie soon struck up a friendship with Colleen who invited Annie to the local church disco on Friday night.

Beth and Dave spent three days together in the first week exploring the local beaches. Beth fell in love with the rocky coastline and the sea views. They drove to a different area each day and walked for miles, finding small coves and hidden beaches. Obviously, due to the time of year, most of the beaches were swarming with holidaymakers enjoying the wonderful, sunny weather, but Beth could envisage a time when there were only the local people about taking their dogs for walks.

At the weekend, Verity and John arranged a barbecue on the Saturday evening to which they invited some of their new friends to meet Beth and her family. They'd got to know several other couples who were also making their living by growing or rearing on small plots of land. Sam and Lucy had also made some new friends at their school and they were invited too. About fifty people enjoyed the barbecue, cooked expertly by John ably assisted by Dave, and the salads and sweets were provided by Verity and Beth.

As the second week began, Beth realised how relaxed and at peace she had become. Even socialising with people she'd never met before on Saturday evening had been pleasurable. John and Dave had hit it off immediately and made a good team, barbecuing steaks, burgers and sausages. The children were all having a good time and slowly developing sun-kissed tans.

Each morning as she woke to another beautiful day, her worries and problems seemed further away. Decisions about mortgages, divorces and jobs faded from her mind.

Dave was planning to work on Monday and Tuesday and take the rest of the week as holiday. They wanted to explore the southern coast line for a few days.

On Monday, Janine telephoned and asked if Annie could look after the children for another four afternoons that week and all day Saturday. They had still not found their ideal house and planned to blitz the estate agents whilst they had a babysitter. Annie was more than pleased at this request. Not only was she earning some money but she thought she'd discovered her future career.

"Mum. I think I know what I'd like to do now I've left school," she said to Beth on the Sunday evening.

"Left school?" Beth was startled. "I didn't know you'd decided not to go back to school."

"Well, I think I have – but don't panic," Annie quickly reassured her. "What I'd like to do is go to college and take a course which means I'd be qualified to look after young children. Pre-school children. If I wanted I could also take a couple of A levels. Colleen has told me all about it. She starts at the local college here in September and she's doing a cookery course as well as English and French A levels. She wants to join a cruise ship as a cook when she's got her qualifications."

"Oh, I see. So you'd like to go to college and do two A levels as well as a course for child minding? I think it is called Nursery Nurse, or it used to be," Beth said.

"Yes, I think I would. I know I've only been looking after April,

Louisa and Jake for a few days, but I've really enjoyed it. I love playing with them and watching them learn new little things. I've been looking after older people for a few weeks now, so I know I can deal with that side of caring. I'd really like to do this," she said earnestly.

Beth smiled. "I'm glad you've found something you'd like to concentrate on. And if you take some A levels too, then if you change your mind you are still getting qualifications that can take you on to something else."

"Yes that's right. And Colleen says that in the holidays you can get a job which help give you experience. I'll be able to help out at a play scheme or in a nursery during the holidays when some of the staff want to take time off."

"That's well thought out. I think it's a great idea. We'll go to the college when we get back and find out all about it and how you can apply for this course. Although I suppose it might depend on your exam results too. Do you know which A levels you'd like to do?" Beth asked.

"Probably English and something else. I'll wait and see how I've done in the GCSEs and then decide. I might do business studies, though, as that would help if I wanted to run a business," Annie said.

Beth couldn't help but be impressed at the amount of thought Annie was obviously putting into this decision about her future. She knew that Annie would be very good at looking after children as she had plenty of patience and kindness which would stand her in good stead.

The boys continued to enjoy their daily surfing lessons and after meeting some of Sam's friends at the weekend, James was invited to join their games of football and cricket which they played most evenings on the village green. A goalkeeper was especially welcome, it seemed, as most of the local lads preferred charging around the field after the ball.

Of course, Beth hardly saw Christina. She was in her element helping to look after all the animals. As Verity and Beth stood by the gate leading into the paddock and watched as Lucy and Christina practised trotting their ponies over the jumping poles laid on the ground, they smiled at each other.

"It's lovely they've got this shared interest, isn't it Beth?" Verity asked her.

"Yes it is. It's a shame it will come to an end though. We've only got another week and then it will be back to normal – all the rushing about. And I've got to make a decision about my job, too. I don't really want to spend another hour each day travelling across town, but on the other hand I can't see me finding another job very easily," Beth frowned as she thought about the problems ahead.

"I don't know what to suggest. It's a difficult one," acknowledged Verity.

"Mmm, and then there's the problem with the house. Phil wants me to sell it so he can have some of the equity, as I told you before. And that all seems as if it will be a lot of hassle for me. Not only would I have to sell the house, which I don't want to do, but also find somewhere else for us to live. I glanced at the local paper before we left and there's not much about in the price range that I'll have to keep within. I think I'll only be able to afford a three bedroom house so the girls will probably have to share. Obviously I want to keep within a short distance of the school, which again limits my choice and I'll still be far away from my new office. When I think about all these things, I just seem to go round in circles," she shook her head as she finished telling Verity her worries.

Verity put her arm around Beth's shoulders but could not find any words to help her older sister.

"Maybe you should just move here," she suggested after a few minutes. "Look at all this peace and tranquillity – it could all be yours!"

Beth laughed and looked where Verity was pointing to the green hills and fields behind their farm.

"Yes it would be ideal if I could move here. But I would still have the same problems of where to live, a job, upheaval for the children and Phil's objections to contend with. So basically, nothing would change," she said.

At that moment the girls arrived at the gate pulling their ponies behind them so the conversation was ended abruptly.

Later, when Beth was on the phone to Dave arranging their plans for the next day's exploring, she laughingly told him what Verity had suggested. But Dave didn't laugh. He went quiet for a few minutes and then suggested that perhaps Beth should think about Verity's idea.

"It would be great if you moved here. All the children love being at the farm so I can't see you'd have a problem there. Ok, so you'd have to find a new job and home, but, as you said, you've got to do that anyway. So what's the problem?" he asked.

It was Beth's turn to go quiet as she listened to his words.

"Oh, I can't," she said "It would be too much to think about. How can I just up and move halfway across the countryside. I've got to be sensible and stay where we are."

"Pity," Dave said. "But just think about it for a few days, Beth. I don't imagine it would be as difficult as you are envisaging. Let's talk about it again in a couple of days."

"Ok," agreed Beth, not really taking any of this seriously. "I'll think about it. Now, where are we going tomorrow?"

The weather was perfect for the last few days of their holiday and before they knew it, it was the last Saturday morning.

"What are you doing today, Beth? Is Dave coming over?" Verity asked as they set the kitchen table ready for breakfast.

"Yes, he'll be over about eleven. We're going to a little cove we found further up the coast. It's very quiet there and we'll probably take a picnic. We'll be back about five, if that's alright?" Beth told her.

"Yes, of course it's alright. You enjoy your last full day here. Do you want to make some sandwiches to take with you? There's plenty of bread and there's plenty of stuff in the fridge?"

"Thanks, that would be lovely. Save us having to find a shop when the roads will be busy today."

"Why don't you ask Dave to stay over tonight?" Verity suddenly said.

"Oh, would that be alright do you think? Will John mind?" Beth asked hopefully.

"No, of course he won't. I mentioned it to him last night and he said he didn't know why Dave hadn't already stayed some nights. I just said he'd been going back to check his emails and work things. But it will be fine," Verity assured her.

"Right. I'll ring him and tell him to bring an overnight bag. At home he's only ever stayed on the dining room floor. I didn't want to rush things with the children, you know,"Beth told her sister.

Verity laughed. "I don't think they'll be bothered now. They're all old enough, even Christina, to know how the world works. Plus they've got so many other things to think about here – they won't be worrying where Dave sleeps tonight."

Beth laughed too. "Yes, you're probably right," she said ruefully, rubbing the side of her nose. "I probably worry too much. In fact, I know I worry too much."

Dave was delighted with the news that he could stay overnight at the farm. "Are you sure it's alright with the children," he asked before his hopes were raised too much.

"Yes, that's fine. We just won't mention it and see what happens tonight. Don't worry, Dave. I'm not," Beth assured him.

"Right, I'll see you about eleven then," Dave finished as he went to pack some essentials into his rucksack.

Beth and Dave enjoyed another idyllic day, walking, sunbathing and paddling in the cool water at the cove. They drove back to the farm in high spirits, singing along with the local radio station, and arrived back just after five.

As they walked into the kitchen, a delicious smell of cooking was wafting around.

"Oh, you've been busy," Beth said as Verity stood up from the Aga with a flushed face.

"Yes, well, I thought we'd have a little dinner party for your last night. I've done a starter, a main course and a choice of two puddings to keep everyone happy'," she said.

"What a lovely surprise," Beth said going forward to hug her sister. "But I hope you haven't spent all of this lovely day inside the kitchen!"

"No, I sat outside for a couple of hours this afternoon and finished my library book. Most of what we have doesn't take long, anyway. I just thought it would be nice to make a special evening before you leave tomorrow."

Beth emptied the flask and put the picnic plates and cutlery into the dishwasher. Then she asked verity, "Can I do anything to help?"

"No, it's all done. Even the table is laid in the dining room as I got Lucy and Christina to help. Annie has made one of the puddings and James and Sam say they've helped by keeping out of the way!" Verity laughed. "Just go upstairs both of you and freshen up. Dinner will be served at six," she announced, shooing them out of the kitchen.

"What a lovely thought," Beth said as they climbed the stairs towards the bedroom. "I just hope I can get through the evening without resorting to tears."

Dave plonked his rucksack on the floor and closed the bedroom door behind them.

"We don't want any tears tonight," he told her pulling her into his arms. "Let's forget tomorrow and just enjoy the evening with your family."

At six o'clock everyone was gathered at the dining room table and Verity brought in the tray of starters. Everyone tucked in hungrily and conversation took a back seat. Verity stood up and collected the nine empty plates and asked Annie to help her serve the main course.

"Can you pour the wine and sort out the children's drinks please, John?" she asked her husband.

Within minutes everyone had a heaped plate and full glass in front of them.

"This is a wonderful meal, Verity," Dave said, raising his glass to the cook.

"Yes, cheers to the chef," they all agreed.

Verity blushed and said she was pleased they were all enjoying it.

"I've done some cooking this week too," Annie told them. "Janine asked me to prepare meals for the children as she'd not had time to stock up the freezer since they'd been house hunting. It was good fun, but I had to put the children in front of the television for half an hour to stop them running around the kitchen."

"Yes, I remember those times," her mother said. "I expect you do too, Verity."

"It's a difficult time of day when you've got young children. Everyone's tired and hungry and irritable. I think it is one of those times you are glad we live in the age of television and can put a cartoon on to keep them occupied for a while," Verity agreed.

"Janine and her husband have found a nice house now. It's just outside Truro and quite near to the school. They've had their offer accepted and hope to move in at the end of September. So their cottage is now up for let again," Annie said.

"Oh yes, I hadn't thought of that. So we'll be getting some new neighbours," Verity said looking at her husband.

"Yes, but they're far away not to be a nuisance to us," he assured her.

341

"I suppose so. But it would be good to have someone nice move in. Someone we could be friends with," Verity said. "Janine and her husband are very nice, but they're a bit younger than us and are busy with jobs and babies. I'd like someone about my age to move in."

"Well tell the letting agents, then," suggested John, laughing at his wife. "Say they can only accept the thirty five to forty five years olds – preferably with a teenage boy and girl!" he added looking at his two children.

Everyone laughed and Verity stood up again to remove the dinner plates.

After they'd all finished both the sherry trifle and chocolate gateau, either with cream or ice cream, the children were told they could watch a DVD and make some popcorn in the microwave.

The four adults removed themselves to the conservatory where Verity served some coffee and chocolate mints. John and Dave also indulged in a small brandy each.

"This is the life," John said as he stretched back in his comfortable chair and looked out at the last few minutes of the sunset.

"It sure is," agreed Dave. "What beautiful colours there are out there. It makes you want to be able to paint, doesn't it?"

"Yes and it means it's going to be another lovely day tomorrow," Verity told them.

Beth felt sad that she'd be spending the day packing up their cases and driving back home. During the past few days she'd thought about Verity's light-hearted suggestion and Dave's urge that she considered it more seriously.

She suddenly sat up straight in her chair as she realised that one of the problems could be solved quite easily.

"We could live in the cottage," she announced loudly, surprising herself as much as the others.

"What?" said Dave. "Who could live in what cottage?"

"We could. Me and the children. We could live in Janine's cottage. It's becoming vacant, isn't it?" she asked.

Verity and John also sat up straight and bent towards her.

"Are you serious?" John asked.

"Well, why not?" she said. "I could sell our house and let Phil have his share. We could rent the cottage and live there. You've been telling me all week how much the children love being here. Well,

Annie could go to the local college and she's already made some friends, including Colleen. James and Sam get on really well together and both love surfing. As for Christina, well she's already told me she doesn't want to go home. She wants to stay

here with the ponies and other animals, and Lucy of course too," she added.

"Ok," Dave said slowly, as he thought about Beth's plans. "What about you though. What about a job?"

"I don't know but I'm sure I'd be able to find something. Maybe at the college in one of the offices. We passed it the other day on the way out to Newquay and it looks a big place. If not, then I don't mind if I don't do accounts work. I could work in a shop or do something different in an office."

Beth found she was talking quickly as the ideas came into her mind. She felt excited and wanted to find solutions to all the problems and issues.

"The school is good here isn't it?" she asked Verity.

"Oh yes. It's got a good reputation and always gets good results and the Ofsted report was favourable," Verity nodded in agreement.

"Well I could get James and Christina in there and, as I said, Annie could go to the college with Colleen. I'll get a job locally and sell the house. That will please Phil and I'll have some money for when I'm able to buy a house down here," Beth listed all the advantages.

"Of course, there is another plus that you haven't mentioned yet, Beth," Dave said.

"I know what that is – I'll be near you too," Beth immediately countered as she grinned at him.

"Yes – surely that's the main factor to be taken into consideration," he teased her.

"And you'll be near us too," Verity wasn't going to be left out.

"Yes. But what about Mum and Dad?" Beth suddenly thought of their parents. John and Verity laughed together wickedly.

When they drew breath Verity said, "Well we happen to know that Mum and Dad would like nothing better than an excuse to move down here. They loved it, as you have, when they visited and saw this area is a wonderful place to retire to. They said they wouldn't do anything for a couple of years until you and the children were better placed and could manage without them. And before you ask, Beth, no they weren't resentful or upset because they couldn't move here now. They like being with your children and helping you. It makes them feel needed. But they could still help out when you're working here, anyway, couldn't they? And with ours too," she finished.

Beth tried to take in all that her sister had said.

"I can't believe it," she finally managed to say. "It seems that the solution to everything has now become clear and everyone is going to be happy. Well, maybe not Phil," she suddenly thought. "He'll not be able to see the children so much if we move here."

"He could always visit for weekends instead of rushing round to your house at the end of each working day," suggested John. "He could stay in a bed and breakfast nearby and take the children out, even if it was only once a month or something."

Beth and Dave were not too sure how that would work and could envisage themselves having to dodge both their ex-partners during the visiting weekends. But that was a small price to pay for all the other advantages, best of which would be their close proximity to each other.

"It sounds an ideal solution and I can't wait to tell the kids," Beth said jumping up.

"Yes, come on let's go and tell them now," Dave said, not wanting Beth to have time to change her mind or think of other problems.

The four adults charged back through the kitchen and into the room where the television was blaring out.

"Hi kids," shouted John above the noise. "Can you just turn the film off for a few minutes as we've got something to tell you."

"What's up?" asked Sam turning down the volume.

"We've got something exciting to tell you and I think you'll all be pleased. Beth, you tell them," John said turning to his sister in law and gently pushing her forward.

"Oh right. Well, we've been talking and I've decided that maybe we could live in the cottage across the field. The one that Janine and her husband are leaving next month," she started.

"But how would we get to school?" asked the ever-practical Christina.

"You could go to Lucy's school, and James could go there as well," said her mother.

"And I could go to the college where Colleen is going," Annie quickly worked out.

"Yes, that's right. And you'll be able to surf and play football still, James. You'll probably be able to keep your pony Christina and I'll get a job here. How do you all feel about that?" Beth asked anxiously looking around at the still somewhat bewildered faces.

"Well I think it would be wicked," James said immediately. "I didn't want to give up my surfing lessons and like you said I can still play football here. I'll miss some of my mates, but I've got new ones here already," he said, pretending to punch Sam.

"And I want to stay here anyway," Christina piped up. "I'll miss some of my friends too and going to the Sanctuary at weekends, but maybe I'll find one here I can help at. And I didn't want to give Silver back – can I really keep him, Mum?" she asked anxiously.

"Yes, I would think so. As long as Aunty Verity and Uncle John don't mind him living here with Toby."

"Of course we don't," Verity immediately hugged her niece to put her mind at rest.

"What about your Annie? How do you feel about living here?" Beth turned to her elder daughter.

Annie thought about it for a few minutes. "Well, I think it will be alright. I'd like to go to the college and do my course and A levels. And I think I could make some new friends here. I like Colleen and her group of friends seem to have accepted me. There's a lot of things going on at the college too so I'd be able to go to things there in the evenings, wouldn't I mum?"

"Of course. It's only ten minutes away in the car so I could take you and pick you up. You'll be seventeen next year anyway, so you'll be able to learn to drive then," Beth reminded her.

Silence fell as they all digested the implications of Beth's decision.

"We're all in agreement then kids?" Beth finally asked her children.

"Yes Mum," they said at the same time.

Beth turned to Dave and smiled. "Wow I can't believe how different I feel now. It seems like a whole big weight has been lifted from my shoulders and that I'm as light as air," she kissed Dave full on his mouth when she'd finished speaking.

"Oh, yeuch Mum. Can we finish watching our film now please," James asked.

The adults left the room and Verity prepared another cafetiere of coffee to take into the conservatory where they continued to discuss the practicalities of the proposed move.

"It will be absolutely wonderful having you live just across the field there," Verity enthused. "I'm so pleased you're coming here and that Mum and Dad may move too."

"Yes, but I've still got to deal with Phil. I've a feeling he won't be too pleased at my taking his children halfway across the country. I just hope he can't do anything legal to stop us," Beth said turning to Dave. "You don't think he can, do you?"

Dave shook his head. "As long as you allow him access to them I don't think he can make you live in a certain place. It's not as if he's made any move to have the children live with him, is it?"

Beth shook her head. "No, and I would always let them go and stay with him if they wanted to. They just haven't said yet that they'd like to go and visit him. Perhaps they will if he buys a house. But that's Ok. I don't mind," she said.

"I think they'll be too busy here with their school friends and interests. I reckon Phil will have to come to them if he wants to see them," John observed.

Beth considered this. "Yes, you're probably right. And knowing Christina she'll want him to see her pony, her bedroom and all her other things. Will you mind if Phil comes to the farm?" she asked Verity.

"No of course not. Will you mind if he comes to your new home?" countered her sister.

"Only if he just comes to see the children's bedrooms and where they live. I won't have him coming in and out of the house as he does now at home. That's another advantage – it's a clean start for me. The new cottage is nothing to do with Phil so it will just be mine," Beth said firmly.

"I hope I'll be able to visit you," Dave said quietly.

"Of course you will. I didn't mean you wouldn't be welcome." Beth turned to reassure him before realising that he'd been teasing her. "Oh you! You know you'll be there all the time!" she laughed.

Dave raised his eyebrows and grinned at her and Beth realised what she'd said. "Oh, I didn't mean you were going to move in and be there all the time. Although you can do, but perhaps not straight away. Not that I wouldn't want you to, but, you know......" She didn't know what to say and was just getting herself tied up in knots.

"It's Ok Beth. I know what you mean. You move in with the kids and we'll take it from there. Sorry, I didn't mean to tease you," he kissed the tip of her nose and hugged her tight.

That night as she lay in bed next to Dave, Beth felt absolutely exhausted. But she couldn't sleep. She got quietly out of bed and tiptoed to the window. As she pulled back the curtain the moonlight streamed into the bedroom. She glanced round but Dave continued to snore quietly.

She perched on the window sill and looked out over the countryside. The full moon cast a silvery light over everything which took on a ghostly aura. She smiled as she caught a glimpse of Janine's cottage through the trees. That would soon be Beth's cottage, she thought.

They had decided that she'd still go back home the next day, with the children, in order to sort out her life. She'd put the house on the market immediately, resign from her job and work out her month's notice, make enquiries about enrolling James and Christina in the local school and Annie at the college. Of course, Annie's exam results were due at the end of August but Beth was confident she would have done well.

The most difficult thing would be telling Phil. Beth had no idea at all of how he would react. He seemed to be very wrapped up in his and Lisa's new life together and often let the children down, either being late or not turning up when he'd said he would. But that was different from not being able to see them at all as they lived over a hundred and fifty miles away. Would he make a fuss and put a stop to their plans? Or would he accept what Beth and the children wanted and be grateful that he would get his money from the house sale without any more fuss and arguments? Beth tended to think that the latter would apply, but she didn't want to get too optimistic in case she was wrong.

Dave stirred slightly in his sleep and turned over, reaching out for her. She stood up and pulled the curtain back. Whatever was going to happen, she'd have to deal with it. She'd come a long way in the past year and now felt stronger and more confident. Some of that was due to this handsome, dark haired man laying in her bed. But Beth also accepted that she'd altered during the past twelve months. She was not taking things for granted any more. She wanted to make changes, become more decisive and choose for herself how to live her life. Not just go with the flow.

From now on, she'd plan and decide what was going to happen to her. She wanted to have a relationship with Dave, she'd find herself a new job, she would move to another part of the country and live in a rented cottage until she decided she wanted to buy a house for herself and the children. Nobody else would make these decisions for her.

Beth slipped into bed between the sheets and snuggled up to Dave. He stirred again and she began to kiss him. As her tongue touched his mouth he woke up and smiled at her.

"Hello my lovely Beth. How wonderful to be woken up in the middle of the night by your sweet kisses," he whispered.

"I love you Dave. And thank you for being here for me," she whispered back to him.

"I love you too Beth and I'm pleased to be here for you. In fact, I'm going to show you now just how pleased I am," he grinned as he began to slowly caress her soft skin in all the places he knew she loved.

Chapter Twenty Seven

--ooOoo--

*B*eth opened her eyes and focused on the open window beside the bed. As her blurred vision took in the billowing curtains and the large bowl of summer flowers on the window sill, she blinked and woke up properly.

She was lying in the middle of the large double bed. A glance at the clock on the bedside table showed that it was three o'clock in the afternoon.

What day was it? Oh, yes. Saturday. A small sound made her turn quickly to the left.

One of the twins lying in the double cot beside her bed had gurgled slightly.

Beth smiled as she looked at them both. She couldn't believe it. Four weeks ago she had given birth to a baby girl and a baby boy. Olivia and Charlie.

She could hear their proud father downstairs preparing some tea. Dave had been astounded and astonished when she'd told him last Christmas that she was two months pregnant. They hadn't been especially trying for a baby but obviously it was meant to be. His wish had come true and she was delighted for both of them.

They had found out that they were expecting twins in January and had immediately agreed upon names.

She thought back to a year ago when she'd decided to move into this lovely cottage. She'd been lucky to find a buyer for the house who'd paid the full asking price and Phil was therefore able to afford a new four bedroom house on an executive estate chosen by Lisa.

As both divorces had recently been finalised, they were all free agents now and Annie had told Beth that Phil and Lisa planned to

349

get married next spring.

Her worries about his objections to their move had been unfounded. Phil was happy enough to visit his children once a month, staying in a local b&b on the Saturday night. Sometimes Lisa came with him, but mostly he visited on his own. He would take the children out on Saturday afternoon and evening and then watch James play football Sunday morning before driving back to his new home.

The children seemed happy enough with this arrangement and, as John had predicted, were kept so busy with their own lives they did not seem to miss him too much.

Annie had completed a year at college and had a part time job in a local crèche. She'd made many friends, both boys and girls, and settled in to her new life quite happily. She was currently saving up for driving lessons and Beth had promised to help her buy a small second hand car when she'd passed her test.

James and Sam were pretty much inseparable. They surfed and played football, enjoyed computer games and were in the same gang at school. James kept in touch with some of his old school friends via email and one had visited him at Easter when he'd been staying in the area with his parents.

Christina didn't seem to miss her old life at all. She also loved being with her cousin, Lucy, and they rode the ponies and helped Verity with the animals every day. She'd quickly made some of her own friends at school as she was in a different class to Lucy, but Verity and Beth agreed this was a good thing. It gave them both a bit of independence.

When they'd moved into the cottage, Beth had applied for a job in the accounts office at the college and had been taken on to cover a maternity leave until Easter. It was ironic, therefore, that she'd had to leave for her own maternity reasons.

As soon as they'd heard Beth's future plans, Jack and Vera had immediately put their own house up for sale and bought a small bungalow situated in the next village. They had been delighted to become grandparents again!

Dave had made changes also. When Beth first moved into the cottage, he'd visited at weekends and a couple of evenings during the week. By hristmas, though, everyone had decided they'd like him to move in permanently so he sold his flat and become part of the Grainger family.

When they found out that they were going to become parents, Dave had immediately asked Beth to marry him. However, she had not agreed at first. She wanted to wait until the twins were born and then make up her mind without hormones coursing through her body and deflecting her from making the right decision.

She smiled as she heard Dave coming up the stairs with the tea tray.

He'd been wonderful since she'd given birth to his babies. He'd taken some unpaid leave for the first three months of their lives in order to help her as much as possible. It had been quite a shock to her system to be the mother of tiny babies again, after dealing with teenagers for so long!

Annie, James and Christina loved the new babies – which was another relief to Beth. She didn't know how she would have coped with jealousy over the new arrivals.

Dave pushed the door open with his foot and entered the room with a smile on his face.

"How are mother and babies doing?" he asked putting the tray down on the dressing table. "Ready for some tea, my love?"

"Yes, thanks Dave. I'm more than ready for some tea. These babies take some feeding, I can tell you!."

Beth pulled herself into a sitting position in bed.

Dave handed her a cup and the plate of biscuits. "Got to keep your strength up," he agreed. "Oh, Amanda rang whilst you were asleep and said they'd definitely be able to come and stay next weekend."

"Oh good. I'm really looking forward to their visit."

They sat in companionable silence, glancing at the twins and then smiling at each other.

When she'd finished her tea, Beth placed her cup carefully on the bedside table and then turned to Dave.

"Dave, you asked me a question a few months ago and I wouldn't answer at the time. Do you remember?" she asked.

He looked at her, startled.

"Do you mean THE question?" he asked.

"Yes, I mean THE question. Well, I've decided on my answer now," she told him. "So do you want to ask me again?"

Dave put his cup and saucer down on the tray and stood up.

"Yes, I'll ask you again. I'm a bit scared about the answer but I hope it's what I want it to be," he said.

Beth smiled so he took heart from that and squeezed through the gap between the cot and the bed and managed to get down on one knee.

"My lovely and beautiful Beth, will you please become my wife?" he asked as he took hold of her left hand.

Beth kept smiling at him and replied "Yes, I will – that's my, Beth's, decision."

****